I KISSED A WEREWOLF
AND I LIKED IT

Cat Hepburn is an award-winning scriptwriter and poet based in Glasgow, Scotland, and Berlin, Germany. Her writing has been featured on BBC Radio 6 Music, STV, and the Edinburgh Fringe. She has written for *River City* (BBC Scotland) and worked as a storywriter for *Hollyoaks* (Lime Pictures). She has also authored two books, *Dating & Other Hobbies* and *#GIRLHOOD*, upon which she based her debut solo show, performed at the Edinburgh Fringe to four- and five-star reviews.

I KISSED A WEREWOLF AND I LIKED IT

CAT HEPBURN

WILDFIRE

Copyright © Cat Hepburn 2025

The right of Cat Hepburn to be identified as the Author of
the Work has been asserted by her in accordance with the
Copyright, Designs and Patents Act 1988.

First published in paperback in 2025 by Wildfire
An imprint of Headline Publishing Group Limited

1

Apart from any use permitted under UK copyright law, this publication may
only be reproduced, stored, or transmitted, in any form, or by any means,
with prior permission in writing of the publishers or, in the case of
reprographic production, in accordance with the terms of licences
issued by the Copyright Licensing Agency.

All characters in this publication are fictitious
and any resemblance to real persons, living or dead,
is purely coincidental.

Cataloguing in Publication Data is available from the British Library

Paperback ISBN 978 1 0354 1988 3

Typeset in 9.80/14.45 pt Hoefler Txt by Jouve (UK), Milton Keynes

Printed and bound in Great Britain by Clays Ltd, Elcograf S.p.A.

MIX
Paper | Supporting
responsible forestry
FSC® C104740

Headline's policy is to use papers that are natural, renewable and recyclable
products and made from wood grown in well-managed forests and other
controlled sources. The logging and manufacturing processes are expected
to conform to the environmental regulations of the country of origin.

Headline Publishing Group Limited
An Hachette UK Company
Carmelite House
50 Victoria Embankment
London EC4Y 0DZ

The authorised representative in the EEA is Hachette Ireland,
8 Castlecourt Centre, Dublin 15, D15 XTP3, Ireland (email: info@hbgi.ie)

www.headline.co.uk
www.hachette.co.uk

CONTENT WARNING

This book contains numerous scenes of a sexual nature, as well as depictions of attempted sexual assault. Reader discretion is advised. Please take care while reading, and prioritise your well-being.

For the lone wolves, the dirty dogs, and everyone in between.

PROLOGUE

There she is. She is smaller than I imagined. Chestnut curls, narrow shoulders and a puny frame. Not what I was expecting. She walks with uncertainty. Like she's not meant to be here. But she is. Her sweet scent overwhelms my senses, even at this distance. Earthy and delectable. I inch closer, the sheer yearning of hunger almost making me lose control. I can't help myself – I am salivating. As I close in on her, I feel the thrust of my appetite, sprung to satiate. This can't be right. My only wish for tonight was that I could see her with my own eyes. But now that I see her, I realise that I must have her. Yet I cannot. She is my forbidden fruit. She is the answer to so many questions. That aroma. It's killing me. I must leave before it is too late. But I stop to smell her some more. Just one second more. Then, despite myself, I transform quickly, my flesh toughening, my teeth turning into sharp fangs. My claws are silenced by the carpet. And then, I simply can't control myself. The human inside me wants her to run. But the other part is stronger. She turns, showcasing a delicate side profile. I leap towards her, my mouth snarling and wide and hungry, and I want to warn her and devour her all at once. My instincts take over as my teeth puncture her beautiful pale neck, and I see her innocent brown eyes, wide in terror as I bite down into her irresistibly tender flesh.

CHAPTER ONE

'Enter freely and of your own free will!'
Discuss the significance of this line in Bram Stoker's
novel **Dracula** *(1897).*

I am splayed on a sticky kitchen worktop in Leith, being inexpertly eaten out by a first-year archaeology student called Gary. I didn't want to get fully naked – I've only just met this man. So my tracksuit bottoms and knickers are twisted around one leg, as if I'm an overused clothes horse on the brink of collapse. Rusty pipes rumble as they fail to heat the draughty apartment, and there are what feels like old toast crumbs creeping up my bum crack. Gary plays rugby, drinks the cheapest available IPA beer, goes skiing in the winter and enjoys watching MMA fights at 5 a.m. And he is not good at oral sex. Trying to guide him to the correct pleasure zone would be mortifying – he is way off-piste – so instead I let out a token moan, hoping he'll give up before I have to fake an orgasm. I was a solid B-plus student in drama, but pretending this feels good would require Oscar-worthy talent. While my wing-woman

Autumn is getting the rattle of her life somewhere from the vampiric model she picked up earlier, I am practically counting sheep here. Poor Gary – with these skills, he wouldn't know what to do with a first-class stamp. But maybe Gary's not the problem. Maybe it's me. This isn't the first time I've found myself wondering whether I have less capacity for fun than the average twenty-year-old girl.

Then again, the average twenty-year-old girl probably didn't kill their sister. So there's that.

I spot a crooked *Pulp Fiction* poster on the greasy kitchen wall and wonder if Gary's even seen the film or if it's just a generic attempt at looking cool. The licks begin to slow; maybe the poor guy has a crick in his neck. I might not be reaching orgasm anytime soon, but at least I'll have a titillating anecdote to share at lunch tomorrow. Cunnilingus in the kitchen wasn't on my first-semester bingo card, but perhaps it should have been.

My eyes wander in boredom to a food processor perched on the floor, not even out of its box, and I think about Gary's mum picking out kitchen appliances for this exciting new chapter in his life. Little did she know he'd be surviving on a diet of microwavable burgers and pussy.

Gary's lazy licks come to an abrupt halt, signalling the welcome end of the act. It is possible that I am even drier than I was before he began. His grip on my thighs loosens and he comes up for air. His alabaster skin is somehow even paler now, thanks to the smears of glistening crimson decorating his mouth and chin. He wipes a thumb across his bottom lip and stares at it before stuttering, 'Y-you're bleeding.'

Let's go back a couple hours. At The Lounge, an underground nightclub at the foot of Cowgate, a hundred or so students dance ironically to a cheesy remix of a screechy electro song that came out the year we were all born. A cohort of fists pumps energetically in the air to the escalating beat. A burly bald bouncer shouts for an adventurous show-off in a miniskirt to stop twerking on a table. An unfortunate soul rushes past me to throw up in the toilet, his fingers cupping his mouth. Two almost identical girls with puffy lips reapply lipstick, using their phones as mirrors. Wallflowers lurk in the shadows. And I am front left of the DJ booth with Autumn.

'I told you I should have stayed at the library!' I shout over the pounding music, now reaching a glitchy crescendo.

'Behave yourself,' Autumn answers in her strong Glaswegian accent. 'I just met a six-foot spoken-word artist with a Prince Albert,' she adds, with a glint in her eye. Autumn dances with ease, her long fiery-red hair swishing behind her as she moves. Her milky face, brushed with a full universe of freckles, shines with sweat. We found each other at registration for English literature last week, where she immediately welcomed me with a million questions over bubblegum breath. When I told her I liked her name, she replied, 'My twin brother is called Winter. Parents are the best, aren't they?' I felt a sudden urge to tell her about my sister Grace there and then. But as always, I managed to resist it, burying her name until the scream became a whisper.

It's only our second week at the University of Edinburgh, but I already feel a strong affinity with my new friend. Autumn is open and fizzing with energy. She has taught me that people can be really nice, and how to make the best spicy margarita (chilli-salt rim). And Zainab, my other new pal, has taught me how to roll a perfect joint (grind furiously before). And here we are, all three of us at a Singles Night. I'd much rather be cosied up with a good book, but I keep this thought to myself. At the door, we were given the choice of a green, amber or red sticker to signify our relationship statuses. As Autumn writhes unselfconsciously to the music, she proudly showcases two green stickers, one on each of her breasts. As if they need any extra attention. 'We are getting fresh meat tonight,' she had exclaimed excitedly on the street outside the club, startling the elderly man shuffling past us.

'No, you are getting fresh meat tonight; I am here for anthropological reasons only,' I'd corrected her.

'We are the fresh meat,' Zainab had added.

Now, Autumn sips her drink and gives me a gap-toothed smile. She is the type of person who always glitters, with her multiple tooth gems twinkling in the swooshing laser lights and her button nose decorated with a gem on either side. Her fashion sense jumps from effortlessly cool to completely outrageous. Tonight's outfit is a faded noughties crop top that accentuates her curves, high-waisted second-hand men's trousers and a giant furry hat, complete with a diamante handbag too small to hold anything. I've opted for my usual look – baggy track pants and a white tank top. Judging by the amount of leg on show, I am not sure I fit in. There's a surprise. I try to move my hips in time to the beat and ask, 'What's a Prince Albert?'

'A dick piercing!' Autumn nudges me as if it's the most obvious thing in the world.

'Of course,' I shoot back in her ear, wondering what the benefits could be. Whatever they are, I'm not sure they outweigh the risk of infection or getting it caught in a zipper. Ouch.

The short yet mighty Zainab shoves her way through a throng of dancers to join us without so much as an 'excuse me'. She is striking, with rich brown skin and wide eyes, adorned with the type of lashes that people pay good money for. Her hair is oil-black, tucked behind her ears in a no-fuss bob that flicks out at the ends. Zainab likens herself to a 'dykey, Indian Wednesday Addams'. Her humour is as dry as sandpaper, and she's quicker than anyone I know. I met her in the library when she asked directions to the romance section. I had already made myself quite at home there. Turns out she was looking for a quiet place to vape. She wasn't really into any of that mushy crap, as she called it.

Earlier this evening, we'd all got ready together at Zainab's townhouse in Morningside, where she lives alone. I say we got ready, but I just brushed through my shoulder-length curly brown hair, chucked on some mascara and sipped my drink as I watched Zainab apply layer after layer of eyeliner, only taking a break to puff on a joint. Autumn sat cross-legged, nursing a wine, remarking that this apartment was bigger than the one she'd grown up in. It's not far off the size of my mum and dad's, either. Zainab just shrugged. I had never understood the phrase 'filthy rich' until I visited her place. Piles of clothes everywhere, *Jenga*-like towers of dishes in the kitchen sink, a bathroom overflowing with expensive lotions and potions, and congregations of old toilet-roll tubes strewn on the floor. Zainab's lived here since she was sixteen. She has the privilege of fierce independence, only granted to people who come from money. She went to the top all-girl's school in the city, and she has private healthcare and a nice car with her name on it – if she gets her degree. But despite her wealthy roots, Zainab is probably the least pretentious person I've met here. And in Edinburgh, pretension is easy to find. She talks straight, makes me laugh and is far too cool for me. Zainab's mum runs a top cosmetic surgery clinic in the centre of the city, but much to her disappointment, Zainab chose to study veterinary medicine instead of following in her footsteps. She shrewdly told me she prefers animals to people. Which makes her interest in me all the more warming.

As Zainab swoops under a dancing man's armpit, I point at the tray of jelly shots she's balancing. 'Are these vegan?'

Autumn swipes two of them. 'Nope, but I can take the spare one to Prince.' She gives us an exaggerated wink and we watch as she swans over to a skinny guy with a neck tattoo, in an oversized denim jacket, leaning on a pillar. His smouldering pose is so manufactured, I am half expecting a group of paparazzi to be lurking a few feet away. If smoking was still allowed inside, he'd be puffing on a Marlboro Red as we speak. It's all too cool for school for my liking, but I guess he's Autumn's type. From our many conversations about dating and sex, anyone and everyone is Autumn's type. She's had them all – her butch football coach, her divorced supervisor when she worked at a supermarket, her pansexual hairdresser. Just about anyone can get her going, it seems. It's quite the skill.

'Let's go,' Zainab suggests, her voice dripping with boredom. 'All the girls wearing green stickers here are straight.'

'Always the way,' I say more knowingly than I deserve to. 'Maybe we should leave.'

Zainab looks pleased, the way she always does when she gets what she wants. Which, thanks to her bad-bitch energy, is often.

'But I haven't found any fresh meat yet,' I add dryly. Just then, I catch the eye of a cute guy with broad shoulders and an even broader smile. Handsome, approachable and, lo and behold, he's wearing a green sticker. The perfect man to pop my university sexcapade cherry with? I look over to Autumn, who is currently kissing the face off Prince Albert.

Zainab sighs and rips off her sticker. 'He looks boring. Come on, shall we find a pub somewhere?'

'At least let me chat to him first.'

Zainab sighs. 'I'm not waiting around like a spare part. Just do me a favour. Please share your location if you go back to his. Safety first.'

'That's why I carry a condom in my bag.' Along with painkillers, a mini torch and an electrolyte sachet, all of which came in one of the starter kits they were handing out at the freshers' fair. If there's a power cut in which I find myself horny and thirsty with a stubbed toe, I'll be covered.

Zainab elbows her way through the crowd and I approach Green Sticker Guy. When Stevo, my first boyfriend at school, asked me out, it didn't occur to me to say anything but yes – after all, I might never get asked out again. Who would want me? I had kissed a few girls and boys before then but never gotten that far, and I was acutely aware of my loner status. Fancying Stevo was easy, but I was never really sure if I loved him, or vice versa. We were just young kids in a small town, doing what everyone else was doing. Cosplaying as a normal teenage couple. We would watch films at the cinema, slowly teasing each other with popcorn-dusted fingers. Then we progressed to shagging in his car on the way home. But soon we stopped caring about one another. He cheated and I stayed with him. I didn't get the hint, so he cheated again. Eventually, he took the initiative and broke up with me via a badly written letter. It started with 'Yo'.

'Hi, I'm Brodie,' I say shyly.

Green Sticker Guy extends a meaty hand to shake mine and introduces himself: 'Gary.'

Two vodka lemonades, some reasonable banter and a spot of oral later, I am filled with red-hot shame – and Gary's chin and previously all-white tee are covered in it.

'Sorry,' I mumble. I take my leg off him, shimmying myself off the worktop. Saved by the bleed. Pulling up my track pants, I notice Gary is now so ghostly white he's practically see-through.

'Sorry, I'm . . . I don't really like blood.' His body starts to sway like he's deflating, eyes rolling back in his head. Then, he has the audacity to faint. I try to catch him in my arms, but being relatively skinny and scrawny, I buckle under his weight. At the risk of putting my back out, I lower him onto the kitchen floor, cradling him on my lap like a giant floppy baby. Panic intensifying inside me, I grab a dish towel, run it under the cold tap, then dab it over his face. I quickly wipe the blood from his chin and wonder if this has ever happened to Autumn. Or anyone else, for that matter. A few painful minutes go by. I imagine him dying right here on the linoleum. Would I have to break the news to his parents? Would I need to speak at the funeral? I'd have to make up some extravagant lie, like saying we met at study group. But luckily, I won't have to worry about any of that, because Gary starts to come around, his eyes eventually regaining focus. Pulling himself to standing, he glances down at his T-shirt, which is decorated in red blotches, and then back at me. He looks as embarrassed as I feel. Almost.

'At least I know I'm not pregnant,' I blurt out. It's meant to provide a moment of levity, but it sounds deranged. Gary doesn't see the funny side and I don't blame him. I wanted the ground to swallow me up before. Now I need an even bigger sinkhole. 'Where's your bathroom?' I ask, grabbing my bag, cursing my period for arriving a day early and wishing never to see this man ever again.

On my walk of shame towards the Old Town, the cool September air rushes up the sleeves of my coat, so I hug myself to keep warm. I pass doorways of bars where drunk men with gravelly smokers' laughs assemble. These places are flanked by more gentrified establishments, artisan restaurants crammed with diners tucking into deconstructed burgers and sipping on overpriced cocktails. Women in fur coats spill out of a wine bar, shrieking as they take a quick selfie before flagging down a taxi. Walking up further, I pass a heaving kebab shop with a zigzag queue of plastered people waiting eagerly to satisfy their calorific needs. A hunched busker belts out an old folk song, accompanied by sporadic accordion-playing.

Coming from Seafall, a sleepy east-coast town about twenty

miles from Kirkcaldy, to suddenly have all of this on my doorstep feels good. I've managed to secure accommodation right next to the George Square campus, in an old Georgian building in Bucky Place. It's within a stone's throw of all the hotspots – the library, cute cafés, the best pubs and cool thrift stores. I got some money to put towards the costs of student life thanks to the Margaret Wallace scholarship, and although my flat's on the shabbier side, this was all I could afford. All I need to do is get straight As and everything will be fine. I feel a familiar spike of shame for going out tonight instead of prepping for my first tutorial tomorrow. Like I've let myself down. And my parents. Again. Anytime I have even the slightest bit of fun, I am tapped on the shoulder by an invisible Shame Goblin who nastily whispers in my ear, *You know you don't deserve that, right?* Just then, my phone beeps with a message from Zainab.

Zainab:

How was the hook-up? Are you staying at his?

I pause, glancing through the window of a quaint indie book-shop called Beyond Books. I've already visited this store three times, chatting to the owner about the new reads that are out. She's what my mum would call a true eccentric – a trans lady in her forties with wild bleached-blonde hair who wears thick seventies glasses and layers of bold jewellery. Seeing the books propped up in the window reminds me I need to go to the library tomorrow to return my most recent haul.

Looking back at my phone, I know I'm not ready to share my humiliating period story yet. It's too raw.

Brodie:

It was OK. Tell you when I see you. Heading home now. Tired. xx

As I approach my block of flats, I see a petite and refined woman walking her pet poodle. I've seen her around a lot: she always wears a long fur coat, almost down to her ankles, her shiny dark hair teased into an expensive blowout. Her mobile phone is glued to her manicured hand. She throws a loud, 'Good evening!' my way before returning to her phone call. 'I told Jeremy to come back to me when he stops feeding me horse shit! The only thing that talks in this equation is money.'

I let her and her poodle pass me.

'Good boy, Pudding, you can wait until we get to the park.' She pulls Pudding's lead and he trots obediently in front of her, his little legs almost bouncing on the grass. I bet Pudding has a nice life. Premium dog food and walks around all the cute parks in Edinburgh. We didn't have pets when I was young. I never asked why, but I always assumed it's because pets inevitably die. And we've had enough death in our family.

As I put the key in my door, I think about how I couldn't wait to move away from my parents and live independently. Leaving Seafall behind to immerse myself in a cosmopolitan life, rubbing shoulders with artists and writers. When I step inside, my new roommate Nathan is heading out the kitchen towards his bedroom, his droopy grey boxer shorts threatening to fall down as he holds a mixing bowl with a tablespoon poking out of it. I try to avert my eyes, but Nathan's tubby figure is covered in tattoos of cartoon characters I have never heard of and kind of hard to look away from. Despite seemingly not caring much for clothes of any description, Nathan has a curiously ever-present blond quiff. No matter the time of day, that thing is styled, standing to attention.

'Oh, are you baking?' I gesture to the bowl.

'No,' Nathan replies, seemingly confused by my question.

Kicking off my shoes, I peer into the bowl and see a melting pot of different cereals, floating in a baby-pink liquid. There must be at least five different types in there.

'Six,' Nathan offers with pride, as if reading my mind. 'I like to call it cereal soup.'

'Is that . . .?'

'Strawberry milk, yes. As an exception, I can make you one if you like?' He scratches his forehead. 'Although we only have one big bowl. I could do it in a pot if you want. However, I would prefer for us to each stick to our own utensils.'

'Tempting, but I already ate.' Zainab had ordered us a yummy Thai takeaway before the club. It pays to have rich friends who can't cook, it seems.

He looks relieved as he disappears into his room, which briefly emits beams of light from his multiple screen set-up. Soon the familiar sounds of explosions from the action films he watches all night reverberate through the walls. I retire to my own room, which is beginning to feel like home. Granted, the peeling wallpaper is the shade of stale chewing gum, and the yucky brown carpet is so cheap and rough it's borderline dangerous to have any direct contact with exposed skin. But I've done my best to decorate it and make it my own. I've stuck some arty photos on the walls, and my crisp new blue bed covers provide a colour pop. My real pride and joys are my books. The bookshelf is bursting at the seams already, so much of my beloved collection lies in piles on the floor. Sure, I need to step over them when I go to brush my teeth, but I wouldn't have it any other way. When I climb under my covers, I habitually reach out to stroke Grace's memory box, an old chocolate biscuit tin that I've kept beside my bed since I can remember. Inside are some tokens from her short life. A purple hair tie and a square of her favourite bumblebee pyjamas. As I try to fall into a much-needed sleep, I am haunted by the strange shadows in my new room. They taunt me, morphing into scary shapes. I ball my hands into fists and gulp down the familiar fear as I hear Shame Goblin's throaty whisper: *You don't deserve a nice life*. The worst thing about this is I know that it's right.

*

I'm at the top of an impossibly high building. So high that when I look down from the window, all I can see is a pit, a deeper shade than black. A never-ending abyss that threatens to swallow me up. Grace is beside me. But she is no age. More like a spirit, or a presence. An impression of her. I start to back away from the window, but then I lose my footing. She reaches out to grab me.

'Be careful!' she begs.

The white net curtains whip in the wind. One curtain suddenly grabs me by my left wrist and yanks me forward. I dig my heels in, but I'm unable to gain purchase and I slide along the floor. I try to step back, but instead I am propelled towards the window as the other curtain snakes around my free arm, pulling my whole body. The wind slaps me for my insolence, rushes down my throat and into my eyes. I try to wrestle out of its grip but it's pointless.

'Brodie!' Grace's voice shouts, strangled with fear.

And then the curtains snatch me outside, and I am suspended over the nothingness, my bare feet dangling.

'Let me go!' I shout. And then suddenly, I am released. I plummet down and down and down and down and down.

CHAPTER TWO

Explore the importance of female relationships in Little Women *(1868) by Louisa May Alcott and how they impact Jo March's character growth.*

This morning I woke up with butterflies in my stomach. A nice change from the knot of anxiety that has made itself at home in there. As I go for a shower, I see Nathan hovering in the hallway. 'Good morning. Please don't use my shower gel – it's medicated.'

'Course not!' I chirp back at him, wondering how long these types of comments will last.

After getting ready, I brush up on my notes that I prepared yesterday and set off for my first English literature tutorial. When I step out into the gloomy morning sun, the wind is especially boisterous, whipping my hair all over the place. I take a big deep sniff, breathing in the hoppy smell of the city as I tread the rain-soaked pavement. Some of the people I went to school with were bonkers enough to stay in Seafall. I couldn't think of anything worse. I always had my sights on Edinburgh, the literary epicentre of the country. So many trailblazing authors and famous poets have lived here, drawing their inspiration from longing and heartbreak; their words of passion and romance dance invisibly in the air to the beat of my walk. Shutting my eyes, I allow the moment to soak in, but I'm swiftly interrupted by a delivery man wheeling a trolley of cardboard boxes towards me. 'Watch it!' he yells, and I spring out of the way apologetically, stepping into an ankle-deep puddle.

I arrive – my hair windswept and with what feels like a developing case of trench foot – at room 3B and settle in early, taking out the book we will be covering today: *The Bell Jar*. Like most of the books on this semester's reading list, I've already read it. In this case, I've read it so many times that my copy is practically falling apart. Worried I look too keen, I second-guess myself and shove it back inside my bag. I rearrange my notepad and pen set on my desk. There are few things in life as satisfying as a new set of stationery. As the room fills up, I shyly observe my new classmates. I reserve the seat beside me for Autumn, although depending on what went down with Mr Cock Piercing last night, maybe she won't turn up.

A few minutes after eleven, a boyishly handsome student in his mid-twenties sporting a shaved head and wearing a holey cable-knit sweater arrives and pulls out the chair I had reserved for Autumn.

'Someone's sitting there.' My words come out clipped and rude.

'My mistake,' he says in a polite Northern Irish drawl, delivering an impish smile. I can't help but notice his stirring bronze eyes and the dusting of freckles on his tawny skin. I blush for my rudeness. And his dimples.

Just as Autumn skulks in, wearing shades and a smug look on her face, he moves to the opposite side of the table and addresses the room. 'Hello class, I'm Killian Maloney. Sorry I'm a little late, I had a run-in with the staff printer.'

I burst into a loud laugh at his joke, clapping my hand to my face as soon as it escapes my mouth. The whole class blinks at me in confusion. Autumn regards me with confused pity.

'What did I miss?' she whispers.

'He's so much younger than I imagined,' I stutter. I know the name Killian Maloney. Anyone who is interested in literature studies knows the name.

'Eh?' Autumn asks.

As Killian quickly delivers our semester handbooks, I say in a hushed tone, 'Killian Maloney. He made big waves in the Belfast lit scene, and has published loads of papers on the role of men in modern feminist literature.'

Autumn removes her sunglasses, her bloodshot eyes staring blankly at me.

'His opinions on men in literature are, like, famous. To be honest, I pictured him being a lot older and crustier when I read his papers.'

'Everything good over here?' Killian asks us.

Autumn lights up like a Christmas tree and flicks her hair flirtatiously. 'Yes, sir.'

'Let's begin. Why do we need books?' As he gazes around the room, Killian shoves his hands in his jeans pockets, adding to his affable charm.

Autumn discreetly mouths 'Fuck' at me, nodding in his direction. Of course, I should have known, an affair with a tutor would be right up her street. I could never be so daring. Killian makes eye contact and I put on my best thinking expression. Autumn flutters her eyelashes and leans back slightly, her shirt with a psychedelic print all over it stretching accordingly in all the right places. 'Because they're fun,' she offers cheekily.

Light laughter spreads across the room like tinkling piano keys.

Killian's smile broadens, showing beautifully crooked teeth. He repeats back to her, in an amused tone that inspires a touch of jealousy in me, 'Because they're fun. You're not wrong.'

'Never am,' Autumn shoots back.

Desperate for him to notice me, I pipe up. 'Books, and literature, connect us to others and help us make sense of the world and . . . ourselves.'

Killian stretches out an arm in adulation. 'Now that is more like it!'

I feel more red heat creeping up my neck and face, but inside I bubble with happiness. I'll tell you what's better than any new stationery set: it's getting an answer correct in class.

After the tutorial, I wait behind until Killian and I are alone. The tall stained-glass window projects a rainbow on the desk in front of me as the midday sunshine pours through it. 'Can I help you?' Killian bundles his laptop into a weathered leather satchel.

'I just wanted to say sorry for being rude at the start of the class. I was saving the seat for my friend.'

'How dare you?' he says, packing away his papers.

I'm not sure if he's joking or not. 'I just don't want you to think I'm a bad student or anything.'

Killian pauses. 'I've seen a lot worse, believe me. It's Brodie, isn't it?'

I nod.

'You made some really valuable points today.'

I feel a surge of gratitude.

'I was actually on the board of submissions, so I read your personal statement to get into the university.'

'You did?'

'Yes. Very impressive.'

And with those parting words, I practically levitate with happiness out the door.

At Café Curiosity in Edinburgh's Old Town, I join Zainab and Autumn for lunch. This jumble-sale-inspired café is a treat for the eyes as much as it is a treat for the taste buds. Fake taxidermy animal heads adorn the walls. At least, I hope they're fake. The wallpaper is different on each side of the room, ranging from hot-pink flamingos to hippie flowers to zebra print. No two pieces of furniture are the same. There is a wooden swing hanging from thick rope on the way to the toilets. The crockery is mismatched in a thrift store/Mad Hatter's tea party fashion. We sit on a battered Chesterfield couch set, elbows grazing in a pleasantly intimate way.

'Before you got here, Brodie, Autumn was telling me about how last night went,' Zainab says in a tone that tells me there has already been many a juicy detail divulged.

'Oooh yeah, Prince Albert. What happened? Did you have the ride of your life?'

'Better!' Autumn glows.

'What's better than that?' I ask.

'So, turns out, he's into tarot card reading. I mean, talk about two souls connecting. It was cosmic, it was explosive, it was celestial.'

'Was it a shooting star or a shag?' Zainab chides.

But Autumn ignores her, excitedly continuing with her story. 'He is my ideal man! We sat and drank cups of herbal tea and chatted for hours. Then he read my cards.'

I am unable to help my own intrigue. 'What did the cards say?'

Autumn takes a pregnant pause. Then: 'I got the Wheel of Fortune!' She claps her dangerously long manicured nails together.

'Congratulations?' I offer. She may as well have said it in Mandarin for all the sense it made.

'Oh please.' Zainab snorts into her cappuccino. 'You don't honestly believe in all that, do you?'

Autumn sniffs. 'Laugh away. I can see right through your jealousy. I have a path of inner peace and joy ahead of me. And with that attitude, you don't.'

Zainab folds her arms. 'Peace and joy are overrated.'

'So what happened after the reading?' I ask, eyeing the dessert counter and already planning a huge piece of vegan chocolate cake for after.

'We fucked, obviously.'

Once our lunch has been delivered by a waitress in a polka-dot dress, Zainab nudges me. 'You didn't share your location last night.'

'I forgot!' I say, my mouth full of a bite of my falafel wrap.

'Anything could have happened.' Zainab points her fork at me before stabbing it into her Greek salad.

I shudder, remembering Gary's blood-soaked chin.

Autumn looks between us as she oversalts her fries.

'Sorry,' I say with a shrug.

'It's really important you do that, you know, especially if you're going home with a stranger.'

'Stranger?' I repeat in faux offence. 'His name is Gary.'

'And his surname?'

'Eh . . .'

'Wait a minute . . .' Autumn hesitates. 'You never asked me to share my location. Prince Albert could have been a serial killer. And you two would have been none the wiser.'

'Come to think of it, he did look a bit dodgy,' I quip.

'Hey!' Autumn protests.

'Well,' Zainab says, 'the point is, I don't need to worry about you as much, do I, Autumn?'

'Why?' I ask.

'Autumn is clearly used to going home with men.'

'And women!' Autumn adds, chomping on a fry.

Zainab nods. 'And women, exactly. Unless you have something to hide, Brodie?'

With their eyes on me, my chest tightens. If only they knew. I twitch, doing my best to look innocent.

'Please. Just send me your location next time, alright?'

'More importantly, how was Gary?' Autumn needles.

I clam up in embarrassment. 'Nothing special.'

'Come on, tell us! Did Gary rock your world?'

'Hardly.'

Autumn grabs a bottle of ketchup and strokes it tenderly.

'Oh, Gary, give it to me, Gary,' she moans, flinging her head back theatrically. She's so convincing I almost take notes for the next time I meet a guy like him.

A group of young students a few tables along stop eating their lunch and stare at Autumn. Zainab grabs the ketchup bottle from her and slams it down.

'Do you have no shame, Autumn?' she says.

'You should try it sometime, Zainab, rather than going about life like you have a pole shoved up your—'

'Can I get you anything else?' the waitress interrupts.

'No, we're all good, thanks!' I reply brightly, grateful that the attention's off me. My phone beeps with a message. On seeing my face fall, Autumn peers over my shoulder to read it aloud.

Gary nightclub:

Hey, it's Gary from last night. Hope you got home safe. This is kind of awkward to ask, but I was wondering if you would mind sending me some money for my T-shirt that got ruined? It was £50. Or whatever you can afford! Cheers, G x

'Girl, what did you do to his T-shirt?' Zainab questions me.

'I bled on it,' I admit frankly, trying to ignore the shame spiral swirling inside me.

Zainab smugly tucks her hair behind her ear. 'A lesbian would never send a text like that.'

CHAPTER THREE

Analyse the inciting incident in Moby-Dick (1851)
by Herman Melville, paying close attention
to Ishmael's journey.

The following day, I check out the university swimming pool, St Leonard's before class. The force with which I hit the water pushes me down so my tiptoes graze the bottom, then I begin to propel myself back towards the surface. As my body surges up, I feel the familiar rush of tiny bubbles flying past me. Through my goggles I see the strip lights overhead, getting nearer and nearer, brighter and brighter. Pedalling my legs as fast as I can, I use my arms to push me up. When my head bursts above the water, I take a huge breath, gasping gratefully as the air fills my lungs. Another swimmer glides past me, reminding me that I'm in the fast lane. This pool is a piece of cake, compared to the chilly Firth of Forth at Seafall. But water is water, and aside from reading, I have always relied on swimming for a welcome escape. My favourite place to swim was always the lido at Thistle Bay. 'Run, Brodie!' Grace would yell, holding my wrist as the thistles jagged our ankles. I could never keep up.

The Thistle Bay lido is surrounded by man-made stone walls, with the water coming straight in from the sea. Salty and freezing. It was a source of amusement that it called itself an outdoor swimming pool, being that it was more of a giant rock pool, but I loved it. Especially when Grace and I were little and I would paddle in the shallow bit, buoyed by my blow-up orange armbands and flotation devices. Our favourite was a giant pink whale which Dad had won at the Seafall Carnival. Grace and I were so excited to test it out on the beach. We jumped up and down and grabbed Dad's hairy calves as he stood in his black Speedos, his late-thirties beer belly going out and in as he blew it up. He had to stop several times because he got light-headed. Probably on account of the number of hand-rolled cigarettes he smoked every night. But it was worth it to have that whale. Though, being the annoying big sister that she was, Grace would always hog it.

Slicing through the water in a front crawl, I make sure I am quick enough not to have anyone else overtake me. But no matter how many lengths I do, how hard I kick my legs, I can't shake off the memory of the pink whale and of Grace. Unfortunately, even nice memories of her are followed by a bitter aftertaste that lingers like off food. I swim so much that I forget the time. And when I notice it on the big clock on the main wall, I shout, 'Shit!' letting some chlorinated water in my mouth. I have a lecture to get to.

I arrive panting at the mostly full lecture hall, a grand room with huge windows looking out to the city, my curls wet and my fingers pruned. Killian's perched near the front, wrapped up in a petrol-blue cable-knit sweater and reading a book. He looks like he's in a cute stock photograph. I decide to sit in his view, but as I make my way down towards him, I hear a sharp whistle. I turn to see Autumn signalling for me to join her a few rows down from the very back.

'We're practically out the door here,' I say out of the corner of my mouth, taking the empty seat beside her.

'If we sit down there, we'll get picked on. Or is that what you want?'

'Maybe,' I reply haughtily.

Forty students watch in painful silence as our lecturer, Dr Jackie Mcallister, a spritely yet slightly hunched woman in her fifties with spiky short silver hair and a penchant for ponchos, footers around with a PowerPoint presentation that looks like it was created the same year the internet was invented.

'What is romanticism?' Jackie finally addresses the room.

I sit on my hands, practically bursting to shout out the answer. But I'm too shy.

Jackie observes the faces staring back at her. 'It is a cultural movement that emerged in the late eighteenth and early nineteenth centuries. It represented a shift towards emotions, intuition and nature with an emphasis on the human experience.'

Speaking of intuition, I have an odd feeling. Like I'm being watched. I gaze around as other students type on laptops, write in notepads, yawn, sip coffee. Then I see him. A man dressed in all black, with his hoodie up, sitting diagonally in the row behind. I can't see his face, but I know he's staring right at us. At me. Strange. I nudge Autumn, who mistakes it for a joke and giggles and nudges me back. I give her a look, which I think says, *Can you see the creepy person that's staring at us?* but despite proclaiming she has a sixth sense, Autumn unfortunately fails to read my mind at this exact moment. She continues to listen to Jackie's lecture as the prehistoric PowerPoint drags on. I glance back at the hooded figure. But he's gone.

I spend the rest of the lesson irked by distraction, turning around momentarily to see if that guy has returned. Sometimes I get my memories and my terrors all mixed up. My mind loves playing tricks on me. Then I end up doubting myself, the lines of reality smudged like charcoal by an artist's thumb.

I'm so bothered by wondering who that guy was that I miss most of the lecture. Craning my neck every few minutes and jumping at the smallest noise. Even when Killian takes to the lectern to discuss one of his papers, I can't concentrate. And this doesn't go unnoticed, as Killian approaches me at the end.

'Hi girls.'

Autumn digs her talons into my thigh so excitedly, I nearly let out a yelp of pain.

'Hi Killian,' she says, the twinkle in her eye almost blinding me. 'Great class.'

'It's a pity not everybody feels the same. Was our lecture boring you, Brodie?'

The comment takes me aback. I want to answer but I stay mute, trying to read his face. Autumn was not wrong: up close, he really is rather handsome. He gives me a brisk yet kind smile, and then he is gone.

His words leave me in a slightly embarrassed, stunned silence. Does he think I'm not taking it seriously or something? If there's one thing I truly can't stand, it's people thinking I am not trying. I've always been a people-pleaser, and the notion of someone thinking I'm lazy or not good enough practically brings me out in hives. The opportunity to come to this uni and study my passion is beyond my wildest dreams. I make a promise to myself to show Killian what I'm made of.

That afternoon, I'm still feeling creeped out by what happened in my lecture. But Autumn has, for no known reason, signed us up for a pottery taster session and I don't want to cancel on the girls. I pull on baggy jeans and a faded denim shirt and scrape my now-dried curls into a bun, letting two shorter pieces frame my heart-shaped face. Or Moon Face, as I nastily got called at school before my body caught up with my head.

The little pottery studio in Edinburgh's Old Town is tucked behind a row of quaint houses. The small windows glow invitingly, backlighting a wooden sign that reads 'Clay it ain't so!' at the side of the door where I meet Zainab and Autumn. Autumn's dressed in a patchwork flowery boiler suit with a bucket hat. Zainab wears a Peter Pan-collared smock dress and an unimpressed look.

As we walk in, Autumn teases Zainab. 'Whose funeral is it?'

'Sorry I didn't get the memo to dress like a deranged children's TV presenter,' Zainab bites back.

'Shhhh,' I say out of the corner of my mouth, smiling politely at the pottery teacher, Vee, a dumpy PhD student with a button nose and tight frizzy brown hair. She seats everyone at small tables, then wrings her hands before going into her spiel. 'Pottery isn't just a frivolous hobby. It's about having a vision in your head and turning your dreams into reality.'

As we sit staring at our lumps of clay, she adds, 'There's no such thing as a bad attempt.'

'That's just as well, then,' I mutter.

'Can we recreate that scene from the movie *Ghost*?' Autumn calls out excitedly.

Judging by Vee's laboured sigh, she likely gets asked this question a lot and finds it neither funny nor clever.

'First you knead and then roll out the clay into large, sausage-like shapes,' Vee trills.

We do as she instructs. 'Looks like a you-know-what,' I note cheekily.

'A big rock-hard cock?' Autumn's voice booms.

Vee's ears prick up and she calls over, 'How's the table at the back going?'

We all reply in unison, 'Good!'

'Yuck, this is gross.' Zainab grimaces, barely prodding her clay. 'How can you stand doing this with your straight-girl nails?' she asks Autumn, who wiggles her clay-covered paws in Zainab's direction, making her squirm.

'I am not straight,' Autumn replies. 'What about you, Brodie?'

I look up. 'What about me?'

'Is it just the Garys of the world you're interested in, or . . .?'

Zainab tuts. 'You've made her go red – leave her alone, Autumn.'

I met my one and only girlfriend working at the Seafall Café. We connected over our hatred of our maniacal manager and love of *Gilmore Girls*. Sally was fun and confident, basically all the things I wished I was. She would steal her mum's gin and read me poetry in the park as we sipped it, pretending it didn't taste like floor cleaner. A rock star in my eyes. Unable to truly accept someone loving me for me, I pushed her away when things started to drift from casual to serious. She quit the café and we both moved on. Aside from the painful ending, she opened me up to what being with a woman could mean. Despite my face feeling like you could fry an egg on it, I reply with what I hope sounds like confidence, 'I am into girls too.'

'Hell yeah,' Autumn says approvingly.

'And what is your type?' Zainab asks pointedly.

I want the attention away from me, but I'm knuckles-deep in a ball of clay.

'I-I . . .' Truth is, I don't really know. Up until now, my type has been whoever thought I was worth paying attention to. They've been few and far between.

'Hey, that's what we're all trying to figure out.'

Vee approaches us, her brow knitted in a frown.

'I'd watch your edges,' she advises Autumn.

'Ah, see, this is deliberate. I am going for a more abstract approach.'

'Nevertheless . . .' Vee retorts.

As she retreats, I whisper to the girls, 'I think our table might be a lost cause.'

'I can think of dozens of things I'd rather be doing than pottery,' Zainab says, pushing her clay to the side.

'Oh yeah, like what?'

'Pub. Pizza . . .'

'Pogo-sticking?' I offer.

Autumn pats her clay. 'Zainab, if you are not open to new experiences, how do you ever expect to meet your soulmate? Or soulmates?'

'Here we go again. Let me guess, we all have a limitless supply of soulmates?' Her lip curls in disgust.

'Sure, why not?'

It's my turn to chip in. 'Sorry, I've read every romance book under the sun. There's no such thing as multiple soulmates. It's your one true love, the one you cannot live without.'

Autumn sniffs. 'You get back to the universe what you put in, girl. That's all I'm saying.'

I purse my lips. I've always hated that sentiment. So, I deserved to lose my sister? Or worse, I'm going to have a terrible life because of what happened?

Shaking off this grim thought, I try my best to fashion my clay together to make a vase. Although a little on the squint side, I am semi-happy with it by the time I sign it off.

Seeing as clay takes ages to dry before it even goes near the oven, Vee delivers us a selection of the previous class's attempts to glaze before sending them off to the kiln. I peruse the various mugs, bowls and vases.

'Wow, that's the runt of the litter,' Zainab says as I pick up the wonkiest-looking vase from the table.

'Nothing wrong with being different,' I reply, stroking its rough form.

Autumn spots a girl in a band T-shirt and goes off to make friends.

'She does it so easily, doesn't she?' I observe.

Zainab shrugs. 'I don't know where she gets her energy from. What's she like in class?'

Her mention of class makes me think about the guy in the hoodie and I pause, attempting to shake off the unsettling memory.

As if sensing something's wrong, Zainab asks, 'You good?'

'Yeah,' I lie.

She narrows her eyes then casually asks me, 'What are we doing tonight?'

'I know what I'm doing.' Autumn returns, looking like the cat that got the cream. 'I have a date.' She waves over at the girl wearing the band tee, who waves shyly back.

'Can you go anywhere without finding someone to hook up with?' Zainab says.

'Girls, if you want a lesson in getting women, just say so.'

We get painting. Autumn utilises a full range of colours, painting different types of breasts all over the wide bowl she's selected. I carefully paint a pattern of open books on mine, their spines purple and orange, with little white stripes of pages flicking out of them.

Zainab swings on her chair, bored.

As we leave our pieces to dry overnight, Zainab links arms with me. 'So . . . pizza?'

'As much as I'd love to, I need to go to the library,' I say apologetically.

Don't get me wrong, I love chilling with these two exciting new people in my life. Especially because in high school I felt like a bit of a loner. Too bookish to fit in with the popular crew, too weird to thrive with the serious study fanatics, too self-conscious for the theatre kids, too shy to join any sports team. Too much inner turmoil to be any fun or appeal to anybody. But despite this new fun flush of friendship, the library trumps it all.

I look up at the university library building, taking in its looming brutalist structure, cutting a jagged silhouette against the brooding September night sky.

When I get to the metal turnstiles, the young male receptionist greets me from behind the front desk. 'Hey!' he says with suspicious enthusiasm. He doesn't look like the average librarian. Seafall's librarian seemed as old and dusty as the library itself, but maybe octogenarian Mrs Templeton isn't the standard against which to measure all other librarians. He is the kind of tall that makes him slightly stooped, even when he's sitting down. He would be domineering if it weren't for his delicate, almost feminine features: small beady eyes, a mop of dark brown hair, a slightly pointed chin and a strong, narrow nose that flicks slightly upward at the end.

'Hi,' I reply quietly as I root around in my bag, finally finding my student card, which had snuck itself into part six of my dog-eared copy of *Anna Karenina*. I try to scan my card but nothing happens. The receptionist rushes around the desk to help me. His general aura is that of a friendly giant. 'There we are,' he says warmly, scanning me in.

'Thanks,' I reply, shoving my student card back in my bag.

'It's Brodie, right?'

My brow furrows. 'Do I know you?'

'No, but you are one of our frequent flyers. First year, right? Let me guess, English lit?'

I nod, feeling a whiff of embarrassment at being identified so easily. What gave it away, I wonder. My slogan tote bag that says 'Get Lit', straining under the weight of more books than is reasonable to carry? That or my general bookish demeanour?

'I'm Sam.'

'Nice to meet you, Sam. Do you always make it your business to learn everyone's names off by heart?'

'Just the regulars,' he says, blinking his floppy hair out of his eyes and giving me a smile that betrays two large, beavery front teeth that make him look mildly like a college football team mascot.

'Thanks,' I mutter shyly.

'Anytime.' He returns to his desk and points at the pile of books I'm now clutching in my arms. 'How are you getting on with those?'

'I've finished them,' I admit.

'Really?' Sam asks, impressed.

'I'm fast,' I say with a shrug. Some nights if I'm lost in a book, I can get through the whole thing. And with this kind of useless flex, no wonder I've always had, shall we say, a limited social life.

'I still need to finish this bad boy, though.' I hold up *The Private Memoirs and Confessions of a Justified Sinner* by James Hogg.

'It's a masterpiece.' Sam flicks his hair enthusiastically. There is something quite cute about him.

'I'll be the judge of that,' I joke, heading for the elevator. As I wait for the doors to open, I wonder if he was flirting with me. No; he was probably just being friendly.

As the lift edges up to the eighth floor, my wavy reflection makes my shoulder-length hair look even more frazzled than it feels. 'Unruly hair, unruly girl,' my mum used to say as she tried to brush it when I was little. Despite her being a hairdresser, I always hated her doing it. It felt like torture. Instead of having poker-straight blonde hair like my mum, I inherited the big curls from the Bells – Dad's side. That and his temper. Grace has the same big curls too. Sorry, *had* the same big curls. Grace being relegated to the past tense burns white-hot inside of me. Sometimes I get on with my day immediately, just bounce on to the next thought or task. And other times I feel the loss pulling me down to a dark place, almost dragging me under. Grief is so weird. One minute you're totally fine; the next minute a can of soup in the grocery store causes you to burst into hysterical tears. 'The price we pay for love,' I saw in looped gold writing on a saccharine condolence card once. Fuck that. Why should I have to pay the price when other people get to glide through life without so much as a pet goldfish passing away?

The reading room is dead. I slowly pad through, gazing at the different-coloured spines. This is my happy place. The smell of old books. The smell of new books. The fusty carpets and glazed walnut shelves that hold the weight of a billion words and stories. The idea that there were many readers here before me and there will be many readers after me gives me comfort. Since I can remember, I've loved reading. Who wants real life when you can live in a different world? I got my love of reading from my fake Auntie Lou. She was an incredible cake-baker and, unlike us, had a lot of pets, who ruled the roost in her dilapidated farmhouse on the hill. There were perpetual cobwebs in the corners of the ceilings and the floors were creaky, but I always felt safe and at home there. Even more exciting than her famous lemon drizzle cake,

Auntie Lou had an unparalleled book collection. My parents did read, or at least I think my mum did. Especially on holidays. But my Auntie Lou had hundreds, if not thousands, of books all over her home. And without the age certification that comes with watching a movie, Auntie Lou could never remember if something was age appropriate or not. 'Is that the one about horse riding? I think you'll be alright,' she would say, stroking her dog Wilbur as she sat in front of her fire. And alright I was, my nose stuck in a Jilly Cooper far too young, sparking a lifelong obsession with books.

It's not my parents' fault that I would rather spend time with books than with them. It's unimaginable what they went through, losing Grace. There's a dull pang in my heart like a guitar string's just been plucked. My childhood can be separated quite easily into two parts: before and after Grace passed away. Before was disco music and hoots of laughter, trips to the beach, slurping on melting ice cream and collecting shells. At home, my dad would play his tambourine, fancying himself as Fife's answer to Bob Dylan. Grace would grab my hands and spin me around the living room until I got dizzy. Even when I screamed for her to stop. She had a wicked side that revelled in taking things too far. Mum would intervene, telling us to 'Be careful!' but with her mouth pulled up in a smile.

Dad would roar as he carried us around on his back, pretending we were two princesses and he was our trusty steed. Mum was never the domestic type but, bless her, she did attempt to follow one of Lou's cake recipes once. Grace got flour all over her nose and I got frosting handprints everywhere. Then Mum had to sheepishly chuck a charred banana bread loaf in the bin and ended up feeding us toast with a mountain of jam and milky tea instead. Life was technicolour. And then, after the accident, it all went grey. Dad's tambourine gathered a layer of dust. Mum looked

more gaunt and tired and far older than she was. No more diabol-
ical baking, or singing. No more laughter, or music. A happy home
to a sad home, in one tragic night.

My fingers stroke the spines of the gothic horror section.
There is safety in books. They can hurt us, sure. Make us cry,
make us laugh, make us question our very existence. But a book
can never leave you.

As I approach my little reading corner, a battered and abandoned part of the library that survived the revamp a few years ago,
there's a sudden icy draught. It wooshes past me, almost through
me, shaking me like a single-glazed window on the night of a
storm. The temperature feels like it's just dived about ten degrees.
I wonder whether or not to say something to Sam on the way out,
but I've never been one to complain. I tighten the straps on my big
navy coat, a vintage find from my first weekend trawling all the
musty thrift stores that Edinburgh has to offer.

The overhead strip lights begin to flicker, a few seconds off and
then a few seconds on. Taking a couple of tentative steps, I suddenly stop dead in my tracks. Below my feet, the carpet is wet and
sticky. There is a pool of some black substance. I move to one side
and bend down to inspect it more closely.

Blood.

I see someone in the distant darkness, a figure bent over. Then
the light flickers again, and they're gone. Am I imagining this or is
somebody playing some kind of joke?

'Hello?' My voice shakes, betraying my fear. My heart thuds
staccato in my chest. Then I hear it. A noise that cuts through
the quiet; it sounds like a guttural growl. Oh man, there must be
people fucking in the poetry section. How ironic. I hear the noise
again. It's veering into the animalistic. Whoever they are, they
are enjoying themselves thoroughly, grinding up against the works
of Seamus Heaney or Maya Angelou. Sorry, Maya.

I decide to let the lovers do their thing and turn back around. Maybe coming here wasn't such a good idea after all. The hairs on my neck suddenly stand up, as if my body knows something is about to happen before my mind does. Before I can move, a streak of silver shoots towards me, and then . . . nothing.

*

I know that she is of great importance. And I am simply here to see her with my own eyes. Florence told me she would just look like an ordinary girl. But I will not blindly trust what she says. I need to find out what this human is capable of.

She is not what I was expecting. Perhaps they got it wrong. Perhaps it's not her. But it must be. Her sweet, earthy smell . . .

Surprisingly delicious. Delectable.

CHAPTER FOUR

In **The Invisible Man** *(1897), H. G. Wells taps in to the fear of the unknown. Please explore the notion of the innate human fear of what lies beneath and how this is shown in the text.*

It's been the hottest July day on record for twenty years. Too hot even to go to the beach and have a swim. I am two weeks shy of my fourth birthday. Grace is six years old and therefore knows everything, obviously. This evening, she has her favourite bumblebee pyjamas on.

Today is Sunday, which means our parents were off work. Dad works at the local car showroom and is the second-top salesperson. Mum is a hairdresser. She says she chose hairdressing because she loves making people feel good, but Dad says it's because she loves talking all day.

Earlier, Grace and I played in the shared garden outside our block of flats with the green garden hose – or, as we like to call it, the 'crazy snake' – spraying each other with welcome water. The air was full of the sound of chirpy gulls, music and the thrilled yells of the other children on our street doing the same. Dad made a barbecue and we had tasty burgers and vegetable skewers – it's still ten years before I watch such a graphic documentary on veganism that I swear never to touch meat again. Mum sat in the shade reading her book and sipping a glass of white wine with an ice cube in it.

Now it's my bedtime. I have a mobile suspended above me with little planets circling one another. After such a fun-filled day, I'm grateful to snuggle my cuddly bear and feel my eyelids get heavy. Grace, on the other hand, has other plans. Mum and Dad have taken it in turns to read her three stories now, and 'time is getting on'! Dad's voice is raised. He's getting angry. He tucks her in and warns her that even if she cries again, he won't come back in.

Grace keeps making a fuss. She shouts that she wants Beebee, the toy Granny Bell got her for Christmas. Dad goes away, quietly shutting the door behind him, but the room isn't so dark. I can see Grace wriggling around, kicking off her blanket and huffing and puffing.

Mum left our bedroom window open to let some air in earlier and she must have forgotten to shut it. The thin, netted curtain boogies in the night breeze. The bright yellow moon smiles at me, with big thick eyelashes and lipstick like Mum wears when Dad takes her out to Mackay's.

I can't remember why, but I jump out of my cot, landing bum-first on our fuzzy rainbow rug. It doesn't hurt. Grace tosses and turns and grumbles. The moon calls me to join her. There's a little wooden stool that sits under Grace's bookshelf. I climb on it. Grace shouts but I just ignore her. And then up on to the windowsill I go. I can see the shiny lights of the town in the distance from our fourth-storey flat. I look down and the ground seems very far away. The cars parked down below look like the small ones I play with at nursery. The moon breathes her gentle hot breath on me and then I see a cow, about to jump high into the sky, and maybe I could jump too?

And then Grace shouts my name, but it's too late because I'm not on the windowsill anymore. I'm outside. I fall and there's a crunch. I can't get *any air in. I cry so loud, I'm sure my dad will hear. And then all I see are Grace's bumblebee pyjamas, and they have turned a deep, dark red.*

*

'Grace!' I wake up sweating and gasping from my nightmare, my eyes scrunched shut in fear. The routine rush of cortisol pumps through my veins, and I try to take some calming breaths. In through the nose, out through the mouth. The haunting memory of that fateful night is nothing unusual. I've had these bad dreams so often over the years I've come to accept them. Like the survivor's guilt that comes with them, they are as much a part of me as my knobbly knees.

Sliding my hands under my covers, I realise I'm wearing a nightie. What on earth? I don't even own one. I snap my eyes open in confusion. This isn't Bucky Place. Fear spikes through me. I don't know where I am. My eyes dart around, searching for the familiar. The room is windowless, sparse, with rough concrete walls, bare apart from a big screen on one side. I hear beeping and see that I have an IV drip in the back of my right hand and a blood-pressure monitor clamped on my index finger. I must be in the hospital. Have I had an operation? Swallowing hurts, like I've gargled shards of glass. My free hand frantically feels my body for clues. I reach for the bumpy scar on my neck, the one I've had since the accident. When I feel the spikes of a row of fresh stitches poking out of my skin like barbed wire, my stomach drops. Where the fuck am I and what the fuck has happened to me?!

A stout woman in her mid-thirties comes into the room. She has a commanding presence. Her afro hair is pulled back in a no-nonsense bun and she's wearing grey scrubs. I sit up, a little too fast. Sinking back dizzily into my pillow, I garble, 'Where am I?'

She gives me a brisk smile, revealing one gold tooth, then looks at the screens on the wall and notes something down on her clipboard. Then she approaches me and shines a little torch into my eyes, causing me to flinch. The woman writes something else on her clipboard. She lifts the silver pendant she's wearing around her neck and speaks into it in a matter-of-fact tone. 'She's woken up.' Seconds later, the door swings open again.

I'm about to ask another question, but my words scurry back into my mouth when a statuesque, athletic woman in a black knee-length kilt and long leather duster strides towards the bed. She has a sleek white-blonde bob, cut just under her silver-stud-decorated ears. Not a hair out of place. She must be in her early forties and has a diamond-shaped face with high-set cheekbones. Her hooded eyelids and slightly hooked nose make her the most interesting person I think I have ever seen. Something about her makes me feel funny, but I'm not entirely sure why.

'Leave us alone,' the blonde woman says in a voice dripping with authority. The other woman nods and makes herself scarce. Once we are alone, the mysterious stranger steps nearer to me, looking at me the way I look at vegan chocolate cake. My body feels on high alert, with all the hairs standing on end so that I feel them brushing against one another excitedly.

'Who are you?' I croak.

'Shhhh,' she says soothingly, taking another step towards me, now looming over my bed.

'Don't you dare hurt me,' I say through gritted teeth.

'I won't,' she says calmly.

'Tell me who you are,' I demand.

She grabs the shiny handrails of my bed with her ring-clad fingers and leans over me, blocking the overhead light. So close, our faces are almost touching. 'I'm Nova.'

'Brodie.'

A smirk threatens to break her cool exterior. 'Yes, I know . . . We read your student card. Cute photo, by the way.'

Autumn helped me prepare for it by tonging my hair, warning

me that a bad hair day is just a day, but a bad photo is for life. Or in this case, four years.

Nova inches even closer to me and I notice the beautiful lines on her face, hinting at a world of experience. Especially the ones leading from her flared nostrils, down the sides of her mouth to her perfectly rounded chin. Her feathered eyebrows are silver-white, with the left one separated by an old scar. On closer inspection, Nova has one green eye, one blue, and I think of my dad blasting Bowie records too loud when I was younger.

'Brodie, do you remember anything about tonight?'

My body starts to shake. 'The lights were flashing. It was cold . . . and I thought I saw . . . something.'

Nova nods encouragingly. 'You were attacked.'

A salty tear runs down my face and into the corner of my mouth, stripping away my tough-girl act. I nod to let her know I understand. 'Was I stabbed?'

Nova looks at me for what feels like an eternity. 'No. You were bitten.'

'By what?'

I watch her candy-coloured lips part to reveal flawless white teeth, and she says, 'A werewolf.'

An uncomfortable laugh escapes me. I shake my head; maybe I was sedated. 'Maybe we should have this conversation when I've fully woken up. I thought you said werewolf.'

Nova doesn't move a muscle. 'You heard correctly.'

I stare back at her blankly, waiting for something that I can make sense of. Or at least for the punchline.

'The werewolf bit you on your neck, where your stitches are. In normal circumstances it would have been a fatal attack, but due to some scar tissue you have already, we think you were somehow protected. Looks like your lucky day.'

'Lucky?!' I spit, my neck suddenly pulsing in pain.

'You've survived something that, frankly, no human should ever survive. It was a highly aggressive assault,' Nova says.

My eyes narrow. This woman is clearly completely mad, and I need to get away from her as quickly as possible. Yet I can't help my curiosity. 'Meaning what?'

'We're going to keep you in for further tests and observation, but we think . . .' She trails off.

'What, that I'm now a werewolf?' I joke.

'We'll see.' Nova's stillness says it all.

'Oh, will we now?' I've heard enough. I need to get the hell away from this raving lunatic. I shakily push myself up, swing off the bed and yank out the IV. This hurts a lot more than I was expecting. 'Aaaaaagh,' I wail in pain as blood squirts up the wall in a manner that would make Jackson Pollock proud.

'Yeah, I wouldn't recommend doing that,' Nova says dryly.

'Oh, would you not? Any other top tips for me?' Finding my clothes folded on a chair, I hastily try to pull on my jeans while holding the back of my hand to stop the bleeding. Then I notice I've pulled them on back to front. The humiliation of the moment crystallises inside me. 'Where's my coat?' I demand furiously.

Nova sucks her teeth like a plumber about to give me a ridiculously high quote. 'It wasn't made of as strong stuff as you I'm afraid.'

As I continue to struggle, Nova steps towards me with a white cloth. She pauses, and for a split second, I wonder if this bitch is about to smother me. Before I can move out of the way, she guides me slowly back to the bed. I sit on the edge of it obediently and she wraps my bleeding hand expertly in the cloth, holding it tight. Something tells me Nova's fingers contain a steely strength from which I would be incapable of freeing myself. Even if I wanted to.

She gestures for me to take over and I press the cloth into my hand to quell the bleeding.

Nova squats, briskly pulls down my jeans and turns them the right way around.

'Foot,' she orders, and I stick my left leg in the hole she's stretched out for me, kicking myself for wearing odd socks today. She does the same with my other leg and guides the waistband up, grazing my calves, then my thighs and finally pulling the jeans over my hips. I lift up my bottom and notice a silver pendant around her neck, just like the doctor's one. It has a wolf engraving on it. We lock eyes. It's like having a staring contest with a pedigree husky. She looks at me with the stillness of a frozen loch and I feel myself slowly calming down as our breathing falls in tandem.

Nova breaks the moment by getting to her feet and clearing her throat. I turn my back to her, quickly whip off the nightie and pull on my torn tank top, being careful to avoid my stitches. Red creeps into my cheeks as I button up my shirt, noticing it's covered in blood. I grab my boots and hastily shove them on.

'It's in your best interests to stay here until you feel better.' Nova's voice is commanding. Her intense gaze has bamboozled me, but my wits quickly come back. I need to get out of here.

'You'll want this,' she adds, holding out my tote bag of books, which I yank from her grip before pushing past her and making my way out of the door.

Like an animal released into the wild from captivity, I'm unsure what to do with myself at first. I'm in a low-ceilinged concrete corridor, lined by green neon tube lights which run alongside the joints in the wall. I look to my left and right, but there's no indication of an exit. If you take a left, you eventually get out, isn't that the case? Or is it labyrinths I'm thinking of? Panic starts to rise in me, so I randomly pick left and run as fast as I can towards a metal door I see at the end of the corridor. When I get to it, I grab the big round iron handle and turn it with all my strength until it eventually creaks open.

Here I find a narrow and twisted stone staircase only leading up. I'm terrified of heights, and this includes staircases that lead to an unknown destination. But who knows what will happen if I go back? Gulping, I look behind me. Nova is nowhere to be seen. This means she's chosen to let me go. I slam the door shut behind me, plunging myself into relative darkness. I can hear water dripping and it smells of warm damp. Trying to swallow my terror, I walk up the staircase, my fingertips dragging along the rough stone wall. I spiral round and round, up and up. And then I feel carvings of some kind. Bringing out my phone to use as a torch, I'm faced with unmistakable claw marks, scoring the stone in a variety of directions. As if a wild animal was in a frenzy. Losing my footing, I gasp, then pause momentarily to calm myself down. I'm starting to feel sick to my stomach. Despite this, I plough on, trying to pick up the pace, taking two steps at a time and praying for something good at the top of these stairs. It feels like they're going on forever. Eventually, I get to a door and bang on it. 'Help! Help!'

It must be a matter of seconds, though it feels longer, before I hear a buzz and then a metal click, and I push out to the cool night air. Slamming the door behind me, I stand panting as my bearings slowly return. I turn around and all I see is a brick wall, as if the door has disappeared. Stroking the brickwork, I can't find anything to indicate where the door might be. But the relief of being away from that place overtakes me and I follow the familiar smell of hot chip oil and battered haddock, surmising that I'm in some kind of back courtyard behind a chip shop. I walk towards where I can see streetlights and hear the murmur of people. As I edge down a narrow close, a door swings open and a tubby man in a blue-and-white striped apron calls back inside, 'And then I said to him, "And what did your wife have to say about that?"'

Before I can move out of the way, he launches a bucket of dirty, warm, soapy water all over me.

'Noooo!' I shout, but he's already disappeared back inside.

My hair and clothes are drenched. The cherry on top of the proverbial cake. Soaking wet and shivering, I stagger out on to the street and look up, searching for a street sign.

A well-to-do couple pass me briskly. 'Someone's had a rough night,' I hear the man mutter.

'I have, as it happens!' I shout back, and they both quicken their pace, a look of fear across their faces.

And then I realise I have my back to Edinburgh Castle. It looms behind me, on top of Castle Rock. I'm on Lothian Road, about twenty minutes' walk from Bucky Place. I rush home as quickly as I can, my boots squelching with the dirty mop water, my thoughts racing. What the actual fuck just happened to me?

When I get home, I find the hallway in complete darkness. Flicking the light on in my bathroom and seeing my reflection in the mirror, I get a fright. My mascara is smeared down my face, my eyes red and blotchy. My hair is all knotted.

And I stink.

I run the shower until the bathroom has filled up with steam, and I have the soapiest, longest shower of my life. Flopping into bed soon after with a towel wrapped around my head, I am exhausted physically and mentally. I can see the sun is about to come up through a gap in my flimsy curtains. Then, just before I fall into a deep sleep, I see Nova's face, smiling at me, lighting up my mind like a projector.

*

There is a blood-curdling scream.

'She's dying!' Mum screams in a pitch I've never heard before. She holds a limp Grace in her blood-soaked bumblebee pyjamas.

Then red and blue lights. Nee-naw, nee-naw. Two friendly women in green jumpsuits put a mask on me to help me breathe.

Some voices I know and some voices I don't recognise.

'Fractured collarbone . . .'

'Lucky to have survived the fall.'

'Lucky to be alive.'

Then hospital. Crisp, hard bedsheets and strong chemical smells. I get to eat vanilla ice cream and jelly, and a funny clown comes in to visit us. One of the boys on the ward is frightened by him, but I tell him not to be scared. There's a really silly nurse who reads me stories. They said I've made a quick recovery, but why is Mum still upset? And I want to know where Grace is. 'She would like this story too,' I tell the nurse.

Back at our home, with all the lights off, Mum sobs and sobs and sobs. Then she screams into a pillow. Dad kicks the telly and the screen smashes like star dust. I'm scared. Dad says sorry, then he sits me down and gives me my blankie to hold. Tells me in a cracked voice that Grace went to the hospital too. That her injuries were worse than mine. She wasn't as lucky as me. She wasn't as lucky at all.

CHAPTER FIVE

In the novella* The Turn of the Screw *(1898) by Henry James, sexuality and repression are seen through the relationships of the characters. Discuss.

What feels like seconds after I close my eyes, the alarm jack-hammers through the air, jolting me awake. Scrambling for my phone to turn it off, dread and fatigue wrestle unhelpfully in my body. My head feels like it's inside a tightening vice. Everything aches. My first thought drifts to a hangover. But then, like a train charging through a tunnel, yesterday rails back. Tracing around the nape of my neck, I stroke my old scar. Not a stitch to be found. No cut, so no bite, surely? Maybe it was just a night terror. I'm no stranger to those. But it felt so real. I give myself a shake.

Sitting up, I check the rest of my body and find a few amethyst-coloured bruises on my legs, but that's it. All I want to do is to curl back into bed, pull the covers over my head and go back to sleep, even if it means more scary nightmares. But I can't miss my lecture. If there's one thing I have always prided myself on, it's being a good student, and that is not about to change.

Dragging myself out of bed, I zombie-walk to the kitchen. Nathan's side of the kitchen has been put into so much meticulous order, it's giving clean freak with nothing better to do. Imagine spending your time labelling and colour-coding all your food. I skipped dinner last night, so I suppose I'd better eat. I shove some bread in the toaster and press it down. The problem is, my mind is whirring, unable to conjure clear thoughts, a jumbled-up jigsaw of memories, moments and visuals. Books. Blood. Neon lights. I stare into space, wanting to make sense of everything but not quite getting there. Maybe I just need a coffee. I quickly rinse and dry one of my mugs from the pile I'd left in the sink and make myself a supersize instant coffee.

The library visit was real, wasn't it? But then that weird place under the castle. And Nova. She was really something. At least it felt like she was something. Sometimes my night terrors are realistic, but this was next level.

Exhausted, I retreat back to my bedroom and lie on the bed, propping myself up with my new pillows. Shutting my eyes, I summon an image of Nova, her chiselled features and full lips. I squeeze my thighs together, feeling a warm tingly sensation start to blossom. Testing myself, I part my knees slowly, then push them closed again, letting my legs brush one another. The tingles get more intense, spreading from my clit all the way inside me to the lower part of my abdomen. It's so intense I start to gently pant. It feels like the embers of a fire are burning hotter and hotter, with growing flames, licking my innermost parts. The breathtaking sensation intensifies every time I squeeze my legs, so much so that it makes me gasp out loud. Teasing myself, I let my knees open again and then press them together as hard as I can. Each time, the fabric of my boxer shorts twists a little more inside the folds of me. Resisting the temptation to put my hand down there and stroke myself to heaven, I squeeze again, the waves of pleasure getting deeper. Now I'm trembling. Thank goodness Nathan always has his headphones on, because now I can't help myself, and my moans get louder and closer together. My hands, which have yet to touch me anywhere below the waist, reach up and grab hold of one of the pillows, threatening to tear it in half. I let my thighs fall open one last time before pushing them together, in one final delicious press. I feel a pulsing sensation so strong and hot it's almost unbearable. The longest, most intense orgasm approaches me, like a mega wave. As it crashes everywhere inside me and around me, I surf it euphorically. My limbs shake as if they have a mind of their own and blood pumps in my ears and my throat. My body convulses as I see stars and white noise fills my ears.

Afterward, I take a huge gulp of air, my head spinning and my face covered in a sheen of sweat. Then it creeps up on me – a strong, distinctive smell, coming from the hallway, I guess. Like burnt food. Nathan must be cooking something. Odd, because I definitely didn't hear him get up. Granted, I was on what felt like a different planet, but still. Looking down at my light grey boxer shorts, I notice a hot wet patch, evidence of that incredible moment I just had with myself. Then through my open knees, I see it. Smoke curls menacingly under my door, creeping into my room like dry ice on a movie set. I jump up, going from post-orgasmic bliss to high alert in a matter of a millisecond. Then the sound of the fire alarm pierces the air. Not just our flat, but the entire apartment block. Hastily flinging on a tracksuit and trainers, I rush into the smoke-filled hallway towards Nathan's room. Coughing and spluttering, I bash on his door. 'Nathan! Fire! Fire!'

The brutal smoke smell fills my nose and lungs as a topless Nathan flings open his door, clutching a hockey stick.

'Where's it coming from?' he shouts.

'I don't know, but we need to evacuate.'

He grabs his coat and leads us to the exit, encouraging me to hold on to his back.

Just as we reach our front door, I let go of him. 'Wait!' I shout, turning back, remembering something I need to grab from my room.

Nathan tries to block me, but I push past him, running through the smoke, which is getting thicker, making seeing and breathing even more difficult than before. Fire engine sirens blare in the distance, letting us know help is on the way. As the smoke darkens to a deeper grey, I cover my mouth and run into my room, wheezing and gasping. I scramble for Grace's memory box and wedge it tightly under my arm. When I rush back into the corridor, Nathan is still there, covering his face with his arm, holding the door open for me. We make our way down the stairs and join everyone else on the grass out the front. Some people are in bathrobes, others in pyjamas, some in their clothes for the day.

As plumes of charcoal smoke come out of our open kitchen window, I can barely look. We congregate like shivering penguins at the fire safety point, and watch as three fire engines screech around the corner and park at an angle. Firefighters rush into the building to tackle the fire. I feel sick, imagining it spreading to our rooms. A ball of fear rolls around my stomach as I think of my new laptop that I bought with my student loan and my treasured book collection being burned to the ground.

Nathan stands stoically with his bare tattooed legs poking out from under his overcoat, looking amusingly like an old-school flasher. If it wasn't such a grim situation, I would tease him about it. He must sense my fear because he says, 'Don't worry, Brodie.'

After ten minutes, the firefighters reappear out the front door. Somebody starts a round of applause and people whoop and cheer. Despite being relieved the fire is out, I am not in a celebratory mood.

'Who lives in the flat on the third floor?' a firewoman bellows. Nathan raises his hand. 'Us!'

The firewoman beckons for us to join her. She holds an unidentifiable charred black electrical appliance in her gloved hand, her smudged brow raised in a scary headteacher way.

'Can you guess what this is?' Her eyebrows wiggle along with the pointed question. I catch Nathan's puzzled look and wonder if it is his PlayStation. He's never off the thing; perhaps he caused the blaze by letting it overheat from overuse.

'This is your toaster,' she says, looking between me and Nathan. 'Looks like someone left a tea towel on top of it.'

Remembering drying my mug earlier, I shrink down sheepishly.

'We left your windows open. But there's significant damage to your kitchen. You'll want to find alternative accommodation until the place is fixed up,' she says.

Riddled with guilt, I follow Nathan to the flat. It stinks. He pulls a face as he leans his hockey stick against the wall.

'You never mentioned that you played hockey,' I say.

'I don't.'

'What's with the stick then?'

'It's for just in case.'

'In case of what?'

'End of the world type thing.'

'You think that'll save you?'

'That's not the only weapon I have – it was just the easiest to grab. I have all sorts. Who knows what we'll be faced with: a zombie virus, vampires . . .'

Werewolves, I think, but I can't bear to say it aloud.

We gingerly step into the kitchen, observing the mess. There are big smoke stains on the countertop and one wall is jet black. Residual smoke hangs thick in the air.

'Sorry, Nathan.' I blot a finger on the charred countertop.

Nathan twitches. 'Not really ideal, is it? Guess I'll be going back to stay with my parents for a bit. What about you?'

'Me too,' I lie. I'd rather stay here in this burnt oven than return to Seafall. I've only just escaped from the place. I want to change the subject. 'Now toast's out of the question.'

'I have just the thing,' Nathan says brightly, swinging his cupboard door open. It's full of ten Mason jars of different cereals. Labelled, of course.

I'm not in a place to judge – I almost destroyed our home and killed us both because I was wanking myself into the high heavens.

And so we sit in our smoky kitchen, eating cereal soup. Until I realise the time. Shoving my bowl in the sink, I thank Nathan for breakfast, then get my things together for class.

As I hurry out of Bucky Place and towards the uni, I see our glam neighbour and her trusty dog Pudding.

'Good morning,' she says in her clipped voice, before going back to her phone call. 'Why has it not been delivered on time? It's just not good enough. Get Colin on the phone and tell him I am livid!'

'Morning,' I say back in a small voice.

'Come on, Pudding!' she shouts briskly, and the little cartoon cloud on legs scurries along beside her, his tiny pink tongue hanging out to one side.

I am about to let them both pass when something very strange happens. Pudding stops dead in his tracks. He can't take his beady eyes off me. Suddenly he bares his tiny jagged teeth in a startling grimace. He looks so silly I let out a small laugh.

My neighbour frowns and holds the phone to her shoulder, tugging in surprise at his designer lead. 'What's got into you, Pudding?'

I give a polite smile and try to walk past. But then, out of nowhere, the dog makes a leap for me, yanking his owner forward. As the cotton ball with fangs soars surprisingly high through the air towards me, it startles me so much that I fall back into the flower bed by the path.

'Pudding!' his owner shouts as I jump up, narrowly avoiding being Pudding's target.

Pudding snarls, a deep, nasty snarl. Part of me is freaked out, but the other part is impressed that something so cute can make such a threatening noise.

Taking a few uneven steps back, I hold up my hands in surrender. The lady looks as shocked as I feel.

'I'll phone you back after my Pilates,' she says into her mobile, then hangs up. 'I'm terribly sorry, he never behaves like this.' She wrestles with the lead.

Pudding crouches down like a little white tiger creeping towards an antelope.

'Hey now,' I protest – then Pudding barks and barks and barks, and launches himself at me once more.

This time, I won't make the mistake of hanging around. So I run. Pudding snaps and snarls. My sneakers pound the pavement. Running as if my life depends on it, I go as fast as I can, with the sound of my neighbour shouting, 'Puddiiiiiiiiing,' getting fainter and fainter.

Turning the corner to my lecture hall, I pause for a breath. Pudding is nowhere to be seen but I am rattled. Gasping for air, I lean against the cool wall, shutting my eyes as my heartbeat slowly returns to normal.

'Brodie?' a voice interrupts.

Killian stands before me, all cute in a crumpled shirt and mustard cardigan, shading me from the sun. Standing up straight, I desperately try to regain my composure.

'Hi,' I say, wiping my mouth self-consciously.

He breaks into such a generous smile, it makes my heart rate start to rise again.

'You . . .' he says softly, gesturing with his hand.

'What?' I ask, trying not to squint.

He points to his lip. Surely, he doesn't want me to kiss him. In broad daylight. Does he?

My own mouth parts to ask a question, but I can't quite summon it.

He looks at his feet, embarrassed. 'Your lip . . .'

'Yes?'

Killian takes a step towards me. He rummages in his jeans pocket and brings out a fresh tissue. 'Here,' he says, handing it to me.

Confused, I accept it.

'You have a . . . something on your mouth.'

I look down at my hand and see my finger is smudged with black from where I wiped the charred surface in my kitchen. I want to explain, but Killian's already heading into the lecture hall, leaving me to fester in my own embarrassment.

After a quick freshen-up in the toilets, I sneak into the lecture hall just as Jackie begins. I'm thankful for Autumn's copper hair, which I can spot a mile off. I slide in beside her and she does a double-take. Her giant reading glasses make her doll-like eyes look even larger than usual. 'What the . . .?'

My jacket is covered in soil marks from the pansies I fell into. My hair is stuck to my face with sweat, my cheeks flushed from the unplanned sprint. And my encounter with Killian.

Jackie continues, 'And that is why the shift to the writer's inner life was so important.'

Autumn talks out of the side of her mouth. 'Why do you look like you've been dragged through a hedge backwards?'

'Honestly, you don't want to know.'

'More to the point, you smell like a barbecue.'

'I've had the morning from hell,' I whisper. 'I almost burned down my accommodation.'

Her eyes widen in horror. 'Deliberately?'

'No, what do you take me for? It was an accident. I had the roughest night. Barely slept. I feel horrific.' I slump down and put my head in my hands.

'You look it.'

'Way to kick me when I'm down!' I snap.

'You girls, who are talking. Could you answer the question?' Jackie's voice booms.

'S-sorry?' I stutter.

'What did you make of what I just said? You are clearly very invested, seeing as you have been conversing since you arrived.'

'Well, the thing is . . .' I'm at a loss for words.

Jackie rearranges her notes. 'Anyone else?'

Another student answers the question eagerly. I'm such an idiot. I've never not known an answer! My stomach curls in shame. I prop myself up with one hand, trying to pay attention, but I'm exhausted.

When Killian takes to the lectern to present his half of the lecture, I blink, willing myself to stay awake. But instead my head slowly falls down and I sink deeper and deeper, his voice soothingly turning to a lullaby.

Autumn gently nudges me awake at the end of the lecture. I open one eye just in time to see Killian climb the stairs beside me, regarding me with what looks like disgust. Wiping the drool from my arm, I sit up, hunched and spaced out.

'Why didn't you wake me up sooner?' I ask Autumn as we make our way to the rec room.

'You looked so peaceful.'

The rec room is a grand, rectangular room in the heart of the university's main building. Extravagant paintings depicting epic war scenes and old dukes with pale faces and rounded bellies sit in chunky, expensive frames. The wallpaper is embossed in gold and red. Comfy old leather couches and chairs sprawl across the room next to an old wooden coffee table where piles of battered board games sit. At either end there are roaring fireplaces, topped up with fresh logs by the janitor. The Persian carpet is worn in by thousands of shoes, from brogues to sneakers. If these walls could talk . . .

Zainab joins us. She throws me off by pulling me into a hug, holding me tight. Then she pulls a face. 'Yuck, you smell like a grill.'

'I know.'

'And you look like shit.'

Zainab's not exactly one to beat around the bush. I usually appreciate this kind of honesty, but today I'm not in the mood. After I tell the girls what happened this morning, they howl with laughter.

'It's not funny, someone could have died.'

'OMG, if you killed someone by having a cheeky wank, how would you ever live it down?' Autumn guffaws. 'Death by diddle!'

'Ha, ha,' I say dryly. 'Nathan just sent me a message. He's spoken to our accommodation officer, who says it'll take a week to fix the damage.'

'Why don't you come and stay with me for a bit?' Zainab offers.

'Really?' Zainab has a bath with gold feet and a fridge that spits out three different types of ice. I try to play it cool. 'I don't want to impose.'

'I have a spare room. No biggy.'

'That would be amazing. Can we have a pyjama party?'

'Sure, why not?'

Autumn whips off her glasses. 'I can't join, I have a second date. All going well, there won't be any need for pyjamas, if you know what I mean.'

I laugh. 'My pencil case knows what you mean.'

After swinging by Bucky Place, I walk to Zainab's with a backpack of clothes. Having very few friends growing up meant I've never had a sleepover. I'm kind of nervous. We decide to watch a cheesy rom-com from the nineties, which I'm surprised Zainab agrees to.

'Is there a hopeless romantic hiding in there somewhere?' I ask her, but before she can answer, the doorbell rings.

Zainab frowns. 'Maybe it's the pizza – that was quick.'

She returns with Autumn, who plops down on the plump teal sofa between us and helps herself to a fistful of popcorn.

'Now the party can really start,' she says, mouth full.

'It's a slumber party. Not a party,' Zainab corrects her.

'What about your hot date tonight?' I ask.

'We cut it short. After I fingered her, she started crying over her ex.'

Zainab shoves the popcorn bowl on to Autumn's lap in disgust. 'That's all yours now.'

'Oh, don't be such a prude!' Autumn laughs.

'Are you going to see her again?' I ask Autumn, who is now digging into a bowl of chocolate pretzels.

She deliberates. 'Not sure. I'm thirsty. Zainab, do you have any wine?'

'Do I?' Zainab grins.

Zainab's kitchen belongs in a fancy magazine at a dentist's office. Huge windows overlook a private garden, where a crab apple tree grows. A marble kitchen island stands in the centre of the room, under different-sized globe lights. Matching copper pots and pans hang from hooks above shimmering green tiles. Something tells me the utensils are more for show than actual use.

Autumn opens a healthily stocked wine fridge that's taller than her. 'Check this out. Your wine fridge is bigger than my fridge fridge.'

Zainab shrugs and offers me a puff of a joint, but I shake my head. 'I've inhaled enough smoke for one day.'

Two movies and far too much wine and pizza later, we all agree on an early night. At this point, I'm both wired and tired. To save Autumn having to catch the night bus home, Zainab puts us both in her spare room, which is decorated in beautiful earthy tones, yet full of junk.

I have to crawl over bags of clothes to make it to the bed.

'Your apartment is so big you have your own landfill.' Autumn laughs.

'I wasn't expecting you.'

'I'm just jealous. It's lush.' Autumn climbs in behind me and wraps her arms around me. 'I'll be the big spoon,' she whispers.

'Night, guys.' Zainab hits the lights.

I nod, happy to be held. I didn't tell the girls what happened last night. Partly because I'm not even sure if it did. If I was bitten, why is there no mark? And also, werewolves aren't real . . . so there is that. As Autumn falls asleep, her grasp on me loosens and she starts gently snoring. My mind, although knackered, goes into overdrive. So many questions. I suppose I could go back to the chip shop on Lothian Road. But that wall just looked like a wall. What would Nancy Drew do? She would return to the scene of the crime and look for clues. I sit upright – the library.

I pull the coat Zainab lent me over my pyjamas, moving as quietly as I can so as not to wake Autumn. Feeling my way down the fluffy carpeted hallway, I trip on a pair of shoes and bite my fist instead of shouting out. I creep out of Zainab's, clicking the grand door behind me as quietly as possible, and head towards the library, which is a short walk across the Meadows, one of Edinburgh's best-known parks. It's a dark night, lit only by the pale yellow moon in the sky. Thank goodness it's not a full moon, or I might be running around town eating people, I joke to myself.

When I arrive at the library, I see Sam is working. He stands up when he notices me.

'You're back!' he exclaims.

'I'm back.' I look around to check nobody else is here. 'Can I ask you something?'

'Sure, hit me.'

'Did you see anything last night? Anything weird?'

He pauses, scrunching his face in thought. 'No, nothing out of the ordinary. How come?'

'You didn't see me leave?'

'No, but I was probably on my break.'

I spot a CCTV camera mounted in the top corner of the wall. 'What about that?' I point at it. 'Do you have access to the tapes?'

Sam looks up at it and shakes his head. 'I'm afraid not, that would be the head of security you would need to speak to. He hesitates. 'Although the footage gets wiped every twenty-four hours.' He shrugs apologetically. On seeing my disappointment, he adds, 'Is there anything I can do?'

'No. It's OK. Thanks, Sam.'

'No problem, Brodie,' he calls after me chirpily.

Frustrated, I head for the elevator. When I step into it, a jolt of fear pierces through me. It was a night terror, it wasn't real, I try and remind myself. But why don't I remember getting home from the library last night, if that's the case? The elevator pings to the eighth floor and I jump. The doors part and dread bubbles inside me. Stepping cautiously and deliberately, I head to the exact spot where I was last night. Standing still, I listen for clues. Strip lights buzz. Wind blows outside. This time, I know I am alone; I can feel it. So I search around. But nothing looks out of the ordinary. Everything looks just the same. Books. Bookshelves, old musty carpet. Feeling something close to relief, I spin on my heels, about to leave, when I spot something out of the corner of my eye. It sticks out of the bookshelf, catching the light. Walking right up to it, I see it, clear as day, poking out between two books. Plucking it from its base, I rub it between my forefinger and thumb, rolling it over and over and holding it up to the light. It is a thick, long silver hair. Too wiry to come from a human. Or a domestic dog, for that matter. Placing it carefully in my wallet, the novice detective in me is triumphant, yet that small win is overridden by an earth-shattering thought.

Maybe I was bitten, after all.

CHAPTER SIX

In 'The Lowest Animal' (1897), Mark Twain writes,
'Man is the only animal that blushes – or needs to.'
Explore what Twain means in relation to the
key themes of the text.

After finding the hair in the library tonight, I go on a frenzied internet deep dive about werewolves. And Nova. But I can't find anything on her — not one old news article or underground blog. Zainab's plush guest bed doesn't spare me from my sleepless nights. And as the night of my supposed attack in the library drifts further and further away, I almost write off the memory. Nathan and I move back into our apartment, which is freshly painted after the fire. Normal service resumes.

Until one dreary Wednesday in October.

'Guys, I have an announcement. I have met the love of my life,' Autumn proclaims with pride. Zainab sighs – here we go again. We are tucked at the back of a new LA-themed salad bar at the top of Victoria Street. It's kitted out in mid-century furniture, and pithy pop music blares through the speakers. Three huge bowls of alfalfa, kale and a whole host of healthy ingredients sit in front of us.

'She is an absolute dream.'

'How did you meet?' I ask.

'Don't encourage her,' Zainab snaps.

Ignoring Zainab, Autumn grabs her cutlery. 'I saw her at the stationery shop; we were both reaching for the same packet of highlighters. I mean, if that isn't fate, what is?'

'Not the weirdest place you've chatted someone up, I'm sure.' Zainab's smirk grows.

Autumn thinks on this. 'No, that would be a tie between the STI clinic and a funeral.'

'Eeeeew,' we say in unison.

'A funeral? Not even I would go there. And I'm dressed like I'm going to one half the time,' Zainab hoots.

Autumn chews thoughtfully. 'It was my neighbour's cat's funeral. She was very old – the whole of Quarryview Estate turned out. I wrote a piece of poetry for the occasion.'

'Please don't tell me you've committed it to memory,' Zainab begs.

Autumn clears her throat for dramatic effect. 'Oh Pussy, you were the finest feline in the land—'

'Pussy?' I cut in, wondering if she's pulling our legs.

'That's right. Pussy Galore. Pussy for short.'

'Pussy the pussy?' Zainab grins from ear to ear.

'I'm more concerned about the clap-clinic pick-up. Were you not worried that the person had something?' I ask incredulously.

'He was only popping in to get free condoms.'

Zainab stares at Autumn witheringly. 'And you believed him?'

'Again, Zainab, if you're looking for dating advice, just ask.' Autumn gives a syrupy smile.

'No need, honestly.'

'Anyway – I think she's The One,' Autumn adds happily.

Zainab and I groan. 'Surely not,' I say, pouring a thick green dressing over my salad.

'And what about the other One, what happened to him?' Zainab asks.

Autumn frowns as she tries to recall.

'You know, the one with the . . .'

I try to fill in. 'Girlfriend? Hearing aid? Trust fund?'

'They are all Ones of the past,' Autumn replies.

'It sort of defeats the meaning of The One if there's loads of them, doesn't it?' I ask before diving into my salad.

'I don't believe in all that crap, and neither should you,' Zainab says. 'It's a function of the patriarchy, used to convince women to wait around to get saved. Fuck that knight-in-shining-armour bullshit.'

'That's not what The One means,' I protest.

Autumn nods. 'Exactly, love comes in many forms. You need to be open to it; it doesn't just fall into your lap. With that attitude Zainab, you'll end up alone.'

'Good, I like being alone. And you, my friend, are falling in lust, not love. There's a big difference.'

'Have either of you been in love?' Autumn wonders. Our silence speaks volumes.

Then I speak up. 'According to all the romance books —'

'Sure, if it's in a book, it must be true.' Zainab's tone is teasing.

'Love, lust, whatever it's called – give me it all.' Autumn leans in, a wicked look on her face. 'Speaking of lust . . . Did you sign up to Killian's book club?'

I move a spiral of courgette around my bowl, trying to act casual. 'Yes, I did. I'm still trying to rebuild my reputation after KO-ing during his lecture. Did you sign up too?'

'Nah, we're not all little bookworms like you.'

Zainab folds her arms, suspicious. 'Does it count towards your grades?'

'No, it's just for . . . fun.'

Her eyes narrow quizzically.

'You're not invited, anyway, it's just English lit students.'

'Killian is a ten-out-of-ten walking ride, in an academic kind of way. In case you hadn't guessed,' Autumn informs Zainab.

She's not wrong. 'I joined the book club for genuine reasons. So what if he happens to be hot? It's not my fault.'

Autumn crunches into a mini cucumber and pulls a face. 'Do they do fries here?'

'No, it's a salad bar.'

'This isn't going to fill me up. Let's get doughnuts after this.'

'It's healthy. Studies show that a vegan diet—' I cut myself off mid-sentence as the most celestial smell fills my nostrils. Sideswiped by it, I drop my fork, and it clunks on the table.

'Calm down, we get it – five a day. Longevity, blah, blah blah.' Zainab exclaims.

But I've already stood up. I'm in a trance. 'Be right back,' I mumble over my shoulder, as I leave the girls and follow my nose through the salad bar. I make it to the front entrance, where the glass door leads out to the curved, cobbled street. Passers-by wrestle umbrellas, bracing themselves in the early October rain. Not caring that I left my jacket at the table, I yank open the door and, nostrils flared, take a big, beastly sniff. Even through the wet air I can smell it, now more potent than before. Seductive, rich and strong, the smell almost drives me mad, it's so good. I don't know what it is, but I have to find it.

Sniffing sharply and quickly, I step on to the pavement in front of a woman pushing a double stroller. 'Oi!'

'Sorry,' I mutter, not giving her a second glance, and she swerves out of the way, tutting as she goes.

My senses are drawn by an invisible hook to an adjacent French bistro.

The sign above the door reads 'Chez Pierre' in gold cursive. Crossing the road excitedly, I step inside and am delighted to find the tantalising smell fills the whole place. The room pulses with the beat of lunch-goers enjoying themselves. Classical music plays under a layer of expensive glassware clinking. A variety of wealthy tourists and high-end business people sit in front of delectable plates of food. They chat in the muted tones reserved only for the rich. 'Rich people have very quiet indoor voices,' my dad once said to me, unable to hide the disgust in his voice. In my dad's book, to be born rich is probably one of the worst things you can do. To become rich, on the other hand, is the most admirable thing a person can do. Drug dealers in shiny people carriers and lottery winners wearing gaudy designer labels garner more respect from him than anyone with a large inheritance. Or 'poshos', as he so kindly nicknames them.

The waiting staff duck and dive past one another like birds, instinctively knowing where each other's next move will take them. A large bill sits on a silver tray as it's delivered to a man and woman. The woman doesn't attempt to pay, instead waits for her husband – or sugar daddy – to take out his bulging leather wallet and cough up. A bottle of champagne is presented in a glistening ice bucket to two rosy-cheeked men in tailored suits. A fork falls to the floor and is discreetly replaced before its user has swallowed their previous bite. Glistening gravy is poured over plates of well-crafted cuisine. A bell rings from the back, signifying food is ready to be delivered. But the thing I am most enraptured by is a solo diner, a man with a huge belly tucking into a particularly sexy plate of food by the window.

I stop a passing waitress, who looks me up and down, which is fair, given I'm clearly not their typical customer. 'Excuse me, but what is he having?'

'Zat, mademoiselle, is ze steak au poivre,' she says in a thick French accent.

I stare, imagining the chunky marbled meat in my mouth. I need it. I want it. I must have it. This thought takes me by surprise, but now is not a time for questioning; it's a time for ravaging whatever meat I can get my hands on.

'If you take a seat, I will bring you ze full menu. Please, right zis way.' She gestures to a table for two at the very back and I sit down. But then I realise I don't have any money. All I know is that a piece of meat needs to be in my mouth asap. It's a deep, animalistic, carnal itch that needs scratching immediately. My legs dance under the crisp white tablecloth in anticipation. Then I see another waiter clearing plates from an empty table, and I watch him hungrily as he carries three half-eaten plates of food past me. Checking nobody is looking at me, I discreetly follow him through the back of the restaurant, down a mauve hallway to the kitchen, which is bustling with noise and even more divine smells.

'I'm away for a quick smoke!' the waiter says, dumping the three plates on a big silver trolley, soon to be collected by a stocky kitchen porter.

Watching voyeuristically from the darkened hallway, I see a woman in chef's whites placing a sizzling brown steak on a plate with some fries, and saliva springs across my tongue. She spins the plate around, dabs it with a white cloth and rings a little bell. 'Check on, table four!' she trills before wiping her hands on a towel and turning her back to tend to some sautéing mushrooms in a pan.

Hovering in the shadows, I know I have to be quick. I wait until the chef's back has turned and grab the plate from under the heat lamps. My fingertips burn on the sides of the piping-hot plate, but I can't let it go, not yet anyway. I can't return to my table, otherwise the staff will see. I spot the toilet door, marked by an old-fashioned image of a little girl peeing into a brass potty, and I push it open with my back. I've never been in a loo this fancy. The piano music plays louder in here, presumably to save people's blushes. There are individual rolled-up towels to dry your hands, and it smells of expensive soap. Luckily, I am alone. Kicking a teal-green stall open with my foot and slamming the toilet lid down, I take a seat on my throne and place the roasting plate on my lap, feeling the heat through my jeans. The steak sits in pride of place in the middle of the plate, the smell now so strong I wish I could inhale it and hold it in my skull forever.

In my haste, I didn't think to grab cutlery, so I pick up the steak like I would a corn on the cob, holding each side with my bare hands, and I take the biggest bite I can without dislocating my jaw. Having been a vegan for so many years, the feeling of my teeth sinking into flesh is unusual but far from bad. It feels so right. Letting the plate slide off me and smash to pieces on the tiled floor, I take bite after bite, moaning as I chew, my boots tapping on the floor in elation. As I gnaw through it, meaty juice squirts out of the steak and drips down my T-shirt, but I couldn't care less. The next few minutes go by in a feverish blur. Masticating and tearing the meat, my jaw gurning in effort, I slurp and bite every last bit of it until my teeth reach the sinewy fat on the bone. That's when I start to lick, my tongue stroking every inch of what is left. Suddenly, I belch, and as the loud noise vibrates around the echoey toilet, I notice that the cubicle door has swung open. Two of the waiters and the chef stand staring at me, their mouths agape, looks of pure disgust on their faces. I feel grease drip from my chin. Looking down at my oil-slicked hands, still clutching the bone, I recoil with disgust. I can't believe I just ate meat! As I grab at the toilet roll dispenser to wipe off my hands, I spot a tampon wrapper sticking out of the sanitary bin. My stomach lurches. I've just behaved terribly. Like an animal.

After convincing the staff at Chez Pierre not to call the police and promising to never return, I rush back across the road towards the salad bar, holding up my arms to shelter me from the rain, which is now falling heavily. When I rejoin the girls, Autumn stands up, her face etched in worry when she sees me.

'Oh my God, what happened?' She slides along the booth, pulling me down beside her. Zainab wears an expression I can't figure out.

Looking down at my T-shirt smeared in meat juice, I think on my feet. 'I went to get money out of a cashpoint and some guy bumped into me and spilled his lunch.' The lie falls out of my mouth as easily as the steak went in.

'Gross!' Autumn shrieks.

They seem to have bought my story, and I head home to clean myself up before the first book club meeting. I feel embarrassed and not in control. How can I have gone from not being able to walk past a butcher's without holding my nose to ravaging a steak on a toilet? Trust me to spend my whole life being a loner wallflower, only to go to uni and become a rabid animal. And with that thought, the supposed werewolf attack – which I've done so well to push out of my mind – comes rushing back front and centre. This cannot be happening to me. Maybe there's another explanation, like a hormone imbalance or an iron deficiency. There are worse things than eating a bit of meat now and again. All I was doing was listening to my body – it doesn't make me a monster. Does it?

For our introductory book club meeting, Killian has suggested an Edinburgh stalwart, a quaint teahouse tucked away through a close in the Old Town. Despite my best efforts, I'm late. I initially left Bucky Place carrying a tote bag that said #vegan on it, and I felt like a #fraud, so I turned back and replaced it with one I got free at the freshers' fair. Entering the warm teahouse feels like stepping into a different world. The air is sweet, cosy and hazy with incense, and I scan the room, looking at the different groups of people huddled on embroidered cushions. Students in knitted hats, old friends laughing and nursing teacups, first dates intently gazing into each other's eyes. The ceiling is low and dripping with colourful glass lanterns. The windows are steamed up from conversation and hot tea. I spot Killian, tucked into a window seat by a big red curtain, his brow furrowing as he thumbs the pages of a book. He sees me too and gives me a wave. A surge of shyness comes over me when I approach him. He looks super cute, wearing a slim oatmeal roll-neck sweater with the sleeves pulled over his hands. It's the first time I've really noticed his physique. His arms look like he works out. He's also wearing those thick black glasses that make him look even more bookish and clever than ever.

'Hi.'

'Hey Brodie. Thanks for showing up.'

'Of course. I love it. Love books.' I shift on the balls of my feet nervously, hating myself more than ever. If that's even possible.

'But this was clearly a silly idea.' He carefully puts a bookmark in his book and tucks it into his leather satchel.

'Where are the others?' I ask timidly.

Killian smiles an impish smile, showing his two irresistible dimples. 'There are no others. You were the only person to sign up.' He sighs. '*The Picture of Dorian Gray* maybe wasn't the sexiest choice.' He avoids eye contact and stands up.

I smile gently. 'Well, I'm here now.'

'It's probably pointless with just the two of us. Sorry, I should have messaged, but I was hoping there might be a few last-minute add-ons. Where do you think I went wrong? Was the flyer too cheesy?'

'Yes, maybe a little.' I stifle a laugh, thinking of the cartoon book with a face, and the speech bubble popping out saying, 'Reading is cool.'

'Thanks for your honesty.' He sits back down, reconsidering. 'Screw it. Can I get you a tea, then, and we can begin? Only if you want, that is . . . You probably have far more exciting things you could be doing than hanging around with your tutor.'

'Yes.' My reply is too eager. 'I mean, no. Yes to the tea, no to the exciting other plans.' Unless you count getting passively stoned and eating tortilla chips as I watch reality TV on Zainab's widescreen telly.

Peppermint tea is the only thing I can stomach right now. As we wait for it to arrive, I bring out the misshapen vase I painted the night I allegedly got bitten and place it in front of him. 'I brought you a gift,' I say, suddenly feeling very silly.

'Oh?' Mild amusement dances on his face.

'It's handmade. I didn't make it, but I painted it,' I blurt out, hoping that justifies the wonkiness.

'The thing is, we're not really meant to accept gifts from students. It could be seen as a bribe, you see.'

I go beetroot. 'Sorry, I didn't realise.'

We both glance at my offering, which from this angle looks even more lopsided.

'I'm kidding.'

'So I *can* bribe you?'

'Something tells me you don't need to.'

I smile modestly. Inside, I'm jumping up and down.

'But is there a reason for said gift?'

My gaze falls to the carpeted floor. 'I want you to know that I am a keen student, I guess. It's not like me to fall asleep during a lecture.'

'Maybe I should put less text on my slides?'

'No, it's not about you. I had a fire at my apartment that day. I barely slept.'

'Well, thank goodness you saved that thing.' He gestures at the vase.

'I know it's crap.' My shoulders tighten. Shame Goblin whispers in my ear, *Of course it's crap; anything you touch turns to crap, you waste of space.*

'I know you are smart, Brodie.'

'Thanks.'

'But smart isn't enough. Everyone who gets into Edinburgh is smart. Succeeding is about hard work, and patience too.'

I nod agreeably.

'It'll take more than a homemade mug covered in random shapes to prove that you are invested.'

'It's a vase. But anyway, I live in the library, I've read every book on the reading list . . . and I'm here.'

'Yes, you are.'

And so we drink tea and discuss the book. At first, that is. Then we veer into different territory. Killian moved to Edinburgh to complete his master's and decided to stay and do a PhD on men in modern literature.

'Please don't call me a freak, but I have read a lot of your work.'

'No!' His amber eyes fire up in delighted surprise.

I sit on my hands and feel my toes squirm in my shoes. 'Yeah, I'm kind of a fan of yours.'

Killian reacts perfectly to my admission. He lights up, seemingly genuinely happy to hear it. 'At least someone is reading my work,' he jokes, but I can see through to the creative in him that he just wants to be loved.

'I've read a lot of it.'

'Stop!'

He taps my leg, quickly and gently, and I glow under the attention. Then he shifts back, as if to remind himself not to do it again. The moment feels awkward, as if neither of us knows what to say.

'Would you ever like to move back to Belfast?' I ask, staring at the tea leaves at the bottom of my mug.

'I don't know. Edinburgh's become home now. You'll feel that too, I'm sure. It's a friendly place.'

It sure is. I tell Killian about Seafall and how desperate I was to leave. And then the inevitable question comes up, the one that is almost always asked in innocence but can turn any conversation from feeling light to heavy.

'Do you have any brothers or sisters?'

'No.' The word leaves my mouth as easily as all of the other times. But it still stings. I swallow the lump in my throat. And in moments, the conversation has moved on.

Before we know it, it's almost midnight and the staff at the teahouse are noisily cleaning the coffee machine and yawning.

Killian lives down the bottom of Leith Walk, so he offers to escort me home. 'I know you're an independent woman, but I've kept you out late; it's the least I could do.'

I don't argue with either of those points. The rain is so heavy, we huddle under his umbrella together. He smells of a nice aftershave. I wonder if he wore it especially for book club.

Killian walks me to the edge of the flower bed at Bucky Place. 'Well, Brodie, thanks for a lovely evening. I would say our first book club was a roaring success.'

I turn to face him, his face dewy from the wet air and the street lamp casting him in a golden hue. 'It sure was.'

He looks at his feet, like he's almost holding in a laugh. 'Well.'

We look at each other affectionately for longer than is probably appropriate. Then I feel the horrible lightning bolt of a reminder not to enjoy myself too much. *He's only being nice to you because he doesn't know the real you yet*, Shame Goblin hisses. I break the moment with, 'Goodnight, Killian,' and then I rush inside, my heart thudding as I leap up the stairs towards my flat, two at a time. When I get in, I find one of Nathan's passive-aggressive notes.

Please stop using MY cutlery. Best, Nathan

I tear it in half and retire to my room.

CHAPTER SEVEN

***Discuss the themes of female sexuality and shame in
relation to Nathaniel Hawthorne's The Scarlet Letter
(1850). Explore at least two different characters.***

A few nights after book club, I'm hunched over my English
textbooks in the library, reading all about the Restoration
period. I find myself reading the same sentence over and over
again. My mouth stretches wide into a yawn. This is my cue to
grab a coffee. A large one. I pack up my books and make my way to
the café on the ground floor. It's run by three battle-axes. The
oldest one, a woman with eyebrows so thin they could have been
drawn on with a biro, takes my order. As she froths my oat milk, I
gaze out the window and see him. The guy in the black hoodie.
He's perched on the concrete wall, watching me.

'Just leave the coffee,' I say to her.

'But I've made it already!'

I've already walked away and headed out the door.

As soon as I step outside and rush down the concrete steps, the guy hops off the wall and breaks into a fast walk. I tail him, quickening my steps to match his, as he heads towards Potterrow. As he picks up the pace, so do I. It's such a dark and gloomy night that I can only really get a good look at him whenever he steps into the orange glow of the tall street lamps. He's a slim build, not especially tall. When he breaks into a jog, I worry I'm going to lose him. So I start running too. Halfway across South Bridge, I start to feel puffed out, my legs tiring and a stitch forming on my right side, but I refuse to stop. Then, as we reach the Royal Mile, the hill gets steeper and steeper and I feel my glutes clenching as I ascend. The iconic silhouette of Edinburgh Castle juts into the sky. The man charges on, and I follow, avoiding well-fed people as they spill out of overpriced restaurants. The sound of bagpipes blares from a shop that sells knock-off kilts at eye-watering prices. A woman comes out of nowhere and steps in front of me. 'Sorry, can you help me? I'm looking for Princes Street,' she says, holding up a paper map, blocking my view.

'Sorry, I'm not from around here,' I offer apologetically, pushing the map away and charging onwards. Frustration rises in me when I think I've lost my mark. My eyes search frantically, scanning through the crowds. And then I think I see him head into a pub called Rock Bar. Rushing up to the entrance, I try and peer through the windows, but they're blacked out and behind cages. Energetic electric guitar music booms from inside. I steel myself and swing open the heavy door.

Rock Bar is cavernous. From the street, you would be forgiven for thinking it was a tiny pub with just a handful of tables. But this bar is deep, spread over two levels. The ground level is so dimly lit I almost have to feel my way through it. The walls are painted black and covered in graffiti, the ceiling is low, and the floor is scuffed with the marks of many a biker boot. As I cautiously enter, the patrons mostly ignore me, but some look at me with curiosity.

Drag queens with high heels and high hair cackle on ripped lea-ther seating banks; women in lace corsets and fishnet bodysuits play a game of ping-pong. An older woman in a catsuit and a young guy with mohawk hair squeeze past me to try and find a seat. There are a lot of smoky eyes, studded boots and, unfortunately for me, black hoodies. The basement floor is bigger, reached via by a rickety metal staircase that looks like a screw could pop out any minute now. My stomach lurches as I peer down to a throbbing dance floor, and a five-people-deep bar. At the top of the stairs, a huge, topless man with a ponytail, so ripped he looks like he's carved out of marble, rubs past me, knocking me by accident. He clicks his teeth at me. The scent of his glistening skin lingers in the air after he is gone. This place is jumping. I spot a person in a black hoodie and tap them on the shoulder, but as they turn around, I know instinctively it's not who I am looking for. It's a guy with stubble and a face like a melted wellington boot. 'What?' he growls. I can't picture him nimbly running across Edinburgh.

'Were you following me?' The uncertainty in my voice is ampli-fied by the fact I have to shout.

'Fuck off,' he says simply. I do as he says.

I make my way down the staircase, clutching the sticky black metal handrail, cursing the person who invented these metal grate stairs. But then I think I see him. The dark hooded figure, lurking by the bar. When I get to the bottom, I can't see him anymore. Pushing through throngs of leather-clad rockers, I lean against a tiny section of the bar and squint out into the abyss, trying to make out the moving shapes I see before me.

'What you having?' a gorgeous six-foot-tall barwoman asks me. She looks like a smoking-hot superhero.

'Eh, vodka lemonade,' I say, before adding, 'Double.'

I sip my drink and lurk about, but there's only so much I can do. And just as I'm about to give up and head home, I get overcome with the urge to kiss someone. A girl, probably around my age, in a black minikilt and a tiny boob tube, dances in front of me like an erratic fairy. She is all pointy edges, elbows and high heels. Her hair is brown and cropped short, letting her angular features and doe eyes do all the talking. She catches me looking and gives me an inviting grin. I down the rest of my drink and step towards her, putting my arms around her bony hips, which jut out above her low-rise waistline. She laughs and tosses her head as I pull her close. Then I don't know what comes over me, but I start licking her. First I lick her neck and I feel her giggle and gasp and shudder in delight. Then, with my fingers gripping into her bare back, my tongue-strokes work their way up to behind her ear. She tastes of wildflowers and fresh sweat. The combination is intoxicating.

She dances into me, letting me know that she's enjoying it. I feel her moans as I lick and lick, saliva sliding all over her. I pull her close, so she's gyrating on my leg. We drag one another to a dark corner of the bar where I hope nobody can see us. Slamming gently against a wall, we kiss passionately in the purple smoky haze. The deafening vibrations of the nearby speaker only spur us both on, licking and sucking one another's bodies, necks and faces. I am so overcome with lust that I get to my knees, feeling the strain of my denim jeans push in between my legs, making me even wetter and more turned on. Pulling up the girl's minikilt, I yank her tiny netted underwear to one side, burying my face in her crotch. The lights flash as I suck on her clit and tongue her to the rhythm of the music. When I feel her shuddering, I grab her petite buttocks hard, my palm filled with her soft, pert flesh, encouraging her to cum. The moment is over almost as quickly as it began.

Getting to my feet, I wipe my mouth with the back of my hand. I can taste her, along with the vodka. The room spins, and suddenly she scuttles off, readjusting her skirt as she pushes through the crowd to presumably rejoin her friends. And now I feel weird.

I'm in a bar by myself, and I've just performed a sex act in public. I could get locked up for this. Kicked out of university, or worse. Shamefaced, I make my way back up the metal staircase, through the throngs of people at the leather booths, until I burst out the door, gasping. The previously inky blue sky is now brightly lit with a stunning moon, so clear I can see the crevices on its grey surface. Staring at it, a feeling deep inside me stirs. At first it's a low hum, and then it gets louder and louder. It's practically ringing in my ears. Something is changing. I know that I am becoming, or have become, somebody else. It's so thrilling, I get the urge to scream into the night air. So I do. My arms outstretched, my head tilted back. Loud and proud. It feels fucking fantastic.

CHAPTER EIGHT

In Alice's Adventures in Wonderland (1865), Lewis Carroll writes, 'It's no use going back to yesterday, because I was a different person then.' Discuss how this statement reflects Alice's journey of self-discovery and growth throughout the novel.

It's Halloween. But most notably, today would have been Grace's twenty-first birthday. The weirdest part of it for me is that with each year that goes by, I'm getting older, but she stays the same age. It feels topsy-turvy to have an older sister who is younger than me. Grace will always be six. I'm sitting on my unmade bed after a disturbed night's sleep, distractedly picking at a hangnail on my pinkie until it bleeds. I can't put it off any longer, so before I can change my mind, I call my parents. I'm relieved when it almost rings out, but then just as I'm about to hang up, my dad answers.

'Hello?'

'Hi Dad, it's Brodie.' I try to be breezy, but there's a strain in my voice.

I can hear him moving through the house. 'Oh, hello my darling. How are you today?'

'Oh, you know.' I don't want the focus to linger on me too long. 'What about you? How's Mum?'

'She's, eh . . . She took today off work. We both did.'

'Can I speak to her?'

Dad lowers his voice. 'She's not great, love.'

'Where is she?'

'Eh . . . She's gone for a nap. We went for a walk down to the beach this morning. But we turned back.' The defeat in his voice is palpable.

Some Grace birthdays have been better than others. When it would have been Grace's tenth birthday, Mum threw a party. She invited some of the kids on our street and we all played games as the adults listened to music and chatted. It was fun, until Mum drank too much and started crying. Auntie Lou cradled her as she sobbed, and Dad ushered everyone out, whispering apologies to their guests. On Grace's sweet sixteenth, Mum refused to get out of bed, so Dad took me out shopping at the Seafall Mall. He bought me a whole new outfit – beautiful indigo bootcut jeans and a matching jacket with flowers embroidered on it. Then we went and got cinnamon buns and strawberry milkshakes. Dad tucked two paper straws under his top lip and pretended to be a walrus, clapping his hands and grunting, and I laughed so hard, milkshake sprayed out of my nose. It was a fun day until we got home and the sadness sucked everything away. As much as I had adored it in the shop, every time I tried on the denim ensemble it made me feel guilty, so I shoved it to the back of my wardrobe until I could claim I had grown out of it. On Grace's eighteenth, Mum suggested we get matching bumblebee tattoos. Dad did not like the idea – I was only fifteen at the time. They argued until Mum got her own way. She took me to Trish's Tattoo Parlour at the top of Dunfermline High Street, and we lied about my age and both got bumblebee tattoos, mine on my inner wrist and Mum's on her ankle. It is, to this day, one of my deepest regrets, because every time I look down at it, I am reminded of what an awful person I am.

My dad and I both try to speak at the same time: 'I was thinking—'

'Are you going to visit soon? She would love that.'

A pang of remorse surges through me as his weighted words hang in the air. 'Sure, yeah. I'll come next month for tea, that would be nice.'

There's another silence. I can't let him know that I don't want to visit home. That home makes me feel anxious, and is full of sad memories.

'That would be really, really nice. How is university going?'

'It's brilliant.'

'Have you made new friends?'

'I have.'

Dad's voice cracks. 'I'll tell your mum that; she'll be chuffed. Are you doing anything special tonight?'

'It's the Halloween Ball. But I don't feel like going'

'You should go. Go have fun.' He clears his throat. 'I better go, love, the fish van's here.'

'Alright,' I say, my own voice wobbling now, the pain stabbing me over and over again. *Sister killer*. Shame Goblin laughs.

After I hang up the phone, I feel like a popped balloon.

It's not the loss of a sister that hurts the most. Grace's life was snatched from her – knowing that and not being able to do anything about it is what kills me. That means everything I ever experience, any achievement or joy, is tinged with at best discomfort and at worst utter horror. Every triumph, big or small, is bittersweet with the knowledge that Grace will never reach any of it. No first day of high school, no first period, no first kiss, no first job. No first anything. Mum's not the only one who finds today almost unbearable, but I have learned the best way to help is to bury my own feelings, push them down until I can't feel their pulse. I didn't lose a child after all. Just a sister, whom I can barely remember, really. As time marches on, I can't be sure if the things I recall about her are actual memories or just stories that Mum and Dad have passed on in an attempt to keep her alive. She loved bees and flowers. She was a notoriously fussy eater. Bossy. Self-assured. She was fearless – except if it came to car washes. She liked to be the centre of attention. She would do anything for me. That's what I struggle with the most. Grace was the better sister. I should have been the one who died.

When I head to Killian's tutorial, I'm glad of the distraction. Autumn senses something is wrong, but when she asks me, I lie and say that I have a headache. Since book club, I have been quietly crushing on Killian, but aside from asking me questions in class, he hasn't been paying me any special attention. Not like I deserve it, but it still doesn't stop me yearning for it. At the end of the class, Killian hands out our prep sheets for our presentations tomorrow. When he passes me my paper, he casually asks, 'Will you be heading out tonight, Brodie?'

'Oh, no.' I shake my head glumly.

Autumn nudges me. 'Are you going anywhere special, Killian?'

'As a matter of fact, yes, I'm heading to the Halloween Ball. I hear it's quite the party.'

'Fancy that, we're going too.' Autumn beams. 'See you there!'

I yank her out of the room by her elbow. 'We're going too.' I mimic her voice in annoyance.

'Thank me later, bitch.'

'I don't want to go out tonight. I have plans. I'm studying for tomorrow.'

'Oh, come on, it's the biggest night of the year. We can prep for our presentations this afternoon.'

'I'll see,' I reply reluctantly.

We stroll over to the library to meet Zainab. She's waiting for us at the steps, looking even more gothic than usual in a long black netted skirt and a black pashmina.

'Happy Halloween,' she greets us, her voice dripping with sarcasm. The reception is covered in fake spiderwebs, and little jack-o'-lanterns full of cheap chocolates and candy sit at the desk. Sam is dressed unusually smartly, wearing a white shirt and a black blazer. His hair is gelled to either side. He looks kind of ridiculous, but I feel bad for thinking that.

'Are you a butler?' I ask, walking past the desk.

He perks up when he sees us. 'I'm Edgar Allan Poe,' he exclaims, his buck teeth looking more prominent than usual.

Zainab lifts her eyebrows. 'Who?'

'Ah, I see it now,' I say kindly.

When we walk away, Zainab chides me. 'Why are you so nice to that guy?'

'He seems sweet,' Autumn says.

'Sure, for an incel.'

'Oh, come on, not all men are creeps.' I take a backwards glance at him. 'I do find him a little much sometimes. But he waived my fee when I lost my bag of books at Rock Bar.'

'Was that the night you ate that girl out on the dance floor?' Autumn wiggles her eyebrows. I had told the girls what happened. God knows, we'd heard enough sexually explicit anecdotes from Autumn to last me a lifetime, so I didn't see the harm in telling them mine. Autumn practically fell off her chair in excitement when I divulged what had gone down in that dark corner of the bar. Even she hadn't face-dived a vulva in a public place.

'Shhh. We're in a library,' I scold her.

'Exactly, it's not a church.'

'It's my church.'

'So what else has been happening with you?' Zainab asks as the three of us find a quiet study booth to share.

'Oh, nothing,' I lie, spreading out my books.

But the truth is, a lot has been happening. Intense sexual desires that have me furiously masturbating in the toilets in between lectures. Meat cravings that wake me up in the middle of the night. Erratic dreams and night terrors even more horrifying than before. I didn't know that was possible. I've spent the last few weeks in a hyper-state of highs and lows, nerves shot during the day and mind racing at night. Not to mention my inability to get the picture of Nova's face out of my mind. Add Grace's birthday into the mix and it's nothing short of a shitshow.

'You sure?' Zainab has her textbook open, but she's watching me.

'Why are you looking at me like I have spinach in my teeth or something?'

'No, it's just . . . If you want to talk about anything . . .' She trails off. Zainab's not the type of friend to have a heart-to-heart with. She's dry and to the point, will tell me if my outfit's not popping, and will give me tough love when I need it. But matters of the heart, forget it. As if I could tell her what has been going on with me – she'd think I've lost my mind. And maybe I have.

'No, I'm good, thanks,' I say, more defensively than I mean to.

And so we sit in silence. I read over my notes for the presentation tomorrow. It's our first graded assignment, so I know I need to nail it. Not just to keep my scholarship; I also want to show

Killian what I'm capable of. I might hate myself, but the least I can do is get good grades.

Autumn raps her nails on the table in boredom. 'What route are you both going down tonight – slutty, scary or funny?'

'I'm not going,' Zainab answers.

'What do you mean? It's the biggest night of the year!'

'You need to stop saying that, Autumn.' But she's kind of right. The University of Edinburgh's Halloween Ball is the party of the semester. Five hundred students are to gather at the city's iconic Macduff Hall, a grand old building with a gorgeous painted ceiling, to have a fancy sit-down meal, followed by a dance with DJs.

'Everyone who's anyone is going,' Autumn protests.

'Like who?' Zainab doesn't look up from her textbook.

'Well, for one, sexy Killian.'

'Please don't call him that.' I feel myself blushing.

'See, you want to go. Just come, both of you! Why are you being so boring?'

'I have a family thing.' Zainab shrugs.

'Can you not get out of it?'

Zainab shakes her head.

Autumn looks to me. 'It's settled, then; you're coming with me. I can't go on my own, can I?'

It's hard enough to get ready when it's just me, but with two of us crammed into my tiny room at Bucky Place, it's an even bigger challenge. As I tie on my frilly white petticoat over my puffy blue dress, completing my Alice in Wonderland costume, I look at Autumn, who, as expected, looks drop-dead gorgeous in a Poison Ivy costume, so tight it looks sprayed on. Her natural red hair is hidden by a lipstick-red wig, flowing over her shoulders in bouncy curls. She's painted her face with green and gold glitter that swirls around her eyes to create a mask effect. Her irises glow an alien green from contact lenses that she got at the dress-up shop in Cowgate. She looks sensational.

'I wish I could pull that off,' I say to her, popping a bottle of supermarket fizzy wine and pouring two mugs for us. Autumn cranks up the music and poses in front of the mirror above the sink.

'You can, babe.'

We cheers to a good night and I take a large sip of my drink, welcoming the bubbles as they race over my tongue and down my throat. It's just a matter of time before they go to my head. Hopefully a night of fun will help me forget, or at least stop me thinking about all of the things that are weighing me down. And I'm right. After my first drink, the ball that's been in my stomach all day begins to shrink.

There's a knock on my door and I swing it open to see Nathan. He looks over my shoulder at Autumn, now curled up like a cat on my bed. He stops blinking, just stares. 'Are you Poison Ivy?'

'Yes,' Autumn chirps. His gaze remains glued.

I wave my hand in front of his face. 'Earth to Nathan!'

'I love that character. From the comics, I mean,' he says.

Autumn beams. I'm assuming this will be the first of many compliments she will receive tonight.

'Anything else, Nathan, or did you just come to gawp?'

'I came to say can you please keep it down? The bass from your music is coming right through the wall. It's distracting.'

'You watch boom-bang movies all night! I need to wear earplugs.'

He yanks up his boxers. 'Come on.'

'Sorry,' I say, and grab the portable speaker and press the volume down a few notches.

'Lighten up, Nathan.' Autumn slinks on her side on the bed like a cat. 'Don't be such a wet blanket.'

He finally blinks.

'Why don't you come join us for a drink and a smoke?' Autumn pats the space beside her and brings out a pre-rolled joint, tearing the tip off. 'Look what Zainab made us!'

Nathan looks startled. 'Maybe some other time. Also, please don't smoke that in here. We've already had one fire incident this term.'

When Nathan leaves, Autumn pulls a face, immediately turning up the music one notch.

'Wow, what's it like living with him?'

'He's . . . quirky. But he's right about the smoking, I'm afraid. He's only just forgiven me for setting the place on fire last month.'

Autumn tucks the joint away and gives me a mischievous look. 'I have something that won't start any fires.'

I take another large gulp of my drink. 'What?'

She sticks her hand into her bra and pulls out a tiny clear plastic bag with five fluorescent-pink love-heart-shaped pills inside. Something tells me they aren't painkillers.

My eyes widen. 'What are they?'

'Eccies.' She sees my face contorted in confusion. 'Ecstasy tablets, if you want their Sunday name.'

'I don't know, Autumn. I've not done a lot of drugs.' Aside from getting mildly high with Zainab, I've done zero. Autumn is the youngest of five and grew up in inner-city Glasgow, so it's safe to say she's lived at least a marginally less sheltered life than me.

'Being stoned is one thing; being high on X is waaay better.'

'Maybe not tonight,' I say, adjusting my blonde wig.

The walls tremble as Nathan bashes three times from his room.

'OK, Nathan, we're leaving!' I holler, then drain the rest of my mug.

*

It's a beautiful evening with a sharp chill in the air. The kind of nip that almost numbs your face. As the sun sets, a giant full moon takes centre stage in the sky. Of course, I knew it was coming, having kept tabs on the lunar cycle since my supposed attack. But so far, I haven't eaten anyone in an animalistic craze. Unless you include the girl from Rock Bar, that is.

With Autumn linking my arm, we arrive at the steps of Macduff Hall a little after six-thirty. Swarms of students walk up the huge grey steps, reaching the grand torch lamps flickering at either side of the entranceway. Seeing this many people in costume is like being in a fever dream. A crazy clown sucks on a melon-flavoured vape; a group of magical unicorns yell at an incompetent Superman as he takes their photo on the steps.

'Do it in portrait, not landscape, you fool!' one of them shrieks.

As we make our way inside, we end up behind a duo of vampires, sipping surreptitiously from a hip flask.

'Oi, have you got a drop for me?' Autumn asks cheekily, batting her green stuck-on eyelashes.

The tallest of the vampires grins and hands her the flask, and she takes a small sip before passing it to me. I take a big glug and balk as the burn of whisky travels down my throat and heats up my empty stomach.

'Are you on the pull tonight?' I mutter to Autumn after returning the flask to its owner, who tucks it under his black cape.

'No, Brodie, this is our night,' Autumn says, and my heart sings with gratitude. Little does she know how much of a life raft this feels like in the storm of my brain.

After we check in our coats, we head into the main hall, where we are greeted with a glass of champagne. It tastes crisper than the cheap stuff I bought earlier, and I drink it quickly before grabbing another one immediately. Autumn squeezes my hand as

I gaze around the room in wonder. It's huge, with ceiling-high stained-glass windows, adorned by flowing drapes. Chandeliers glitter from the ceiling, which is painted in a stunning mural depicting different animals against a starry sky. My eyes focus on a wolf baring its fangs. I bare my teeth back. The hall is filled with round tables, with snow-white tablecloths and classy Halloween decorations, including jack-o'-lanterns whose eyes and mouths flicker with tealights. A live harpist plays creepy movie music as people take to their seats.

'I've never been anywhere like this before – do we just sit anywhere?' I ask.

'Let's sit at the Michael Myers table!' Autumn squeals. We locate it and take a seat. Autumn's to the left of me, and to my right is a woman with exceptional posture and a long, thin face. She's dressed as a witch. Original.

'What are you studying?' she asks me before I can even pull my chair in.

'English lit. I want to be a writer.'

Her nose twitches. 'What kind of writer?'

'I'm not sure yet. Maybe a novelist. Or a playwright.'

'How quaint,' she says.

Patronising bitch, I want to say, but instead I smile sweetly. 'And you?'

'Law.' She flicks her hair in pride.

'And what do you want to be?' I joke.

Her lip curls. 'Where is your accent from?'

'I grew up in a little seaside town on the east coast.'

She does a head tilt that makes me want to lamp her. 'I didn't catch your name?'

'Brodie,' I say, dreading sitting here for the next hour or so. 'And you?' I'm betting that she is called Beatrice or something equally twatty.

'Penelope, but friends call me P. P.'

I pause, wondering if she is winding me up. 'As in pee-pee?'

'As in Penelope Pembroke. P. P.'

'Excuse me,' I say politely, before turning to Autumn and giving her ankle a swift kick under the table. She seems deep in conversation with the person next to her, a guy in a banana suit.

'Ow!' she yells, and the rest of our table gives her a funny look.

'Maybe I will have one of those things,' I hiss.

Autumn shoogles her shoulders in delight. 'Buckle up, baby!' She discreetly bites a tablet in half and drops it into my cupped hand. I stare down at it, a little pink triangle, smaller than a mint. Here goes. I fling it into my mouth and guzzle it down with the remainder of my champagne. Then I help myself to a very large glass of white wine from the cooler on the table.

The starter consists of 'Bloody Beetroot Soup', with a side of judgemental and strained conversation with P. P. in which, no joke, she asks what my mum and dad do for a living. When she starts talking about bonds and shares, I elbow Autumn. 'I'm not feeling anything, are you?'

'It can take a while to kick in. Usually it should have by now, though. Do you want another half?'

'Anything to take the edge off Miss Trust Fund,' I mumble, and swallow it down with a generous gulp of white wine. And we all share a laugh at the mummy at our table, trying to navigate a soup spoon with bandages trailing off his arms.

Then I start to feel it. The music becomes out of focus. And so does P. P. Her witchy face blurs like it's sitting behind frosted glass as she tells a story I'm not really paying attention to.

'. . . so then Daddy decided I should get my own horse, so that Victoria and I didn't have to share.' She frowns. 'Are you OK?'

I stand up, shoving my chair away, and walk towards the bar.

'I need water,' I shout over my shoulder.

Making my way across the room, I push past anyone who gets in my way, almost bashing into several tables. A waitress holding a tray of bread rolls swerves me. 'Woah, watch yourself.'

'You watch yourself,' I say under my breath. *I have a dead sister, so fuck you. Fuck everything.* My body has started to tingle. From my toes, up my legs, into my stomach, my lungs, all the way to my fingers and the tip of my scalp. I want to dance – why is nobody dancing? A few small groups of people are waiting at the bar in between the first and main course, but not one person is dancing. I am charged and ecstatic, and I start to move and shake to the music. A couple of guys notice me and start to clap, egging me on. Are they bodybuilders or are they wearing bodybuilder suits? I feel like I am made of hot wax, being poured in circles and swirls. I gyrate my hips and swing my arms, and the claps and laughs get louder and louder. I'm a star, shooting through the sky. I'm the universe, the Milky Way, all the planets. Planets. The little planets spinning on the mobile above my bed the night she died. Now I'm not sure if the room is spinning or if I'm spinning, but something is going around and around and I need a drink. This is the best and the worst I have ever felt in my life. I might have to start doing this more often. Why isn't everybody taking X every day? I feel sick. Grace never had her first eccie. And never will. Now I definitely need a drink. My jaw clenches and swings to either side, as if it has a mind of its own.

I sway up to the bar and see people throwing me a mixture of dirty and concerned looks. They are clearly jealous of my dance moves. Idiots. My face tenses and gurns and my eyeballs feel like they are vibrating, like marbles rolling around in the boot of a car. Maybe the barman will have a pair of sunglasses that I could borrow. I stumble to the bar, leaning my elbows on the wet surface, arching my back because it feels nice.

'What the fuck are you looking at?' I snarl at a particularly judgemental gothic ballerina. She clicks her tongue and turns away. My mouth is as dry as sandpaper, so I get the barman's attention and order a double vodka lemonade, downing it in one.

'What's up with her?' I hear somebody say. Or is it Shame Goblin? Hello, are you there?

'None of your business,' I shout, knocking into a big guy in a Mario costume.

'Hey! Watch it!' he exclaims, his beer spilling down his dungarees. I grab the bottle out of his hand and take a swig, finishing it and then releasing it, watching it smash on the fancy floor. Green crystals everywhere. Beautiful and shiny. I lean down to get a closer look and someone pulls me back.

'Hey, come on,' a voice says.

But I am sick of people telling me what to do. I feel red-hot rage rise inside me, bubbling up and up.

'Is she OK?' a girl in a lion costume asks.

Nosy Lion can go fuck herself, that's for sure. And to let her know this, I give her a big shove. Even I am shocked by how far she flies across the room, landing on her back, the wind knocked right out of her.

'Brodie?!' The voice shouts this time. I'm aware of an arm around my back. I spin round at the sound of my name and see Killian in a ringmaster costume, his expression one of deep concern.

Fleeing the hall, I stagger in the direction of home, zigzagging across the streets. Trick-or-treaters laugh and point as I meander towards the Meadows, which is decorated in little pop-up stalls to celebrate Halloween. The orange glow of lanterns and pumpkins bounces in front of me. After bumping into a few annoying children in fancy dress, I decide to get off the main path and walk behind the stalls and across the grass, which squelches slightly under my black buckled shoes. The park is lit up by the bright moon and I stop to stare at it in awe.

'Incredible, right?' a deep voice says. I twirl around and come face to face with an old man with wild white hair and tiny spectacles, wearing a lab coat. He holds a test tube in his hand. I reach out to touch his hair. It feels like candyfloss. Stroking it, I giggle.

'It's a wig,' he offers, and I burst out into peals of manic laughter. Focusing on his face, I realise he isn't old at all; he's just wearing a crazy scientist costume.

'Happy Halloween,' I slur.

'Where are you going, Alice?'

I'm about to correct him and tell him my name is Brodie Bell, but then I remember I am in costume.

'I was at the ball . . .' I point behind me.

'And then what, you followed a white rabbit?' A wide smile spreads across his face.

'Maybe *you're* my white rabbit.' I lean into him, our bodies pressing together. He's good-looking, in a posho kind of way. At the University of Edinburgh, men like him are ten a penny. Handsome, tall, well spoken. Boring. Probably has a double-barrelled name.

'I can be if you want me to be.' He smirks, pulling me close. His breath smells like cider, sweet and hot on my face. He's so tall I have to arch my back to look at him. His eyes shine hungrily in the moonlight. Not caring if anyone sees us, I pull him to a nearby tree and press even harder against him. I feel his dick stiffening through his trousers, thick and long. Autumn told me that tall skinny guys always have massive ones. Maybe she was right. White Rabbit grabs my hips with big, spade-like hands. I grind on him, rubbing myself, letting out a little moan of pleasure. I arch my back fully and let myself bend back until my blonde wig is almost touching the ground. My head swims.

'Woah,' he says, cupping the back of my neck and pulling me up. I feel dizzy and horny.

'Do you not want to kiss me first?' he asks, as I ravenously undo the top button of his trousers.

'Not really,' I admit.

He lets out a small laugh, but then, seeing I'm serious, he shrugs and lets me pull out his giant throbbing dick. I enthusiastically grab it with both hands.

'Oooooh, your hands are cold,' White Rabbit exclaims, stepping from one foot to the other.

'My mouth's warmer,' I say, getting to my knees. White Rabbit leans against the tree and grabs my blonde wig as I take him inside my mouth. It's so big I almost choke. I can feel the exposed root of the tree as it grates against my knees. Looking up at the stranger I am sucking off, I almost burst out laughing. He looks, quite frankly, ridiculous, with his lopsided white hair and bargain-bin wire spectacles. After a few minutes, I stand up and pull him away from the tree, encouraging him to stand behind me. Steadying myself by putting a hand on the damp bark, I yank my silky wet knickers with the other hand and let them drop down to my ankles. My previously white pop socks are muddied and bloody at the knees. I pull White Rabbit's hand to reach under my puffy blue dress and feel my dimpled, cold cheeks. Grabbing his dick, I cram it inside me with such force I let out a gasp.

'Does it hurt?' he asks, concerned.

'No.' I push my bum back to let him know to keep going, and as he starts to thrust inside me, I let myself forget who I am for a few blissful moments. The fast and hard pumps, alongside the thrill of the sheer spontaneity of the fuck, are enough to edge me close to an orgasm, but I'm suddenly distracted by a spotlight, beaming on the back of my head. I turn around with my bare bum exposed and my knickers at my ankles, and squint at the culprit.

'Shit,' White Rabbit says, hastily tucking his dick away and buttoning up his trousers. I shield my face, confused. Then I hear the crackle of a police radio. 'Oi!' a policeman shouts. I quickly yank up my underwear and bolt as fast as I can across the park. White Rabbit runs the other way.

'You!' I hear the policeman shout, but he sounds quieter than before. The radio gets quieter too. I run until I can't anymore. I've reached a street made up of townhouses with expensive cars parked outside. Ducking between two cars, I hug myself and pant until my breathing becomes regular and I am sure the coast is clear. When I stand up, I pull off my Alice in Wonderland wig, shove it in a nearby trash can and make my way to the kebab shop. I'm starving.

CHAPTER NINE

Explore the concept of nature vs. civilisation in **The Hound of the Baskervilles (1902) by Arthur Conan Doyle.**

'What the fig!?' I hear Nathan shout.

My gritty eyelids slowly part. The first thing to hit me is the atrocious taste in my mouth. This is closely followed by a sprawling sting from a cluster of fresh ulcers on my tongue. I can feel uneven ridges down each side from where my teeth have dug into it, and the insides of my cheeks feel chewed up. My teeth themselves feel coated in gunk yet exposed and sensitive at the same time, and my neck and jaw throb with a dull pain. I am not in my bed, rather I am face down on my coarse bedroom carpet. Trying to lift my heavy head, my body and mind feel separate, as if both are coming out of sedation from two different drugs. I roll around and prop myself up on my elbows to face Nathan, who hovers in the doorway, a judgemental sneer plastered on his face. I'm still wearing my previously baby-blue Alice in Wonderland costume, now soiled, ripped and stained with a rusty brown substance all down the front. I gingerly take a sniff, noting the acrid stench of red kebab sauce and something else, indistinguishable. Both of my knees have scabbed over, caked in old dirt and blood, and I'm still wearing my buckle shoes, now scuffed and covered in flakes of mud. The room looks fractured, like a frozen puddle after a booted foot has stamped on it. I attempt to put the disparate pieces together.

'What time is it?' I croak, noticing my throat feels like I've swallowed a cheese grater.

'Time you took a long hard look at yourself,' Nathan snaps. 'You have a visitor, by the way.' He casts one last disgusted glance down at me and then leaves. That's when I notice that my room has been ransacked. My study calendar is torn ferociously from the wall, my wardrobe door hangs at an angle off its hinges, and my clothes have been pulled off their hangers and ripped to rags. The mirror that's drilled to the wall above the sink is cracked and the curtains have been slashed, revealing beams of menacing sunlight from outside. 'My books!' I howl, observing with sadness that the pages of many of my favourite reads have been yanked away from their spines with such force that they're now as good as scrap.

Zainab comes in with a more solemn demeanour than usual. She locks the door behind her, seemingly unperturbed by the crime-scene-adjacent mess. I realise the back of the door has been scratched, with deep grooves exposing flakes of the inner wood.

'The books are the least of your worries, babe.' She hovers for a moment as I try to get up, feeling like I've been hit by a truck. I eventually muster a laboured move from the floor to my exposed mattress, which is wounded with what look like stab holes. I lie down, narrowly avoiding the sprigs of white stuffing and jagged springs sprouting out of it.

'Remind me never to take drugs ever again,' I moan.

'Noted,' Zainab says. She perches on my desk chair, which has almost been snapped in two, and swivels to face me. Her expression is stoic.

'Do you know who did this?' I ask shakily.

There's a long pause before she replies matter-of-factly, 'Yes . . . it was you.'

Deep down, I know she's right. Salty tears sting my face. 'Zainab, I don't know what's happening to me,' I start to sob. 'I'm really scared.'

She just blinks at me.

I sniff. 'There's something I need to tell you. I-I . . .' I can't get the words out.

'You were bitten by a werewolf and now you don't know what to do.' Zainab looks at her nails.

'You know?' I'm incredulous.

She nods. 'I know.'

'How? Why?'

She hesitates. 'Do you need a water or anything?'

'No, just tell me what the hell is going on!'

She purses her lips. 'The reason I know you were bitten by a werewolf is because I am one too.'

I stare at her, unable to compute. 'You are one what?'

'A werewolf.'

My eyes narrow. Is she pranking me? But something about Zainab's vibe tells me she's being serious. The air feels as if it's been sucked out of the room.

'Did you bite me?'

She shakes her head fervently. 'Don't flatter yourself; I did not bite you. I promise. But I may have accidentally set it up. I was only following orders, telling them you would be in the library. I'm a Scout. I didn't know what was going to happen. The werewolf who bit you is under observation, to figure out what happened. But they were keen to meet you.'

'Why do they need to figure out what happened?'

'The bite was so deep, it should have been fatal. We thought you were immune at first. Nova ran tests on you at the Den. The place under the castle, you remember?'

'Fatal? As in, someone tried to kill me?'

'Not so much kill as eat.' Zainab looks almost embarrassed.

Suddenly, I am taken over by a feeling of anger and injustice so strong it gives me the power to get to my feet. All I want to do is rip this bitch's head off. Even though I'm sure I look like a murderous Disney character, Zainab doesn't even flinch.

'I thought you were my friend.'

'Please calm down. I am.'

Anybody with any sense knows that a surefire way of getting someone who is riled up to get even more incensed with anger is to tell them to calm down.

'But you would have been happy to let me become some beast's dinner?' I lurch towards her.

'If I'd known, I never would have passed on your location.' She shields herself with her forearm and pushes me away. I sway backwards, weak on my feet.

'Why should I believe a word that comes out of your mouth?'

I lunge at her again, this time my hands grasping around her neck. My fingers snake through her silver necklaces and start to squeeze. I catch one in particular – a silver pendant with a wolf engraving, the same as the one Nova was wearing.

'Please, Brodie!' Zainab gasps. Her eyes shine with something near to desperation.

I loosen my grip and take a step back, my chest heaving.

Zainab disdainfully clears her throat and fixes her hair. 'We thought the attack had left you with a tiny bit of werewolf in your blood, but not enough . . .' She trails off, biting into her bottom lip.

'Not enough for me to trash my room?' Anguish squeaks out of me.

'And all the other stuff that's been happening to you. It appears that it's only going to get worse.'

'In what way?' I spit.

'Have you felt any different?'

'No.' I stick out my chin stubbornly.

Nathan's voice suddenly booms through the door. 'That's the third time this month you've eaten all my bacon and sausages, Brodie. Buy your own or find somewhere else to live.'

Zainab raises an eyebrow. 'How's the veganism going?' She leans forward. 'First, it's your room, then it's – you know.'

I sit on the edge of the bed for a few moments, hugging my knees. 'Leave me alone.'

'You are going to hurt yourself, and others, if I leave you. You know that, right?' She clears her throat. 'Nova's summoned you to the Den. We need to monitor you. Work out what you are.'

'Summoned? Fuck off.' My blood boils with anger. 'I know who I am. I'm Brodie fucking Bell. I'm a first-year English lit student who . . . who likes rom-coms and chocolate cake and . . . and reading and I . . . I-I'm not an animal. I'm not one of you. I'm not.'

Zainab casually rests her feet on a pile of books as if it were a foot stool. 'That person you are describing is gone, Brodie,' she says flatly. 'She died the night you were bitten.'

'Just go,' I say, almost pleading now.

'That's not an option.'

'If you think I'm going to come to a literal dungeon with a bunch of rabid creatures, then you are mistaken.'

Zainab leans forward. 'Let me make this crystal-clear for you. I'm not asking you to come with me. I'm telling you.'

I sniff sullenly. 'And if I don't obey?'

We're interrupted by a knock on my bedroom door.

'Go away, Nathan!' I yell.

'It's me, Autumn.'

I catch Zainab's look of surprise. 'Don't tell me – she's one too?' I press.

'Brooooodie, I know you're in there!' Autumn's voice sing-songs.

'No, she certainly is not one too – and you need to keep quiet about all this, if you know what's good for you,' Zainab warns me as I stand up to unlock the door.

'No worries, Judas,' I hiss.

Autumn bowls in wearing a hot-pink velour sweatsuit and her usual cheeky grin. Her expression changes when she sees the state of me and my room. And me. I return to the mattress of shame.

'What the actual . . . !' she exclaims. Then she notices Zainab. 'Oh, hope I'm not interrupting?'

'Not at all,' Zainab says.

Autumn gingerly presents me with a paper McDonald's bag.

'I got you breakfast. In case you were feeling a little rough today.'

'Rough? Understatement of the year,' Zainab scoffs.

I glower at her as I tentatively accept the food bag. 'Thanks, Autumn, that's really sweet. But I'm not sure I can stomach food just yet.'

'It's vegan,' Autumn reassures me, mistaking the shock on my face for trepidation. She almost looks scared of me. 'What happened to you last night? One minute you were at the table, next minute, you'd done a runner. And you didn't answer my calls. Did you have a party here without telling me?' She sticks out her bottom lip.

'Something like that.'

Autumn looks to Zainab for more of an explanation, but she just sits there.

'Sorry about last night. I guess I went a bit overboard.'

'You dark horse, I never knew you had it in you. Did you fling your telly out the window too?' Autumn tries to lighten the tone.

'Ha,' I say meekly.

'Why don't you shower and we'll head to uni together?'

I twitch. 'Uni?'

'We have our presentations in an hour.'

I put my head in my hands and utter a statement that neither Autumn nor Zainab nor I believe. 'Let me have a coffee and I'll be good to go.'

'Just a little comedown,' Autumn calls it as we approach our tutorial room. The shirt I've chosen in an attempt to look smart is soaked in a layer of sour-smelling sweat and sticks to my back. My hands are shaky and my throat is dry. To make matters a million times worse, Killian asks me to wait behind after class, to 'discuss last night' – presumably me pushing his, I guess, girlfriend at the Halloween Ball. Even through my waves of shame and anxiety, I can't help but feel a little judgemental about him wearing a couples Halloween costume.

'Please do your presentation first,' I beg Autumn, who successfully explores the key similarities and differences between Shakespeare's *The Taming of the Shrew* and the film *Ten Things I Hate About You*. After a smattering of applause from our group, Killian calls out my name. As I stand up, I avoid eye contact and step to the front of the class with the enthusiasm of somebody in line for their own beheading. In fact, at this point I'd choose my own beheading over this presentation. Looking down at my prompt cards, now damp from my clammy palms, I struggle to focus as my own handwriting dances in circles.

'Motherhood, in Toni Morrison's book, eh, *Beloved*.' The words come stuttering out, like they're not sure if they're in the right order.

Killian looks strained. I open my mouth to speak more, but the ball of nerves in my stomach has turned into nausea. I suddenly feel even worse than before. Who knew this was even possible?

A few painful moments of silence go by. 'Brodie?' Killian asks, and I politely smile, willing the surging feeling up my throat to retreat. But it's too late. As I attempt to rush out the door to go to the toilet, the feeling of an imminent puke takes over my body faster than I can move.

I don't make it to the door. I don't even make it to the waste-paper bin before a shower of rancid spew sprays out of my mouth and all up the cream walls. The smell makes my fellow students gasp and gag. One girl rushes out of the room to be sick herself. I stand, shaking and numb from humiliation, as Autumn grabs me and guides me to the bathroom. As she ushers me out the door, I turn around to see Killian giving me a look of sheer pity, his knitted sweater sleeve covering his mouth to avoid the stench.

Autumn is a good friend. She pretends not to be repulsed as she helps remove my shirt and passes me stacks of paper towels to clean the sick off myself.

'How can you stand doing this?' I wail.

'Didn't I tell you I have three brothers?' She hands me a comb and I brush my hair back into a ponytail and splash my face.

Facing myself in the mirror is worse than I thought. I'm sheet-white, with pink eyes. 'I think I'll take the rest of the day off.'

As I hurry down the steps of the university building, I call Zainab. 'I'm still fucking furious with you,' I spit when she answers.

'What exactly is it you're most upset about?'

'Where to start? Keeping a secret from me! Lying to me. How do I know you're not trying to lure me to my death?'

'Oh, come on, now you're just being dramatic. Everybody has secrets,' she says defensively.

I know this more than anyone. I bite my lip. 'Whatever . . .
I need to know more. Take me to the Den.'

'When?'

'Meet me at Bucky Place in an hour.'

After I shower and clean the sick smell off myself, Zainab collects
me and we walk through the Old Town in relative silence. I have a
million questions, yet I am too exhausted to ask any of them.
When we head up the Royal Mile, I welcome the light spritz of
rain on my face. As we near the top, a small Jack Russell tied up
outside a candy shop starts barking at us.

Zainab turns to it and stares it out until its barks become
whimpers and it cowers back, trembling. 'Scaredy cat,' Zainab
jokes as we approach Rock Bar.

'Here?! Really? I'm not in the mood for a drink.' I hesitate as
she approaches the door.

'Trust me,' she says with her back to the door.

'You're kidding, right? You tried to have me killed. You and
those animals.'

'You're one of those animals now,' she says plainly before pushing the door open.

I follow her inside. I couldn't be sure that the guy in the hoodie
came in here that night; nevertheless, it doesn't stop me glancing
around the seating banks for him. It's not as busy as the night I first
came here. But it's just as dingy. Rock music plays as a few day-
drinkers congregate in the booths, sharing loud, alcohol-fuelled
stories. A woman in bondage gear sips a red cocktail as she reads a
well-thumbed book. I get a glance at the spine as we walk past.

'She's reading *Rosemary's Baby*!' I say to Zainab, but she's not
listening. An older couple snog enthusiastically by a cigarette
machine.

Zainab leads me down the scary metal stairs and we head

towards the bar, where one member of staff, a short and broad-shouldered man with a bald head, stands, knitting.

'Good afternoon,' he says, putting down his needles and wool. 'What can I get you?'

I tug on Zainab's sleeve. 'Just get me a Coke,' I beg. 'Full fat.'

Zainab hops on to a shaky bar stool and gestures for me to do the same.

'We'll have two Moonlight Martinis.'

They sound too strong for how delicate I'm feeling, but I'm too weak to argue.

The barman shakes the drinks, sets two napkins on the bar and places the martinis in front of us. Zainab sips hers and pulls a face.

'You know, I don't usually make a habit of drinking in the afternoon,' she tells me.

'Me neither,' I say, hunching over mine, not yet ready to touch it.

'But, as my mum says, some situations in life demand a hair of the dog.'

'It's a well-known phrase. It's not like she coined it.'

'Sorry, Miss Dictionary.'

I suck my teeth. 'Maybe this was a bad idea.'

Zainab changes tack. She cocks her head sympathetically. 'I know yesterday was a difficult day for you.'

I shrink down in my seat. 'Navigating the last while has been hard.'

'Believe me, I know.'

'Were you also bitten? Is that how you became one?' I ask in a hushed voice.

Zainab perks up. 'There is only one route to life as a werewolf. You are bitten. If you are more than bitten – for example, if you lose a limb or a main artery is punctured – it's game over. In that case, you are not bitten, you are eaten. Dead, you understand?'

My stomach flips like a pancake. 'When were you bitten?'

'When I was fourteen. On my walk home from clarinet practice. I'd been hanging around with the wrong crowd, so my mum used music lessons as an attempt to control me. Quite ironic, really. At first she thought it was my hormones. But I fucked our neighbour's nanny and then ate the entire contents of their pantry. That was a fun night.'

'Does your mum know, then?'

'She knows something's up. But her approach to life is when you throw money at the problem, it usually goes away. That's why I have my own place. She loves me, but from a safe distance.'

Even though I'm so mad at Zainab, I can't help but feel a pang of sympathy for her. Without her mum, she must have felt so disorientated and out of control. Teenage angst is bad enough. As an adult, this werewolf business is melting my brain; I can't imagine how awful it would be to go through this on top of puberty, and all alone.

As if sensing I have softened on her, Zainab adds, 'After my mum and dad's divorce, he got married again straight away. Now he has two normal daughters with Felicity the yoga instructor.'

My brow crinkles in pity.

'I don't need him. Or my mum. Not in that way, you know.'

We sit wordlessly, until she adds, 'When you're a werewolf, you gain a whole new family. One that accepts you for who you are.'

Ha! Wouldn't that be nice. A worrying thought wriggles its way into my mind. 'Wait, is that why you're studying vet med?'

'It was either that or become a butcher.'

Zainab's mum was right: the hair of the dog does perk you up. After drinking two martinis, I feel a little more relaxed about everything. But Zainab's hesitance to share any other information has left me wanting more. When I suggest a third round, she shakes her head and asks the bartender if she can put it on 'Nova's tab'. He nods and takes a large keychain out of his pocket, with at least ten different keys. Checking nobody's watching, he beckons us to follow him through a doorway to the back. He whistles as we walk in single file down a narrow corridor until we get to a door marked 'Keg Room'. The ceiling's so low we have to duck our heads. He unlocks the door and Zainab steps in first, with me at her tail. It's not really a room, but an old-fashioned elevator inside an ornately decorated, cage-like brass enclosure. Zainab grabs my hand to pull me inside and gives the bartender a nod. He shuts the gates behind us, and Zainab presses a weathered gold button marked 'D'. The elevator comes to life, spluttering and rattling as we sink down and down. I start to tremble with anticipation.

The elevator finally shudders to a halt and Zainab pulls open the brass doors from the inside. We step out together into a large concrete wonderland. 'The Commons,' Zainab calls it. Concrete walls, with those familiar neon lights snaking around the room. It looks like a refurbished nuclear power plant. Or how I would imagine a Berlin sex club to look. The room smells of stone and wood. The floor is uneven, exposed concrete, powdered with dirt. The ceiling is low by the entranceway, but as I walk in, the space opens out, stretching up to reveal an angular maze of different levels. At the very top of the highest point is a round glass porthole, letting the only streak of natural light beam down. Just below it, a cubed glass room juts out, full of giant green plants, overlooking the Commons. Then, as if out of nowhere, Nova stands before us. She's even more remarkable than I remembered. The face of an angel – no, a queen – her silvery-blonde hair immaculately slicked back, her eyes glowing. I suddenly feel a pang of fear, muddled with something else.

'Brodie Bell,' she says coolly. 'Better late than never.'

I look to Zainab for support, but she's frozen to the spot, an atypical submissive look on her face.

'I tried to get her to come along earlier, but . . .' Zainab catches my fearful expression. 'But she wasn't feeling well,' she finishes.

Nova hasn't taken her eyes off me. One green, one blue. 'That will be all, Zainab,' she commands in a whisper.

I side-eye Zainab, knowing how much she would hate someone speaking to her like that, but she's looking down at her brogues.

'Yes, Nova,' she says compliantly.

As Zainab retreats, fear of the unknown spurs me to reach out for her hand, silently begging her to stay with me, even though I am still pissed off with her.

'Sorry,' she says apologetically.

'You're leaving me?'

Nova places a cold palm on my cheek, gently but firmly guiding my attention back to her. 'Girl, say goodbye to your friend.'

'She's not my friend,' I spit out bitterly. And just like that, Zainab is gone.

Nova steps nearer to me and I feel my heart thudding faster. A jolt of excitement flashes between my legs like a lightning bolt. 'We have some catching up to do; let's go to my quarters,' she says briskly and turns around quickly on her heels. I have no choice but to follow her.

Nova leads me down a set of tunnels reminiscent of the ones I ran through like a headless chicken the night I was bitten. She clearly knows the place like the back of her hand and I have to quicken my steps to keep up with her as she strides confidently ahead. We pass a canteen where people in cargo pants and vests tuck into metal trays of food and exchange loud banter. When they spot me, they fall into silence. I go hot with shyness as they stop what they're doing to ogle me. 'There she is!' I think I hear somebody exclaim.

'No way, that's not her,' another person whispers.

Techno music thumps as we walk through a gym area, full of intimidating metal workout machines and mirrors. I try not to leer, but I have never seen bodies like this in real life. Muscley, throbbing, rippled flesh pumps and pounds. One person in particular catches my eye. Tall and broad, with dark hair pulled into a messy ponytail; his bulging muscles look like they're trying to escape his glowing, sweaty skin as he does bicep curls. He has a jaw that could cut glass, a wide-set nose and deep sepia eyes. One eyebrow is pierced. He puts his weights down and approaches us like an alley cat with big swinging balls.

'Who, may I ask, is this?' he says in a deep, velvety timbre, giving me a sharp sniff. I frown – I'm sure I've seen him before somewhere. I know! He pushed past me that night at Rock Bar. How could I forget those abs?

'Not now, Shadow,' Nova scolds him in the tone of a headteacher to one of her favourite naughty pupils.

He bends over to whisper in my ear, 'Maybe later then?'

I open my mouth to reply, but Nova puts an arm around my waist and guides me down one final corridor and up a narrow staircase, where we reach her quarters. We enter via a thumbprint security system. I thought those only existed in movies.

As we step inside, I realise we're in the glass room at the top of the Commons. Big exotic plants sit by the window. It smells like a greenhouse, hot and wet. 'That's Shadow,' Nova says, encouraging me to take a seat on a wide angular couch.

She sits opposite me on a big black leather throne by an unlit wooden stove. 'He's one of our best warriors.' She claps twice and the fire bursts into life, its flames a bright purple.

'Warriors?' I repeat.

'Yes, but you mustn't worry about any of that right now,' Nova says reassuringly.

What a warrior has to do with me, I have no idea.

'What exactly has Zainab told you?'

'That she's a werewolf. And I'm a werewolf too?'

'You're a bit of an anomaly, truth be told.'

'Meaning?'

'I think I mentioned to you before, the vicious attack at the library was so brutal, it should have caused your demise. Typically, a non-fatal bite would turn someone into a werewolf. But in your case, that didn't happen. The bite just left a tiny bit of the werewolf gene inside you. Not enough for you to be howling at the moon every twenty-nine-point-five days. On average.'

My shoulders relax. 'So what you're saying is . . . I'm not a werewolf.'

'It's not black and white. You see, it has come to our attention that you have been displaying werewolf-adjacent tendencies.'

'I mean, I guess.'

She licks her lips.

I unexpectedly feel a throbbing between my legs so strong I cross them to try and push the feeling away, but it just intensifies.

Nova sees me squirm. She leans back in her leather chair. I try to control the sudden need I have to pounce on her. The yearning in my crotch is pounding now; it's almost painful.

'I believe you are one of us. But you are resisting something, holding something back. Which means you are not able to reach your full potential.'

'Ah.' I breathe heavily, rocking forward. 'What does that mean, exactly?'

'What do you think, Brodie? Is there a beast in there waiting to get out?'

'What if I don't want there to be?' I ask distractedly.

'You could have strength beyond your wildest dreams, instincts that would make a human look as deep-thinking as a jellyfish. Not to mention, we werewolves play by our own set of rules.'

Given how turned on I am, it is really hard to tell if she's flirting with me or not. I want to jump on her and kiss her, but the moment's thwarted by a woman swinging open the door. It's the doctor from the night I was bitten. Nova doesn't break her gaze.

'Juniper?'

'I thought we could do the chipping now?'

I gulp. 'The chipping?'

'We need to implant a tracking device in you, so we know your whereabouts. The whole pack has it done.'

'Zainab too?'

'Yes. Did she not tell you about this?'

'Nope,' I say through gritted teeth.

I'm back in the hospital room, lying on the bed, with Nova leaning over me. Even upside down, her face is handsome. Still, it's not fully distracting me from the growing feeling of terror in my gut.

'It's really important you don't jump, Brodie,' Juniper says, applying a cold, wet cream to my neck. Fear surges through me.

'That's right,' Nova says, her grip tightening. 'Remember that poor boy. What was his name?'

I start to shake in fear.

'Toby? Tam? Terrence?'

'Terry!' Nova and Juniper shout in unison.

'Yes, poor Terry jumped out of the way, and we chipped his right eye by mistake.'

'It wasn't fun for him or me,' Juniper says sagely, manoeuvring a metal machine towards me that looks like a robot's arm. I wince.

'She's scared. See, that's how we know she's mostly human still,' Nova says.

I try to sit up, but Nova pushes me back down.

'You need to stop wriggling around, Brodie.' Nova presses her hands over my clavicles, her fingers pinning me down. Every breath I take pushes against her, but she is so strong it doesn't make a difference.

Juniper jovially agrees. 'A werewolf would be far more chill. Now, Brodie, I need you to take three big, deep breaths for me. I'm going to insert the chip on the count of three.'

I let out a whine. How has it come to this? Haven't I been through enough?

'Tell me you understand,' Juniper says to me like I'm a five-year-old. Which is fitting, because all I want is my mummy.

'I understand,' I say, cold, white terror rising inside me. This could be the end.

'Remember, the microchip is tiny.' Juniper presses some random buttons on the machine and it beeps. 'The size of a SIM card. And it will live under your skin. You won't even know it's there.'

'Ready?' Nova whispers into my ear. Her fingertips press, deeper and harder.

'Not really,' I say, my jaw clenched.

'Oooooone,' Juniper says in a soothing tone. I obediently fill my lungs. I push the air out through my teeth.

'Twoooooooo . . .'

As I take my second breath in, there is a flash like a paparazzi camera.

'Aaaaagh!' I yelp in shock. 'Is it done?' The only experience I can liken this to is getting my ears pierced in Seafall Mall when I was twelve. The searing hot pain in my temple is only just catching up.

'Yep, all done,' Juniper says, hoisting the metal machine away. Nova's hands are no longer on me, but I still feel their imprint.

'You told me you would do it on three,' I say, my hand flying to my head, where I can feel a tiny raised rectangular bump. 'What now?' I sit up and twist around to see Nova.

'We recommend you go home for now. It's a bit of a wait-and-see situation with you.'

'Wait for what? Till I maul someone to death?'

Nova purses her lips.

'I'm not joking. Am I just meant to saunter back into my life now everything's changed?'

'Everything changed some time ago, Brodie.' Nova puts her hand on my shoulder, and I feel electricity pulse through me.

As I walk towards the exit in a daze, I see Shadow again. He jumps up and grabs hold of a metal bar, then swings from it playfully. His muscles are so prominent, they create a V shape pointing down to his crotch. Autumn affectionately calls these lines 'cum gutters'. I can't help but imagine licking them, feeling the grooves with the tip of my tongue. I turn the corner, and as I wait for the elevator, I feel fatigue, lust and confusion churning inside me. Maybe there is a beast in me waiting to come out after all.

CHAPTER TEN

*In Jack London's **The Call of the Wild** (1903), the laws of nature are contrasted with the human-imposed laws of society. Please compare and contrast these ideas, using examples from the text.*

It's a biting late-November afternoon outside, with temperatures low and scarfs and hats aplenty. I'm flicking through the chapters of *A Clockwork Orange* in the rec room before class when I spot Autumn curled up on one of the big couches by the roaring fireplace, wearing a flowy white dress with biker boots and a big leather jacket. I've been avoiding Zainab for the past month, and unfortunately that has meant avoiding Autumn too. I sink down in my seat, praying she doesn't see me, but it's too late. She gets up and bounds towards me like a Labrador.

'Brodie!'

I paint a look of surprise on my face. 'Oh, hey.'

There's a painfully awkward pause. 'I've not seen much of you. Zainab and I were saying we miss hanging out.'

'Is that right?' It's difficult to know how to react when I don't know what story Zainab's spun to Autumn. One that paints her in a good light, no doubt.

Autumn takes a step nearer. 'Look, I don't know what happened between you two, but surely you can figure it out.'

I haughtily suck my cheeks.

'It's just not as fun without you,' she adds.

Yeah, right. Swallowing down the lump in my throat, I feel a pang of wanting to forgive and forget.

But then Zainab appears out of the toilets and a spear of anger spikes through me again. When she notices me, her expression changes to a warm smile. It doesn't suit her.

'Are you joining us for coffee?' she asks me, her voice laced with hope.

I look between them and stand up abruptly, grabbing my bag. 'No, thanks, I better get to class.'

I push past them, more aggressively than I intended.

'But it doesn't start for twenty minutes,' I hear Autumn protest as I go.

I make my way to the lecture hall in what I hope looks like an empowered, nonchalant way, but my legs are shaking.

Zainab has tried to make up for her betrayal, in a low-key Zainab way. But the more I've thought about it, the more I feel lied to and cheated on. All those times she was asking to hang out, was she really wanting to spend time with me, or was she just wanting to know my whereabouts so she could secure me as one of her crew's next meal? The phone tracking suggestion, the daily messages asking what I was up to; it's all just made me feel so yucky. That bitch set me up – it's going to take a lot more than a few voice notes to make it up to me. More than annoyed, I'm embarrassed for thinking she was interested in being my actual friend.

By all accounts, I'm better off without Zainab. I don't miss her annoying rants about basic men, or her eye rolling, or her quick-witted sarcastic comments. I don't miss my study buddy. Not one bit. I've gone practically my whole life up until now without good friends, so I'm sure I'll manage without them now. My focus is on getting the grades I need. At least, that's where I want my attention to be. It's been difficult, waiting to see if some dreaded change happens, something to confirm what Nova told me. My concentration has been drifting, but I'm determined to get it back.

I take a seat at the back; I've not been as keen on making a goodie-two-shoes impression recently. The lecture hall slowly fills up with people, and I find myself sitting beside a guy I've seen around a few times. His side profile is well drawn, handsome with a strong chin that juts out, like a comic-strip superhero. He has pouty, pillowy lips. It's difficult to pinpoint why, but he seems like the type of guy who phones his mother once a week, but never calls girls back after he fucks them. I spot the back of Autumn's head and squirm in discomfort. Avoiding someone takes a lot of effort. I know none of this is her fault, but I can't pretend things are fine and dandy, and just sit and have lunch with her and Zainab as if nothing has changed when it has.

Jackie approaches the lectern and gets her PowerPoint about the works of Sylvia Plath up and running, her patchwork poncho swishing as she moves. As I sit and listen to her, phrases like 'alienation', 'inner turmoil' and 'self-destruction' hit a little close to the bone. I wonder how Sylvia would have dealt with being bitten by a mythical creature. I uncross my legs, and my foot accidentally brushes the sneaker of the guy beside me.

'Sorry,' I whisper.

He gives me a forgiving nod, and I notice his gaze lingers on my thighs. As Jackie goes into the main themes of *The Bell Jar*, I let my foot graze against his once more.

At first, I regret going back a second time, but after a few moments, I feel a swift nudge back. A sideward glance shows me he's now chewing his pen playfully. His jaw grinds as he takes it between his teeth. I wait a few moments, then nudge his strong calf with my leg. He nudges back harder. Feeling a familiar pulse of anticipation between my legs, I slowly move closer to him, and then a few moments later, he moves close to me. Soon we are locked side by side, my leg snaked around his, my right hand stroking his rock-solid dick through his jeans. His hand reaches across and he gives my upper thigh a forceful squeeze, like he's pinching a tough piece of fruit. It almost hurts, and I love it. We take it in turns for me to rub then him to squeeze. Staring straight ahead I feel the blood rush between my legs, pulsing and throbbing like a drum.

As Jackie's voice warbles along, I feel him get harder and harder in my grasp. I am so slippery wet, I undo my jeans myself and, as discreetly as I can, guide his hand inside my underwear. Thankfully it's not laundry day. It's not an easy task to wank each other off without anybody noticing. The odd rustle of paper or cough from another student makes us both freeze on the spot momentarily before continuing on. His finger rubs my clit over and over, pushing me to a shuddering orgasm. A matter of seconds later, I rub him to silent completion and get a feeling of deep satisfaction knowing he has spunked in his pants.

Who the fuck do you think you are, you tramp? Shame Goblin cackles as a wave of embarrassment washes over me. I get paranoid – what if everybody in that lecture hall knows what I have just done? I lean over my notebook, letting my curly hair curtain my flushed face. Stricken with guilt, I can't so much as glance in his direction. I wonder if he's experiencing the same levels of mortification as I am, but I doubt it. Most men just saunter around feeling deserving of a hand job, don't they? I excuse my way past the knees of three other students and flee the lecture hall. I may have finished, but Jackie hasn't.

Outside, the cool air bites at my hot cheeks as I make my way to the library, head down, still feeling the wetness between my legs, a stark reminder of what I just did.

'Oi!' a voice shouts.

At first I ignore it, although somehow I know it's directed at me. I keep walking, picking up a faster pace.

'You!'

I spin around and see it's my mutual masturbation buddy. I stop on the spot, unsure of what to do. He jogs up to me, his nose turned pink in the cold.

'That was mad,' he says with the giddy excitement of someone who has stepped off their first roller coaster.

I want to die. I don't know what I was thinking in there. In the middle of a lecture – what the hell is wrong with me?! But I smile tightly in agreement.

'It sure was.'

He observes me expectantly. I spot a bit of mustard or some other condiment on his aviator jacket and my stomach lurches. It's funny how somebody can go from the sexiest thing in sight to giving you the ick in a matter of minutes.

'Well, bye,' I chirp, desperate to get away from him.

'Can I at least have your number?' he asks, a note of expectation in his voice.

'Uuuuuh,' I stall as I try to think what to say. Sensing my reluctance, he stands up taller, bracing himself.

'Don't tell me, you have a boyfriend. Man, this keeps happening to me,' he huffs like a petulant child.

'No,' I say so quickly I regret it. Should have said, yes, I have a boyfriend with a black belt in karate and a wildly jealous temper.

'What, then?'

My mum told me once that lies are allowed if they protect people. Sometimes the truth can do more harm than good. But my mind draws a blank. I can't come up with an excuse.

'To be honest, I'm not interested in you.' As soon as the words have left my mouth, his teen boyband face contorts into a nasty grimace.

'You just let me finger you. What the fuck is wrong with you?' He shakes his head in disgust.

And as he walks away, hands in his pockets, I notice swirls of shame circling around inside me. But even bigger than that feeling is another. It's something edging towards satisfaction.

Once at the library, I check my student portal to see if any of my grades have been uploaded, and I stop dead in my tracks.

'I got an F?' I challenge Killian, accosting him as he makes his way into his office. He removes his coat and pulls off his knitted hat, hanging them both on the coat stand.

'Brodie, nice to see you too. Come in. I only have ten minutes, but remember we have our one-to-one in a few days as well.'

'I don't want to come in. I'm pissed off.' I hover in the doorway. 'There has obviously been some kind of clerical error.'

'You projectile vomited across half your classmates.'

'I sent you my study cards. The ones I didn't spoil, anyway. I had done the prep.'

Killian sighs, as if he's torn. 'But you didn't do the presentation. That was ninety per cent of the grade.'

'I was sick; surely you can make an allowance?'

'For actual sickness, yes. But for hangovers, I'm afraid not.' He busies himself with some paperwork.

I begrudgingly step into the office, anger bubbling.

Killian gestures to the chair, but I remain on my feet.

'How do you know I was drunk? Maybe I was spiked.'

His expression has changed from sympathetic to cold and hard.

'You were out of your mind. And you pushed my . . .' He trails off, his fist balled in frustration.

'Your girlfriend?'

'She's not my . . .' He stops himself saying more.

I stand, awkward and frustrated. He looks bashful. It's a whole big mess.

'I'm expecting better of you, Brodie.'

And with that, I spin on my heels and storm out of his office. So I'm failing at being a student, I've failed at finding friends. *One. Big. Failure.*

By the time I was ten, I had adopted a habit of running away from home. I would pack my little orange backpack with a juice box and cookies, my dog-eared copy of Enid Blyton's *The Famous Five* and the torch that lived in the bottom kitchen drawer. I'd tiptoe downstairs, being careful not to stand on the third one from the bottom, which always made a loud squeak. My mum would often be on the phone to Auntie Lou, telling her all about her day and gossiping about the annoying or funny clients she'd had. It was easy to sneak past her. My dad liked watching TV, nature documentaries mostly, so if one of them was on, I'd wait for the loud bit where a lion was enthusiastically mauling an antelope, then sneak out the door. I would run to the local woods up on the hill and fashion a den from old bits of wood. Once I found a huge piece of blue tarpaulin and stretched it over a hunched tree branch, creating a little tent. I would sit and read my book and eat my cookies. And I would wait. And wait. It would start to get dark, or cold, or both. Or I'd get hungry for something more substantial than sugary treats. I would begin to regret my decision, so I'd head home then. Mum would either still be on the phone or drinking wine. Or both. Dad would have another nature documentary on. Or the sports channel. They'd ask me if I'd had fun. They always assumed I had been out playing. Looking back, I don't think I wanted to run away; I wanted to be found.

This time, I'm running away for real. I have no friends, and I've fucked up my first uni assignment. And Killian has a hot girlfriend who wears matching Halloween costumes with him. What is the point of me being here – to wait around until I grow fur and eat Nathan when the full moon's out?! No, thanks.

This time I have my grown-up backpack with my laptop, a book, underwear, pyjamas, a few T-shirts, deodorant, toothbrush, toothpaste and Grace's memory box. I decide on London because it's far away enough to escape this madness, and it's a big enough city that it will be hard to find me. I'm sure Nathan will be happy to see the back of me – I just seem to stress him out. Hell, I stress myself out. I need to leave and start afresh. As for the chip in my temple, I will just need to cut it out. The thought curdles my stomach, so I push it to the side.

After securing the cheapest ticket I can find, I climb on the bargain Edinburgh to London night bus to find a combination of lone travellers, couples and families rustling candy-filled bags, all settling in for the ride. I'll be sitting upright for the entirety of the nine-and-a-half-hour journey, but that's the price you pay for savings. Sleep's overrated, anyway. I search for two seats that are free together, but the bus is packed to the rafters. Eventually, my only option is to perch beside a heavy-set man sporting a big blond moustache and a trucker hat, who is sitting with his legs spread wide, watching a very loud kung fu movie on his phone, with no headphones. He bites hungrily into a sandwich whose main job appears to be making the whole bus stink. On closer inspection, I see the filling is some kind of flaked fish. Because of course it is. Giving the aisle one last scan to make sure this is in fact the only option, I reluctantly take the seat beside him, brushing a couple of his stray crumbs away first. He ignores me and continues to chew his sandwich with his mouth open.

A frenetic fight scene plays out, and he lets out a guttural laugh, spraying tiny bits of food in the air. Maybe I *was* killed that night in the library, because this feels like literal hell. There is a sliver of hope that he is about to plug in his headphones, but somehow I doubt it. As the bus pulls out of Edinburgh, I stare at the captivating skyline, the perfect mixture of tradition and modernity. Never before have I felt such confronting disappointment. I had such high hopes for uni. I wanted to learn and read books and make friends. Instead, I've found myself alone, yet again. Maybe I am destined for a life of solitude. Some people just are. Driving further and further away from my hopes and dreams, I fixate on the silhouette of Edinburgh Castle, sitting atop Castle Rock. Giving me the metaphorical finger. I think about Nova, Juniper and Shadow. And Zainab. *You'll never fit in with any of them*, Shame Goblin reminds me.

My bus friend has finished his sandwich, but the pungent notes will undoubtedly hang around for hours. And he still hasn't put his headphones in. I bite my tongue. It's not worth getting into an argument with a stranger. Especially not one I am forced to sit so close to for the whole night. As I reach into my backpack to find my own headphones, I am zapped by an overwhelming pain that sears through my body like a steak knife. It gives me such a fright, I go to gasp but nothing comes out, as if the pain has hit me with such force it's rendered me speechless. Unable to breathe. I stiffen, adrenaline rushing through me, and I know that something isn't right. The pain stabs through me again and again, and it is so bad, it feels like I might be dying. The man beside me shifts in his seat and has the audacity to throw me a look of annoyance. And then everything goes dark.

CHAPTER ELEVEN

In The Awakening *(1899), Kate Chopin explores the ideas of female independence and self-discovery. Please discuss Edna Pontellier's journey as she breaks free from the traditional roles of wife and mother to seek autonomy and self-fulfilment.*

Before today, the most embarrassing moment of my life occurred when I was fifteen. The whole class had to do solo presentations in geography. When it was my turn, I walked to the front of the classroom and heard horrible sniggers and titters escape from the rest of the students. Trying to ignore the sea of smirks, I attempted to shake off my nerves and did my best, but it was really hard. After my presentation, my teacher kindly informed me in front of everyone that my school skirt was in fact tucked into my bright blue striped knickers. My whole bum had been exposed. The laughs and jeers echoed around the room, ringing in my brain, as my face turned beetroot. I wanted to die. But instead I kept my head down, burning in my own humiliation until the bell eventually rang. The next day, I begged my parents to give me the day off school, but they were having none of it. Stacy, a bony assassin with a block fringe, was my biggest antagonist throughout school, and she teased me so much I ended up running to the wooded area by the science huts, where I pulled off my school sweater, balled it up and let out a silent animalistic scream into its folds.

Now, here I am, standing buck naked in the middle of Edinburgh zoo, shivering in the frosty morning. What the fuck happened to me last night?! I was on the bus and then . . . and then I woke up in a wolf enclosure. No big deal. Instead of my usual alarm, I came to with something licking my face. Big, thick strokes that felt rough and slobbery. At first, I thought I'd let one of my one-night stands stay over, which was very unlike me. The past few months, I've been very much in favour of going our separate ways after I've got my rocks off. But then I felt bits of straw sticking into my ass and I realised I wasn't in the safety of my single bed at Bucky Place. When my eyes snapped open and I saw a wolf, much bigger than any four-legged creature I've come close to before, I jumped up, half-asleep and freaked out. Now, here I am. Several other wolves who've been loitering around in the background have noticed I am up and come trotting over. They appear friendly, but I suspect what they are capable of. I've already been almost eaten once this year, and that was enough.

I look down, almost laughing at the ridiculousness of shaving my bikini line the other night. The soles of my feet are scratched and cut, along with bruising and cuts up my arms. I'm not wearing a watch, but I know what time it usually gets light, so I'm guessing it's around 8 a.m. All I need to do is get out of the enclosure, find some clothes to fling on and get the hell out of here without being caught. Then, once I am safe, I can piece together the rest of last night. The distinct toot of an elephant sounds in the background, and I know that if I wait any longer, I risk being seen.

The wolf enclosure is huge, with sprawling grass, trees and plenty of vegetation. I've always felt conflicted by zoos. All those poor animals taken from their natural habitats, and ending up in grey and gloomy Edinburgh. But then there's the argument that the animals are being protected and studied. The wolves seem happy enough in here, but it's not for me. Climbing a fence at the best of times is no fun; however, sans underwear, it poses a troubling task.

I find an old barrel and roll it to the lowest point in the fence. At first, I try stepping on it sideways, but it keeps rolling away from me. I'd prefer not to break my neck today, if possible. I imagine the headlines – 'Promising English Literature Student Found Naked and Dead at Edinburgh Zoo'. On second thoughts, maybe it would read, 'Failing English Literature Student Found Naked and Dead at Edinburgh Zoo'. Sitting the barrel upright, I shakily hoist myself on to it, feeling damp flakes of wood scrape against my bare bottom. At this rate, I'll be joining the baboons. I stand on the cask, my toes curling to keep me steady, and then I reach out to touch the fence, half expecting an electric shock. As my fingers touch the cold, wet metal, a surge of relief pumps through me. It takes a few goes, but after a couple minutes I'm folded over the fence, trying to ignore the shocking discomfort of metal digging into my bare stomach. I swing myself over the top and land, as gracefully as could be expected, on the concrete path on the other side.

Pain ripples through my shin bone. I see signposts for the penguin enclosure, and the meerkats, before my sights land on a portacabin with a sign that says 'STAFF ONLY' on the door. Bounding up the winding concrete path is easy when the ground is this cold. My feet are so frozen, they feel like they're about to fall off. I try the door several times, only to find it's locked. Keeping an eye out for anyone around, I walk around the back and find a small window, presumably for the toilet, is open a crack. I find a twig on the ground and push it open wider. Then, for the second time in one morning, I'm hoisting myself up, balancing on a helpfully positioned bench. I climb through the gap as fast as my hips will allow, praying that nobody is walking past and happens to spot my naked behind hanging out the window.

I roll on top of a toilet, which thankfully has the lid down, and sit for a moment, naked and panting. The room is almost as cold as it is out there, and I can still see my breath, making itself visible in little clouds as it pours from my mouth. Pushing my hair out of the way, I frantically look for the door and make my way towards it, but just as I'm about to swing it open, I hear the distinct sound of a kettle boiling and movement on the other side. I'm not alone. The portacabin creaks and heaves under the weight of the person, who sighs and shuffles, jingling their keys. I stand shivering behind the door until I hear the kettle click and the clatter of a drawer opening. I wait until I hear them move across to the other side of the hut, and then I push the toilet door open a tiny crack. Just enough for me to peer through. There's a person, a middle-aged woman with a tight bun on top of her head, sitting at a desk, scanning a newspaper. 'What is the world coming to?' she says, and for a split second I worry she's talking to me. She slurps her coffee loudly and lets out another dramatic sigh, evidently unaware there is a naked girl a couple of feet away from her. I watch as she slowly reads the morning paper, licking her fingers to turn the pages. She pauses to unwrap a packet of biscuits and dunks one in her mug.

'Dang!' she shouts as it breaks off, and I can't help but jump, bashing my elbow on a pipe. But thankfully, she's so concerned about half of her biscuit drowning, she doesn't notice. When her phone rings, my nerves are so shot, I almost jump out of my skin in fright again. Despite the freezing cold temperature, I feel hot blotches of panic form on my neck and face.

The woman seems annoyed that her paper reading and biscuit ritual has been interrupted, and she takes her sweet time answering the phone.

'Yello, Barbara . . . You what? What do you mean . . . Slow down . . . A what woman? Did you say naked? I'll be there in two.' She slurps her coffee one last time, pulls on a green body warmer, grabs another biscuit for the road and rushes out of the portacabin, her keys jangling as she goes.

As soon as the coast is clear, I rush into the poky office and fling open the first metal cupboard I find. It's full of stationery and paperwork. I hit the jackpot with the second cupboard, discovering a cardboard box full of staff uniforms. I hurriedly climb into a pair of medium-sized cargo shorts and pull on an oversized khaki polo shirt that has the word 'STAFF' in big yellow letters across the back. I find a pair of plimsolls and quickly shove my feet into them. The finishing touch is a forest-green baseball cap, which I stuff my curls into.

Stepping out of the cabin, I walk tall, but not too tall, and as if I know exactly where I'm going. Two members of staff walk up the path towards me. My heart thuds as they approach.

'Morning!' one of them says brightly. I tip my cap in relief and shuffle off before they notice anything odd. I glance up at the wooden signposts, searching for the way out. It appears the quickest route is back the way I came, past the wolf enclosure. I pull my cap over my face, and, as I turn the corner, I see Barbara and two security guards at the gated entrance.

One of them talks animatedly. 'Then she jumps over the fence. It couldn't have been longer than fifteen minutes ago . . .'

'She must still be on the premises. Put an alert out for all staff.'

They pause as they see me trying to stride confidently past.

'Excuse me. Miss?' one security guard shouts after me.

I pause, as fear ricochets through me. 'Yes?'

'Where is your staff I.D. badge?'

'Oh.' I tap my head dramatically. 'Silly me, I forgot it.'

'But you need it to scan yourself in,' the other security guard says with suspicion as they both step towards me.

'I-I . . .' I'm trying to think of the next thing to say when I'm interrupted by a howl, which pierces the air with its sheer volume. Barbara looks inside the wolf enclosure. Then another howl. And another howl. Soon, the air is filled with the almost deafening whines and howls of a whole wolf pack. By the time the security guards have turned back around, I have darted towards the exit.

When I get to the bus station, I search for the ticket desk for the company that runs the buses to London and enquire about the driver from last night.

The cashier is about my age, with chubby cheeks and a piercing right above her Cupid's bow. She chews gum like it's going out of fashion and is clearly counting down the minutes until she can clock off.

'Is the driver around who did the 11.05 drive to London last night?'

'He should be in London?' she answers, confused. Her supervisor, a willowy man, pushes her chair out of the way and leans down to talk to me through the glass.

'Jerry needs a bit of R and R after the incident last night.'

'What happened last night?' I pull my cap down, deepening my voice.

'He'd barely got on to the A1 when one of his passengers had a meltdown and they had to turn the whole bus back. Wait a minute.' He narrows his eyes, his grey eyebrows kneading together. 'Are you a journalist?'

'No, but I am the woman's sister. She's diabetic, didn't feel well. And I think she left her backpack behind?' I say hopefully.

He regards me with suspicion.

'Can you name some of the contents in the backpack please?'

'Sure, there should be a laptop, some clothes . . . and a copy of *The Goldfinch*.'

'A what?'

'It's a book.'

Once he hands it over to me, I turn on my heels and walk, as quickly as I can, out of the bus station and towards Morningside.

When I bang at Zainab's door, she opens it with a suspicious look on her face.

'No, thanks,' she says, about to close the door on me.

'Wait, wait, please!' Peering behind her, I see the lights are all off and, more importantly, she looks a mess. Tired and withdrawn, her hair unbrushed, with big circles under her eyes. Her clothes are old and baggy. She clearly wasn't expecting any visitors today.

'Look what the cat dragged in,' she says, before leaving the door sitting open for me to follow her in.

We take a seat in her living room, which is strewn with empty takeaway boxes. The curtains are pulled shut, giving it extra crackden vibes. Zainab slumps on her sofa and takes a large bite of an old slice of pepperoni pizza. She chews, loudly and unselfconsciously. Only when she's finished does she comment on my Edinburgh Zoo outfit.

'Did you fuck a safari park guide last night?'

As I tell her what happened, she barely reacts; instead, she waits for me to finish, and then reaches for another slice of pizza.

'Let me guess,' I say eventually. 'What happened to me is completely normal. For a werewolf.'

Zainab tears off the corner of the pizza, takes a huge bite and replies with her mouth full. 'It was a full moon last night. This shit can happen. What I want to know is why you were on the night bus to London in the first place.'

'I was planning on, eh, visiting family,' I lie.

Zainab smells a rat. 'Your family are from Fife, aren't they?'

'Do you know what's going on with me or not?' I ask her.

She swallows, her mouth now glistening with red oil. 'Forgive me if I'm a little slow today. Last night took it out of me.'

'Were you out, like, eating people?'

'As if.'

I roll my eyes. 'Back to me.'

Zainab licks the pizza grease from her fingers one by one. 'Your experience is unique to you. It isn't one size fits all.'

'Is that it?'

'Being a werewolf isn't like this big awful thing that destroys your life. Sure, we go a bit loco when it's a full moon. But it's freeing.'

'Which part of it, exactly? The part that turns you into a rabid dog once a month? Mauling people, is that fun, is it? They chipped me like I was livestock!' I know I'm getting shrill, but I can't help myself.

'Didn't stop you from trying to run away, did it? If you want to know what I think – you are better off embracing it, Brodie.'

'But what if I don't want to? All those people I saw at the Den, they look like athletes. You said yourself, I'm not even a full one. I'm not one of them.'

'You could train too.'

'Train for what?'

'To look like them,' she says, curling up smaller on the couch.

'But you don't.'

'I told you my role is more comms-based. I'm a scout. I report things.'

I can't deny a big part of me is intrigued to see Nova again. And maybe Shadow. I start to salivate.

'It's a gift. And I truly believe that.'

'What if I don't want the gift?'

Zainab lets out a belch. 'Doesn't matter if you want it or not, you have it. Last night, you tried to run away from who you truly are. And look what happened. One thing I know is, you can try to do all this alone' – she gestures with her hand – 'but you need other people. And I'm not saying that as a werewolf, I'm saying it as a friend.'

We sit in silence. Zainab grabs a wet flannel, leans back and rests it on her forehead.

'I get you're mad at me – you think it was my fault, that I fed you to the wolves.'

'Literally!'

'But there's something way bigger at play here. Way bigger than you or me.'

I fiddle with the buttons of my Edinburgh Zoo polo shirt.

'And instead of feeling overwhelmed with unanswered questions, you can just ask me.'

I sit up straighter. 'Quick-fire round?'

She rubs her sunken and bloodshot eyes. 'I didn't mean right now.' Then she catches my hopeful expression. 'Fine. Shoot.'

'When you change, do you feel it? Are you, like, aware of being one?'

'No, for me it's like blacking out. But very special ones can change and remain lucid. Like Nova. Now that, I hear, is a good buzz.'

I tuck my feet under me. 'How does it feel the night of the full moon?'

'Everyone meets in the Den before sundown. We eat a hearty

meal, then go into our lock-ups. It's mandatory. If you don't adhere to the rules, you aren't allowed to be in the clan.'

'Lock-ups?'

'They're individual cells. That keeps us contained.'

'How often do you bite or eat people?'

'We try to be respectful – after all, we were all humans once. So we avoid that as much as possible.'

'How many people have you . . .?'

Zainab shrugs, tossing the flannel down, then picking out a half-smoked joint from a brimming ashtray and sparking it. 'There's no way of knowing your own body count. Unless you're an elite.'

'And how do you feel after the full moon?'

'The day after is the worst. We call it Day Zero. Zero energy, zero patience. Think your worst period meets your worst hang-over times a hundred. That day is for rest.' She looks at me pointedly, but there is warmth beneath her cool exterior.

'What's your favourite thing about being a werewolf?' I watch her think on this for a long time, blowing smoke out the side of her mouth, then chewing a random piece of pepperoni. She turns to face me.

'Life is all about boxes. When you're born, what percentile are you? When did you start talking? Can you spell or write your own name? Are you in the square, circle or triangle group? Have you passed your exams? What do you want to be when you grow up? What do you want to study? Who do you want to marry? We are institutionalised, whipped into submission, and we don't even know it. Then, before you can say two-point-five kids, you've spent your whole life scrambling to get to the next level. Reaching for the next step. And for what? To lose the plot in an old folk's home, with a dwindling retirement pot in the bank and kids that hate you? Being a wolf means we can be as wild as we want. And nobody can tell us otherwise.' Her eyes flicker momentarily with life, and for the first time in months, I feel better. I sideswipe her with a hug, then I check the time. If I leave now, I'll make it to Killian's tutorial.

Autumn looks delighted when I take the seat next to her in class. She writes me a note on the corner of her pink notepad, and I crane my neck to read it.

Hey babe!

She's such a sweet, nice person that she's immediately welcomed me back into her life with open arms. I feel relief at this kindness, but a stab of sorrow too. *She wouldn't forgive you if she knew the truth*, Shame Goblin whispers.

I try to shake off the voice and listen to Killian, who is lecturing about *Frankenstein* by Mary Shelley. 'Let's look at the alienation and isolation caused by being a monster.' When he has finished his explanation, I stick up my hand.

'Something to add, Brodie?'

'The isolation isn't because he is a monster, though, is it?'

Killian's face twitches with a smile. 'Go on . . .'

'Well, the Creature has monstrous qualities, yes. But he is capable of moral reasoning and emotional complexity. He has humanity. It's the way society treats him that causes the most isolation. You could argue that humans are the real monsters.'

Killian folds his arms and tips his head approvingly. Autumn clicks her manicured nails and whispers under her breath, 'Yes, girl.'

After class, Autumn asks me to lunch at Café Curiosity. 'Sure, I'll meet you there in fifteen minutes,' I tell her.

When Killian and I are alone, he sits on the chair next to me. 'Have we cooled off, then?' His tone is light and teasing. I feel embarrassed for coming in so hot yesterday.

'Yes,' I reply shyly, instinctively nibbling at one of my ragged cuticles. It tastes foul, so I sit on my hands instead.

He waits for me to say more.

'Sorry for losing my temper. Good grades mean a lot to me, that's all.'

'I can see that,' he replies. Then his eyes drift towards my arms, which are decorated in scratches.

'My friend's pet ferret got a bit fresh,' I offer defensively.

He doesn't believe me. 'Brodie, I'm here for you. I hope you know that?' Killian looks at me. Really looks at me, his gaze penetrating my soul. For the first time in months, I feel seen. I stare into his amber eyes, glowing like a cosy fire. So warm and inviting, they make me want to wrap myself in a blanket, curl up beside him and bury myself in a book.

Unsure of what to say, I just keep staring. And then I think he leans forward, and so do I. My face pushes into his, my lips finding his mouth, but instead of kissing me, he pushes me away and lets out a gasp. 'What are you doing?' I feel the place on my shoulder that he pushed with his fingertips throbbing in shame. He stares at me in disbelief, then leaps up from his chair and stands behind it, as if it were a shield.

Before this morning, my most embarrassing moment was the skirt-in-my-knickers incident in school. The zoo briefly took the prize, but this has swiftly overtaken it. I get to my feet, shaking my head in regret. All I can say is, 'Sorry.' And then I run out the door, getting as far away from him as I can, ignoring him calling my name.

CHAPTER TWELVE

In Thomas Hardy's **Far from the Madding Crowd** *(1874),
the line 'A resolution to avoid an evil is seldom framed
till the evil is so far advanced as to make avoidance
impossible,' captures a tragic irony. Analyse how this
sentiment reveals the complexities of human nature.*

Over the next few days, the awkward moment with Killian
plays over and over in my head, like a Christmas song in a
fast-fashion store. Relentless and dementing. I am kicking myself
for being so stupid. Coming on to my tutorial leader – what a prize
idiot. I'm so mortified by the whole thing that I can't even bring
myself to share it with Zainab and Autumn. I sit in a quiet corner
of the reading room at the library and attempt to bury myself in a
copy of *Little Women*. But not even Jo March and her sisters can
soothe me.

'Hey there.' A voice pierces through my shame spiral.

When I look up, I see Sam. He stands, lopsided, a goofy smile
spread across his face.

'Hi,' I say plainly.

'What you up to?' he says.

I feel bad for being so standoffish and return the nearest thing to a smile that I can muster. 'Just doing a bit of reading.' I gesture to my book.

'That has been around the block, eh?' he remarks, taking *Little Women* from my grasp and inspecting the well-thumbed pages.

'I've had it since I was a little girl.'

'How many times have you read it?' Sam asks, with a tone that tells me he is impressed. It's pathetic, but I feel myself going red.

As he hands me back the book, I sit up straighter. 'At least twice a year for ten years.'

'That is so cool.' His hand grips the table for a second, and I pretend not to see that he's left little sweat marks on it. I notice he's stepping from one foot to another. He seems a little nervous. This relaxes me a little.

'I was wondering . . .' He clears his throat and then flips his hair out of his eyes like a donkey at a fair.

'What?' I look up at him, waiting patiently for him to spit it out.

'If you would like to meet up. Tonight?'

This question takes me by surprise. 'For what?'

He flips his hair again, quicker this time. 'For a drink.'

'Oh.' I blink, realising he's asking me on a date. Maybe it's because I found myself naked in the wolf enclosure at Edinburgh Zoo this week. Or maybe it's because Killian pushed away my advances. But something tells me I have nothing to lose.

I shrug and smile, a more genuine one this time. 'Why not?'

Sam has suggested meeting at the Student Union, and I am happy to take his lead. I decide to wear a plain top and my favourite dark blue jeans, but I don't want to look too datey, so I've kept make-up to a minimum. Cool and casual.

When I arrive, Sam is perched on a high stool by a jukebox. He waves at me awkwardly and I join him. He's even more nervous than earlier, twitching and looking around, as if his eyeballs want to do anything but focus on me.

'You look nice,' he says quickly as I climb on to the stool opposite him.

'Thanks,' I say, tucking a curl behind my ear.

There ensues a gaping awkward silence. So I fill it, by asking him questions.

'How long have you worked at the library?'

As soon as he hears the word 'library', he lights up, and that gets him talking.

We sit and talk and drink cheap, watery pints, and then he suggests tequila shots because why the hell not. And I drink faster than usual, as if I'm trying to drink away my week, pretending that I'm a normal girl who didn't sleep on a bed of straw at a zoo a few nights ago. And certainly didn't fire into my tutor.

In three hours, I go from not fancying him at all to thinking he's alright. He's no Killian. But he wanted to spend time with me. He likes me – it doesn't take a detective to figure that one out. Maybe Sam is a slow burn. You hear about people who didn't fancy one another at first, but then they end up married. I shudder at the thought of marrying this chump, but ignore my instincts. *Do you really think you could do better?* Shame Goblin whispers.

When it gets to near midnight, Sam invites me back to his flat for a nightcap. I don't really want to; my gut is telling me to call it a night. Go home. Maybe it's the cheap tequila, or the fact that Sam hangs off every word I say, but I reply, 'Why not!' with faux enthusiasm which he seems to buy. In fact, he seems very pleased indeed. We walk through the streets and he takes my hand, and even though it's freezing out, his palm feels sweaty. His winter coat looks too small for his lanky frame, and I start to wonder if this is such a good idea after all.

When we get back to Sam's flat, it smells of cat litter, damp and roll-up cigarettes. And his idea of a nightcap is a healthy dose of limoncello out of a chipped mug that has the ring stains of countless cups of coffee around the inside. He encourages me to down mine in one, and now the room is spinning. I start to feel a little queasy, and tell him I've had a long day, that maybe I should be getting home.

'I've had a long day too,' he says, peeling my winter coat from me. His place feels draughty and uncomfortable. 'Why don't we go for a little lie-down?' The same tone of voice I imagine he uses for his pets.

He guides me into his bedroom, which is dingy and dirty, and I shake my head. This is not what I want. I squint when he flicks on the main light.

'Mood lighting!' Sam exclaims quickly, as if he just invented the concept. I watch as he scrambles to turn on his bedside lamp. Then he guides me to sit on the corner of his unmade bed. My head feels fuzzy, so I comply, but I am not doing anything with him. I try to work out how long it might take me to walk home. Or maybe he could call me a cab.

My tongue feels thick in my mouth. 'I'm jusht gonna sit here until I feeeel a bit besher.' The words stumble out of me, holding on to one another like drunk friends.

Sam tops up my mug and puts it in my grasp. 'Drink up,' he purrs, putting the mug to my lips.

I shake my head. 'I want to go home,' I mumble.

'Why don't you crash here?' He looms over me, and suddenly I'm on my back. I feel the pain of my hair twisting from my scalp as he grabs a fistful of my curls. The mattress below me feels paper-thin as his weight presses me down.

'Ow!' I shout out.

'Shhh, you'll wake my roommate,' he whispers in my ear, clasping a damp hand over my mouth. His breath is hot, boozy and wet on my cheek. I panic and try to shove him off me, but the more I wriggle, the more he stiffens and pushes. He grabs my hands and pins them above my head.

'No. No!' I squirm more, trying to get out of his grasp, but he just increases the weight he's pushing down on me and tightens his grip. My wrists burn.

'Get off!'

'Oh, come on,' he spits venomously. 'You've been flirting with me since the moment we met. Everyone at uni knows you're a sure thing.'

Recoiling at his words, I feel sick. As he tries to plant a wet kiss on my mouth, I flatten my lips into a line and turn my head.

'Nobody spends that much time in the library. I get it, you were coming to see me.' He takes one hand away to fiddle with my jeans button. He struggles with it before undoing it, and then I hear his zipper going down. I go cold. *Not this. Please not this.*

Then things come into sharp focus. Something inside me snaps. I stare angrily into his dark eyes and, out of nowhere, I find the strength to push him off me, his torso hunched like a rag doll. His hands, a moment ago pressed on mine, flail as he tries to get his balance. Pathetic Superman. Using my legs to push his, I feel my eyes bulging and my arms shaking as I lift his body weight. Sam's expression goes from astonishment to fear.

'Woah, now. This isn't funny. Come on, put me down.' He sounds like a scared little boy.

I lift him further so my legs and arms are stiff like steel rods, propping him up, and he lets out a frightened laugh.

'OK.' I smile, then with all my might, I throw him across the room. As he crashes against the wall, it cracks, and puffs of dust appear. He falls to the carpet and then groans like a wounded animal. As he lies there, twisted, I see his white collarbone jutting out of his skin at an odd angle. *Whoopsie.* His jaw is contorted in shock and he twitches; his mouth opens and closes, making him look like a stupid goldfish.

'Where's your phone?' I growl.

He points with trembling fingers, to his bedside table.

I grab it, noticing his screensaver is a photo of himself reading a book upside down, a pair of glasses perched comically on the end of his nose. *Yuck.* I watch him jerk in pain before dialling the emergency services, leaving the phone beside him as he whimpers. On my way out, I bang on the door of his roommate and then leave, exiting into the biting-cold winter air.

Having now sobered up, I walk home, taking big strides. Snow starts to fall from the low, velvety sky. Tiny snowflakes at first, but they soon get bigger and bigger, thicker and faster, twirling from the inky blue, as if a giant is up there, shredding bits of paper. At the corner of Bucky Place, I pause and tip back my head, opening my mouth as wide as it will go. I squeeze my eyes shut and feel the little wet snowflakes fall into my mouth and melt on my tongue, savouring the sensation.

CHAPTER THIRTEEN

Madame Bovary (1856) by Gustave Flaubert follows Emma Bovary, a woman who is unsatisfied with her married life. Explore how Emma's pursuit of her desires leads to her downfall.

*G*race and I are in matching dresses. They have little blue bows and white lace around the trim. I love dressing like my big sister, but this outfit is annoying me. We're sitting on the floor waiting to leave for Granny Bell's party. My tights are itchy and my hair smells funny. Mum sprayed something sticky on it to keep the curls bouncy. It made me cough and splutter and I could feel it at the back of my throat. I don't want to go to the party, I don't want to leave my toys. Crossing my arms, I push out my bottom lip and huff. Grace pulls me in for a cuddle. She guides my head to hers and gives me a 'nosey', rubbing our little button noses together. It instantly makes me feel safe.

*

Autumn: Where are u?

The message is brief enough that I can read it without opening

it. I don't want her to know I've seen it. A crippling feeling of anxiety has plagued my whole morning so far. Nothing has made me
feel better – not a family-size bar of my favourite chocolate, nor
an episode of *Gilmore Girls*. Every time I blink, Sam's grimace
appears, leering at me with hot limoncello breath. The snow continued to fall through the night, encasing the whole city in a thick
layer of white. It's a perfect day to snuggle under the covers and
fester in my hangover in peace. But I don't feel at peace. Not one
bit. Hot and cold, I toss and turn until my bedsheets are damp and
twisted. Not only did I miss my lectures this morning, I am meant
to have my one-to-one with Killian later. My stomach heaves with
the embarrassment of my last interaction with him.

For hours I have been rolling around, trying to unpick things.
But it's all too much. Even though all I can taste is tequila, I am
too numb to brush my teeth. I wonder, in the cold light of day, if
Sam will press charges. Or worse, try to seek his revenge. Maybe it
was my fault for leading him on. I knew he had a crush on me. He
did give me special treatment, lending me more books than the
library cap of ten allowed, letting me get away with late returns
and lost books without so much as a slap on the wrist. Speaking of
wrists – mine are achy today. As I circle them clockwise then anti-
clockwise, my bones creak, and I notice fingerprint bruises all
around my forearms. Little purple reminders of Sam's touch that
make me want to throw up.

The scene in his bedroom unfolds in my head like a bad play,
over and over. Sam's unfamiliar smell, his thin lips, curled in a
sneer, his spindly fingers wrought with hangnails. I feel like an
idiot for trusting him to be a nice guy. And for going back to his
when I felt so drunk like that; I should have gone straight home.
Or said no to the shots we did. I shouldn't have agreed to go out
with someone I didn't even fancy. *That's what happens to bad girls*,
Shame Goblin whispers.

Imagine if Sam had taken things further, or if I hadn't been able to fight him off. Imagine if I had to go to the police. Or go through a trial? I've heard horror stories of sexual assault victims being questioned by the defence, their previous sexual history wheeled out to be used against them. I'm not exactly ashamed of the amount of sex I've been having the last few months, but I don't want a room full of strangers picking it apart. Or my mum and dad hearing it. Self-reproach flips in my tummy like a pancake. That's why so many women don't press charges, or report assault in the first place. Our embarrassment or fear of a teardown keeps us silent, and those fuckers get away with it time and time again. What if I go to the police and I end up having to explain my where-abouts for the past week? The last thing I want is to be exposed as the Zoo Streaker, which the news outlets are treating as a titillat-ing fluff piece. It's pretty confronting to see a pixelated photo of yourself scaling a fence in the nude. The classier broadsheets chose the least-degrading stills from the security cameras, but the trash sites went for the worst out of the selection. At least the images are so grainy, I can't be identified. Hopefully. The image of a criminal line-up pops into my head, but instead of variations of me standing there, it's all vulvas. From fully waxed to full bushes, and everything in between. I can picture the two security guards having a field day trying to narrow down which one belonged to me. This thought tickles me – before my mind drifts back to Sam. At least I was able to retaliate to that sick fuck in my own way.

Nathan raps his knuckles on my door, interrupting my daydream.

'What?' My voice is thick and deeper than usual.

I've put a poster on the back of the door to cover the scratch marks from Halloween, and it flutters as Nathan pokes his head in. I gesture at him to come in fully and he does, narrowly avoiding standing on a stray sneaker and a pile of books. His nose wrinkles at an unpleasant smell, which I am clearly immune to. I don't bother sitting up, but prop my head up and wait for him to talk.

'This is awkward, but we started that cleaning rota for a reason.' His large white belly spills over the waistband of his boxers. Even in teeth-chattering December, he still doesn't put on any clothes; I seriously don't get it.

'Yes, Nathan; the reason was you wouldn't get off my back,' I retort. His face falls. He's not used to me being this cranky. And to be honest, neither am I. I instantly feel bad. 'Sorry,' I add. 'I'm not feeling so good today.'

Nathan observes me with pity as I lie here, tired and ropey. 'Another late night, was it?' He may have meant it in a jovial way, but this comment hits a nerve.

'It's called having a social life.'

'I have friends,' he says, his chin quivering.

My head slumps back down on my bed and I reach for a bag of spicy crisps. We both know all of his friends are online. I'm not cruel enough to say it, but he knows I'm thinking it.

'Fine. I'll do the bathroom later.'

'And the vacuuming?'

'And the vacuuming,' I repeat before shoving a handful of crisps in to my mouth.

I toss and turn for an hour or so more, then decide the only way for me to get out of my slump is to face the music and go to uni. Showering gets rids of the smell of last night's events, but the bruises stay put. I wrap my big thrifted tartan scarf around me, pull on my winter coat and head out, enjoying the awakening feeling of the bitter cold whipping my face.

When I get to Killian's office, the hangover still thrums, a low level of anxiety swimming through me. I stomp my boots, ridding them of chunks of snow, before stepping through the door.

'Come in!' He beams, gesturing to the armchair across from his desk. 'I'm glad you're here.'

I frown, unwrapping my scarf from around my hair, which is covered in little water pearls from the air outside.

'Put that on the heater if you like,' he says, and I place the scarf over an ancient-looking radiator. Taking a seat, I rub my stiff fingers together in an attempt to warm them up.

'When you didn't turn up for class this morning, I was worried.'

'About what?'

We give one another a wordless glance.

He goes first. 'Let's just get the awkward thing out the way, shall we?'

I wait for him to continue, unsure of what to say myself.

He looks out the window for so long, I wonder if he's ever going to speak. 'I'm fresh out of a divorce.'

Oh. That was not what I was expecting him to say. I let him continue.

'I won't go into the details, but I moved here with my wife. She has family here and wanted to be near them.'

'You don't need to explain yourself,' I say kindly.

Killian turns to me, his expression pained. 'She encouraged me to make new friends, so I did. Anyway, long story short, she cheated on me with one of my new mates. They are getting married this week. And I am not doing well.' His voice cracks. 'Far from it, actually.'

I'm stunned by this admission of vulnerability.

'I know you're probably thinking, why the hell is he telling me all this?'

'Kind of.'

He lets out a ragged breath. 'I am pretty concerned about you. I know that you have the makings of a fantastic student. You are smart and have a genuine love of literature, which is quite frankly amazing to see. More important than any of that, I have seen changes in you over the last few months – you seem withdrawn and not yourself.'

I stare blankly and finally ask, 'Is this conversation about me or you?'

He nods as if he is saying a rehearsed speech and intends to stay on course. 'Both. This is all to say, I wanted to know how you were doing the other day. But for a moment, I let my professionalism waver and I let my feelings of inadequacy and jealousy about my ex-wife take over me. And I leaned in to kiss you.'

My mouth falls open in surprise.

'It would have been easy to pretend that it was all your fault. But I signalled for it to happen. I know I did. Because I am having a freak-out about Kristine marrying a guy I met at a fucking pub quiz.'

He draws air into his lungs and blows it out slowly and deliberately. We lock eyes. And I see sorrow. I feel bad for him.

It's my turn to speak. 'Thanks for sharing all that,' I say, and I really mean it.

He continues: 'I'm truly sorry. I crossed a line. And I'm in no way using this to get you to open up to me, but I would hope that if something's going on with you . . . I hope we have built enough trust, adult to adult, that you can tell me. If you want to, that is.'

Maybe it's his truly sincere tone, or the fact that I'm feeling extra delicate today. But something he says awakens something in me. A part of me I have been ignoring. I start to cry. And not cute little rolling tears down one cheek like in the romance films I love. Big, heaving sobs. Once I start crying, I can't stop. I let go of all of the emotions that I have been pushing down for months. I cry for all the times I've lost control recently. For being bitten and being pulled away from the thing that matters to me the most – my studies. I cry angry tears over how Sam treated me last night. I cry tears of grief for Grace. I cry for the time that I thought Zainab was using me. And I cry at the sweet way Autumn welcomed me back into her life after I avoided her for a month. I cry and I cry and I cry.

Killian comes around from behind his desk and hesitates before he puts a friendly hand on my shoulder. And being touched by somebody who truly cares for me, as opposed to the harshness of Sam's touch in his skanky bedroom, just makes me cry even more. I go until I can no longer go. It might be two or twenty minutes, I'm not sure. Afterwards, my face feels swollen and I can only imagine it is peony-pink. My eyelashes are all criss-crossed and wet. My nose is snotty. I feel great. Killian passes me a box of tissues and I make my way through them, blowing my nose and dabbing my face. He doesn't rush me, or ask me to tell him what's wrong. He just lets me be. I fling at least ten crumpled-up tissues in to his wastepaper bin, and he nods at me sagely.

'Thank you,' I utter in a small voice.

When I step back outside, I feel lighter, as if I've been carrying a backpack of heavy rocks, and have finally got the chance to take it off. It's still biting cold. Despite my snow boots, I am unsteady on my feet. Bristo Square is slippery with black ice, and I grip the handrail along the steps as I exit the university building. Then I see him. The guy in the hoodie. Standing at the other side of the square, looking straight at me. I look down and feel the cold wetness as I breathe into my scarf. My heart begins to pound in fear. I don't want him to know I've seen him, so I keep my head down, but slowly move my gaze up. Thinking on my feet, I choose to walk the wrong way home, in the hopes that he'll follow me. And he plays right into my hands. Cautious and deliberate, I pad along the path that winds around the side of the sandstone building. I walk for about a minute, then I spin around on the spot and catch him about five feet behind me.

'You!' I yell, before lunging towards him. He tries to run away, but, fortunately, the group of students walking behind him blocks him so I can catch up. I reach out, grab his hood and yank it down, then let out a huge gasp of surprise.

CHAPTER FOURTEEN

**Wuthering Heights (1847) by Emily Brontë portrays
intense and destructive forms of love, particularly
between Heathcliff and Catherine. Please explore
the notion of destructive love in the text.**

'You?!' The padded air swallows my question.

Nova stands statuesque, not one silvery-blonde hair out of place. Her nostrils flare, and her eyes glitter like two lost diamonds in the snow.

'Calm down.'

'Calm down?!' I yell back, my voice startling even me. After the few days I've had, I have zero fucks left to give. So no, I will not calm down.

She stares at me, her still energy in opposition to my growing hysteria.

'Has it been you? This whole time? Stalking me! Like a creep.' I spit out the words, flinging up my arms animatedly. I feel some curious people stopping to look.

'Let's go somewhere more private,' Nova offers in a quiet, clipped voice.

'Why should I do as you say?' I shout, hating myself for sounding like a petulant child.

Nova regards me in a way I cannot put into words. It stirs something deep inside me. So deep it's a place I feel like I can't reach unless she's there.

'Because I am in charge,' she says with confidence.

My legs buckle at her command.

'Follow me.' She pulls her hood back up and turns. This, I imagine, is not a request.

As we head together towards Leith Walk, thunder claps in the distance.

'Looks like a storm's coming,' I babble, filling what feels like an uncomfortable silence.

She gives me a withering look as if to say, *No shit*. I curl my toes in my snow boots, berating myself for not being able to remain cool and calm. She's the one who has been following me, but she's making me feel small and insignificant.

'You've been on quite the adventure over the last few days,' she remarks, striding along the frosty sidewalk.

Remembering I'm chipped, I feel myself blush with embarrassment. Does she know I went to Sam's?

'Yeah,' I say uncertainly.

Nova pauses and turns to face me. Her nose has turned pink, like that of a freshly born kitten. I have to resist the sudden urge to lean in and lick it.

'I saw you on the news.' Nova starts to walk again, crunching the snow underfoot, a smile dancing on her face. 'Nice bum.'

I redden even more, and can feel my armpits and the backs of my knees sizzling with the heat. Thank goodness I'm swaddled in winter clothes.

'Have you ever woken up in a strange place?' I ask.

She raises an ashy eyebrow, and I instantly regret the accidentally intrusive question.

'I didn't mean . . .' I trail off, hyper-aware that everything I'm saying sounds utterly foolish.

We go back to not talking. But I have so many things I want to say. Nova walks at a naturally quicker pace than me; I have to double up my strides to keep up.

When we reach Newhaven Harbour, I remove my scarf and pull my hood down, enjoying the cold air as it dances around my now-warm ears and neck. Nova nods to a little waterfront café with a giant plastic ice-cream cone above the door.

'Fancy a coffee?'

'Yes, please. Black.'

Nova heads into the café, the bell on the door tinkling. I don't know whether she wants me to wait outside for her. Something about her makes me unsure of myself. Even more so than usual. I fiddle with my coat, wondering if I look OK. She's caught me on a bad day. Hungover and post-hysterical crying. I wish I'd stopped at the toilets on the way out of uni and checked my face. I smooth my hair in the reflection of the café window, then turn to the water. The air is so cold and wet and thick, I can't see that far out, so I concentrate on the nearby boats, bobbing on the icy water, covered by a layer of freshly fallen snow. *Not a good day to be sailing*, I think as the bell tinkles again and Nova returns to my side.

'There you are.' She hands me a steaming hot cup of coffee. I take an enthusiastic sip and burn my tongue.

'Agh,' I yelp.

'Watch it, it's hot,' she says.

'No kidding,' I shoot back, my already bloodshot eyes watering in pain.

Nova grabs a handful of fresh snow. 'Open up,' she instructs.

'What?'

'You heard me.'

I open my mouth self-consciously and she tips a small scoop of snow on my tongue. It provides a welcome, cooling relief, and melts almost instantly, dripping to my back molars.

Not sure what to do next, I swallow. An icy drip escapes and dribbles down my chin. Nova wipes it with her thumb, which is softer than I expected it to be.

'Good girl,' she says coolly.

I take a sudden interest in the positioning of my gloves.

Nova points at the little white lighthouse at the end of the stone jetty, which is getting pummelled by energetic waves on either side.

'Let's go there.'

'Why?' I ask her, feeling a knot of anxiety form in my chest.

'Why not?' she counters, and walks towards it. Like before, I feel I have no choice but to follow her.

The sky has now turned the colour of a bruised apple, bathing us in a weird golden light. As we plough forward, the wind that we were protected from in the city takes jabs at us, and sea foam sprays from either side. Now I've cooled down, I feel chills creep into every gap in my clothing, from my collar to my sleeves.

When we reach the little lighthouse, I think of the loneliness of a lighthouse keeper, and wonder what kind of person would choose that job. 'Will you talk now?' I eventually say, over the increasing gusts of wind.

'What do you want to know?' Nova says.

'Why are you stalking me?'

Nova shakes her head. 'I'm not.' She is matter-of-fact when she speaks. As if everything is obvious. But everything she says just makes me feel more muddled than before.

'I need to be near you.' A dagger of truth slices through me when she says that.

'Why?' The ball in my stomach expands and contracts.

She ignores me and keeps striding along, getting to the foot of the lighthouse and stepping to the side as a particularly big wave crashes at her feet.

'Why?' I shout again.

'Because,' she says.

'Because what?'

Nova turns around. Her hood twitches with the gusts of wind, her jaw set with grit and poise.

'I was the one who bit you.'

My body turns as icy cold as the water looks. She tried to kill me that night in the library, and now she's taken me on this remote walk so she can finish the job. My instincts kick in. I will not be prey, not again. Thinking fast, I quickly survey my surroundings. On the left, waves crash and foam, and on the right, there is a rock formation that would be sure to turn me to pulp if I fell anywhere near it. Nova sees me eye the water and takes a step towards me. Panicking, I fling my coffee in her face, but she swerves it expertly and the brown liquid sloshes on the concrete. The wind picks up and shrieks and howls, as if it's agitated too.

'Brodie, stop it,' she commands. But I don't trust her. How could I?

'You tried to kill me!' I spit, anger vibrating through me, from my toes to my scalp.

'I didn't.' She stands with her arms spread, as if to say she comes in peace. But I know she doesn't. She takes another step towards me.

'You did! Murderer!' I scream, but the wind picks up my words and sweeps them away. Only one of us is making it off this jetty, and given I've already almost lost my life once, I sure as hell am not letting this happen again.

I crouch down on the ground and hug my knees, curling myself into a ball.

'Brodie?' Nova steps near me. I keep still until I see the toes of her scuffed leather boots at my feet. 'Brodie,' she repeats, this time with a gentle, coaxing tone. But she won't fool me. I count to three slowly in my head and then spring up, standing tall, and attack her in a capricious frenzy. I claw at her face and try to grab her by the hair, but her responses are quick and she ducks and dives out of the way. I keep jabbing and attacking, but I'm losing control. Thunder rumbles, loud and menacing.

'You don't understand!' Nova shouts. But I won't accept her bargaining. She's just trying to buy time, and save herself. Another thunderclap booms so loud that I jump. And then a huge fork of purple lightning stabs through the sky. As Nova turns to look at it, I give her a swift kick and she trips over an old rusty anchor chain, her heel catching on it. As another fork of lightning slices through the sky, she stumbles back. As if she's in slow motion, she falls backwards. I watch in shock as she falls into the dark water, her pink mouth open in an 'oh' shape, and she goes under just as a huge wave crashes, pulling her down.

It hits me like a slap in the face. Although I'm the one on dry land, I may as well be drowning. I have no reason or logic playing in my mind. Just the instruction, the primal need for Nova to reappear. But she doesn't. Seconds stutter by and I don't take my eyes off the spot where she fell in. As the ominous thunder claps again, there is no sign of her on the foamy surface of the water. I can't wait any longer. I desperately rip off my boots and fling my coat to the side, and without a second thought, my hands in a diamond, I bend my knees and dive in. The cold feels like a thousand knives cutting through me. I plunge as far down as I can through the murky water. Opening my eyes, the burn of sea salt stings like hell. It's so dark I can barely see, but I must keep them open. Then the whole of the sea bed lights up as another crack of lightning fills the sky with a bright neon flash. Shapes of seaweed and wood and glimmers of tiny fish appear in front of me, but no Nova.

As I run out of air, I propel myself upwards. When my head bursts out of the choppy water, the clouds above are now a threatening charcoal grey. The waves fling me from side to side as I suck in my breath and dive under again, thinking of the news headline: 'Edinburgh Zoo Streaker Found Drowned'. The bossy current is putting even my best efforts to the test as it pushes me away from the concrete walkway. It's indescribably cold; moving my limbs is a struggle. If I don't find her this time, then I will have to call off the search and admit defeat. Then I surprise myself with the thought that I'd rather die than return to the jetty alone. Which doesn't make sense. The second time going under is harder than the first. I'm fatigued. My eyes are burning. I can barely see. Another rumble of thunder rolls. It's so loud I worry for a second that a huge shipping container is moving towards me.

My fingers get caught in some seaweed and I shake them free just as another blast of lightning lights the way. And that's when I realise. It's not seaweed; it's Nova's hair. I'm so happy and shocked to see her that I let out a slew of bubbles from my mouth. Her skin is even paler than usual; her eyes are open but have lost their sparkle. She looks so peaceful, like an angel. Is she dead? Maybe she hit her head, or swallowed water. I swim under her, looping my arms around her taut waist, and kick furiously to the surface. The waves have no qualms about sloshing us back and forth as I drag her to the side of the jetty. When we reach it, I find a wedge of stone to balance my foot on as I heave her up. It is annoyingly slippery, and it takes all the strength I have left in me to push her up and pull myself up after her. Then, like clockwork, huge snowflakes start to twirl furiously from the sky.

Nova lies lifeless on her side and I gently turn her head, open her mouth, pinch her nose and breathe into her cold lips, which have turned blue. She's dead. Now the headline will read: 'Edinburgh Zoo Streaker Gets Life in Prison for Murder'. What am I meant to do now? I can't give her back to the sea – she'll become fish food. I can't just leave her out here. But I'm not strong enough to lift her. Fuck. My life's over, isn't it?

Then she splutters and gasps. I almost don't hear it over the roaring of the wind. The relief makes me shake. I cradle the back of her head, see the life slowly return to her eyes, and she grabs the scruff of my sweater, which is now heavy with seawater.

She stares at me, her expression wrought with intensity. She bares her teeth, her bottom lip sticking out, shiny and glistening wet.

'If you dare think about killing me after I just saved your life, I will fling you back in there, bitch,' I mutter to her, surprising myself with my ballsy tone.

'I was wrong about you. You have barely any wolf in you.'

'What?'

'If you had any power at all, you would have transformed there. But you didn't.'

'Screw you. I rescued you, isn't that enough?'

'No.'

And then Nova grabs more of my sweater in her fist and yanks me down so our faces are millimetres apart. Even though I am leaning over her, I feel vulnerable. She could easily flip me over or strangle me in this position. She could do anything to me right now.

Her lips part and instantly find mine, and we smash our mouths together in a kiss I didn't realise I had been waiting for my whole life. Our tongues find one another and dance and stroke. She tastes salty and sweet. She grabs my face, pulling me further into her, and I obediently climb on top of her. My mouth moves around the edges of hers, feeling her sea-soaked skin. Her moans ring through me like a guitar string being strummed for the very first time. We kiss for what feels like hours, yet only a millisecond too. Too much yet not enough. I feel like I could never get enough of her. It's otherworldly; thousands of sparklers of pleasure ignite inside me. Then Nova stops. My mouth stays open, but she's pushed me off, leaving me shaking, dizzy and drenched. She gets to her feet, her sodden hoodie clinging to her athletic body. We don't break our lustful gaze for what feels like an age. Then she shakes her head as if gravely disappointed in me.

'We can't do this.'

She turns on her heels and runs away from me, back to the harbour, in a black streak, moving so fast I know I wouldn't be able to keep up. I am left shaking and wet, with just the delicious taste of Nova on my lips. And something metallic. I lick my bottom lip and taste the unmistakable flavour of blood, then rub it with the back of my hand, where a deep-red smear shines. I don't know what the hell just happened, but I instantly want more.

CHAPTER FIFTEEN

In Pride and Prejudice (1813), Elizabeth Bennet and Mr Darcy experience a complex emotional dynamic following his initial proposal. Analyse how their denial and subsequent behaviour affect their relationship and the novel's progression.

Christmas comes and goes. It's just as well I have some time away from school, because I have been driving myself wild. The taste of Nova stays on my lips for days. Instead of fading, the memory of our kiss, wrought with passion, wet and hard against the cold stone walkway of the jetty, seems to be tattooed on my mind.

Like most of the other students I know, I go home. Zainab doesn't celebrate Christmas, so she nips over to Bali for a vacation with her mum. When I message her to ask how it is going, she replies, 'Too hot. I hate sand.' My holiday season consists of my parents and I watching a lot of old movies, playing many games of *Monopoly* (Dad is the reigning champion) and countless rounds of *Scrabble* (I am the reigning champion), as well as drinking a lot of wine (Mum is the reigning champion). On New Year's Eve, we go down to Thistle Bay and watch the fireworks display with the rest of the community. As the explosion of whites and pinks and blues and greens burst in the dark sky, I watch their shaky reflection on the choppy sea, wondering what new things this year will bring me.

Beyond the kiss, Nova's words have been ringing in my head. What did she mean when she said she was wrong about me? That she thought I was something I'm not? This statement has sliced right through to my core, the feeling of not being good enough spilling out of the hole it has made in my insides. *Of course you're not even a proper werewolf – you're not a proper person*, Shame Goblin whispers. Another voice appears in my head. Small and timid, but there nonetheless. *But what if I am?* it replies.

I'm relieved to get back to Edinburgh and return to student life. And to be near Nova. I reunite with the girls at Café Curiosity on a downright disgusting January morning, and while Autumn is busy chatting up some guy who is dressed like a mime artist, I pointedly ask Zainab if she knew Nova was the one who bit me. Her expression falls, and then she begins to choke on a bite of carrot cake, spluttering and reaching for her water.

I pick up her water bottle from the table and hold it out of reach as she coughs, spraying crumbs in every direction. Eyes bulging, she signals for me to pass it to her, opening and closing her hands like a confused crab.

I hold the bottle further out of her reach. 'Tell me the truth, yes or no?' I demand. 'I mean, you as good set it up, didn't you?'

She finally swallows and looks at me, wiping her mouth. 'Yes, but you don't understand—'

'I got his number! And his star sign. Sagittarius.' Autumn rejoins us, plonking herself down on the couch beside me. 'He's in a band,' she adds, flashing her best smile as he saunters away.

'What's up with you? Do you need water?' She passes Zainab her flask.

'Thanks,' Zainab says after sipping it, throwing me daggers. 'Something went down the wrong way.'

Autumn looks between us. 'What's going on with you guys?'

We both answer too quickly. 'Nothing.'

Autumn lets out a laboured and heavy sigh. 'I can't cope if you two fall out again.'

'We won't, promise,' Zainab answers, searching my eyes for forgiveness.

'I wouldn't be so sure.' I stab my chocolate cake with my fork. 'What kind of band is it?' I ask, feeling bad at the thought of Autumn getting dragged into our spat again.

'Urban psytrance new wave,' Autumn chimes.

In class, Killian talks about the importance of this semester's grades. He addresses the whole room, but it feels like he's talking to me. I'm not exactly sure if it's his vulnerable admission of his failing romantic life, or my emotional breakdown during our one-to-one, but I am seeing him in less and less of a sexual light. Before, I would fantasise about him asking to speak to me after class, bending me over the desk and having his wicked way with me. Now, as he goes into the key objectives of the term and explains the rubric grading scales, I see him for what he is: a very clever, very handsome, completely nice guy. And I have bigger fish to fry. This morning, I masturbated eight times in a row, thinking about Nova, resulting in seven orgasms and a sore wrist. I wonder if anyone has ever had to go to the doctor for a repetitive strain injury from wanking. But aside from the kiss, there is the small fact that she admitted to trying to kill me. All I know is that I need to see her again soon. Maybe we could even pick up where we left off . . .

'Brodie, what do you think about that?' Killian's voice shatters my fantasy. I blink, shaking myself out of my daydream. I hadn't realised I'd been staring into space. Autumn wrinkles her nose, unable to save me.

'Eh. Eh . . .' I stumble my words, the heat of my classmates' stares burning through me.

'Let's start as we mean to go on,' Killian says kindly. 'You all have a chance to pull your grades up from last semester. With your upcoming essays and then exams, I'm confident in each and every one of you. It's time to step up and realise your full potential.'

Sensing my worry, Autumn nudges me, and I give her a tight smile.

After the tutorial, I probably should go to the library. But I can't help myself. I visit Rock Bar alone. It's throbbing with people. I squeeze past a group of leather-clad goths playing darts and smoking cigars. They observe me with mild interest as I make my way down the rickety stairs, pausing cautiously as one step feels a little shakier than the others. The guy who was here last time stands behind the bar, his knitting needles moving furiously.

'Cute scarf.'

'It's a snood. What can I get you?'

'Just a lemonade, please.' I look around to check nobody is listening in. He slams a coaster on the sticky bar and places the drink in front of me. Leaning forward so he can hear my lowered tone, I add, 'And put it on Nova's tab.'

'Wow, the standards are in the gutter these days,' he says sassily, chewing gum.

I'm so keen to be allowed into the Den, I don't hit back with a remark. He looks me up and down, grabs his keys and takes me through the back to the keg room. This time, entering the elevator alone, the blood pumps around my body in a marriage of fear and anticipation. When the elevator pings, I can hear the commotion before I see it. I pull the gate open, and I'm shocked to see the Commons full of hordes of people all jeering and shouting, from the ground floor, spilling over every concrete level, all the way up to the dome. And these aren't your run-of-the-mill folk. They all look like Olympians, godlike athletes; most are strong, tall, chiselled. Most look like they could snap me in half. Some stand in the Commons, shouting and cheering. Others clap and holler from the elevated levels. Everybody's focus is on the middle of the floor, where the crowd has formed a ring around two people who are kicking the shit out of each other.

I try to squeeze through to get a better view, but the swarms of muscle and strength create a barrier that's near impossible to penetrate. Saying, 'Excuse me,' in a mousy voice doesn't get me anywhere. There is a loud crash as one of the opponents is flung against one of the metal grates separating the main area from the next. The crowd swells in apparent delight at this move. I find a metre-long rectangular concrete block, climb on top of it and see the focal point – two women in tight leather outfits. The taller one, a Viking-esque woman with tight side plaits going down to her bum, leans over the small one, who lies curled on the floor. The tall one leaves her for a moment to beckon the spectators surrounding them to clap encouragingly. An MC's voice booms from the speakers in each corner of the room.

'It was close until now, but it looks like this fight will be over soon!'

The smaller of the two uncurls herself and sits up. She has short spiked black hair and feline features, but she is far from dainty. Rolling away from the grate, she jumps to her feet and ducks and dives as her broad-shouldered opponent throws aggressive punches.

'Come on, Coco!' a deep voice echoes.

'Fuck her up, Willow!' another person yells. The crowd vibrates with excitement as the taller one – Willow – picks up Coco and flings her to the ground. As she crashes down again, the audience winces in thrilled empathy.

'Coco's down,' the MC hoots. Gasps ripple through the throng of people. Coco lies in the foetal position, crumpled up like a wounded animal. She shakily tries to get to her feet, her mouth crimson with blood.

'I think we have a winner,' the MC's voice crackles through the sound system. And just as Willow gestures dramatically for the crowd to hype her up, Coco steadies herself, then jumps on Willow's back, looping her arm around her neck and choking her from behind.

The MC's voice gets more excited. 'Coco is back from the dead, proving that it's not over yet.'

They spin around until a dizzy Willow stumbles back and falls. Coco rolls on top of her, puts one foot on Willow's heaving chest and lifts her hands in victory. The audience explodes in a fever of excitement. Willow punches the air in weak annoyance.

'Who would like to challenge Coco next?' the MC booms.

That's when I spot Shadow, leaning against one of the metal grates, shirtless. His smooth chest catches the light as he chats jovially to his mate, a toothpick sticking out the corner of his mouth. Somehow, through the swathes of meaty shoulders, he notices me too.

'Hey!' he shouts. 'What are you doing here?' His voice thunders across the Commons.

I feel a hundred pairs of eyes stare at me as a spotlight shines from above. There is nowhere to hide.

'Who, me?' I say quietly, and feel a ripple of laughter and whispers.

'Are you here to fight me?' a voice taunts. It's Coco. She spits out a mouthful of blood and it splats red and shiny on the concrete floor. She rewraps her dirty hand ties, looking hungrily at me.

I fervently shake my head. 'No, no, I'm not.'

'What are you doing then?' she chides.

I swallow. I can't find the words to explain myself. I search the crowd, looking for a friendly face. What was I thinking, coming here alone without Zainab? I'm so stupid.

Then I see her, standing on the balcony of her quarters on the upper level, looking down at us all like a hot, sexy Roman emperor. Is she going to watch me as I'm flung to the lions? Or wolves, rather.

'What the hell is going on?' Nova roars, cutting through the hyped-up atmosphere. Everyone suddenly disperses, scurrying off down different corridors, or busying themselves with tasks such as cleaning weaponry or tying rope.

I am left exposed and alone, standing on the concrete block, sticking out like a giant sore thumb. Nova whispers something to Juniper, who stands behind her. Juniper nods and disappears.

'Wait there, Brodie,' Nova commands, and I do as she says. People have gone back to whatever they were doing before the fight, but some are still stealing glances at me, and I get the sense their hushed whispers are about me.

Coco swaggers towards me and gives me a wide smile, showing her bloody teeth. I attempt to smile back, but she's so intimidating it comes out as more of a grimace.

'Next time, Wolf Walker,' she snarls as she saunters past me.

When Juniper collects me and takes me to Nova, I'm not sure why I'm here. To confront her? Or finish what we started on the jetty? Nova stands in the corner of the room, poised and reserved. She looks more intimidating when she's in her leather kilt, compared to the last time I saw her, in jeans and a hoodie. Grabbing me and kissing me. I try to shake off the thought. Nervous sweat prickles at the backs of my knees, and despite the brave face I'm putting on, I am trembling from within. Juniper looks between us and casts me a dismissive look before leaving us alone.

We stare at one other. I think she's waiting for me to explain myself. 'Did you ask Zainab if she had any friends at university who would be dispensable?' I eventually say in a shaky voice.

Nova doesn't seem surprised by the question, but busies herself by watering a massive potted cheese plant with a copper watering can. Sensing she'll need more buttering up before she answers my questions, I change the subject. 'That's a lovely plant,' I offer, hoping to coax her into a conversation. '*Monstera deliciosa*,' I add.

Nova's head turns to me. 'What did you call me?'

'No, nothing, it's just the Latin name for . . .' I kick myself. *Shut the hell up, Brodie.*

Nova puts down the watering can and starts wiping the proud green leaves with a sponge.

'Were you always this smart?'

I'm unsure whether to take it as an insult or not. I decide to take it at face value. 'Yes,' I respond plainly. 'Can we talk about what happened, Nova?'

'Let's just forget the little blip at the lighthouse,' she says casually, plucking a dried yellow leaf from the stalk. 'Pests,' she adds.

'What?'

She twirls the leaf. 'Pests. Or disease. Either way, it needed to be removed.'

Despite myself, I'm really hurt. She may as well say kissing me was one big mistake. It triggers an all-too-familiar self-hatred in me. But what am I going to say? That it was the hottest kiss I've ever experienced? That joining mouths with her was better than any fuck I've ever had? That she's been consuming my thoughts day and night ever since?

'I agree,' I reply quickly, sticking out my chin in defiance. 'About the lighthouse. Let's forget it. But why did you bite me?'

Nova puts down the cloth and gestures for us to take a seat on the leather couch. Sitting near her shreds my nerves. I become so aware of every movement my body makes. I cross and uncross my legs, sit on my hands, play with my hair, unbutton my coat. Anything to stop me imagining pulling her black top and ripping it off her. Pursing my lips, I wait for her reply.

'The truth is, the bite was an accident.'

I let out a scoff, but she still holds all the power and we both know it.

'I wanted to meet you, but I was overcome. I'm not usually so . . .' Nova looks at me. I'm unsure if she's expecting me to finish her sentence for her or not.

I wait for her to find the words.

'Animalistic.'

We catch each other's gaze. Then there's a flash of excitement between my legs, strong and sudden, like the lightning bolt from the storm. Electric and hot. It makes my left knee buckle. Nova eyes me, from my boots to the top of my head. She licks her plump lips. Our breathing falls into tandem.

'As a werewolf who holds a higher power, I can transform at will – and when there's a full moon. But I didn't mean to that night. You bring something out in me that I can't quite explain,' she adds.

I swallow. Then I blink. She stands up suddenly, as if she's heard her phone ringing and is in a rush to answer it. Now she has her back to me, looking out at the Commons. Or avoiding my gaze. Maybe coming here was a stupid idea. But something makes me stay. I can't leave, not yet.

'So it's my fault you attacked me?' I ask, my voice coming out at a higher pitch than I would have liked. 'Why did you want to meet me in the first place?'

'None of that matters now. As I said, I was wrong about you.'

I know there's something she's not telling me.

'What is a Wolf Walker? That girl downstairs, Coco, she called me it.'

Nova bristles.

'Well?' I wait.

She turns to face me again. 'It wasn't her place to say that.'

'All I want is a straight answer.'

Nova sighs, as if she's wrestling with herself about something. 'A Wolf Walker is what we call hybrid werewolves. Mostly human, but with a little bit of feral blood in there too. They are still part of us, and we invite them to join us, in the same way we would any werewolf. Some werewolves are less welcoming than others, of course.'

'As much as I appreciate this drip-feeding of information, you need to tell me what the fuck is going on! And now!' I demand.

Nova seems unimpressed by my little explosion. 'If I were you, I wouldn't speak like that to your superior.'

'Why don't they like Wolf Walkers?'

'Jealousy. Unlike pure werewolves, Wolf Walkers are not beholden to the full moon every month. They might still feel a bit off, but the force within them is a lot weaker than pure werewolves. Wolf Walkers control their power, rather than letting it control them. Which is a blessing, if you ask me.'

I frown, trying to process what she's said. 'If I am a Wolf Walker, why can't I just transform at will?'

Her eyes twinkle. 'You tell me.'

'How would I know?'

'Something is holding you back.'

The familiar pulse of shame envelops me, and I look away, scared she can see all the way through me to my insides, black and rotten.

'Nobody is forcing you to come here, Brodie. But at some point, you have to address whatever it is that's getting in your way. If you want to be one of us, that is.'

I sniff. She sees right through me. Like she knows that the thing holding me back is myself. Accepting who I am as a human has been hard enough, let alone as a werewolf or a Wolf Walker. No matter what happens in my life, I will always be plagued with a sense of not being good enough. A shame so deeply rooted, it is as much a part of me as the blood that courses through my veins. Because if it weren't for me climbing on to the window ledge that fateful night, my big sister Grace wouldn't have tried to save me – and she would still be alive.

Slumping down on the couch, I feel beaten. 'If I'm so useless, then why were you following me around?'

Nova steps nearer to me. 'I think that the night in the library when I bit you, a little piece of me went into you.'

'Meaning what, exactly?'

'That we will be forever linked.'

'Until I die?'

'We die. If one of us dies, so does the other one. You are what we call my soul spirit. And I am yours.'

Her words hang in the air, which is thick with questions. I am speechless.

'I'm sorry,' she adds.

Nova stands over me and lifts my chin. I look up at her: handsome, strong and tall, yet her ring-covered fingers are soft. She extends her hand and cups my throat. A thousand tiny jolts of electricity run through my body. I close my eyes and obediently let her tilt back my head and open my mouth. I moan in anticipation, the noise escaping me uncontrollably. My eyes snap open to see her looming closer. I open wider and stick out my tongue, silently begging her to touch it with hers. She leans down, blocking the neon chandelier that glows from the high ceiling. And then our lips join like magnets. I move my tongue around as it dances with hers. Her lips feel even softer and more sumptuous than at the harbour. She moans too, then she pauses to take a big, long sniff of my neck. The pendulum swings from pleasure to danger.

My instincts tell me to push her away, and when I do, Nova regards me as if she's never seen me before.

'Fuck!' she shouts suddenly, slamming her hand on the table. 'You are my biggest test; you know that, don't you?'

Shaking, I glance at the door.

'It's locked,' she offers.

I keep quiet, and still, waiting for her move. Nova seems perplexed, pacing the room as if she's trying to figure something out.

Yelling from downstairs interrupts the moment, and Nova looks through the glass to see what's going on.

'Is it another fight?' I ask.

'Play-fight, yes. It's good for them. It helps keep morale up.'

'Can I stay here tonight?' I ask in a small voice.

'I'm not so sure that's a good idea.'

'Please.' I don't care if she thinks I sound pathetic.

Nova nods. 'If you want, you can sleep in one of the bunk rooms.'

'Not with you?'

Her face crinkles into a kind smile. 'No.'

Smoothing my hair, I avoid Nova's gaze. 'Actually, I just remembered I need to study anyway.'

Nova doesn't beg me to stay or try to stop me leaving.

'Wolf Walkers have something we werewolves don't.'

'Which is?'

'The choice of a normal life. If they want. That's why the others were taunting you down there. That's why they will never accept you.' She looks resigned.

'What would you do?' I ask.

'I'm not your mummy or your therapist. You either want to join us or you don't.'

I ignore the slight. 'No, come on. What would you do? If you had the choice.'

She smirks. 'That's a pointless question. I've never had the choice you have.'

'But I want to know. If you were me, and had to choose which path to go down, what would you do?'

She folds her arms. 'Alright, I'll play along. If you gave me a million lives, I would pick this one every single time.'

I hover by the door. 'I'm not the only one holding back, by the way.'

'Hmm?'

'You're happy to point out my shortcomings, but have you thought about looking at your own? What are you so scared about with me?'

Nova looks at me with a piercing stare. 'I am not afraid of fucking you, Brodie. I am afraid of killing you.'

CHAPTER SIXTEEN

Geoffrey Chaucer's dream poem The Parliament of Birds *(also known as* The Parlement of Foules*) (written between 1372 and 1386) features the line 'The lyf so short, the craft so long to lerne'. Explore what this means in the context of a person's lifespan.*

Despite my scholarship terms being reliant on me achieving high grades this semester, my grades have slowly faded from the forefront of my mind. Instead of burying myself in books, I wish I was buried between Nova's legs. I would kill to have one more moment with her, to feel her touch, her kiss. To taste her, inhale her, eat her. And there must be a way to get through to her. Even if it means risking my life. She's had a few chances to kill me, but it's no surprise she's so conflicted. If I'm to believe her – and let's face it, at this point, I have no choice but to trust what she's told me – then should I die, she'd be toast too. No wonder she hasn't finished the job. And, just maybe, being a human is over-rated. It has caused me a life of feeling shitty most of the time.

Could being a Wolf Walker be better? If Nova thinks I'm not werewolf enough, then I will prove to her that I am.

But with our exams approaching, I need to at the very least make an attempt to study. I've been avoiding the library since my awful date with Sam. As much as I would like to, I can't avoid it forever. Ignoring the horrible knot forming in my gut, I walk through the front entrance, trying to hold my head up high. When I scan my student card through the turnstiles, I can't bring myself to look anywhere but straight ahead, in case I see Sam. Any shape I see out of the corner of my eye looks like it could be him. Then I slowly shift my gaze to the reception desk. I'm flooded with relief to see that he's not there. I exhale, not realising I'd been holding my breath. But just when I think the coast is clear, I hear his goofy laugh: he's there, to my right, chatting to a girl. Even the thought of his name makes me feel sick. Being three metres from him shakes me to my core. He has one of those ghastly metal back braces on. *Run, girl!* I want to scream at her. *Run for the hills; he's a sex pest!* Cortisol pumps through my veins as I edge nearer, over-hearing the conversation.

'You could take the stairs by the door there – and anything else you need, just give me a shout,' he chirps, gesturing robotically. There is a small bit of comfort to be had seeing him all bashed up. Swallowing, with my head down, I head straight for the elevator, praying he doesn't see me, but it's too late.

As I try to hide amongst the other students waiting for the elevator, Sam approaches me, as discreetly as a walking highlighter pen. I feel a pinch of pity as I take in his healing body. But it's quickly replaced with anger.

'Brodie, can we talk?' he says, his sunken eyes pleading with me. On closer inspection, he looks terrible.

'Sure, we can chat here,' I reply, knowing there's safety in the strangers that surround us. Monsters like him don't dare do bad things in the light of day; no, they wait to pounce in the shadows like the cowards that they are.

'Eh, sure.' Sam is practically whispering. His voice sounds wobbly and a few octaves lower than usual. 'Last time I saw you . . .'

I purse my lips, enjoying seeing him struggle to find the language.

'It was just a misunderstanding – right?' He blinks nervously.

As the elevator doors part, I eventually give him a quick nod of agreement, and a smile. A flash of relief spreads over his face as people file in. I step into the elevator last, still facing him. 'Sure.' I beam.

He meets my smile with an even broader one. And just before the doors shut, I add in the sweetest voice I can muster, 'If you ever speak to me again, I will fucking bury you. Rot in hell.'

His face is stricken with shock as the elevator doors shut, and I feel the others staring at me. But I don't care. My heart thumps with the thrill of saying that to his face. I have never spoken to anyone like that. Not in my angriest moments. Maybe it comes from having a hot-headed dad or a tragedy in the family, but I've always thought that biting my tongue was the best thing to do. But why should I give a fuck? Why should I be quiet? Why shouldn't I be angry? Instead of pushing it down, I feel good about letting it spill out. I'm still shaking with fury, but I feel great. Rage doesn't mean I am weak. It means I am powerful.

My heart's still pounding when I find Zainab sitting with a pile of books in our usual study corner. She wears a crisp collared shirt and a black paisley head scarf. I join her and give her shoulder a squeeze.

'Yo,' I say, sitting opposite her.

'Yo yourself.' She flicks the pages of her book and sighs.

'How's your studying going?'

'It's pretty interesting. Animal behaviour.'

'Anything about wolves in there?'

She sniffs haughtily, then lowers her voice to an almost whisper. 'I didn't know Nova was going to bite you, by the way.'

I stare her out, and she matches my stare with her maple-syrup-coloured eyes, her thick black eyelashes smudged with black kohl.

'Why did you not tell me she bit me? Or that she wanted to meet me? It's a bit suss.'

'She just asked to see you.'

'Why, though?'

'How do you expect me to know?'

'You question everything. Have you never stopped to wonder?'

'She's the Sovereign of the Scottish Werewolves. I have to put her orders before anything. Surely you know that by now?' Zainab lowers her voice. 'I heard you visited the Den without me.'

'Great, have you been spying on me as well?'

She sucks her cheeks in. 'I have better things to do with my time.'

I busy myself with my books and pencil case, laying them all out on the table, paranoid that she can read my mind, or that maybe she's heard a rumour about my kiss with Nova.

'If you must know, I took all your advice onboard. From now on, I think I'll be spending a bit more time at the Den. Embracing it. What have I got to lose?'

Your life! a voice yells in my head, but I ignore it.

Zainab brightens up. 'For real?'

'Yes, I want to be more involved. Embrace my inner wolf.'

'Cool.' Zainab acts nonchalant, but I can tell she's excited by the prospect.

'So, any tips on how I can get more into the fold, let me know.'

'You've probably gathered by now, it's not all twiddling our thumbs waiting for the next full moon. It's nearer to an army training camp than anything.'

'But how come you get away with dipping in and out? I don't see you pumping iron.'

'We all have our jobs.' She thumbs the pages of her textbook. 'Have you met Shadow already?'

'The oiled-up guy who loves himself?'

'He's not my cup of tea, but he is the key. You make friends with him, get him to train you up a bit, you're guaranteed a seat at the table.'

'He looks like he could crush me with one hand.'

'Some people are into that.'

'And you didn't have to train with him?'

'Babe, I'm just a scout. Now, if you don't mind, I need to brush up on equine behaviour.' She goes back to reading her book, but mine remains shut, as the thrill of what could be in store for me crackles in my thoughts.

Later, I skip my lecture to pay the Den another visit. This time, I am not here to see Nova. What with her warning that she might kill me, I think avoiding her for a while will be good for both of us. But I still want to prove to her that I'm worthy. I'm not some puny, helpless girl. When I enter the Commons, there's less commotion than last time. I stop a ghostly pale guy with short bleached hair and two nipple piercings carrying huge planks of wood, and ask him where I can find Shadow.

'Shadow?' He smirks. 'He's always easy to find.'

I walk down the corridor Nova took me through, following the snaked neon lights, and find the gym behind a massive metal door. When I push it open, the smell of fresh sweat and rubber mats wafts up my nostrils. Techno music thumps as I pad through the mirrored room, doing my best not to look self-conscious. I tell myself over and over that I belong here, but I don't quite believe it. To my right, I recognise Willow, the big woman Coco defeated.

She's in a tight unitard doing shoulder presses with huge dumb-bells. A stout Black man with bulging biceps stands behind her, his hands hovering under her elbows. Her face contorts as she pumps the weight in the air, letting out a loud groan.

That guy was right. It is very easy to find Shadow. Not only is he physically big, but there's also something about him that ensures he is the centre of attention. Like he's the point of focus in any space he inhabits. The opposite to me. He's doing one-armed pull ups, surrounded by a small audience. His abs glisten under the strip lights, his thick dark hair pulled into a messy bun on top of his head. When he sees me, he carries on, moving in time to the music, and I stand awkwardly as he finishes his reps. Buoyed by a smattering of adulation from his entourage, he pounces on the mat and swaggers towards me. When he gets near, I'm taken aback by the sheer size of him. He towers above me, so much that I actually have to tilt back my head to look at him square on. Now he's close, I notice his strong fresh sweaty scent, woody and tangy.

Dabbing his thick neck with a small towel, Shadow gives me a surprisingly cute smile for someone so big and tough-looking.

'Well, if it isn't the famous Brodie.'

I frown. 'Famous?' I repeat, confused by the taunt.

'We've heard all about you.' His cronies nudge each other conspiratorially.

Feeling shy, I stand my ground. 'What have you heard?' Embarrassment floods me as I wonder if he knows about the blip at the jetty.

'I've heard rumblings about a new Wolf Walker joining the crew, that's all, Little One.'

Being called 'Little One' would usually rile me up, but he's not wrong: compared to him, I am tiny. I brush a rogue curl out of my face and try not to stare at his body. His skin shines in the light, and I imagine what it would be like to run my tongue along the ripples in his chest.

'That's actually why I'm here. I wondered if you could take me under your wing.'

Now he looks even more amused. 'I'm not a babysitter.'

'And I'm not a baby.'

A few more guys circle around, sensing something building between us.

'Hunter, grab me a sandbag,' Shadow orders. The guy who was spotting Willow picks up a cylindrical sandbag and passes it to Shadow.

'Put your hands out,' Shadow demands. And I do. He slowly places the sandbag in my arms, and I buckle under the weight. As it thuds to the floor, I hear hoots of laughter ripple around the gym.

'Come back when you're a bit stronger, Little One,' Shadow taunts. I want to rip his head off. But there's an undercurrent of sexual tension between us – I feel it, and I know he must feel it too. He is a specific type of irresistible asshole and I hate him for it.

'How can I get stronger if you refuse to help me?' I kick the sandbag in frustration, and Hunter shouts in glee.

Shadow seems tickled by this. 'Got a temper on you, Little One.'

He reaches out and pushes my front curl behind my ear. His hands are big, and his fingers rough. Goosebumps prickle all over my skin. I look down at his crotch and lick my lips when I see a bulge. I imagine getting on my knees and taking him in my mouth. Feeling his cum drip down my throat. I lift my gaze up to meet his dark eyes, glinting with hunger and delight. We fixate on one another for far too long. The group surrounding us disperse. The music pounds like my hammering heart.

'Why don't you train me?' I say through gritted teeth.

'I ain't your PT,' Shadow replies plainly, breaking our moment to drink from a water fountain, and letting little drops trickle down his smooth chin.

'Please,' I say, attempting to turn on the female charm, trying my best to channel Autumn – although it's safe to say she'd be doing a much better job if she were here. I drop my tote bag to the ground and it makes a thud with all the books I've been ignoring for the last few weeks. 'Woops,' I say.

Shadow eyes me, now perplexed.

'Come on, it'll be a good challenge. You look like you're no stranger to those,' I add, now sounding dangerously pathetic.

He clicks his tongue and jumps back on to the bars, swinging with the grace of an acrobat. His muscles twitch and pulse under his shiny skin.

'What's in it for me?' he says. He's toying with me, enjoying the chase.

In a quick flash, I run up to him and leap on to him. I manage to wrap my legs around him, hooking my feet around the small of his back to steady myself. And now we are eye to eye, closer than before. His skin is waxy and soft. Perfectly imperfect. With that finesse and agility, I took myself by surprise, but he's taking it in his stride, swinging his body to hoist me up and nearer to him. My bum sticks out in the air as my back curves. Shadow's breath is hot, and he has a sheen of sweat on his forehead. He searches my face for motivation.

'This is in it for you,' I whisper. I'm sort of shocked by my own boldness, but shy kids eat last, as they say. And I've been eating last for far too long.

He blinks, barely breaking eye contact. 'Deal. But you need to work on your strength outside of here.'

I lean in and press my small nose against his, as if we are two wild horses sparring. He presses back with such force, I lose my grip and land with a thud on the mat. Some of his crew laugh and jeer. I get to my feet, pushing my hair out of my face.

'See you soon, then?' I say as I saunter out, pretending my ankle doesn't hurt like crazy. I need to head home to get ready for a night staying with my parents. As I leave, I spot a little black security camera in the metal ceiling. I stare into it for a few moments, wondering if Nova's been watching me.

CHAPTER SEVENTEEN

James Joyce's Ulysses (1922) features the line: 'Think you're escaping and run into yourself. Longest way round is the shortest way home.' This illustrates the theme of self-discovery in the novel. Discuss.

A year after Grace passed, Mum and Dad decided it was best to sell our fourth-storey flat and move to a new house. We had tried to carry on, as families do, but it was too painful. They needed to get away from the memories. The corner of our bedroom where her little bed was. The living room where we would watch cartoons. The kitchen where we ate countless breakfasts. The concrete path that finished everything. I didn't want to move, I didn't want any disruption, but they had made their choice, and, as with most things in our family, I didn't get any say in the matter. Even though I lived in the new house for far longer than I did the old flat, that's all it is. A house. Not a home. And now I've moved out, it feels even less familiar and warm. But seeing as I stayed for the bare minimum over the festive period, my mum has guilt-tripped me into another visit.

After the scenic train ride from Edinburgh over the Forth Road Bridge, where I watch the moody waves crash on the rocks below, I catch the local bus from the train station, and half an hour later, driving along the winding coastal road, arrive at their house. It sits in a quiet street in the middle of a row of identical modest bungalows. As an act of individualistic protest, Dad has painted our front door bright yellow. 'Like sunshine,' he says. When we all know that all we feel are clouds.

I step through the door. It smells like Mum's spaghetti bolognese and Dad's hand-rolled cigarettes.

'Hello!' Dad shouts over the blaring TV. A glazed hippopotamus bares its gargantuan teeth on the screen. He mutes it as I walk into the living room, and he gets to his feet.

'There she is!' He stands, unsure whether to hug me or not. I walk into the light and wrap my arms around him, feeling his beer belly, which is expanding by the year. Dad has had the same hairstyle since he was a free-spirited twenty-year-old, playing in bands all across the UK. His chestnut-brown curls sprawl down to his shoulders. At work, he wears it in a little ponytail. Mum cuts something resembling a fringe every few months. He has a small, crowded mouth and a cheeky look in his eye.

'What's all this?' I point to a dozen blue squares of sample paint on the wall by the TV, which flashes as the hippo is seen attacking something in the water. The shades of blue are so similar to one another, it's comical.

'Your mum's getting into *interior design*.' Dad emphasises the words 'interior design' as if he's saying 'demonic worship' instead. His tone tells me it's another one of her mad projects. Since I can remember, Mum's always had a habit of getting really invested in a new hobby, living and breathing it for a few weeks, even months, then abandoning it. Reformer Pilates, choir singing, rollerblading, jazz dancing, knitting, growing her own vegetables and ceramic art all spring to mind. Her favourite hobby is finding another hobby.

Mum comes through from the kitchen, wiping her hands on a dish towel. She's a bottle blonde with a big open face, and her welcoming smile reveals a gap in her front two teeth. Her glasses have steamed up from cooking. She was never much of a hugger, so instead she pauses and looks at me as if she's choosing a new sofa.

'Your hair!' she exclaims. I freeze, unsure if she's being nice or not. 'You should have let me cut it at Christmas. You look like your Auntie Gemma,' she adds. That'll be a no then. Mum was never a fan of Dad's little sister. She called her a cheapskate grifter behind her back. Auntie Gemma was fun at least; whenever she visited, she would slip me a ten-pound note and give me a wink. Perhaps it was a bribe for keeping quiet about her raiding their drinks cabinet, but I didn't care. Dad called her lost, as if it's the worst thing a person can be.

'Are you eating well?' she asks, putting our bowls of food at the pre-set table.

'Oh, yes,' I say enthusiastically as I take my seat.

'Get that off.' Mum nods to the TV. Dad throws her a look of disdain, but he presses the remote, turning it off obediently.

'So, what's new?' Mum asks.

I don't meet their eyes, for fear of them somehow realising what I have been doing the last few months. A staccato of naughty images flashes in my head, and I take a sip of water to distract myself.

'I've been telling everyone all about how you're now in your second year at Edinburgh, studying writing,' Mum chirps.

'Well, English literature. And it's the second semester, not year,' I correct her.

Mum nods over enthusiastically. They're acting supportively now, but they were more than a little worried when I told them what I wanted to study. Dad was concerned about the job prospects of an arts degree. Mum wondered if I was better off just going straight into the workforce. But I'd already worked as a waitress at the Seafall Café on the high street for five years by the time I applied for Edinburgh. I'd had a taste of adult life, of schedules, disappointing pay cheques, mopping floors and disgruntled customers. Reading and learning seemed like a holiday compared to all that.

'He tells all his customers about his clever daughter,' Mum teases, topping up her glass of wine.

'How's the garage?' I ask before taking a mouthful of spaghetti, ignoring the overly salted tomato sauce laced with undercooked chunks of garlic.

'Sales are steady!'

Then there is a silence between us, punctuated by scraping forks and chewing. Three is a weird number of people. No matter how you frame it, there is bound to be an odd one out. The worst thing is, we aren't just a three, we're a four minus one. And the spare part has always been me. I don't only feel this in my family; it's a notion I've carried around my entire life. Every room I've stepped into, I'm not sure if I belong there. I certainly don't fit in with the posh people living off Mummy and Daddy's money at Edinburgh Uni. And I've hardly been welcomed with open arms in the Den. Because of losing Grace, I feel anchorless, like an odd jigsaw piece, not sure of where or who I'm meant to be. My baseline is hanging around the fringes, not knowing where to put myself. Never fitting in. It's exhausting. And being around my parents is draining too. Mum polishes off four glasses of rosé at dinner. Maybe it's the excitement of my visit, but she barely asks me any questions. However, she has a lot to say about her clients.

A great deal. The stories are funny, and at least they lighten the mood. And maybe there's not much to say about Edinburgh Uni. I'm not sure it's been what I had initially hoped. Maybe I was naive to think that I would feel at home anywhere new.

After dinner, Mum serves us each two large scoops of the cheapest supermarket ice cream that we all agree tastes the best. Mint choc chip. Grace's favourite. I swallow it down, with the regret.

'It's such a relief you're not vegan anymore. What a pain that was.' She gives me a jovial smile. Too right, I'm not a vegan anymore. I ate a whole roast chicken, squatting behind the post office, on my way back from class last week.

We sit in front of the TV straight away and learn about humpback whales. Dad sits in a cloud of persistent smoke from the roll-ups, giving his live commentary.

'Would you look at that? Nature's marvel.'

I'm pretty sure he used exactly the same phrase to describe an earthworm last time.

After an hour, I excuse myself and head to my room. Calling it 'mine' feels like a lie, given it now appears to be the dumping ground for all of Mum and Dad's miscellaneous stuff. 'We're going to convert the attic,' Mum had told me excitedly. Yet another project. I'd glanced at Dad, who gave me the surrendered look of a kidnap victim.

The room is small, with a single bed in one corner and a little desk on the other side. Posters of boy bands I pretended to adore are still tacked to the walls. Funny how, even in my own private space, I still felt like I couldn't be myself. Despite my taking as many books as would fit in the boot of my dad's car to Bucky Place, my bookshelf here is still full. I stand staring at the dusty spines, with certain books reminding me of the different chapters in my life. Jacqueline Wilson got me through the loneliness I felt at school. The *Sweet Valley High* collection gave me wildly unrealistic ideas of what adolescence was going to be like. Judy Bloom taught me about what relationships should look like. The raunchy Jilly Cooper books nicked from Auntie Lou provided the springboard for many a night of self-exploration.

Then my attention shifts to a pile of cardboard boxes. The first one I grab is full of thrift-store cookery books. One is dedicated to baking cakes in the shapes of animals. Just what I've always wanted: an alligator-shaped Victoria sponge. When I try to place the box back where it was, the whole pile topples, spilling books and photos and old newspapers on to the worn-out carpet. I'm scrambling to tidy it all up when I happen across a shoe box, and nausea grips my throat as I see the word 'Grace' scrawled across it with a Sharpie in Dad's handwriting.

Poking my head out into the hallway first to check Mum and Dad are still glued to the TV, I carefully empty it and spread its contents out on the bobbled bed covers. I hold Grace's birth tag in the palm of my hand. It's made of white plastic with her name and the date she was born, 'Grace Bell' written in tiny letters with a ballpoint pen. I hold it like it's spun gold. Next, I thumb through a series of photos. Sunny days at the Seafall lido in matching red swimming costumes. Arts and crafts mornings in the flat, with Grace holding up her paint-smeared hands, grinning from ear to ear. Being the older, more outgoing one, Grace is the focus of most of the photos. She was always pulling a silly face, or had her arms outstretched with a carefree confidence. I'm usually in the background, with a more serious and earnest look on my face. A stick in the mud, even as a toddler. Poor Mum and Dad, being lumped with me. And then I find one of me as a freshly born baby, swaddled in a white blanket, eyes shut. Mum looks happy but tired in the background, and Grace holds me like the buzzing big sister she was. I gulp. I can still hear her adorably childish voice shouting my name without the 'r': 'Boddddddiiiieee!'

Grace was light and fun. She was a happy, outgoing kid. I hold the photograph to my chest, my breathing ragged as grief swells. My parents would never say as much, but I know deep in my soul that they would rather I had died that night. I know that I would maybe get some closure or at least some clarity if I talked to them about the accident, but how would I even begin – can you tell me about the night I killed Grace, oh, and pass the salt please?

The next photo I find is from a holiday at Butlin's, a matter of weeks before her death. I am smiling for once, eating an ice-cream cone, the corners of my mouth upturned and glistening. Grace is in the background, looking like she's in the middle of having a temper tantrum, her face contorted as she clutches her cuddly toy Beebee. She wasn't herself on that holiday, I heard Mum say once. I continue to look through the belongings, and wonder whatever happened to Beebee. There's no way Mum would have given it away, or handed it down to another kid on the street. Maybe it was beyond cleaning after the accident. My stomach lurches at the thought.

Then I pick up a little bracelet with tiny plastic bumblebees on it. I remember this bracelet. Twirling the little beads in between my forefinger and thumb, I notice a row of them are covered in a thick black substance. Scraping it off, I smell it, and as the foul, metallic scent fills my nose, I realise it's blood. Grace must have been wearing this the night of the accident. I scrape and scrape, embedding my dead sister's blood under my fingernails. I don't wash my hands. I'm not ready to let go of the last trace I have of her living body. I slide the bracelet on to my wrist. It's definitely designed for a smaller arm, but the elastic stretches to fit me in. I carefully put everything back in the box and then curl up on top of the covers, falling into a quick and welcome sleep.

*

I'm in a dark hospital room. At least, I think it's a hospital. The concrete walls are wet, as drips from the room above travel down in zigzagged streams. There is one bright light illuminating the old Victorian bed in the middle of the room. I have a bad feeling about this, but I step, shaking, towards the bed. There's a small person in there, tucked under the covers, tiny and sleeping. Or maybe they're dead.

I walk and walk, but somehow this doesn't take me any nearer to the bed; in fact, I am getting further away with each step I take, as if an invisible elastic band is pulling me back. The bed looks smaller and smaller, and the light fades as I am sucked into the darkness.

'No!' I shout, fighting the invisible claw that's dragging me into the shadows. Pushing with all my might, I'm able to scramble and step nearer. I'm awash with relief as the bed gets closer and the room feels brighter.

'Grace?' I say. Nothing.

I step nearer to the bed and say her name again. This time louder. 'Grace?'

The lump in the bed stirs. And then, faster than I can fathom, the person flings off the covers and springs towards me. It's Grace, but it's also not Grace. It's her pale and cute chubby moon face. And it's her curly hair, just like mine. But her arms are longer than they should be on a child's body. They are red and wet with blood, her hands outstretched, reaching for my throat. Her eyes are not their usual hazel brown, but glowing and demonic-looking. Her mouth is open as if she is screaming, revealing a set of razor-sharp teeth, and she jumps on top of me, ripping my flesh. I scream the loudest I've ever screamed.

*

'Ow, it's me, Brodie! It's Mum!'

Snapping my eyes open, I see it's dark outside, but the room is lit by a street lamp. The inside of the window is wet with condensation. It's cold, but I'm damp with sweat. Mum clicks on the lamp on my bedside table, her face drawn with worry lines and kindness. She has a glazed look in her eye from the exhaustion of her day and the wine she's drunk to forget.

'Shhhh, it's me.' She strokes my back as I turn to lie in the foetal position, facing away from her. She's never been a tactile mum. Which is odd, because she touches people for a living. But I don't remember her ever cuddling me, or soothing me the way she is now. Mum was always very contained. It was dad who was big, a hugger, a kisser, playful and loud. And angry, yes, but at least he showed emotion. Mum had her moments, but they seemed to come from bottling stuff up before it had no choice but to explode, like the lid flying off a bottle of soda, unable to take the pressure anymore.

A few moments go by before I sit up, the terrifying images of the bad dream slowly fading.

'I was dreaming about her,' I offer quietly, my wet hair clinging to the back of my neck in sweaty tendrils.

'It happens to me too,' she says soothingly. And I know that is meant to make me feel better, but it doesn't. Not one bit.

'Does it? What are you doing in the dreams?'

'Oh, silly stuff. Walking around the supermarket, dropping her off at the ice rink or at a boy's house, or watching her at a dance recital.'

'How old is she in these dreams?'

'All ages.'

'Do you talk?'

Mum sniffs and says simply, 'Sometimes we talk. Yes.'

'And what's that like?'

'I say sorry.' These words come out choked and scrambled.

I wait a few moments before speaking slowly. 'What are you sorry for?'

Mum clears her throat. She looks strained, her glassy eyes filling up with tears.

'For . . .' She takes a sharp intake of breath, struggling to get any words out. Or wondering what to say next. 'For causing the accident,' she says quietly, unable to look at me, her focus seemingly anywhere but on me.

I'm frozen, but I force more words to come out, trying to sound as relaxed and inviting as I can. 'How did you cause it?' I ask her, looking up at her rounded chin.

Her mouth opens, the remnants of dried red lipstick blotted around the edges of her lips from a day of chatting. Then she shuts it again, as if she was about to say something, then decided against it.

'Mum?'

She turns to look at me then, her face etched with deep grooves of worry and years of carrying around grief. 'The night of the accident . . . I left the window open, didn't I?'

CHAPTER EIGHTEEN

In Mary Shelley's **Frankenstein** *(1818), the Creature says,
'I am malicious because I am miserable. Am I not
shunned and hated by all mankind?' Analyse how this
quote reflects the Creature's struggle with being
misunderstood and isolated.*

As the stirring sounds of morning drift through the walls at Bucky Place, I slide my hand over the naked curves of the woman in my bed. I pull her close to my own nude body, and she lets out a little snort as she wakes. Pressing my pubic bone up against the round of her bottom, I shake off the guilt of the stark fact that I know I cannot fully enjoy this moment. Because she's not Nova. She is a criminology student with pink hair whose name I didn't bother to ask for when we met at Autumn's current man's gig last night. The music was what you would call experimental. Although it wasn't exactly my favourite genre, it had a certain produced-in-a-bedroom type charm. Even having slept on it, I'm not exactly sure what I witnessed on that stage. But it was fun, nonetheless. The woman and I got chatting when we were waiting to order drinks at the bar and both laughed over the weirdness of the lead singer using samples of angry voicemails from an ex-girlfriend while playing an electric keyboard in a jockstrap. 'Sounds like he was the one in the wrong there,' I said, and Pink Hair laughed heartily, which I liked. I enjoyed her vibe. She carried herself with the lightness of a girl with confidence. She was self-deprecating and made an astute observation about the tambourine player in the Cuban heel.

It's not often I let my one-night stands stay the night. Zainab wholeheartedly agrees with that rule, especially after a previous squeeze of hers ran off with the Rolex she got for her sixteenth birthday. You don't know who you can trust. Don't let them get attached. Autumn thinks we're being ridiculous. But that's easy for her to say – she's so at ease with intimacy, it comes naturally to her. She has fucked people then become their best friend. I, on the other hand, am still not sure how to play things. Yearning for closeness, for pleasure, yet not wanting to be attached, I've tied myself up in many knots. After Pink Hair and I kissed and rolled around in my single bed last night and made each other cum, I didn't have the energy to ask her to leave. I fell asleep in her pillowy arms. Too comfortable, or too tired to move.

She backs into me and moans gently, and I climb on top of her. Last night's blue eyeshadow is caked in the creases of her eyelids, and smudged mascara sits on her lashes. The remnants of her face glitter are still stuck on her temples. Her face is round and smooth, with a top lip that curves up, making her look like she's always on the cusp of asking a question.

'Morning,' I say, tasting her skin as I kiss her bare neck. Her generous breasts sit majestically to each side, nipples pink and proud. As she moans deeper, I lick and suck them. Then, I go down on her, my tongue flicking her most private parts, as she rubs herself with one hand and digs another into my head. I wish she would do it harder. After she orgasms, she pulls me on top of her, and I sit on her face and stare out the window. The dull February morning outside provides a blank canvas for my thoughts. It's ironic to not feel in the moment with someone's tongue inside me, but here we are. The only way I am climaxing is if I imagine Nova, and picturing her face, body and hands makes me cum quickly, hard and deep. Pink Hair looks very pleased with herself. But I don't want her to get too comfortable. As she pulls on her shirt, jeans and boots, I sense she's about to ask for my number – or worse, my surname, so she can look me up on social media.

'Gosh, would you look at the time!' I exclaim, springing out of bed in an effort to look like I'm in a rush. And it's not exactly a lie. Killian's running a special essay surgery today.

I give Pink Hair a peck on the cheek and hurry her out of my room. I should have been studying this morning, but instead I was sitting on someone's face. As I brush my teeth and splash my face with water, I hear her bump into Nathan in the hallway and introduce herself as Tilly, 'short for Matilda'.

When I slide into class, I notice Autumn's wearing a green eighties power suit, making her fiery hair pop even more than usual. Killian gives me a silent but friendly acknowledgement. The sexual tension between us has been well and truly dissolved, like an aspirin in water, dissipated into something a lot less distracting. We can still taste it, but it's notably less strong and in no way near as consuming.

'Last night was fun, wasn't it?' Autumn beams.

'The gig . . . Sure it was, pretty unusual.'

'I ended up in a three-way with Joe and the bongo player,' she whispers, but it's loud enough for the person beside us to throw us a disapproving glance.

'You better watch out, you might end up in one of their songs.'

'I feel like I would make a good muse, actually.'

'More like a groupie. Wow, you are literally glowing. Is that all it takes? So who was it, the one in the top hat or the one in the gimp suit?'

'No, silly, that was the flute player. It was the guy with the giant flares and the mohawk.'

'And? How was it?' I lean towards her, hungry for more, details.

'You know what they say about dicks. The more, the merrier.'

I frown. 'They do?'

'Anyway, I know I'm not the only one who got lucky – who was the girl you left with?'

'Right, let's begin.' Killian cuts through the chatter. His unironed shirt collar pokes out of his knitted sweater as he stands at the top of the table. I wrinkle my nose, remembering once more what I would have given to ride him on his office desk as he choked me with said sweater. Now, he looks like a teddy bear. And nobody wants to shag a teddy bear.

'Thanks to everyone who submitted their essay for feedback,' he says, handing out our essays. When mine reaches my desk, I am disappointed to see I only got a B-minus.

'I was impressed overall, but there is always room for improvement.'

Autumn got a B-minus as well and looks positively delighted.

'You're not on a scholarship place,' I remind her and she rolls her eyes.

'Do you want to go thrift-store shopping later?' she whispers. But I can't take my eye off the red pen that decorates my essay. Phrases like 'confusing', 'needs work' and 'consider changing' leap out. Not good enough. I shove it in my bag, trying to pretend I'm not completely livid with myself.

'I can't; I need to go for a swim.' Since I went and saw Shadow,

I've been swimming any chance I get. I've become a little obsessive.

'Can't you take a day off?' Autumn asks. I shake my head. Nothing will get in the way of my training. The next time I see him, I want to show him that I can be strong enough to lift two sandbags without even flinching. As for the essay rewrite, I'm sure I can salvage it.

Killian continues delivering papers around the room. 'I saw some of the same mistakes in a lot of your essays, so I've made these essay checklists to help you on your way.' He hands them out. But instead of thinking about my essay, I'm wondering if the same rules can be applied to studying to be a werewolf. Nova isn't sure I belong, and Shadow thinks I'm just a skinny weakling. But if I apply these tips not only to my studies but also to joining the werewolf crew, then I could prove to them, prove to Nova, that they can take me seriously.

I scan Killian's top tips. The very first bullet point reads, 'Get to know your subject material.' Maybe that's where I have been going wrong all along. I haven't been treating werewolf life with the seriousness that I normally treat academia. But if there's one thing I know how to do, it's how to cram and research. That much is certain.

Before my swim, I head for Beyond Books at the top of Leith Walk.

A bookshop to me is what a doughnut shop is to a sugar addict. When I walk through the door, I get a visceral surge of excitement. I love the vibe – the smell, the stillness, the warmth, everything. The owner is crouched at the checkout, nursing a giant mug of steaming coffee. Her bleached mane is teased in all directions and she greets me with a huge, toothy smile.

'Come in, darling! Make yourself at home.'

'Thanks,' I say in a hushed voice. It's a low-ceilinged treasure trove in here, with every bit of wall crammed with books. The different sections are displayed with little rainbow name cards: Queer, Scottish Authors, Feminism, Black Voices, Radical Activism, Trans Liberation.

'Are you looking for anything in particular?' she calls over to me in a nasal voice.

'No,' I lie. Then, after looking around some more, I eventually approach her. 'Actually, yes. Do you have any books on folklore, mythical creatures?'

She doesn't miss a beat. 'Yes, we have a slew of titles. Vampires, fairies – what sort of mythical thing are you after?'

I shift uneasily, as if I'm buying a dirty magazine for the first time. 'Werewolves,' I eventually say, and then, thinking on my feet, I add, 'I'm studying fantasy as part of my English literature degree.'

She arches a well-plucked eyebrow. 'They put all sorts on the syllabus these days, don't they? Give me a moment; I might have just the thing.' She wheels her stool over to a giant metal filing cabinet and flings it open, balancing her glasses at the end of her nose.

'Werewolves, werewolves, werewolves,' she mutters, as her long fingers, topped with lacquered magenta nails, flick through the files with the deftness of a classically trained pianist. Even though we're alone in the shop, hearing a normal person say those words out loud puts me on edge. I look around shiftily.

'Aha!' she exclaims. 'I remember this one. *The A to Z of Werewolves.*'

I let out a laugh. She must be joking.

'Something amusing, darling?' she says, slamming the cabinet shut before getting to her feet. She is a tall woman who stands a little hunched. It's hard to tell what kind of body shape she has, because she's swathed in a colourful kimono. Maybe she shops in the same place that my lecturer Jackie does. She has multiple garish necklaces looped around her neck, and her arms are filled with bangles. They jingle against each other every time she makes a slight movement. She walks gracefully to the back of the shop.

'Mind the step,' she warns, signalling for me to follow her.

At the back, the books are so tightly crammed together it's a wonder anybody can find anything.

'I know, I know, it's a mess back here,' she says, flinging up her arms dramatically.

'No, no,' I protest.

'And you're probably thinking, who does this woman think she is, having everything in a filing cabinet, when she could go digital like one of the big chains?'

'Well, yes.'

'Screens are the enemy,' she says passionately. 'Never forget that, darling.'

She reaches up to a top shelf and pulls out a big grey book with silver writing up the spine: *The A to Z of Werewolves*.

I leave, forty pounds poorer, with the weight of the chunky tome under my arm. I couldn't believe the price of it, and have committed to eating beans for every meal for the rest of the week – no, month – to justify the purchase. I take it to the library, find the most secluded spot, where I hope nobody will find me, and open it. The dedication says simply:

For the misunderstood beasts.

Each letter of the alphabet is accompanied by an intricate painting. I start at the beginning.

A – Alpha

The alpha is often depicted as the dominant leader of a werewolf pack, typically possessing greater strength, and having authority and control over other werewolves in the group.

I mull this over. It wouldn't take a genius to figure out that's Nova. The head honcho, the queen bee. She speaks and everyone listens. I turn to the next page. I used to love devouring a book cover to cover. Recently, I've been lucky to get through a chapter in a week. But I read it in one sitting. Snapping the book shut, I get a familiar pain in my neck. It aches from bending over the book, so I head for my swim at St Leonard's pool, grateful for the chance to stretch out my body and try to process what I've read. I go for more lengths than usual, imagining Shadow's amusement at my efforts to spur me on to gain strength.

My wet hair attracts a cool breeze and I hug my coat around me, noticing my stomach rumbling with the delicious hunger that appears after a big swim. I turn up the bottom of Potterrow and barely register the black van parked with its side door open, about ten feet ahead. Two people clad in brown leather are crouched down, inspecting the van's front wheel.

As I near them, I realise they're wearing balaclavas. It's not completely bizarre – it is February in Scotland – but something in my gut tells me to give them a wide berth. I cross to the other side of the street, walking in and out of the shadows of the oak trees that flank either side. My steps quicken. So does my heartbeat. At a glance, it appears that they've retreated into the van, so I let out a little sigh of relief. But before I can even take another breath, one of them is standing right in front of me, blocking my next step. 'Excuse me,' I say.

She's cocky in her stature. 'I wonder if you can help me,' the woman says. She speaks softly, but her voice is laced with menace. I need to get as far away from her as possible. She notices me glancing nervously at the nearest lane and takes a step closer to me. Fear pounds through me. And then someone grabs me from behind.

'No! Help!' As I open my mouth wide to shout again, a cloth is shoved over my mouth and nose. I wrestle and fight, as hard as I fought back against Sam in his room, but I am weak. Ingesting the toxic smell of chemicals, I feel dizzy. And then there is nothing.

I wake up and everything is still black. I blink three times, slowly and deliberately. Have I gone blind? Where am I? It doesn't feel like we're moving, so I don't think I'm in the van. But maybe they've parked. What if they've buried me alive? Oh my God, where have they put me? I take a short, panicked breath and feel the hotness of it fill the scratchy material that's stretched over my head. It's heavy, with rough threads poking into my ears and brushing my forehead. I gulp. My mouth and throat are as dry as toast. When I try to move, I realise that my hands are tied together behind my back. I can sense I'm not alone, but I can't be sure. I move my body, wiggling my fingertips and toes. I'm on my knees, hunched with something soft and springy beneath me. I move my fingers again, and they brush against straw. Suddenly, I hear a whispered woman's voice. 'Phoenix, she's up.' I start to tremble in fear.

Who is Phoenix? I feel a hand on the back of my neck, and I'm terrified I'm about to be shot, or strangled to death. *You are finally going where you belong*, Shame Goblin whispers.

'No,' I protest in terror. But then I hear a rip, and whatever was on my head is pulled off, grazing my earlobes on the way.

It takes a few moments for things to come into focus. Hay bales. Straw. I'm in what looks like a wooden barn. I spot a pitchfork, leaning against one of the wood-panelled walls, and gulp. An old potato sack lies on the ground.

I cast a glance around me, looking for signs of life.

'Where am I?' I croak, my lips dry and cracked.

'Hello, Brodie,' a woman's voice says from the shadows.

Then she steps into the light. She is small and toned, and wears a suede waistcoat with tight jeans and cowboy boots. Her pale arms are covered in the types of scars that tell me she's been in her fair share of fights. The straw rustles as she steps nearer to me.

She bends down in front of me in a squat and I look into her eyes, a blend of green and brown. Her cheekbones are high and her heart-shaped face is framed by two auburn waves. The rest of her hair is scraped back at her nape. I notice a couple of gold chains around her neck, a locket and a grey pendant, the same one that Nova, Zainab and Juniper have.

'Welcome,' she taunts.

I suddenly become aware of a sharp burn in my wrists where they have been tied, and start to wriggle my body again.

'If you stop squirming, it will hurt less,' she offers.

Throwing her a dirty look, I do as she says.

'Where am I?' I ask again, my tongue fuzzy with dehydration.

'You are exactly where you are meant to be.' The woman springs to a standing position, and the sudden movement makes me jump. A flicker of sympathy passes over her face. 'If I untie you, you promise me you won't run away?'

I nod agreeably.

'Because if you do, there are two guards waiting at the other side of that door who will not think twice about chopping your head off.'

A boulder of dread rocks from side to side in my stomach.

'Do you understand me?' she asks, kicking a ball of straw and lighting a cigarette. The grey smoke curls up towards the barn lights.

'Yes,' I say, my voice thick with fear.

'Untie her!' she commands. The women in brown leather from the van at Potterrow approach me, their balaclavas rolled down at their necks to reveal identical pinched faces and shaved heads.

They must be twins. The only difference between them is that one of them is holding a knife.

I start whimpering. For a second, I wonder if she is going to slit my throat instead, but soon my wrists are on my lap, the rope cut. I take turns massaging the deep pink ridges that the rope has left behind on my skin.

As the twins leave, Phoenix grabs one of my wrists and I cower. 'Is that a bumblebee tattoo?'

'Yes.'

'Aw, how cute,' she snarls. 'And a bumblebee bracelet, too?! I'm sensing a theme here.'

I try to pull away from her, but she whips it from my wrist and chucks my limp arm back to me.

'Give that back, you bitch!' I screech.

'What did you call me?'

I shrink in fear, and try to change the subject. 'What do you mean, I'm where I'm meant to be?'

Phoenix smirks.

We're interrupted by a noise from outside. Phoenix frowns as the barn door shakes and two people shout at one another on the other side.

Maybe it's the police. This might be my only opportunity to escape. 'Help! Help!' I yell at the top of my lungs. I open my mouth to shout again, and then *crack*! Phoenix strikes me with her hand. The blow is swift. And then, a few seconds later, hot pain. It takes me right back to school, when Stacy lamped me for looking at her boyfriend a certain way. It's a shock. At first, I'm too stunned to react. My entire cheek pulses and throbs from the force, and I feel wetness under my eye. What if she's sliced my face open? Phoenix shakes her hand, as if annoyed I forced her to take such a drastic measure.

'Ow,' is all I can muster, and a drip of saliva pours out of my mouth and on to my lap. I look down and see tears fall into the straw.

The shouting at the barn door has stopped, and Phoenix regains her footing. 'Sorry about that.'

I open my mouth to reply, but am interrupted by the two wooden doors flying open. My heart sings when Nova strides in. She looks around and sniffs as if she's picked up a bad smell.

'You ought to get better security, Phoenix,' she calls, boldly walking towards us.

My eyes widen in gratitude and I silently beg Nova to look at me, but she doesn't take her gaze off Phoenix.

'Well, if it isn't her Royal Uptightness,' Phoenix says in a playful tone laced with menace. She does a dramatic curtsy and then spits on the ground at Nova's feet.

'Is this how you welcome all your guests?' Nova says as she reaches us. I am hunched over, face red-raw, eyes watering, nursing my wrists. I know I must look an absolute state, but the relief of her arrival overtakes any embarrassment.

'To what do I owe the pleasure of this visit?' Phoenix mimics a posh voice, and the pair glare at one another.

Nova pulls off her leather gloves and looks Phoenix up and down disdainfully. 'You have something of mine. Something that means rather a lot to me.'

My heart skips a beat.

Phoenix rolls her shoulders back and puffs out her chest. She cracks her neck and then cocks her head in my direction.

'You must be mistaken, Nova, because she's not yours.'

'Yes, she is,' Nova snarls, her voice echoing up to the high ceiling. A harassed bird flies out of its nest on one of the supportive beams, causing two feathers to flutter down to the ground.

'She's one of us,' Phoenix says, looking at her square in the face.

I glance between them. 'What do you mean?' The words spill out of my mouth before I can stop them. They both turn their heads to face me.

'You're a Wolf Walker,' Phoenix says plainly. She turns back to Nova. 'She knows that, at least?'

'Yes, she knows,' Nova replies in a clipped tone.

'So why she wants to skulk around under the rat-infested floorboards of Edinburgh Castle with your gang is beyond me.'

'Coming from someone who shares a living room with donkeys, that's rich,' Nova snarls back.

'They're horses. Bitch.' Phoenix puts her hands on her hips. 'She needs to be with her people.'

I shift uncomfortably. What are they talking about?

Nova's fist clenches and unclenches in annoyance. 'Thanks for your time, but we must get going. Brodie?'

My face is throbbing from where Phoenix struck me. I'm frozen to the spot, scared she might do it again, or worse.

'See? She wants to stay with us.' Phoenix's smug face is enough to make me shakily get to my feet.

'No, I'm going with her,' I say boldly, and scurry to Nova's side. She gently pulls me behind her to protect me.

Phoenix sneers, 'If you think I'm just going to lie back and let you walk out with the key to—'

Nova interrupts, her voice raised, nostrils flaring. 'Brodie, step outside and wait for me.'

I eye the open barn doors. Outside, it's dusk. I can't leave her.

'No,' I say bravely.

Phoenix laughs bitterly. 'Then I'll fight you both.'

Nova pushes me with force. 'Brodie, it's an order. Go. And shut the doors behind you.' Hearing the severity in her tone, I do as she says, giving Phoenix one last glance before I make my way over the straw to the door. When I'm outside I push the doors shut, only to find the twins and what must be Phoenix's two guards lying bloodied on the ground.

In a matter of moments, I hear snarls and bangs. It sounds

horrific in there. Against my better judgement, I peek through the keyhole and see a flash of white and a flash of brown. Two beasts, far bigger than any normal wolves, are tumbling on the ground together, twirled around each other as if they were one, snarling and growling. The larger one has fur that is effervescent, shimmering silver and white. I remember the hair I found in the library the day after my attack, and my blood runs cold. That must be Nova. Seeing my attacker in this terrifying form makes all my hairs stand up on end. I try to shake the blood-curdling thought of her leaping towards me in the library. She pins down the other werewolf, whose fur is rusty-brown with cream patches. Phoenix. Nova lets out a loud, guttural growl that reverberates across the barn. This is the most disturbing thing I've ever seen, but I can't tear my eyes away.

Phoenix shakes under the sheer force of Nova, then strikes her with a paw the size of a beach ball. It makes a huge thud, and makes the slap I received look like a tickle. Nova winces and leaps away from Phoenix, who spins around on all fours. The pair circle each other, glaring and snarling. I'm terrified of what will happen next. Nova's hackles are raised, her shoulder blades moving going up and down as if they're being manoeuvred from above by a puppeteer.

Then Phoenix has Nova pinned to the ground, and she's poised to sink her jaws into Nova's neck. Nova winces in pain. I can't let her die. Us, die. I don't even think, I don't even decide, I just do. As quietly as I can, I push open the barn door and creep stealthily to the corner of the room where the pitchfork is. It's heavier than I'm expecting, so I rest it over my shoulder as I creep quietly and deliberately behind Phoenix, who has Nova pinned, about to sink her razor-sharp teeth into her neck. I lift the pitchfork over my head and crash it down on top of Phoenix's skull, making a loud crack that thunders through the air.

CHAPTER NINETEEN

In Shakespeare's Othello (1622), Iago says, 'Men should be what they seem; Or those that be not, would they might seem none!' How does Shakespeare use this to explore themes of jealousy and the destructive potential of misplaced trust?

Phoenix howls a deep, guttural howl and immediately jumps away from Nova, almost knocking me off my feet. Her hind legs buckle as she shakily limps to the shadowy corner of the barn. Nova remains on her back, but her four legs shrink back into human form, with the rest of her face and body soon behind. She lies twisted in pain, her face sheet-white, her naked body covered in goosepimples. I yank my sweater off and quickly pull it on her, feeding her bloodied arm as delicately as I can through the sleeve, my hands brushing her milky thighs. It reminds me of the night she helped dress me when I woke up in The Den.

'Are you hurt?' I shout, getting to my knees and cupping her head under my hands.

'We need to go – now.' Nova pushes me away from her and gets to her feet unsteadily. She looks like all the energy has been squeezed out of her, like a twisted tube of toothpaste. I grab her elbow to try and bolster her up. At first she's hesitant, but then she has no choice but to lean on me. Sliding an arm around her slim waist, I help her walk towards the exit. She's hunched, with a limp and a sore knee, her mouth in a straight line. At the door, a small group of people have formed, their expressions twisted in disdain. They sneer at us as we walk out; one of them even spits at our feet.

'Move out the way!' I shout angrily, and they part, allowing us to walk through.

When we step outside, I try to get my bearings. Water stretches out in front of us, and Edinburgh's skyline is behind. The low February sun is on its way out, which isn't great news for us. Tonight is going to be a full moon.

The urgency with which we need to return to the Den hangs unspoken between me and Nova. But I can't help myself; question after question is racing through my head like a fast train. 'Why was Phoenix so desperate to have me join them?' I say in as brave a voice as I can muster.

But Nova's not in a talking mood. She looks towards the skyline, which is a sorbet pink. It would be beautiful if it didn't mean we were close to darkness. Close to the night. And if there is anything I've learned over the past few months, it's that strange things can happen anytime, but especially at night.

'Is there no way we can go underground?' I try to reason as Nova, despite her limp, storms ahead of me, her leather kilt swinging with her big strides.

'The only way is through town, on land,' she growls.

'Why did you come to rescue me?'

But there's no reply.

Within ten minutes, we reach the main road, which is busy with pedestrians on the sidewalk and cars humming past.

'Brodie, listen to me, I need you to do two things for me: flag down a taxi . . .'

'And?'

'Shut the fuck up.'

I can't lie, her words sting a little. Within minutes, we are in a taxi, but unfortunately our driver didn't get the memo about shutting the fuck up. By the time we have crawled up Leith Walk to the town centre, we have learned all about our driver Billy's underactive thyroid, his holiday to Disneyland Florida for his fiftieth birthday, and his exacting opinions on whether or not aliens exist. I wonder what his thoughts on werewolves are, although I don't dare ask him for fear of Nova opening the door and shoving me out of the moving car.

In between Billy's anecdotes, we sit in a charged silence. Her jaw is clenched, making her look even more dominant. Even hotter than usual. If that's possible.

'You OK?' I whisper gently.

'Yes.'

I consider reaching across and touching her leg to comfort her, but I'm scared of her reaction.

The sun is now sinking behind Edinburgh Castle, and we both know we don't have much time. The taxi has sputtered to a standstill, gridlocked in traffic. Billy toots his horn and shakes his head in vain. 'It's a Friday night,' he offers by way of an explanation.

I catch Nova's eye and she tilts her head briskly, signalling for us to jump out of the cab and cover the rest on foot.

'Sorry, Billy!' I shout apologetically as we climb out of the car and slam the doors. Who have I become? This girl who runs away from taxis and doesn't think twice about bashing someone over the head with a heavy metal object.

Nova strides up the street and I do my best to keep up. We find ourselves in the midst of an inebriated bachelorette party. The bride wears a veil and a white minidress, and sips from a mini bottle of champagne through a penis straw. The women cluck and coo as they discuss which bar to hit up next. Nova is in such a rush she gets herself caught in the bride's veil. She wrestles her way through it in annoyance, which, despite the severity of the situation, amuses me.

Nova catches my smirk. 'What?'

'Nothing.'

She charges ahead. I follow, a couple of steps in her wake.

We arrive at Rock Bar and go as fast as we can down the rickety metal staircase, Nova's boots thudding loudly with each step. When we reach the sassy barman with the shaved head, he immediately grabs his keys and leads us to the back. Nova goes in before me, and I see obnoxious blotches of blood decorating the concrete floor. She clamps a hand over her arm to stop the bleeding.

We get to the Commons and it's eerily empty.

'Where is everyone?'

'In their lock-ups, preparing for their transformations for the full moon,' Nova says plainly.

We head up to Nova's office. 'Tell Juniper I'm here,' she barks at a shocked-looking Coco, who pins her back against the wall to let us past before rushing away.

Nova and I step into her office and look at each other in relief. The scent of the room stirs a feeling of yearning in me that I try to squash down. Now is not the time. Nova staggers into her side table.

'Woah, watch out.' It must have taken all of her energy to fight Phoenix, and my heart swells in gratitude to her for coming to save me. God knows what would have happened if I'd been left there.

I try to help her as she lowers herself on to a chair, but she waves me away just as Zainab appears in the doorway, her face scrunched in worry. She rushes up to me.

'I just saw Coco. Are you hurt?'

I shake my head. 'Not really.' I look at Nova, who sits stoically holding herself up by the corner of the table.

'Zainab, pass me the gauze,' Nova instructs.

'Sure.' Zainab answers quickly, grabbing a little medical kit and shakily unzipping it. I've never seen this side of my friend. She's normally so cool and calm and uninterested; it's unsettling to see her spring into action like this.

'And fetch me some whisky.'

Zainab spins around and rattles about in Nova's drinks cabinet, squinting at the label of a half-drunk bottle of whisky. 'Is single malt alright? I'm more of a weed person.'

'It doesn't matter.' Nova's voice is strained with pain. She's gone paler than usual, and I notice inky blood spreading down her arm. Zainab shakily pours a generous whisky and passes it to Nova, who drains it in one.

'Now get out!' Nova roars. I jump a little at the sudden outburst, and Zainab gives me one last look of support before making herself scarce.

'Use the rest of the bottle on my cut.' Nova peels off her jacket.

I've never tended to an injury before. Concentrating so hard my tongue pokes out the side of my mouth, I hover the whisky bottle over the two giant puncture wounds on Nova's arm.

'Just do it,' she says, barely moving her lips, her gaze set straight ahead.

'They look like drill holes.' I steal a glance at her to see if her face gives away any signs of pain.

'It'll heal fast; it always does.'

I remember how quickly my own wounds healed the night of

my attack. I wonder how they got me back to the Den, or who sewed me up. I pour the amber liquid on to Nova's arm and the hoppy ethanolic scent fills my nostrils.

'How can people drink this stuff? It smells like alloy wheel cleaner.'

Nova sniffs. 'I love whisky.'

'Do you think she's dead?' I ask after dabbing the wound clean.

'Who, Phoenix? Ha, chance would be a fine thing. No, she's like a cat with nine lives. Or a cockroach. It will take more than a pitchfork to the head to exterminate her.'

'What would it take?' I reply, curiosity getting the better of me.

'Fire. Being shot with a silver bullet. Or . . .'

'Or?' I press gently.

'At the hands – or teeth – of her soul spirit under a blood moon.'

As her statement sinks in, I pause.

'Why would her soul spirit want to kill her?' I ask after a moment.

'Love can make people do crazy things, you know.' She sucks the air through her teeth as I press the gauze as hard as I can, wrapping it tightly.

'Sorry; I'm no nurse.' I let my fingers linger over her forearm, and I feel her body tighten. 'What did Phoenix mean about "my people"?'

'She's the leader of the Faol People. They are an all-women, vigilante group of Wolf Walkers with radical ideas. They are hell-bent on ascending to become the dominant species on the planet. Above humans. Which undermines us. Acting like we are a disease or something.'

'What's the problem?'

'They're idealistic at best, dangerous at worst.'

'Why do they want me?'

'She just kidnapped you to get to me.'

'Why, were you . . . Is she your ex?'

Nova almost laughs. 'No. We've never seen eye to eye. The Faol People are extremists that believe in an all-or-nothing approach. The more power given to their silly ideas, the more our existence is at risk.'

I watch Nova's expression cloud. 'But they will be the least of our worries soon enough.'

'How so?'

She stares ahead. 'The Illvirkjar . . . Never mind.'

I probe no further, pinning the bandage around Nova's arm. 'All done.'

She turns, drinks me in for a few beats, her chest moving up and down. Leaning into her body, I feel an electricity between us so strong that I'm surprised I can't see it. She gives my neck a big, sharp sniff, as if she's trying to get as much of my smell as possible in her nostrils. I reach out and grab the back of her neck.

I feel a kiss coming, and I pulse with excitement. Then suddenly, as if out of nowhere, she bites me. It's quick. Like a viper from a bush. My hand flies to my neck, and I feel the tiny incision where she's broken the skin. Now Nova's eyes glow with danger.

'Ow!' I exclaim, shocked by the sudden attack.

'Leave. And shut the door behind you,' she snarls in a deep, strangled voice.

I don't need to be told twice. I imagine being stuck in a room with her when she's a wolf again – I wouldn't stand a chance. She could rip me to shreds. Tear my flesh like wet paper. Annihilate me, crush my bones between her teeth. Use my ribs to floss afterwards.

I look down at my hands, now smeared with her blood and mine. It courses through my veins, hot and fast. My neck stings at the small puncture she managed to make.

I flee the Den, clutching my neck. I walk down a corridor in search of the quickest exit. Then I turn a corner, and realise I have reached the lock-ups. Like a row of dog kennels, each one separates me and them with thick iron bars. An orchestra of sliding metal locks plays. At first I don't dare look up, as each member of the clan hides themselves away in preparation for what's to come. But as I walk towards the exit, my knees knocking in terror, I hear jeers, snorts and snarls from the people behind the bars. Near the end of the corridor, when I've almost reached the door, I steal a glance into one of the lock-ups, and I see Zainab crouched on the floor, her face covered in sweat and her eyes bulging.

'Go,' she says to me in a choked voice. Terrified, I find the staircase that I know will take me to Lothian Road, and I rush up the cold stone steps. Then I hear it. Like the noises that helped distract the guards at Edinburgh Zoo. A cacophony of howls, all overlapping each other.

I reach the door at the top of the staircase and push it with all my might, rushing into the sharp air. I walk home, quick as I can, letting the boastful moon guide my way, bright and alluring in the velvety winter sky.

CHAPTER TWENTY

In **The Scarlet Pimpernel** *(1905) by Baroness Orczy,*
the protagonist Sir Percy Blakeney puts himself
in danger. Discuss how his actions are brave
or otherwise.

*G*race and I are having a tea party with our dollies and teddies. The
sky is a gorgeous blue, with not a cloud in sight. Beebee sits at the top
of the table, with a little plastic teacup. We giggle and laugh at the idea of
a bumblebee drinking tea. Then the sky turns a threatening grey, thunder
claps, and out of nowhere Phoenix appears and grabs Grace, wrapping
her up in the chequered picnic blanket. I stand up and try to grab her back,
but Phoenix suddenly strikes me, and the force of it makes me roll down
the hill. As I flip and flail, the image of Grace kicking and screaming gets
further and further away. I open my mouth to shout for Mum, but nothing comes out . . .

*

Nova's bite heals, but it's still fresh in my mind. I toil over whether
it's something I hated or loved. The thrill of the chase between us

is one thing. But her actually going in for the kill . . . that's a different ballpark altogether.

In an attempt to carry on my little charade of a normal life, I visit my mum in Seafall to get my biannual haircut. It's free, after all. After a long and dreary winter, spring is promising to come soon. The grassy mound at the top of Seafall High Street is decorated with sprigs of green, soon to be huddles of budding snowdrops. Hairways is a modest salon, perched by the little roundabout, opposite the greengrocer's.

I used to come and hang out here after school while Mum finished up with her afternoon clients. When I got old enough, I helped sweep the hair and fetch people coffees. The sounds and smells of the salon have always felt comforting to me. The hair dryers blowing, the layers of different conversations going on. The gentle clicking of scissor blades slicing. The aroma of coffee mixed with perfume and ammonia.

But as I sit in the weathered leather chair, staring at my own reflection, I feel awkward and unfinished. My mum stands behind me and lifts my dark mop of hair before letting it fall to my bony shoulders. She's looking at me in the mirror.

'You've let yourself go a bit, love,' she says, her voice as cutting and as sharp as her scissors.

'I have not.'

'What you have been getting up to, I really don't know.' She tuts, inspecting the hair closely, lifting whole sections to the light and shaking her head at the split ends.

'One of the women in here says her son piled on the pounds when he went to university, but you've shrunk.'

Unsure of what way to rebut, I sigh, my whole body tensing up. Maybe this was a bad idea.

'Right, let's take you to get this washed.' She leads me over to the sink and I rest my neck against the cold porcelain. I stare up at the ceiling and notice one of the lights is out and there's a small cobweb in the corner.

When I was younger, Hairways felt like the height of glamour. But all these years on, the salon is starting to show signs of disrepair. The owner, Diane, lives on the hill in one of the big fancy houses. She's a kind woman who seems to take great pleasure in running Seafall's flagship hair salon. But lately she has been going through what Mum describes as 'marital issues'. She can't hide her enjoyment of the phrase. As if gossiping about someone else somehow negates all the yucky stuff you have going on in your own life.

Mum washes my hair with such aggression it makes me flinch. She notices my scrunched-up face, and this winds her up.

'Sit still, Brodie. Always so dramatic.'

Are you this rough with all your clients? I want to ask. But I say nothing. The ends of her fingers scrub at my scalp and I shut my eyes and think about her combing mine and Grace's hair. Memories have blurred as time has passed, but I can still hear the lightness of Grace's shrieks and giggles. She was always so much happier than me, even when she was uncomfortable. The good child.

Mum rinses my hair, puts conditioner through the ends, then rinses it again, before wrapping my head in a towel and taking me back to my chair.

We haven't spoken since her admission that she blames herself for Grace's death. It's the Bell family way. Swallow it down and it will go away. Or at least it will seem like it's gone away. Even if it's so heavy that it pins us to the floor, the main thing is that everything on the outside looks fine.

As I stare at my mum sectioning then cutting into my wet curls, I have the urge to ask her questions. She was tipsy the night she opened up to me – maybe she doesn't remember. I used to try and talk to her about things, but she would let me know in her own way that she wasn't ready. She wouldn't or couldn't engage. The kettle needed to be put on, or was that a knock at the door maybe? But she can't run away from questioning when she's in the middle of doing my hair.

'Can I ask you something?' I say, over the buzz of the salon. Diane is giving the old lady next to me a trim. She's so short, her feet don't touch the floor – her wrinkled ankles are suspended in the air, with her orthopaedic shoes pointing slightly inward.

Mum pauses briefly and looks disdainfully at me in the mirror. 'Let me guess, you've run out of money,' she says.

'No, nothing like that.' I'd rather sell feet pics than ask her for another loan.

She visibly relaxes.

But then I say it. 'You know how you said you feel guilty?'

Mum's eyes widen. Like she's just been slapped unexpectedly. 'Not here.' Her words exit out of the corner of her mouth. Her expression has changed. It's giving air hostess at the end of her tether.

'I just mean . . . if you blame yourself, then maybe do you blame me as well?'

I observe her closely in the mirror. Nowhere to hide. She looks pained, suddenly older than her years. She shuffles on her feet, blows the bleached strands of her fringe out of her eyes with a sharp breath.

'What do you mean?' She has one hand on her hip, her scissors hanging off her thumb.

I repeat the question. 'If you blame yourself, then does that mean that you also blame me?'

She sniffs. 'Of course not. You were a child. It's not your fault.'

My palms are sticky with sweat under my gown. 'Because I don't blame you. So you shouldn't either.'

She smiles; it's weaker but more real than the last one.

'Well, that's good, love.' She cuts the rest of my hair in silence as we listen to Diane's client talking about how she suspects that her best friend has been cheating at Bridge.

I spend the train journey back to Edinburgh mulling over Mum's words. Logically, she's saying she doesn't blame me. All this time, I was convinced she did. *Or maybe she was just trying to make you feel better. You KNOW you are to blame, that's what matters*, Shame Goblin taunts. I pull out a miniature bottle of wine that I bought for the trip, unscrew the cap and take a few glugs of the vinegar-adjacent beverage, willing the voice to leave me alone.

When the train pulls into Edinburgh, I take a big sniff of the familiar hoppy scent and feel something near to relief. I enjoy climbing the narrow steps of Fleshmarket Close; even the distinct smell of burger-shop fat, urine and cigarettes is welcome to my nose. My sense of smell is so strong now. I can detect myriad scents from miles away. This newfound strength has its benefits – and, unfortunately, its costs too.

I can't wait to get back to Bucky Place. But I want to see Nova first. It's been weeks since she rescued me from Phoenix's grasp. Since our kiss. Since her bite. All my womanly, humanly and otherwise instincts are telling me I need to stay as far away from her as possible, but I just can't help myself. Without even going to my flat to drop off my belongings, I head straight for Rock Bar. Stepping nervously down the stairs, I clock the bartender from the first time I visited here. Hoping she doesn't recognise me as the girl who gave cunnilingus on the dance floor, I approach a little sheepishly and order a lemonade. Then a second later, I ask for a shot of vodka in it. She clicks her tongue in the side of her mouth, as if I just asked her to make nineteen more drinks. When she serves it, I ask to put it on Nova's tab.

'I don't know what you mean,' she says, folding her scrawny tattooed arms.

'Nova's tab?' I repeat.

She shrugs. 'We don't do tabs – now, can you pay for your drink or not?'

'I'll get this one.' A deep voice rumbles behind me as a big beefy arm stretches across the bar and hands the barmaid a crisp note. She swipes it out of his hand.

'Keep the change,' he adds, and she nods with a reserved gratitude, dropping some coins in to a big Mason jar with 'Tips' scrawled on the front.

I crane my neck and see who my kind benefactor is. It's Shadow. He's wearing cargo pants, a tight black top that shows off his muscles and a cheeky grin.

'Thanks,' I say in a small voice. He tips his bottle of beer towards my glass and we clink them together in a cheers, which causes a bashfulness in me that I can't stand. Every time I try to fixate my gaze on something ordinary, it lands on something hot and sexy on him. His pierced nipple under his vest, his trap muscles bulging as he moves, his big hands, which I know could pick me up and spin me every which way. I try to distract myself with the lonely slice of lemon in my drink, twirling it around with my straw.

'Come join me, Little One,' he says over his shoulder, striding towards one of the tables at the edge of the empty dance floor. We sit opposite one another, and I feel a rush of gratitude for my new haircut. Maybe Mum was right – maybe I did let myself go, just a little. I tuck one of the strands behind my ear self-consciously.

'What brings you here?'

'Same reason you're here, I guess. I fancied a drink.' I laugh before shyly taking a sip.

Shadow leans forward, his chiselled features illuminated from below by a flickering candle. It should be illegal to be this hot.

'Hmm,' he says slowly, drinking me in with his eyes.

He makes me so nervous, I know my voice is starting to shake. 'Can't a girl have a drink on a Wednesday night?'

His face doesn't change; instead, he looks even more intensely at me, as if he's studying every centimetre of my skin. 'Maybe Nova was right.'

'About what?' I ask quickly, desperate to know what she's said about me.

'You're not special.'

I gulp, choking on his words like they're pieces of food I forgot to chew before I tried to swallow them down. 'I'm sorry?'

'Not in a bad way. But you, Brodie Bell . . .' He lifts my chin with his forefinger until our gazes meet. Even sitting down, I have to look up at him. 'Are perfectly ordinary.'

'Okaaaay,' I say. 'That doesn't sound like a compliment to me.'

'Believe me, it is.'

'Please, will you take me to see her?'

He shakes his head. 'Orders from the boss, sorry.'

'I thought you were the boss,' I flirt, hoping it will get me further.

'Nice try. Nova doesn't need you in the Den. If she told you to stay away, then maybe you should listen. Enjoy your life. Focus on partying and kissing boys.'

I let out a small, bitter laugh. 'But what if I can't? Enjoy my life, I mean.'

Shadow glugs his beer and starts to peel off the label; he looks preoccupied.

'I've been training, you know.'

'You have?'

'I've been going swimming every day.'

'You look like you might need to up your protein, to be honest.'

'Shadow's a cute name,' I tease, hoping to lighten the mood. But his face clouds, his jaw jutting out.

'I chose it. Most of us choose our new names.'

'You do?'

'Usually, but not always – the name relates to your bite story.'

'Go on, tell me your bite story.'

I watch as he considers opening up. 'Maybe some other time.'

'Come on, I'll tell you mine.'

Shadow deliberates.

'Go on!'

Then he leans forward. 'I went out on a hike with my dad one day. We loved hiking. Happiest when we were climbing hills, or exploring mountains. My mum used to laugh at how similar we were. The older I got, the more I looked like my dad, and sounded like him too. People couldn't tell us apart on the phone.'

I wait as a flicker of self-consciousness crosses his face.

'I don't know why I'm telling you this.'

I give him an encouraging look to let him know I won't judge him. 'You don't have to,' I offer, and his mouth curves into a grateful smile.

'Forget it.' He sips his beer and looks away.

'You can trust me,' I gently prod.

'We climbed Ben A'an. We'd done that walk at least ten, fifteen times before. Long story short, I hurt my ankle, my dad went to fetch help. And . . . that's the last thing I remember.'

'Did your dad survive?'

'No,' Shadow says, his tough-guy mask slipping for a millisecond. 'It looked like he fell and broke his neck. I guess he was trying to run away from the wolf.'

'Sorry,' I say, and I understand that I really mean it but, at the same time, I know those words don't mean much at all.

'It's fine.'

'Why "Shadow"?'

Shadow grins. 'My dad was the toughest guy you'd ever meet. He was built like a tank, legs like tree trunks, arms so big I used to swing off them when I was a little guy. I looked up to him so much. I used to follow him around like a shadow. At least, that's what people would say.' He gulps, a flash of pain tightening his features.

I nod in understanding. 'How's your mum now?'

'She's passed now. But . . .' He rips the label off the beer and folds it into a tiny square. 'That's why I'm Shadow.' We sit in silence. I grab his giant hand and wrap my fingers around his. I stare at his handsome face, and I don't see a big, muscular gym guy anymore. I see a scared little boy.

'It's good to meet you, Shadow,' I say tenderly.

He smiles, even going a little red. Then he finishes his beer and slams it on the table. 'Look, I'll take you to see her, but I can't promise it'll go well, Little One.'

'Don't you want to know my bite story?'

He grins, getting to his feet. 'I already know it.'

'How come?'

'You were bitten by the most powerful werewolf in the country. Everyone knows it.'

Arriving at the Den, I look up and see Juniper observing the Commons from Nova's glass room. I give her a little wave, then instantly regret it. Shadow stays with me, throwing dirty looks at anyone who stares at us as they saunter past. Juniper appears quickly, looking very cross with us.

'What is she doing here?'

'She wants to speak to the boss.'

'Absolutely not. Nova is too busy for visitors.'

I hover behind him.

'Come on, I'm sure she can spare a minute,' he says.

Juniper sighs, regarding Shadow with a resigned weariness. 'Fine, but make it a short one.'

Shadow steps into Nova's office first, and she snaps at him. 'Shadow, who do you think you are—' She stops when she sees me. Takes a step back.

Everything stops. Time. My heart. We stare at one another for a few long seconds.

'Brodie. I told Juniper I was too busy . . .'

'I brought them up,' Juniper remarks, standing in the doorway, arms folded, already ready to fling me out of it.

Now I feel self-conscious. 'I want to join you. Be a part of all this.'

Nova remains still.

'Will you let me?'

'I could take her under my wing, train her up?' Shadow offers.

Nova looks through the glass to the Commons, then back at us, an unlikely pairing. 'Maybe in the future, but not now,' she finally answers.

I scan Shadow's face to see if I should be deflated or excited. He looks down at his feet.

I linger, waiting for Nova to ask me to stay. To tell them to leave us alone, and to rip off all my clothes and eat me alive. But she doesn't.

'Time's up,' Juniper barks and Nova nods.

'I'll be in touch, Brodie.'

I smile politely, but I can't help but feel a surge of disappointment.

Shadow walks down one of the hallways and I follow him out, but I'm swung back when Juniper grabs my wrist and pulls me close.

'Ow!' I say, trying to pull it back.

'Listen to me,' she says, her mouth pursed in a straight line. 'You are not a proper werewolf. You are a human being. A puny human being at that. I could snap your wrist in half right now if I wanted to.'

'Juniper, get off her,' Nova commands from the doorway. I yank my arm back as Juniper retreats back to Nova's room.

Nova steps nearer to me, and I want to surrender so badly to her. Her nostrils flare. 'Juniper's right, you know. You're not a proper werewolf. You're just an ordinary girl.'

'Why does everyone keep saying that?'

'Because it's true.'

With Shadow striding ahead, I storm into the Commons. Anger boils inside me like a forgotten pot of stew. How fucking dare Nova string me along like this? One minute I'm welcomed into the fold, the next minute she's trying to kiss me. Then bite me. Then she tells the Rock Bar staff not to let me through. Now I'm some plain Jane who she can't be bothered to see anymore. Fuck her, and fuck this place too.

As Shadow walks me to the exit, I spot Coco sitting on a concrete block, laughing about something with a couple of friends.

'You! Coco!' My voice echoes around the room, which is scattered with people. I feel everyone's ears prick up in interest.

Coco juts out her chin, amused with me. Then she stands up. 'Yes?'

'Fancy a fight?' I bellow, letting my bag slip off my shoulder and drop to the floor with a thud.

Shadow puts his hand on the small of my back. 'Little One, no.'

'Who with – you?' she mocks, her voice loud enough to let everyone else hear.

Shoving Shadow off, I extend my arms and beckon Coco with my hands, just like Willow did that time they were fighting.

Coco sneers as she walks towards me, elegant and predatory, like one of those big cats in the documentaries Dad likes. *Let go of what you're holding back*, I tell myself. *And then you can become a were-wolf. Summon the power. You know you have it in you*. Squeezing my eyes shut, I clench my fists and growl. Nothing. When I open my eyes, Coco is heading straight for me. Frightened, I step back and stumble, losing my footing. My legs buckle as she prowls towards me, quick and agile on her feet. The good news is, it's over quickly. She trips me up, somehow making me fly through the air like I'm a cartoon character who has just slipped on a banana skin. When I land, the wind is knocked out of me, and I roll and cower in a ball, panicking that I can't breathe. My hands press into the cold concrete floor to steady myself. Coco waits for me to catch my breath as a small crowd forms around us. I look up and see Shadow, biting his nail. He shakes his head at me, and this makes me feel even worse. As soon as I sit up, Coco grabs me by my underarms and swings me to standing. Then she punches me, right under the ribcage. I wheeze and drop down to my knees, the pain of the blow spreading across my abdomen. The pièce de résistance is a headbutt, which sends an explosion of pain across my whole face.

'Enough, Coco!' Shadow bellows and grabs me, pulling me to my feet, dragging me away as some of the people watching boo and cheer.

He carries me to his quarters like we're newlyweds. Unlike Nova's sprawling and grand space, Shadow lives in a low-ceilinged bunk room in the lower levels of the Den. There are a few personal items littered around. A crinkled photograph of Shadow as a boy holding a fish, presumably with his dad. A few weights. A pile of dirty laundry. It reminds me of a jail cell I saw in a documentary once. As if he can read my mind, he pipes up, 'It's small, but I don't spend much time in here.'

I walk towards a full-length mirror and stare at myself in it.

They're right. I'm tiny. He comes up behind me and gently pulls my hair to one side. Tingles dance across my skin. This probably isn't the best idea, but I don't care. I shut my eyes and enjoy the feeling of his dense body pressing against my back. When I open them, I see his form behind me in the mirror. He towers over me, and his frame is at least double the width of my own.

'Little One – that was silly, picking a fight with her.'

'I'm done talking,' I say back, making eye contact in the mirror. He gruffly spins me around so I'm facing him, taking me in his arms, squeezing me. He's so strong, he could probably crush my bones with his bare hands. A moan of pleasure escapes my mouth, and I feel delicious, hot wetness between my legs. He flicks the tops of my jeans and undoes them with a swift hand movement. This, evidently, is not his first rodeo. I move my hands to touch his rippling abs, but he grabs me by the wrists and playfully shakes his head. He forces them behind my arched back.

'Don't move,' he whispers in a cunning voice, tickling my ear. I do as he says, and tremble in anticipation as he yanks my jeans down. On his knees, Shadow looks hungrily in between my legs, but then he shakes his head and gets to his feet.

He turns me around again so that we are both facing the mirror once more, my hands still pinned behind my back. I let out a little squeal at the force of his touch. The ache from Coco's punch has melted away, and something else far more palatable has taken its place. Shadow's hand reaches up my top and cups my left breast. As it spills out of my bra, he nods in approval. Then, in one fell swoop, he tears my top clean off. My mouth drops open in shock. The arrogance, the sheer entitlement of his actions, turns me on to an outrageous degree.

'What am I going to wear home?' I ask, insolently.

His spade hand cups over my mouth. His skin is rough like a brick, from years of fighting, training and whatever else he gets up to in the Den. Saliva springs out the corner of my mouth in anticipation, and I hungrily lick the inside of his hand. He pulls my body into his, so his gargantuan dick presses in between my bum cheeks, my cotton underwear yielding with the pressure. I didn't even notice him pulling it out of his cargo pants. I stare at myself in the mirror, a bruised and bony body, with one breast exposed and my jeans at my ankles. My hair is wild from my tussle with Coco. Then he slides his fingers inside me as I watch him in the mirror. We don't dare break eye contact, and I observe his handsome face and feel the heat of his body, the strokes of his fingers, until I reach orgasm. My knees knocking in pleasure, I let out a raw and earthy groan.

Then he spins me around again, and as quickly as Coco tripped me up in the Commons, he lifts me over to a wooden desk and balances me on the edge, yanking my cute underwear to the side and pushing himself inside me. The length of him makes me gasp. At first it feels too much, I'm not sure I can take it, but a few rocks and I begin to savour the sensation: one of being filled up and feeling whole. He thrusts with the precision and expertise I'm sure he must use at the gym, pulsing in a rhythm that rides me to my second orgasm in a matter of minutes. This one is deeper and longer than the first. I feel pleasure spread all across my body in little electrical tendrils, sparking along the way. And then it's his turn. He grabs me close – I feel like a china doll, about to be crushed into a million pieces. He pumps his body, getting deeper and faster. When he gets close to orgasm, his grip tightens. Then he lets out a noise, husky and coarse, into the nape of my neck. We hold each other, sweaty and breathless. As his grasp slowly loosens, he pulls out of me, pulling up his pants, and drinking me in, half-naked and tousled, perched on the edge of his desk.

I glance around and locate my jeans, pulling them on as quickly as I can. I don't want to hang around.

I speak first. 'I better go.'

'Probably,' he agrees. Then he pulls me in for our first kiss. It's sloppy and quick. The corners of my mouth are left slick.

Once I'm dressed, I let myself out, clutching my ragged top closed. Just as I'm about to shut the door behind me, Shadow calls after me.

'It was a compliment, by the way. When I called you ordinary.'

CHAPTER TWENTY-ONE

Explore the themes of independence and empowerment through the character of Jane Eyre in Charlotte Brontë's 1847 novel.

We're in our childhood bedroom, but it's a lot bigger than I remember. It sprawls like a gladiator arena. Thousands of people are watching a fight from the tiered seating. I am standing in the shadows, and Grace is getting the shit kicked out of her. She's my age. Looks like she could be my twin. It's like having an out-of-body experience, watching myself get beaten up. I would be lying if I said I didn't fantasise about this sometimes. Getting kicked and punched, the visceral nature of it, grounding me. Getting what I deserve. But seeing a loved one go through it – it's agonising.

'Get off her!' I shout. But my voice is silent, the words blown away by the wind from the window being left open.

'Leave her alone!' I plead. Now even she has stopped screaming as the kicks and punches continue. Beating her to a pulp. And I have just stood by and let it happen. Useless, yet again.

*

People in the library are staring. I shake my head as yet another person hastily looks away and scurries past.

'You should have seen the other guy,' I throw over my shoulder.

'Have they never seen a black eye before?' I say to Zainab. My bottom lip is so fat, I now have a slight lisp.

'What possessed you to start a fight with Coco?'

'I was trying to prove myself.'

Zainab looks lost for words.

'Try and wipe that judgy look off your face, please.'

'And I heard someone saw you sneaking out of Shadow's bunk room . . .'

I blush. Busted.

'I get you wanting to join the crew, but whatever you're up to, it's not the way to go about it. People are talking.'

'I thought embracing my inner animal was all I had to do?'

'That doesn't mean fighting and shagging your way through the Den.'

A girl at a nearby table looks up from her textbooks.

Zainab lowers her voice. 'Animals don't just follow their instincts; they engage in deliberate and calculated behaviours.'

I squirm in my seat, my cheeks hot with the embarrassment of being called out. 'Well, if you don't mind, my first exam is tomorrow – so let's cut the wolf chat. Unless it's Virginia Woolf, that is.'

'Fine by me.' Zainab bites the lid off her highlighter and slides the pen over her page.

I watch her for a few moments. Her hair is gelled and tucked behind her ears. The crisp collar of her shirt is pulled up in a chic fashion. The image of her crouched and poised to transform flashes in my mind. She sees me recoil.

'What is it?'

'How do you do it all? Wolf life and student life?'

'I thought we weren't mentioning the "W" word?'

'How do you reconcile these different parts of yourself?'

She sighs. 'Everybody's complicated. Even straight-up humans. You can either sit back and let things overwhelm you, or you can just get on with it.'

'Have you seen Nova recently?' I say casually, busying myself with my pencil case.

'Yes, why?'

Being shunned by Nova has triggered the worst feelings in me. I'm not good enough, and I'll never fit in. Some days, I get so mad at her for biting me in the first place, for allowing our kiss to happen. She told me that we will always be interconnected, then she banished me from the Den. Was she negging me? I hate how pathetic she makes me feel. Despite – or maybe because of – that, I miss her. I want her, even if she makes me feel like shit. When we met, she filled a hole in my life that I didn't even know existed. And when she told me to stay away, it hurt even more because she took a piece of me with her. At this stage, I'd do anything to see her again. Breathe in her scent. 'No reason,' I chirp.

Autumn joins us, dressed in an oversized see-through sweater and knee-high boots. Her long hair is pulled behind her in a tight pony.

'Wait, are you a hologram? I thought you were allergic to the library?' Zainab teases.

'I like to study in the comfort of my own home, so what?' Autumn empties her bag on to the table. Packets of nuts, fresh fruit, dried fruit, chocolate and candy gather in a rainbow-coloured heap. 'I come bearing gifts.'

Zainab and I exchange a look.

'Thanks, Autumn.' I gratefully tear into a packet of candy.

'It's also a little bit of a bribe,' she admits, as I shove the sweet into my mouth.

Zainab and I brace ourselves.

'There's a girl I've been chatting to who is going to this club night tonight. I really want to go, but I need someone to buddy me.' She looks pleadingly at me.

I shake my head earnestly. 'We have our finals tomorrow – no way.'

Autumn purses her lips. 'True, but you have barely done anything fun with us for weeks.'

I mean, that's not strictly true, but there's no way I'm sacrificing being fresh just so she can get her rocks off.

'Come on, Brodie. You've been studying your ass off for months.'

I flinch at this untruth.

She continues, 'You've barely even come to the pub. We've hardly seen you. Living in the library isn't healthy. Do you not think you deserve a little bit of fun after that random girl mugged you?'

'Hmmm,' I say, avoiding eye contact, hating that I had to tell yet another lie to Autumn.

'Plus, how much more can you possibly learn today that you haven't already studied?' Autumn adds. She makes a valid point.

Zainab's unusually quiet. 'Would you come as well?' I ask her.

She shrugs. 'What nightclub is it?'

'Chemistry,' Autumn replies quickly.

I've heard of it. It is an old relic of a nightclub by the train station, one that the older, non-studenty types would go to. Probably to avoid first years like us.

'Fine,' Zainab agrees.

'I guess fine as well,' I eventually say.

Autumn looks ready to burst with excitement. 'Good. We all deserve a night out. Let's get ready at yours tonight, Zainab.'

'No way, my place is disgusting.'

'Even more so than usual?'

Zainab flings an apple at Autumn, who catches it with one hand and takes a big bite out of it.

The plan is to go in early for a dance, hang around until Autumn has met the girl, and then slink off into the night. My exam is at 10 a.m. tomorrow, so as long as I am home by 1 a.m. at the latest, that should give me enough time to sleep and get up feeling refreshed.

We arrive at the bricked arches by Haymarket train station. The sounds of trains rumble on the railway below as the ground shakes. There is a queue forming already, and the thrum of people huddling in groups, chatting, smoking and laughing, fills me with anticipation.

Autumn is positively glowing. 'I'm so happy I have my girls with me!' she says, pulling me and a reluctant Zainab in for a cuddle.

'You know I don't like physical contact, get off me,' Zainab says, gently pushing her off.

'What does the girl look like?' I ask, trying to peer over the heads of the other people in the queue.

'She's tall, with long dark hair.'

When we get inside, the pounding music thumps through my bones. We head to the bar to grab a drink. 'Just a lemonade for me!' I yell over the music.

'Boring!' Autumn chides.

'My scholarship hangs in the balance,' I remind her, but she's already preoccupied with her gin and tonic. She leads us to the dance floor and we dance in a little triangle. At first I feel awkward. Like everyone's staring at me. But soon I let myself get lifted up by the tunes. The rhythmic beat of the music floods through my body as I move my hips and arms and legs, letting them lead the way, and allowing my mind to shut off for once. And then I see her. Appearing and reappearing like a ghost, in and out of time to the music, the flashing lights illuminating her. I freeze, suddenly unable to move. Then I rush towards her, breaking the little force-field I have with Zainab and Autumn on the dance floor, pushing people out of the way to get to her.

'Nova?' I shout, my voice sounding so insignificant under the volume of the music.

She turns, surprised to see me.

'What are you doing here?' I shout over the pounding beats.

She takes this the wrong way, looking me up and down. I feel silly and young. Standing before her now in my baggy jeans and a cute top I borrowed from Autumn makes me feel vulnerable and insecure. *Stupid, ugly outfit for a stupid, ugly girl.*

'Can we talk?'

She shakes her head, but I see a yearning in her eyes.

'Please, Nova.' I reach out for her hand. Electricity sparks as she lets me hold it for a moment before pulling it away.

'Not here.' She says it so quietly, but I can read her mouth.

I glance over at Zainab, who is distracting Autumn by dragging her to the toilet. The lights continue to flash as I follow Nova outside into the cool air, my heart pounding in my throat. A bouncer puts his arm out, stopping me. 'You need a stamp if you want to come back in.'

'Fine,' I say distractedly, letting him stamp the back of my hand.

Nova strides away and turns a corner down an abandoned alleyway.

'Are you embarrassed by me?' I call out, my voice startling a big city rat that had been hiding behind some rubbish bins. It scuttles away into the shadows.

Nova spins around. 'You never know who is listening.'

I get close to her and stare into her pale face, half illuminated by a street lamp. Pure beauty.

'I forgive you,' I blurt out. 'For biting me. I don't know an awful lot about this werewolf business, but what I do know is that I want to be one of you. I want to have the power.'

Nova looks me up and down again. 'But . . .'

'What? You warned me that I'm holding something back, but you are the one who is holding something back! You are all half sentences and borrowed looks. I'm going crazy because of you!'

Nova's face is flooded with a steely sorrow. 'I need you to stay away from the Den, alright?'

'Just because I'm not strong enough to fight yet? You're cutting me out?'

'It's not as simple as that. I told you I was afraid you'd get hurt. And so far, you have proven me right.'

'You said you were worried about being the one to hurt me though.'

She raises her voice now, cutting through the cool spring air. 'I still might! So stay away.'

'Give me a test; let me prove myself. Please!'

Before I can get an answer from her, she's gone, into the darkness, just like the rat.

I kick a metal trash can with all my might although the clanging sound of metal does nothing to quell my anger. My big toe throbs in pain. But it's nothing compared to the pain in my heart. I storm back to the Chemistry entranceway, hurry into the dark folds of the club and head straight to the bar. I order a tequila shot. Then another. And as the feeling of the liquid goes down my throat and warms my belly, my fury dulls. I stop caring. I dance and drink and Autumn meets the girl. Zainab's tired and wants to walk home together, but I'm not ready. I want to dance some more.

Just one, maybe two more songs. Maybe one, two more drinks. I lose myself in the music, and then I have another drink. And another. And like most other times when I edge near to something resembling happiness, just as I am as close to euphoria as is humanly possible in this moment, Shame Goblin rears its ugly head. *It's all very well having fun. But remember Nova doesn't want you. And why would she? You killed your sister. You should have died that night.* And so I have another drink to shut the voice up, but it gets louder and louder. And I bob and sway in between strangers' faces, contorting in fright at me. It's hard to tell at this point: are they scary or scared? And then I stumble to the bar and order another drink, but I've lost my purse. And the bartender gives me a look of disgust and tells me I've had enough. So I head for Bucky Place, walking in zigzags. When I get home, I ransack the cupboards for more booze. I find a case of beer in the fridge and write a note to Nathan.

To Nathan

I am sorry I stole ur beer. Will replace!

Lots of love

Brodie

(don't hate me)

I go into my room, and I sit on my bed and drink and drink and drink until finally the voice shuts the fuck up.

The next morning, my alarm doesn't wake me up. My anxiety does. When I drag myself out of bed, everything hurts. My cheeks are puffy and my eyes gritty. My tongue throbs with a layer of scum that even two rounds with a toothbrush fails to remove. Not to mention my head. It's throbbing, just like the music in the club last night. *Doof. Doof. Doof.*

I stand, hunched in my kitchen, waiting for the kettle to boil. Although, given how awful I feel right now, I know coffee isn't going to scratch the surface. My eyes well up in regret. Why did I drink so much? The sound of Nathan clearing his throat startles me, and I spin around to face him. He's clothed, for once.

'What were you staring at?' he asks, giving me a very odd look.

'Nothing, actually. I'm guessing the lack of insulation in here has finally got to you?' I mean it as a joke. It comes out snarky.

Nathan's nose twitches awkwardly as he reaches into his cupboard. I watch him as he methodically prepares his trusty bowl of cereal soup.

'How are you?' he asks in a clipped fashion.

'I can't be bothered. I have my first exam today. I just want to go back to bed. I had a bit of a late one.'

Nathan offers me a tight smile. I'm paranoid he can smell the tequila on me. It feels like it's oozing out of every pore. At the very least, I know he can sense the shame that ripples out of my aura. So large and weighty now, I'm convinced that everyone can see it.

I busy myself with making my coffee. I know I look rough as a carpet. When I glanced in my mirror this morning, I got a fright. My two black eyes have almost faded away, but I have big bags underneath them. My skin is pale and dry. Even my frame feels smaller, and I've noticed my jeans have been feeling looser recently. A few months ago, I never understood the women who would 'forget to eat'. The same women who always have perfect hair, and brag about eating as much pizza as they want. These types of women have always made me suspicious, and I was sure they were lying. Recently, however, I have actually forgotten to eat some days. That's where my similarities with this breed end, however. I am about as far away from the clean-girl aesthetic as one can get. My stomach suddenly rumbles, making a noise akin to a giant steel bridge groaning under the weight of hundreds of cars.

'Someone's hungry,' Nathan remarks as he opens the fridge.

My drunken note swooshes out, drifting to the floor. Nathan reads it, then sighs.

'Sorry about that.' I grab an old apple from a dusty bowl on the window ledge. I inspect its puckered skin from being left beyond its prime. It'll do.

'Where did you go last night, then?' Nathan is nice enough to change the subject.

'Just having a bit of fun,' I say in a light tone, taking a gulp of my coffee, which incinerates the roof of my mouth. 'Suppose I better get to uni – I'm meeting Autumn to do some cramming before our exam. Wish me luck!'

Nathan's spoon hovers over his bowl, and he gives me a polite smile. 'Good luck, then.'

I pull on my coat and grab my bag, checking I have my notepad and pens.

As I fill up my water bottle, I distractedly ask Nathan, 'When are your exams?'

There is a pause. 'Mine started last week. And I have one today,' he says.

Almost halfway out the door, I stop. 'Oh! Good luck to you too, then.'

'Thanks.'

'Sorry, I didn't know you had your exams.'

He blinks at me. 'You never asked.'

The rec room is dotted with people studying alone or in little huddles. I arrive before Autumn, plonking myself down by the newly lit fire, which spits and sparks. Even the smell of woodsmoke makes me feel nauseous. I lay out my papers and books, but can't bring myself to look through any of them yet. I stare instead at the growing flames of the fire, allowing myself to get lost in the beauty of them. Soon myriad unhelpful images flash in my mind: my kidnapping, Grace on a swing, the fall, screams, Nova and Phoenix practically ripping each other to shreds. My fingers brush the bumpy scar along my neck; I know all too well that even when the outside heals, it's the inside that keeps on hurting. When Autumn approaches me and taps me on the arm, I jump in surprise at her touch.

'Woah, it's only me.' She smiles brightly at me, taking off her coat to reveal a preppy outfit, complete with a shirt with a big flouncy bow. Her efforts highlight my own dog-eared appearance. Getting ready didn't so much consist of picking an outfit; it was more a case of grabbing whatever clothes smelled the least bad. Which, it turns out, aren't many, since I haven't been to the laundromat for weeks. I am a mere day away from having to turn my underwear inside out.

'Look at you,' I say, trying not to sound as flat as I feel.

'I'm channelling academic chic.'

'I'm channelling nervous wreck,' I reply.

'I can see that. What time did you get home last night?' she teases.

I snap my head around to face her and bristle defensively. 'Why?'

Autumn roots around in her bag and hands me a hairbrush full of her orange hair. 'I'm only teasing.'

I want to tell her about what's been going on. I want to tell her about being bitten, and being drugged and taken to the Faol People, and the rest. But I can't. Secrets really do eat you up. You think they won't, but they do. They're sliding around inside me, like toxic sludge. Moving from limb to limb. Never going away, even when I think they have. I swallow the lump in my throat and take the hairbrush, dragging it through my hair obediently, wincing at the knots. My mum would be ashamed if she saw me right now. Another pang of guilt.

'That's my girl.' Autumn pats me on the leg.

I can't even muster a smile.

'It's normal to have exam jitters, you know,' she adds.

I nod, grateful for something I can project my worry on to.

She continues, 'But you've done the work.'

'Have I?'

'You were obsessed with books and studying when I met you.'

'Were,' I repeat.

Autumn changes tack. 'You know what I mean. Well, my mum and dad have threatened my murder if I fail, so I have that looming over me.'

My parents don't know it's my first exam today. I deliberately didn't tell them. A well-meaning good-luck text would be enough to push me over the edge right now.

Before we know it, we are piling into the freezing cold examination room, a brightly lit hall with cavernous high ceilings and rows of individual desks and plastic chairs. The invigilator is a short, balding man with incredible posture. He looks like he has an iron rod up his back. And one up his arse, too. His nose is tipped up in the air, his cheeks sucked in, as if he has just popped a sour candy into his mouth. His beady eyes observe us as we take our individual seats. I am in the middle row, facing a large clock on the freshly painted wooden wall. Autumn sits to my right. I watch her fondly as she gets out her rainbow pencil case and empties a bunch of gel pens in a variety of colours on to her desk. When she notices my gaze, she picks a violet-coloured pen and offers it to me.

'I'm good – I have one.' I hold up my ballpoint.

'Take it. It's good luck.' Autumn smiles at me, her freckled face filled with so much warmth, I want to fling my arms around her.

I accept the pen, grateful for the gesture. But as the sounds of everyone else in the room – settling in, removing their jackets, rifling through their stationery – simmer down, I'm left with a feeling I can't shake. I am screwed.

You've not studied enough.

You're not good enough.

You've not studied enough.

You're not good enough.

You've not studied enough.

You're not good enough.

You've not studied enough.

You're not good enough.

You've not studied enough.

You're not good enough.

You've not studied enough.

You're not good enough.

The sense of dread in my stomach grows from a grain of sand to a marble, from a marble to a tennis ball, on and on and on. It grows so big that I swear I can feel the weight of it, the heaviness of it pinning me to my seat. Holding me hostage. I think about Nova at the nightclub last night. She's trying to push me away; I know she is. But why? Maybe it's because of what I have known all along: I truly am not good enough.

The invigilator clears his throat. 'You may now begin!' he says, in a posh timbre.

I turn my paper over and read the question.

Explore the themes of independence and empowerment through the character of Jane Eyre in Charlotte Brontë's 1847 novel. How does Jane's journey from a disadvantaged orphan to a self-reliant and morally

principled woman reflect broader societal attitudes towards gender roles and empowerment in the Victorian era?

A year ago, I could have answered it in my sleep. How is it possible that my time at university has made me more stupid? My mind has drawn a blank. The rustle of papers and scratching of pens and pencils beginning to make notes is even worse than the silence that had me so on edge just a moment ago. The words swirl around like melted raspberry-ripple ice cream. I tap Autumn's purple pen and shake my foot in a frenetic rhythm, until the guy in front of me turns around and throws me an exasperated look. I mouth *Sorry* at him. The invigilator walks over to us and stands behind me. Sweat gathers at the nape of my neck and under my arms and on my palms. I blot them on my thighs and take a ragged breath. I jot some random words on my paper, but I'm not even sure if they make sense. The clock ticks. The room fills with the sounds of everybody else writing. Their scribbles serve as a reminder of my own ineptitude. Time refuses to stand still for me, even though it would be oh so very helpful right now.

The invigilator starts to move along, casting his eyes from left to right as he walks down the aisle, like a nosy bridesmaid. I start to panic. I look to Autumn, who has stopped biting her lip in thought and is now penning her answer with her scrappy handwriting, pausing every few paragraphs to check she's on the right track.

The invigilator has reached the front and begins to snake up the aisle to my left. I focus on his presence without looking directly at him. A few minutes go by until he is walking down the outside of the furthest-away row and has his back to me. Then I do probably the stupidest thing I've ever done in my life. I crane my neck to read Autumn's paper. At first, I can't make out what she's writing, but then some keywords start to jump out: 'self-discovery', 'romantic equality' and 'Moor House'. Autumn feels my stare and catches my eye. At first, she cocks her head and gives me a confused smile. Then I flick my gaze, moving it deliberately from her paper to my paper, followed by a pleading expression. Autumn is taken aback. She can't believe I'm asking her to do this. I hate myself for taking advantage of my friend's good nature, but I am desperate. I know the answer, I just need a bit of help. Autumn looks very pissed off, but she shifts her body to make it easier for me to look at her paper, leaning the opposite way. She moves her left arm to her lap. Other words jump out and I start writing them down. I start to remember a tutorial with Killian where he asked us to discuss Jane Eyre. And it all begins to trickle then flood back. All I needed was a kickstart. Just as I am writing the words 'social commentary on gender and class', I feel a hefty hand firmly but gently tap me on the shoulder. I turn to face the invigilator, who looks very angry indeed.

He bends down to whisper in my ear. 'I've been watching you for the last five minutes. I know you were cheating. I'm going to move you to another seat. And this isn't the end of it, but please, for now, do not disturb your hardworking classmates.'

I am numb as I gather my things and move as quietly as I can to the front of the room. I notice Autumn's cheeks have flushed a deep red, and she refuses to look at me. The invigilator gestures to a seat right by his desk and I skulk into it. I see a guy in the front row looking particularly interested in me, then I realise it's the man I jerked off in my lecture. He stares at me like I'm in a freakshow. This truly is one of the worst moments of my life.

By the time the invigilator announces, 'Ten minutes left,' I have accepted my fate. Not only am I going to fail this exam, I'll also get in trouble for cheating. I don't dare look in Autumn's direction, so I hunch over the desk for the final ten minutes and let my disappointment in myself brew inside of me.

When time is up, I watch as other people high-five, shake out their wrists, let out audible sighs of relief and share satisfied smiles and mutterings of 'Well done' and 'Phew, thank goodness that is over.' Autumn stands up, her head stooped, rams her pencil case in her bag and rushes towards the exit.

'Wait!' I shout, causing people to turn and stare. 'Autumn!' I shout again. But she has pushed her way to the front, and I watch helplessly as she rushes out the door, her hand flying to her mouth as she bursts into tears.

I catch up with Autumn as she walks briskly across Potterrow, her bag swinging dramatically against her hip. I reach for her shoulder to stop her walking away. She violently shrugs me off, her face wet with tears.

'Go away,' she spits at me. Her usually open and beautiful face is contorted in disdain.

'I'm sorry.'

'Sorry isn't enough. You really threw me off in there. Like, not even a tiny bit – completely.'

'I know it's not cool. Not cool at all.'

'It's alright for you, Miss I Read Two Books a Night.' Her impression of me is so nasty and childish, it catches me off-guard.

I frown, unsure where she's going with this.

'For someone who is so clever, you really don't get it, do you, Brodie?'

I continue to stare at her, genuinely not understanding. 'Please tell me what you mean.'

'You think you're the shit. Always going on about being a straight-A student. Sure, I've not read as many books, and sure, I don't know as many big words. And sure, I didn't have the confidence to apply for a scholarship, and I definitely didn't know all the right things to say. But I did well in school, really well. And I worked two jobs, and so did my mum, to help pay for this semester. Next semester, I'm on my own. I've worked really hard to prep for this exam. I don't live in the library like you, but the only apartment I could afford is halfway out of the city. I've been studying my brains out.'

With each point she makes, I feel myself shrink smaller and smaller. With any hope, I will fade away into nothingness.

'I'm truly repentant over this—' I start to say.

'See! There you go again, using a big fancy fucking word to make me look like an idiot!'

She takes a sharp inhale through her nostrils. 'And then you, the brainiest person I know, the person who I always look to for answers and advice, you put me in the position to help you to cheat. To let you copy my answers. Because you know I can't say no. Pushover Autumn, she'll do anything you say, just walk all over her!'

The last few words tumble out in a shrill shout. She's livid. The truth of what she's saying curls around me like a thick smoke.

I open my mouth to apologise again, but she points a long, manicured nail at me.

'No! You do not get to have the last word. You used me. What if I fail? Or what if I get in trouble because of this? What if I get kicked out of uni?'

Sensing these are rhetorical questions, I look at my feet.

'You think I was joking about my mum killing me. She would hang me out to dry. Maybe your parents think the sun shines out your ass, but mine are realists. Hard-working people from an estate. You don't know how good you have it.'

I shake my head. 'That's not true.'

'Yes it is. I can see I've hit a nerve.' Autumn's cheeks are shiny with fresh tears, her eyes wild with anger.

I hop from foot to foot, stomping my feet to warm them up. I take a deep breath. 'Autumn, I need to tell you something.'

'Get fucked, Brodie!' she snaps. And then she's gone, giving me the middle finger as she disappears into a crowd of students.

CHAPTER TWENTY-TWO

In H. G. Wells' The War of the Worlds (1898), please explore the notion of 'nothing to lose' and how it resonates with the characters' experiences of and reactions to the alien invasion.

'So, the thing about investing is you never allocate more than you are willing to lose ... Hello? Are you listening?'

'Hmm?' I zone back in. I am on a date with a final-year finance bro called Jethro. He has steely blue eyes, short blond hair that swirls in little angelic curls around his head, and a Cupid's bow so prominent it almost looks sharp. His tanned skin has an oily sheen to it, thanks to a combination of expensive skincare and habitual drug use. Jethro's proclivity to talk about himself, his frequent trips to the toilet and the abundance of phone calls he's not only taking but making have all ensured that this will be our first and last date. We have fucked already, in the back seat of his sports car after he stopped to give me directions last week. And, perhaps against my better judgement, I agreed to see him again.

As Jethro excitedly goes into excruciating detail about joining his dad's financial analyst company when he gets his degree, I pass the time by doing some maths in my head and working out that the bottle of champagne he just ordered is more expensive than my entire outfit. I thrifted a long black dress and wore my only pair of high heels for the occasion. I would have borrowed something hotter from Autumn – if she were speaking to me, that is. But she's not. This outfit, paired with a deep red lipstick, is not exactly my style, but then neither is Jethro. What have I got to lose? The woman I am pretty sure I am in love with wants nothing to do with me. My best mate thinks I'm a scumbag. And she'd be right. My roommate hates me. And I am potentially getting kicked out of uni, pending a cheating hearing in the next few weeks. So I may as well eat lobster with a fuckboy.

After the overpriced starters are cleared, Jethro goes outside to vape and probably text other women. I entertain myself by checking out all the other couples. An older woman feeds strawberries to her toy-boy; an elderly couple laugh into their napkins at a private joke. The presence of other people's love cements the lack of any in my own life. Who knows, with Jethro there is a possibility – albeit small – that I'll fall head over heels in love and become a trad wife, fleeing my university course and committing to a life of popping out little blonde finance kids and filling my time with yoga and day-drinking.

Suddenly, I get the feeling I'm being watched. I turn around and see Shadow, taking up the entire doorway. I signal to him as if to say, *What are you doing here?* He points towards the toilets and disappears. My heart pounds in anticipation and excitement. I can barely sit still.

'Sorry about that. I had some business to attend to,' Jethro says, returning to his seat, a telltale crusty white ring around his right nostril betraying his lie.

'No problemo,' I say brightly. 'I need to powder my nose.' *Seeing as you have*, I add to myself as I slink away, grabbing my handbag from the back of my chair.

I step into the men's toilet to find that it's empty, then, out of nowhere, a spade-like hand grabs me and yanks me into the cubicle. Shadow looks hot as hell. He's freshly shaved, his long hair tucked behind his ears, and he smells, quite frankly, delicious.

'You missed me so much, you have to turn up to a date I'm on?' I stroke his chest teasingly.

He lets out a laugh and flicks my hand away. 'Not quite, Little One.'

I take a step back, affronted by his dismissiveness. 'What are you doing here, then?'

'Nova has asked me to take you for some training.'

The hairs on my neck prickle. 'What kind?'

Shadow strides out of the cubicle. 'Well, are you coming?'

'I need to get my jacket,' I call after him.

'Where we're going, you won't need it,' he laughs.

At the mouth of Loch Aidan, at just after 11 p.m., I stand shivering in a wetsuit, backlit by the blinding headlamps from Shadow's truck. The engine runs, sputtering out the smell of petrol into the otherwise fresh air. A rubber mask presses tightly around my forehead, pulling at my skin, and I hold a snorkel in my hand. Two black rubber flippers sit at my feet, ready for me to put them on. The water is still and murky, boasting the pixelated reflections of the moon and the clouds in the sky. My stomach twists in fear of the unknown.

'Repeat back to me what I've asked you to do,' Shadow says, tussling with a loop of thick rope in the open boot of his truck.

'I have to swim into the middle of the loch and fetch a broken sensor.'

'Exactly.'

I can't take my eyes off the murky water. The loch is, give or take, the same length as St Leonard's swimming pool, and maybe double the width.

'How deep is it?'

'At the centre point, it's fifteen metres deep.'

That's three times the depth of the pool at the university. Piece of cake. I hear the wings of a little insect buzzing around. 'Any wildlife I should worry about?'

'Nothing you can't handle.'

I pull my mask over my face, wishing I was still sitting opposite Jethro, laughing at his thinly veiled misogynistic jokes, letting him look down my dress and counting down the minutes until he fingered me in the car park.

'You're an outdoor swimmer, right? You told me you've been training.'

'Well, I . . . Yes.' I sit down on the cold, gravelly ground and pull the rubbery flippers on to my feet one by one.

'Then this should be a walk in the park.' He faces me. 'Now, the sensor looks like a silver cube. It should be tied down with an iron weight, so you will need to unlock the chain that attaches it to the weight and then bring the sensor to the surface.'

'Is it heavy?'

I observe his reaction carefully. 'Yes.' He returns to the boot of his truck, which has an open metal suitcase inside, showing a little monitor. 'The main thing you need to be wary of is the reeds. But I'll be here, so if anything goes wrong . . . Remember, it's just a training exercise. You ready, Little One?'

Am I ready? Absolutely not. I look back to the black water. It looks terrifying. A frog ribbits and I jump. My nerves in shreds, I give Shadow two thumbs up. I'm evidently unable to actually utter the words, *Yes, I'm ready*.

Shadow holds his pendant and speaks into it. 'She's about to go down.'

And then I readjust the mask and place the lower end of the snorkel in my mouth, aware of the sounds of my breathing echoing through the plastic tube.

I gingerly wade in, feeling the cold water bite at my feet and soaking into the wetsuit at my ankles, dampening my skin. Then I force myself to sink the rest of my body into the water, taking a sharp intake of breath as the cold envelops me. I hear Shadow shout, 'Atta girl!'

And then I start to panic. Maybe it's the champagne I had at dinner. Or the fact that it's pitch black and freezing cold. But I start to feel sick. Panic spirals. I'm freaking out. I'm not ready. I can't do this.

'Get me out!' I shout, splashing around erratically.

'What?'

I thrash in the water with the elegance of a dying seal. Slimy reeds catch between my fingers and I whimper. Shadow pulls me out of the water by my armpits, and I lie on the gravel, panting.

'Sorry,' is all I can say. Over and over.

I can tell Shadow is pissed off. He mumbles into his pendant about me not being ready and I yank off the flippers and chuck them into the lake.

'Why can't I just get something right, for once!' I scream into the night.

I get dried off and we drive back to Edinburgh in silence, Shadow concentrating on the road, and me concentrating on the fact that I am still the biggest fuck-up I know. I read a text from Jethro.

Jethro: *You nasty cunt, leaving me in that restaurant. I had to eat all those oysters myself.*

Heart pounding, I quickly block his number.

When we park, Shadow pats my leg. 'Better luck next time, Little One.'

I stare straight ahead. 'Take me back to the Den.'

'That fuck we had was good, and I'm not going to lie, I have a high success rate with returning customers. However, I think it would be for the best if we cooled things off—'

'Not to have sex with you. To see her.'

Shadow sighs, tapping his fingers on the wheel. I turn to face him, and he must see how serious I am.

'Fine.'

Shadow helps sneak me into the Den through a different entrance. After we park his truck at a car park, we climb through a hatch and down some stairs that take us to the side of the Commons. I head straight for Nova's quarters. She's sitting on her big leather armchair, playing a game of solitaire, when I arrive. She looks very surprised to see me.

'Why did you set me up for failure?'

Nova stares at me in annoyance. 'You need to stop turning up here. Shadow, you can go, but I'll be having words later.'

Shadow leaves me. I stand there, my fists balled in anger. I know I look crazy, with wet tangled hair and smudged mascara. 'You set me a challenge, knowing I would screw up.' I feel my chin tremble. *Pull it together, you wimp!*

Nova takes a sip of her drink. 'You asked for a test.'

'Are you doing all this to deliberately mess with my head?' My eyes narrow.

She shakes her head. 'It was one final chance to see if you could summon your power.'

'Right.' I fold my arms, cross beyond words.

'There's a real threat on the horizon. One that, honestly, I'd really rather you weren't a part of. Juniper and I are going to visit Glasgow to figure out some stuff in the coming weeks.'

I move nearer. She stands up, moving away from me.

'Why can't I be involved?'

'Believe it or not, I care about you.'

'Bullshit!' I shriek, my fingernails digging so hard into my palms, I might draw blood.

'You are not ready for what is to come.'

'Stop talking in riddles. What is it?'

Nova jingles the ice cube in her glass. Takes another sip. 'The Illvirkjar are, apparently, launching a surveillance mission on us, the werewolves of Scotland.'

'The who?'

Nova says the word again as if she's spitting out poison. 'Illvirkjar.'

'What's so bad about them?'

Nova lets out a small laugh. 'They're a Norse army. You wouldn't want to meet them in your wildest nightmares.'

My mind fleetingly goes through a carousel of all my nightmares. If only she knew how bad they are. 'What has that got to do with me?'

Nova bites her lip. 'Please trust me when I say I am doing this for your own protection.'

I step closer and reach out to her, pulling her into me. She breathes in my scent and my skin tingles with anticipation, but then she pushes me away.

'If they find out about you, they will slay you quicker than you can even open your mouth to shout for help. You need to lie low. Stay away.'

'And us?' I ask bravely.

'There isn't, and there never will be, an us.'

CHAPTER TWENTY-THREE

In Fyodor Dostoevsky's Crime and Punishment (1866), how does Raskolnikov's psychological torment represent the concept of the 'long dark night of the soul'?

The cherry trees that line the Meadows are in early bloom and the sky is a perfect blue. But my mood is as dark as the moodiest rain cloud. I am so wrapped up in my own miserable thoughts that I don't even recognise Killian as he strolls towards me. Stewing deeply in my own pot of misery, I almost bang right into him.

'Brodie?' He looks a little different. His hair is slightly longer, and he has a moustache. I wonder if he's trying to impress a girl.

'You've missed your last couple of tutorials.'

If I wasn't feeling so shitty, I'd be embarrassed right now.

'So?' I shoot back, hating myself for being so insolent, but also not able to help it.

Killian is clearly taken aback by this attitude, but pretends not to be. 'I think it might help your cheating case if you are able to keep everything else on track.'

I look around the park, refusing eye contact. 'Well, maybe I'm not.'

He tuts. Not in an annoyed fashion; in a pitying way. 'What possessed you to copy Autumn's answers? She's a smart girl, but you must have known what to write. It was *Jane Eyre*, for Christ's sake.'

'Some things just aren't meant to be. Maybe coming to uni wasn't such a good idea.'

Killian is genuinely shocked. He takes a deep breath, gathering his thoughts, before pointing a finger in the air to make his argument.

'Remember, I was one of the people on the panel to read your personal statement for your scholarship. You wrote about experiencing a loss at a young age.'

Now he's got my attention. My focus swings back to him, his stupid kind face etched with concern.

'You said that this tragedy had changed you forever, and you couldn't wait to come and study in Edinburgh. To honour that person's memory. Whatever you are doing just now is not that.'

His words cut me like a knife.

'Go fuck yourself,' I spit, then I push past him and stride away, instantly feeling terrible.

Killian was trying to help, but him bringing up Grace has hit a nerve. And I'm already feeling at the end of my rope.

As I walk towards my new place of work, the Palace Hotel, I almost laugh at myself. Why on earth did I ever believe that I could have an ordinary life? Or that Nova would want me? I'm a cheat, a bad friend, a bad werewolf and, if the last few months are anything to go by, a bad student too.

In the hotel kitchen, the air is stifling, what with all the heat lamps and sizzling stoves. The smells of bacon fat, congealed eggs, old avocado and sickly tomato ketchup hang in the air, partnered with the smell coming from my underarms. The unreasonably thick purple shirt that all the waiting staff here are required to wear is made the type of material that immediately makes the wearer perspire like it's going out of fashion. Post-breakfast is my favourite time of the shift. The snooty guests are no longer complaining about their sourdough toast being below a certain temperature, or asking me to fetch them sugar when it's sitting right in front of them. Sundays are the most treacherous. Sprawling bottomless brunches, where women with taut faces and fresh manicures drink their body weight in mimosas and screech across the tables at one another while their fat husbands do a round of golf on the course behind the hotel.

At least today is a Monday. After clearing the breakfast plates, it is my job to take all the used silverware from breakfast service and carry it in a big red plastic box to the little hallway at the back of the kitchen and tip it all into a cutlery cleaner. As it cleans the knives, forks and spoons, it clangs and groans so loudly, I can feel it vibrating through my bones. It's a slow process. I offered to do this task because I get to dissociate while I'm doing it. I can close my eyes, even steal five minutes on a chair, rest my feet, which are throbbing from the thousands of steps I've already covered. In these moments, I can pretend my life has worked out the way I had planned. I can pretend that I sat and passed my exams with flying colours. I can pretend that I didn't muck up my finals on account of being treacherously hungover. I can pretend that I got a really cool writing job to tide me over the summer months while I enjoy living it up in Edinburgh.

My manager, Ross, is a ferret-like man with nicotine-stained teeth and brown hair that he likes to gel back with what I can only assume is some kind of superglue. The way he says my name, like he's licking each letter, gives me the total creeps. The silverware cleaner is so loud that I don't hear Ross approach. He eventually turns the machine off, rudely interrupting my daydream, dragging me back to reality.

'I've been calling your name,' he says, breathing his acrid ashtray coffee breath on me.

I wipe my oily brow with the back of my hand. 'Sorry, I didn't hear you.'

This place and everyone in it sucks. But it was the only job I could find that had an immediate start date, and with this term ending in a month, I need as much money as possible to continue to live in Edinburgh over the summer. At this stage, I don't even know if I'll be returning to uni after the summer, but I do know that I can't go back to Seafall.

'We need you to fold napkins after this,' Ross says. Then he hovers.

'Anything else?'

'A few of us are going for pints after work, if you fancy joining?'

I stare at Ross, unsure I've heard correctly. Is he asking me out?

'You can decide later. No pressure.'

'Oh, OK.'

'I'm a terrible flirt when I'm drunk,' he blurts.

I let out a small laugh, hoping he'll leave me alone so I can wallow in peace. I have had sex with my fair share of weirdos this past year, but even at my lowest ebb I would never go near someone like Ross.

'Maybe,' I say politely. Once he's gone, I get out my phone and scroll indiscriminately through my contacts. I land on G. The first name that pops up is Gary Nightclub. I quickly send him a message asking if he's free later. He replies quicker than I expected. And now my mood has slightly improved, because I have secured an evening plan. And anything will be better than listening to Ross's sexist jokes.

*

I am far more irritated by Gary than I was during our first interaction. It was only September that we had our encounter on his kitchen worktop, rudely derailed by my menses, but it feels like a lifetime ago. Was I really this tolerant to someone talking over me? Did I just not notice it before because I was blinded by the excitement of joining university? I cringe deeply at the old me.

Gary is so annoying that I hurry the date along, rushing our drinks and teasing his foot with mine under the table at the chain pub we've met in until he gets the hint. He seems more than happy to bring me back to his.

To my relief, we go to the bedroom this time, and we land on his bed in unison, kissing each other's faces off. I can't believe I didn't notice before, but Gary isn't a great kisser at all. His tongue is going round and round like it's in a spin cycle in a dryer. His bottom lip is a few centimetres south of what is comfortable, and I can't help but feel repulsed by my chin getting wet from his dribble. It's going to be red-raw at this rate.

I push him off and instead lie him on his back, pulling his jeans off and taking his dick out of his boxers. I wank him off. Quick and mechanical. He comes fast, which is a relief. Now it's my turn. I pull down my pants and let him tease me through my lace underwear. And then he goes to town. And it all comes flooding back. The sluggish tongue movements. The unsexiness of it all. I feel like I'm getting less and less turned on with every move.

'Could you try going . . . this way?' I try my best to position his head further down in lieu of having a big sign with an arrow that says, Here's my clit. But he doesn't take the hint. He's nowhere near. If it's possible, he now feels further away. This is fruitless.

I gently push his head away and he scoffs in annoyance.

'Don't tell me you're on your period again?' he says, his glistening lips giving me the ick.

I yank up my knickers and swiftly swing my legs off the bed.

'I could tell you that. I could say it's my time of the month. To relieve you of any further duties.'

'Eh?' He sits up, perplexed. Watches as I pull on my jeans and jacket, check my hair in the mirror.

'The thing is,' I continue, 'that would be a lie. You're just not very good at giving head.'

CHAPTER TWENTY-FOUR

***Please interrogate how the theme of self-acceptance is explored through the different characters in* The Wonderful Wizard of Oz (1900) by L. Frank Baum.**

This morning, I was feeling so restless and edgy before my cheating panel meeting that I went for an aimless walk, and before I knew it I found myself in the library. Books have always been my saviour, and I've been feeling so rudderless. I gravitated like a ghost to the spot where Nova bit me. I observed my surroundings, paying attention to the little details, the strip lights, the worn brown carpet, the comforting smell of old books. Then I thought long and hard about what might have happened if she hadn't bitten me that night. Would I have continued presenting as an ordinary, happy girl, dying on the inside? I wondered what would have cracked me open instead. Something far worse, maybe. The irony is my own self-hatred has held me back more than any werewolf bite. Maybe Nova's attack wasn't one of the worst things to ever happen to me. Maybe it was the best.

*

At the meeting, it's painfully awkward as we file in one by one. Autumn stood ignoring me in the hallway beforehand, so I'm not surprised that she avoids looking in my direction when she takes her seat at the end of the oval table. She looks great today in a baggy suit, her hair pulled into a big bun on the top of her head. I'm so embarrassed it has come to this. I sit with my back to the window, facing the committee, and Zainab rushes in, spouting an apology. I'm just relieved she's here. Directly opposite me is the chairperson, a woman with a pointy chin and sharp, black, shiny bob. The invigilator who caught me looking at Autumn's paper is beside her. He regards me with a self-righteous and brisk nod, and I stare back at him, unblinking, until he eventually looks down at his lap, brushing an imaginary piece of fluff from his trousers. There is a younger woman with a laptop who is warmer than the other two. She has red lipstick on, and her long, lacquered nails click and clack on the keyboard.

After an agonising minute of silence in which I guess nobody wants to make small talk, Jackie and Killian walk in soberly and sit in the two remaining empty chairs. I busy myself with a drink of water. I steal a subtle glance at Killian, who is presenting as unusually smart in a navy suit. It randomly makes me wonder what he wore to his wedding. A stab of regret shoots through me when I realise how nasty I was to him in the park the other day.

The chairperson clears her throat to begin. 'Hi everyone, now we are all here, let's start. My name is Cassandra, and I am the chair of the disciplinary committee. Julie will be taking notes; this is Ted, the invigilator; Jackie, head of department; and Killian, you are Brodie and Autumn's tutorial leader and—'

'I'm here in support of Brodie,' he says firmly, his hands clasped.

'Very well.' Cassandra sniffs.

I slowly lift my head and thank him silently.

Then I realise the whole panel is staring at me, waiting for me to introduce myself. 'Oh, sorry,' I mumble, clearing my throat to start again. 'I am Brodie Bell, obviously. I am here to defend myself. And I brought my friend Zainab with me, for . . . for . . .'

'For moral support.' Zainab gives the panel a cool nod and, under the table, squeezes my thigh. It's eye-wateringly painful, although welcome all the same.

The room looks expectantly to Autumn, who taps the table haughtily. 'I'm Autumn Ferguson. I am obviously involved. Even though I'd rather not be.'

'Great, let's see how this goes,' I mumble out of the side of my mouth. Zainab gently taps me with her elbow and I fold my arms. 'Let's just get this over with.'

Cassandra raises two thick black eyebrows. 'Alright, does anyone else have anything to say before we begin?' she says in a clipped tone. Someone's stomach rumbles. Nobody dares even smirk.

'Let's dive in, then, so we can be done by lunch. Brodie, you know why you are here today. You were caught cheating during your English literature exam on' – she casts a brief glance at her notes – 'Tuesday, March nineteenth of this year. You were appre-hended by the invigilator, Ted Smart, as you were attempting to copy the answers from your classmate Autumn Ferguson's paper. Now, Autumn, in your initial communication with us, you stated that this attempt at cheating was not a premeditated plan between the two of you. Additionally, your tutor Killian has insisted that both you and Brodie have the capabilities to pass on your own merits.'

'With flying colours,' Killian interrupts.

'Eh, Mr Maloney, we will get to you in a minute, please. Where was I? Ah, yes. Today's panel is not about whether or not you tried to cheat, Brodie, because it is very evident that you did. Today is about deciding whether or not we believe that you deserve to keep your place here at the University of Edinburgh. As you will already know by now, the most severe penalty for cheating is expulsion from both your course and the school.'

I knew that this would be the worst-case scenario, but hearing it out loud makes me feel sick.

'Do you understand?' Cassandra needles.

'Yes, loud and clear,' I reply quietly.

'So we want to know, why does a seemingly high-performing and promising student decide to copy someone else's answers? And how confident can we be that you won't repeat these behaviours?'

I look down at the desk, lost for words. Zainab gives me an encouraging smile. Autumn checks her nails, feigning boredom.

'I think I . . .' I trail off.

Killian offers me a supportive nod. Julie, the note-taker, is typing away, *click-clack click-clack*. Then she pauses.

Zainab speaks up. 'She's had a couple of tough semesters. But she is super smart. She really felt desperate.'

Cassandra folds her arms. 'We would prefer it to come from Brodie herself.'

As much as I am grateful for Zainab's help, Cassandra is right. It needs to come from me.

'I have had a difficult time,' I confirm, fiddling with the top button of my shirt.

I see the blank stares. They need more of an explanation. I have nothing to lose. There is only one thing for it – honesty. I take a deep breath.

'When I was little, I did something. No, something happened to me. To my family. It left me with deep scars. Mental and physical.' I catch Autumn's eyes widening in surprise, but I keep going. 'I've never felt safe, not really. I've certainly never felt good enough. And as time went on, instead of getting stronger, and tougher, I began to feel weaker. More and more worthless. Almost like the world would be a better place if I wasn't here.'

Autumn lets out a short gasp.

'I never dealt with any of it. I internalised, told myself a story. I'm not good enough, everyone hates me. That has played in my head, daily, over and over.'

The *click-clack* of the keyboard has softened. I stop fiddling with my button and look at Killian. He gives me the silent support I need to continue.

'I thought coming to university would help with the internal shit-talk, but it just made everything worse. People who study here tend to be posh, wealthy, from academic backgrounds or a combination of all three. Instead of my feelings of unworthiness dissipating, they crystallised. So, in answer to your question, why did I try to cheat that day? Because I felt worthless. It wasn't pre-planned; Autumn is way too smart to have agreed to that. My mind drew a blank. It's ironic, because I've read *Jane Eyre* three times. I could reel off the answer to that exam question any day of the week. Usually. But I used her. I'm deeply sorry. To you, Autumn. To the university. To Killian, who has been so support-ive. To everyone.'

I look down and a tear drops on to the desk. I wipe it away. I didn't even know that I'd started to cry. I hear a sniff and realise Zainab's started crying beside me. 'Oh, Brodie,' she whispers. I feel a hand on mine and I look up to see Autumn is shiny-eyed, leaning over the table. Killian clasps his hands together and mouths, *Are you OK?*

I nod, gratefully. And I think I am OK. I feel lighter than I have ever felt before.

After the meeting, Zainab, Autumn and I walk to Café Curiosity and order three obnoxiously large slices of chocolate cake and a scoop of homemade vanilla ice cream each. Once we're all settled in our favourite corner, I start to reel off an apology.

'I'm so, so sorry for what I did to you, Autumn.'

She stops me by wrapping me in a sudden and fierce hug. Her perfume smells like she's run through a spring meadow. 'I'm so done being mad at you. It was my idea to go out the night before the exam. I shouldn't have let it unfold like that.'

I hug her back, grateful. And then I feel a second set of arms reach around, and the three of us sit, huddled together like kid's modelling clay.

'I thought you didn't do hugs,' I tease Zainab as we break apart.

'Yeah, well, extenuating circumstances, isn't it?'

Autumn starts to well up.

'Hey, what is it?'

'I'm sad that you felt you couldn't talk to me. That you couldn't tell me what was going on.'

'Hey, it's not a reflection on you. I was getting in my own way.'

'What happened to you?'

And then I tell them everything I can remember about that night. From climbing on the window ledge, to Grace's scream, to her bloodied pyjamas, to the ambulance.

Autumn speaks first. 'It's not your fault, Brodie. You were an innocent little girl.'

Her words carry more meaning than she'll ever know. I don't reply, I just let them wrap around me like a blanket.

After some tears and then a few delicious mouthfuls of chocolate cake, I set down my fork and nudge Zainab. 'There's something else I need to tell you about, Autumn.'

She rolls her eyes so hard, I'm surprised when they come back to focus. 'Oh, cut it out,' she says lightly. 'Like I don't already know.'

My mouth opens in slack surprise. Zainab eyeballs me, warning me not to utter a word about you-know-what.

'What do you know?' I ask with uncertainty.

'The late nights, the looking like shit. You both act like you are being so smooth, but I can spot it a mile off. In fact, I've known this whole time.'

'Y-you have?' I stutter. Zainab drops her fork.

'Yep.' Autumn crosses her arms triumphantly. 'You two have been hooking up.'

I can't help it; I burst into uncontrollable laughter.

Zainab tucks her hair behind her ear. 'As if. She's not my type.'

'If that's not it, then what is it?' Autumn's quizzical gaze flicks between me and Zainab.

Zainab shrugs. 'Brodie, are you sure this is a good idea?' she says through gritted teeth.

'I can't be honest about one thing and not another. Come on, it's Autumn.'

'Now I'm getting freaked out.' Autumn's voice is strained with impatience.

'Fine,' Zainab says to me. 'Autumn, if we tell you something, you must swear on your life that you will never repeat it. Swear it on Winter's life, on the lives of everybody you've ever loved.'

'I swear.'

Zainab looks satisfied with Autumn's earnest reply and nods at me to continue.

'The thing is, Zainab and I are werewolves. Well, I'm a Wolf Walker, which means I'm part-human, but for all intents and purposes, we're werewolves.'

Autumn's expression becomes pensive. She's wondering if we are winding her up, trying to make her the butt of a joke. We wait for a reaction.

'Prove it,' she says finally, her chin sticking out defiantly.

'What do you want us to do, bite you?' Zainab asks.

I grab Autumn's hand and feel her long nails twitching in my palm. 'There have been a lot of lies and dishonesty. But this is real. I promise.'

'This is crazy.'

'You're telling us!'

We tell Autumn everything that she needs to know.

Eventually she says, 'Fine. I believe you. Thanks for opening up to me. It actually makes more sense than you two being an item, to be honest.'

'Oi, I'm a catch,' I protest, feeling the freedom that telling the truth brings washing over me for the second time today.

Now, I have a favour to ask Zainab.

'I need your help. I know that Nova and Juniper are going on a special mission to Glasgow soon.'

Zainab thinks she's already heard enough. She shakes her head. 'No way.'

'All I'm asking is for you to find out where they're going. That's all.'

'Then what?'

'Let me worry about that part.'

'Nova would have my head on a platter if she thinks I'm being any kind of informant.'

'We're on the same side. I'm done tiptoeing around. I'm over being underestimated. I'm going to show her I am enough, with or without your help.'

Zainab isn't used to me sounding so assertive. She deliberates, chewing on a piece of cake. Her tongue darts around the corners of her mouth. 'Fine. But on one condition . . .'

'What?'

'I'm coming with you.'

I am so happy I almost jump out of my seat. I go in for a high-five, which she ignores coolly. Then I notice Autumn's petted lip.

'What's up?'

'This past year, I knew you two were leaving me out. Even when you had your falling-out, you were both protecting one another's secret.'

I cast a guilty look at Zainab.

'Let me help you with your plan tomorrow.'

I pause for thought. Autumn is usually the loudest person in the room – she loves being the centre of attention, and she wears eye-catching clothing. She is not one for a covert mission. But maybe, just maybe, she could be our secret weapon.

CHAPTER TWENTY-FIVE

Explore how King Arthur's quest to fulfil his prophecy
in Le Morte d'Arthur *(1485) by Sir Thomas Malory*
launched the 'Chosen One' trope in literature.

The following morning at dawn, Zainab and I meet around the corner of the car park tucked behind Lothian Road. We wait, crouched behind a parked people carrier, hoods up, in silence, barely talking, barely moving. After a long twenty minutes, we see them emerging from a little bricked alleyway. From afar, they're unrecognisable, but as they come closer, it's unmistakably Nova and Juniper, wearing hats and dark glasses like two celebrities attempting to foil the paparazzi.

Juniper climbs in to the front of a black 4X4 pick-up truck and gets the engine running, and Nova surveys the car park before jumping in to the passenger seat. It's all happening so fast. I gulp and tap Zainab on her shoulder, signalling for her to follow me as I creep nearer to the truck. We don't have much time.

Hunched down, I look around, but I can't see anything or

anyone. Then a morning jogger appears. Zainab and I duck back down until they've gone. When we slowly rise, we hear her before we see her.

'Hellooooo!' Autumn's voice, shriller than usual, rings across the car park. Autumn turns the corner, springing into Nova and Juniper's view, a vision in neon pink and orange, holding a giant boom box on her shoulder, telegraphing unrelenting bassy EDM. I would love to see the looks on Nova and Juniper's faces right now. As the music gets louder, Zainab and I edge our way to the back of their truck.

'Coooooeeeeee!' Autumn shrieks over the music. I fling my hand up to my mouth to stop myself from laughing, as she dances in front of the truck, blocking their way.

Juniper toots the horn angrily.

Autumn calls again, 'Helllooooo!'

As Zainab reaches up and pulls the back door handle as gently and as quietly as possible, I peer around the side, just in time to see Autumn shake a pink feather boa in between her legs. I realise then that she's wearing her wig from her Poison Ivy costume.

'The handle won't open,' Zainab hisses quietly at me. I stand up and try it, once, twice. On the third try, it finally clicks open. Phew. As planned, Zainab climbs into the bay first, and I slink in second, accidentally rolling on to her hand. She bites her other fist to stop from yelping out in pain. There are a few big plastic containers and a pile of velvety blankets. We wedge ourselves between the boxes, keeping our heads low, and bury ourselves under the blankets. If we keep down, they won't see us in the rear-view mirror. We debated over whether they would pick up our scent, but we're hoping that because we're in the bed of the truck, we won't get sniffed out. The tunes helpfully get louder and louder. Over my heart thumping in my chest, I hear Nova's window slide down.

'What the hell do you think you're doing?' Nova shouts at Autumn.

'Maybe it's an immersive theatre piece?' suggests Juniper.

'At six in the fucking morning?!' Nova shoots back.

Over the thumping beat, we hear Autumn shout again, 'Fancy a dance with me, girls?'

'If you don't move out of the way, you'll end up as roadkill,' Juniper shouts out of the window.

Autumn goofs around for another minute, until she's sure we are in the truck, and then she retreats.

'Go back to the Fringe where you belong,' Juniper snarks as she pulls out of the car park and we get on our way. I give a thumbs-up to Zainab and she returns it with an exhilarated smile. Part one of our mission is complete.

As the truck speeds along the motorway, triumph is quickly replaced by dread. What if Nova is so mad that we've snuck into the truck that she becomes violent? I turn my attention to Nova and Juniper to try and get a sense of what to expect on the other side. The only information Zainab could get was that we were headed to a place called Clyde Cove – the HQ of the Glasgow cohort of wolves.

'Rex will try and get you to agree to his strategies. Just remember who is boss,' Juniper says.

'Don't worry about that.' Nova laughs. 'I've brought precautions, just in case.'

I glance at the plastic box that my feet are pushed against. It has a little skull and crossbones sticker with 'DANGER' on it.

A precaution for what, I'm not exactly sure. We pick up pace, and I slump down further as trees and fields fly by in a green smudge.

*

As we pull into Glasgow, Nova asks Juniper where the cloaks are.

'In the back,' Juniper says. Then I realise we're not wrapped in blankets – they're cloaks. I wriggle around, and find myself almost nose to nose with Zainab, who throws me a grumpy look.

'Five hundred years, and they still haven't updated the uniforms,' Nova says wearily.

'That's tradition for you,' Juniper replies, hitting a pothole. Against our will, Zainab and I knock heads.

A loud 'Ow' escapes from me.

Juniper screeches the truck to a halt. I hear a revolver click.

'Who's back there?'

The terror in Zainab's face reflects my own.

'It's us!' I say in a shaky voice.

In a flash, Juniper leaps out of the truck, flings the back door open and grabs me by the scruff of my neck.

'Hey!' I yell as she swings me out and I land on the ground, the breath knocked out of me. Zainab's close behind, and I wince, hearing her hit the concrete with a smack.

I writhe around in pain.

'Juniper! What happened to keeping a low profile?' Nova shouts.

'I can explain!' I plead to Juniper, my hands in the air. Nova appears behind her.

'Everyone, get back in the truck!' Nova's words echo. I hadn't noticed my surroundings yet – I was too busy hoping that I wasn't about to die. We are under a bridge with cars passing above us. It smells of damp and looks exactly like the type of place a young woman should avoid at all costs. Scrambling up, my left knee throbs in pain, and I limp towards the truck as fast as I can. Zainab, who has a bloodied nose, follows me, and we climb into the back seat. We sit with our palms in our laps like naughty schoolchildren. Nova gets back in to the passenger seat and Juniper goes behind the wheel. Both of them twist around to face us.

'What possessed either of you to hatch this plan is beyond me. Idiotic, senseless . . .'

I flinch at every insult, worrying that I am further than ever from proving I mean business to Nova.

'. . . but I kind of love it.' Nova turns around and gives us a wicked smile.

'Eh?' Juniper's expression is priceless.

Nova shrugs at her. 'Nothing wrong with having a couple watchwomen with us, is there?' she says to Juniper, who catches on, her mouth curving into a wide smile, her gold tooth catching the light. 'True.'

'Watchwomen?' I repeat. My bravery is depleting by the minute.

'We need to show the Glasgow clan that we are in charge. So you two can come with us, but you mustn't speak unless spoken to.' Nova hands Zainab a handkerchief, and she tilts her head back and holds it to her nose.

'Juniper, get them a couple of cloaks.'

'Sure thing.' Juniper isn't best pleased, I can tell.

'You OK?,' I whisper to Zainab as we unfold the inky blue cloaks.

'Never better.'

I trace the intricate silver braiding and stitching with my fingers. If I wasn't shitting a brick, I would probably be marvelling at the craftsmanship.

As we walk towards the city centre, Nova warns us to keep our heads down, avoid eye contact and not speak to anyone. 'People are especially talkative around these parts, so don't give them an excuse to converse.' We do as we're told. I keep my eyes on my boots and concentrate on taking one step at a time.

We get to the large bridge connecting the north and south of the city and take some crumbling stairs down to the metal railings below. The River Clyde's water is relatively serene, save for the odd empty plastic bottle bobbing along. Nova scans the area, muttering something to herself, before crouching down beside a small patch of brickwork, where the railing meets the ground. She grabs hold of a little red brick and pulls it out, leaning towards the hole.

'Madadh-allaidh.'

I look quizzically at Juniper, who is keeping watch, casting her view from left to right.

Zainab whispers in my ear, 'It means wolf.'

Then, as if out of nowhere, a small motorboat appears, with a tubby man with greying hair at the helm. The deckhand is a middle-aged stout woman with bleached hair, extending her arms as a welcome. 'All aboard!' she shouts in an abrasive, nasally voice. I watch as Nova and Juniper climb over the railings and hop on to the boat, which sways from side to side under the new weight. Zainab's next. She jumps on quickly, tripping into Nova's arms. I can't help but feel a stab of jealousy.

The water looks dark and scary. 'I can't!' I shout, terrified of falling.

'You have to!' Nova yells back, pulling her hood down.

'Stop wasting time, Brodie!' Juniper snaps. The deckhand opens her arms for me to jump towards her. And so I jump, landing with an ungraceful thud, rocking the boat from side to side.

The skipper does a one-eighty, and the force of the boat makes my knees buckle, throwing me into Nova's lap. She grabs me, pulls me close and holds me as we pick up pace, slicing through the water as we head west.

'The Glasgow werewolves also live in an underground system,

but it's linked to the abandoned train lines,' Nova tells us as the boat enters a pitch-black tunnel. The air is warm and wet, and the dripping water plays like a piece of classical music turned down low. Nova must sense my anxiety, because she reaches out and gives my hand a comforting squeeze under the folds of my cloak.

After about ten minutes, I clock a glimmer of light. As the boat purrs nearer to it, I realise it's a static fire torch, its amber flames lighting up a wooden doorway. The skipper pulls the boat in, just by a small set of steps, the water lapping at the lower ones. The deckhand jumps off the boat first and ties the rope to a metal stub. Nova steps off next, refusing the deckhand's arm. Juniper gestures for me to go, and I leap into Nova's arms. We are face to face for a few blissful seconds, then she turns around and faces the door. Zainab climbs out after me and throws me an accusatory look.

'What?' I say innocently.

The metal door knocker is shaped like a wolf howling at the moon. Nova raps it three times.

The door swings open immediately and the welcoming amber light draws us in. An elegant, muscular man in his fifties stands in the doorway. He's well-groomed, with raven-black shiny hair down to his shoulders, taut tawny skin and a hooked nose. He moves with purpose and grace, gesturing eloquently with hands covered in chunky gold jewellery. His smile shows white teeth, and betrays an undercurrent of resentment.

'Welcome,' he says, bowing to Nova.

'Rex.' Nova greets him with a hint of reservation in her voice.

Beside Rex stands an extremely tall Amazonian goddess who looks like she's both stepped out of a lingerie campaign and could kill me with her bare hands.

'Gigi,' Juniper says, shaking her hand.

'Great to see you all. Come in.' Gigi takes our cloaks from us and hangs them up.

'These are our lookouts,' Nova adds, as Zainab and I try to puff up our chests and look as hard as we can.

'Get into a tussle on the way here, did we?' Rex gestures to Zainab's bloody nose.

'Nothing the girls couldn't handle. They could both kill a man with their bare hands,' Nova boasts.

I stifle the urge to break character and laugh.

'Let's hope it doesn't come to that,' Rex retorts. 'We may not be funded as generously as the Edinburgh factions or live under a castle, but we still take pride in our base,' he says, guiding us through the main hall.

Nova and Juniper share an eye roll at his thinly veiled dig. The interior of Clyde Cove is pokier than the Den. It's more rough and ready, with makeshift tables and light fixtures, like an old junkshop showroom. We reach a large meeting room, which has a huge shiny wooden table in the centre. Sitting around it is a mixture of people chatting amongst themselves. Like to the Edinburgh cohort, they are all very fit and athletic. And some of them look a lot scarier.

'Wait for us at the end of that corridor, please,' Nova orders me and Zainab as she and Juniper step in. Everyone gets to their feet when they see Nova. Some whistle, some bow.

'Why?' I demand.

'Keep a lookout,' she replies over her shoulder, and closes the door.

Once the door is shut, Zainab and I stroll down the corridor.

'What's the deal with you and Nova?' Zainab pries, checking nobody is around to listen in.

'Nothing,' I lie.

'So the honest new you is only honest about some stuff, I see.'

'What? No,' I try to protest, but my voice is a few octaves higher than usual, and my neck and cheeks are flaming hot. I've been busted. I lean against the wall and look up at the row of exposed bulbs strung above us.

'We've kissed,' I eventually admit, unable to hide my smile.

Zainab's eyes practically pop out of her head. 'Nova?!' she asks, her expression wild with wonder.

'More than once.'

'I thought maybe you had a little crush or something. Never, ever did I think . . .' She's lost for words. It's a rarity.

I fold my arms. 'What, you didn't think a woman like her would go for someone like me? Be careful, Zainab, because it sounds like you're about to insult me.'

'Well, no offence, but yeah. She's one of the most powerful werewolves in the country. Wait a second. Is this whole charade just to get you closer to her? Roping in me and Autumn, after everything that's happened?'

'No, no. I genuinely want to prove myself to her. She keeps telling me to go away.'

'Why?'

'Because she's worried that I'm not strong enough. And also she's afraid she might attack me again.'

Zainab's about to ask another question, but we're interrupted by a loud swell of shouting from the meeting room. I quickly creep towards the door and peer through a small panel of glass, where I see Rex trying to control the room. The attendees seem riled up about something.

'Silence!' Rex's voice cuts through the excited chatter. 'We are delighted to welcome Nova and Juniper from the HQ in Edinburgh.'

Nova remains steely as the group bursts into a round of applause. 'It is a shame I am not here under more positive circumstances. But I have it on good authority that the Illvirkjar are coming back.'

There is a collective intake of shocked breath. Zainab and I share a terrified look.

An alarmed statement pierces the air, seeming to carry the shared sentiment of the room. 'So much for a bloody ceasefire!'

Nova remains calm. 'Now, before we start panicking, we must remember that we suspected this day might come. Rex and I have been planning for the worst-case scenario. And, unfortunately, it looms.'

'What does all of this mean?' I whisper to Zainab.

'War.'

I flinch at her reply.

Then, another voice from the group: 'I heard that you have found the Chosen One.'

A different person shouts out. 'The rumour is he's a young student at the University of Edinburgh. Is it true?'

'If he is, then we must protect him at all costs. He is the key to the survival of the Were species,' another person trills.

'We are protecting the Chosen One, don't worry about that. And she is a she,' Nova adds.

There's another ripple of chatter. Juniper catches my eye through the glass, and rushes to the door. Suddenly the window is covered and the sounds of talking are muffled. Even with my ear pressed against the glass, I can't distinguish what words are being said. But that doesn't matter, because I've heard the only two words that I need to. Chosen and One. I turn to Zainab. Her surprised expression tells me that this is news to her too.

Something clicks into place. Like I have been trying to view my life through shades and I have finally taken them off. I am not the odd one out because I am bad. I am just different. 'They mean me. Don't they?'

Despite the news of the ceasefire being broken, Rex insists on continuing the banquet that he had planned for our visit. He wants to show the Edinburgh clan some good old Glaswegian hospitality. After the meeting, about fifty of us take our seats around a long wooden table in Clyde Cove's mess hall. Candles flicker and people cross-talk nervously as they tuck into the spread of roast chicken, hearty vegetables and wine. I can't eat a thing. Zainab and I are on either side of Nova and Juniper so I've not even had a chance to talk to her properly. But it's Nova who has the answers. Aware that we're being watched, I lift up a bread basket and offer it to Nova. 'Roll?'

She shakes her head.

'I'm the Chosen One, aren't I?'

Nova bristles, wary that there are dozens of eyes on us. 'Not here, please.'

'Then where?'

'I didn't know it was really you.' Nova manages to speak while barely moving her mouth.

'What do you mean?'

'I was told you existed, by a prophet. You were marked as an ordinary university student, capable of extraordinary things. But I didn't believe it. I needed to see you with my own eyes. Make my own judgement.'

Rex interrupts by passing down a silver gravy boat along the table. 'Nova, have you tried the gravy? It is to die for.'

Nova accepts the jug politely. 'Can't wait.'

'And then?' I demand, taking the jug next and pouring it over my food.

'When I went to suss you out, I bit you. And then I wasn't sure if it was you at all. You just seemed so . . .'

'Weak?'

'Normal.' We catch one another's eyes. Time stands still as we stare at each other.

'Is it weird that I have the overwhelming urge to kiss you right now?' I say.

I see a flicker of fire in her face before she turns cold again. 'Don't be so silly.'

'When were you going to tell me I was the Chosen One? What does the Chosen One even mean?'

'The prophet told us you would come to us . . .'

'And?'

'A toast!' Rex gets to his feet, holding up a goblet of wine. 'To our dear friends from the capital.'

Nova lifts her glass, relieved to get out of my line of questioning. The room vibrates with a loud 'Cheers!' although the news about the Illvirkjar hangs in the air like a bad smell.

Rex is about to take his seat when Gigi runs in, a look of panic across her face. 'Rex!' She rushes up to him and whispers something in his ear. His expression turns grave. He lowers his wine to the table.

'We just got word that the Illvirkjar have indeed launched a surveillance mission. It is likely they are going to look for Nova first. Everyone, Operation Silver Claw has now begun.' A loud siren pierces the air, and everyone gets up from the table and scatters with purpose.

Nova pulls me, Juniper and Zainab in to a huddle. 'Listen to me. Rex is right; they are going to go after you too, Brodie. The main priority is keeping you out of harm's way. I suggest that we all leave for Edinburgh immediately and go into hiding there.'

'What if they beat us to it?' Juniper asks.

We wait, our minds whirring. Nova stomps her foot as an idea forms. 'We have a safe house up north.'

'What about Zainab?' I ask, having to speak extra loud over the wailing sirens.

'Juniper will stay here with Zainab as a decoy then.'

'No, we have to stick together!' I protest.

'Nova's right, Brodie. We need to separate. We all need to protect you,' Zainab says.

An uncomfortable feeling surges through me. 'I'm not leaving you.'

Nova grabs me by the back of my head like a boxing coach. 'This is bigger than what you want.'

I let out a big exhale and reluctantly nod in agreement. I give Zainab a tight, quick hug. 'I love you,' I whisper in her ear, fighting back tears.

'I love you too.'

CHAPTER TWENTY-SIX

In **The Adventures of Huckleberry Finn** *(1884) by Mark Twain, Huck Finn and Jim go on the run to escape their respective troubles. How does Twain use their journey to explore themes of liberation and identity?*

After a tense, four-hour-long journey, during which I hear Nova give orders via her pendant and otherwise stare determinedly at the road, one hand on the wheel and the other looped through a handle above the window, we turn off the main road. The truck bounces as we navigate the uneven and winding country track, driving us towards a horizon of purple. It looks like a child has taken a giant crayon and scribbled all over the fields. Nearing closer, I see thousands of bluebells twitching in the warm wind.

Eventually, we reach a little wire fence. Nova encourages me to unclick my seatbelt. 'Get out, I'll join you in a second.'

I do as she says and climb out of the truck, stretching my arms and cracking my back. My knee still hurts from being flung on the ground earlier.

Then she revs the engine and drives under a little bridge. She's abandoning me! Leaving me to fend for myself.

'Hey!' I yell. But she's gone.

I stand in stunned silence, welling up. I don't even know where I am.

Then, after a few torturous minutes, Nova reappears, striding towards me with a large bag on her shoulders.

'Had to hide the truck.'

'Where is the safe house?' I ask, flooded with relief. Nova points up a steep hill.

We climb over a wooden stile in silence, and then tackle the hill. Nova is always a few steps ahead of me. It would, on any other day, be quite a pleasant hike. But I am swarmed with uncertainty. What does being the Chosen One entail? Will I be wheeled out like a sacrificial lamb? Will Zainab be safe at Clyde Cove? If she dies, I don't even want to think about what I would do.

We reach a forest, sprawling with mighty oak trees, with trunks so thick I'd need ten of me to wrap my arms around them. The air is a lot cooler here, and we walk in the dappled shade to a quaint, moss-covered wooden cabin in the depths of the woods. The leafy green trees surrounding the cabin are so tall and wide-spread that we are in complete shade, save for a few tiny spots of sunlight that have crept through. The cabin has a large porch area, complete with a huge stack of chopped wood. Nova yanks the axe that juts out of a tree stump and hands it to me before taking a rusty key from her boot and unlocking the door.

Inside, it's dark and musty. The walls are varnished wood and the ceilings are made of chunky wooden beams. It's giving bargain après-ski vibes. We yank big dust sheets from the vintage furniture. In the heart of the kitchen-living room is a small fireplace, a low table covered by a retro flowery tablecloth, an old couch and an armchair. It's cosy and twee. I inspect the kitchen area, with a tiny gas stove and ancient sink. I pull aside a chequered cloth to reveal dozens of tinned provisions. At least we won't starve out here. In the bedroom, I notice there are twin beds – so, no spooning tonight, I guess. I nosy in the big wooden closet and find folded bedding.

Back in the kitchen, I find Nova rooting around under the sink, fetching a large packet of matches. She lights a series of candles that are dispersed around the room. Then I notice the cabin has a back door.

'You won't believe what's out there,' Nova says, noticing my interest is piqued.

'Is it south-facing?' I joke. There's a little metal key sticking out of the keyhole already so I turn it clockwise, and as the door swings open, I let out a gasp. A large wooden mezzanine stretches out, following the edge of the back of the house. It would be perfectly normal if it weren't for the fact that the decking juts out above a deep, rocky valley. So deep, that when I glance over the wooden railing, I can't see the bottom. It taunts me with its vastness. I am suddenly confronted by the image of me and Grace falling; it hits me like a slap in the face. Maybe I would always have hated heights, or maybe it was the accident. But even when I've scuttled back indoors, my feet tingle in fear of that drop. And Grace's little round face, contorted in horror, hangs around for way longer than I want.

I slink beside the fire, which is now crackling, as Nova wipes the thick layers of dust from an ancient-looking radio. She regards me with a playful grin. 'Didn't fancy sitting out the back?'

'Heights aren't really my thing. I didn't realise we were at the edge of a cliff. Is it safe?'

'Sure. That decking is as sturdy as can be. The valley has been around since the Ice Age – pretty cool, huh?'

I'm not really in the mood for a history lesson. I go queasy just thinking about the bottomless cavity, and steady myself by leaning on the wall. 'How high is that drop?'

'High.' Nova twists the knob of the radio until an old country song crackles out. She goes over to a small drinks trolley and pours herself a generous whisky from a crystal decanter. 'Want one?' She notices my hesitancy. 'We're safe here, so we can relax. For now.'

'Why not?' I sit on the armchair and watch as the fire gains momentum, cracking and popping.

Nova takes a seat on the couch and visibly relaxes.

'My mum loves country music,' I say, swirling the ochre liquid in my glass before tipping it to the back of my throat.

'Three chords and the truth.'

As the heat spreads around my belly, I feel brazen enough to ask the question that has been running through my mind since Clyde Cove.

'When were you planning on telling me I was the Chosen One?'

Nova takes a steady sip from her glass. After a few moments, she sits up. 'For years, werewolves have existed in more or less harmony. The odd human life is a small sacrifice for us to survive. We don't answer to anyone. But we have a long-standing relationship with the Sìthiche Tribe.'

'The who?'

'Sìthiche Tribe. Fairy people. They inhabit the forests in the Highlands. They mainly keep themselves to themselves, but their leader Florence is something of an oracle. A prophet.'

My mind is still trying to process the idea of fairies being real, but I'm desperate to know more. 'She sees the future?'

'More or less. And she can also tell us things about the past. It was she who warned us that the Illvirkjar would be coming after us again. The brutalist Norse army that wants our heads on a plate.'

'What has that got to do with me?' I press.

'Florence predicted that they would rise again and try to obliterate the werewolf race. But one person would end up being our saviour. Not just any person. A young woman from humble beginnings, with special powers.'

'What are they, then? Because last time I checked, balancing a spoon on your nose isn't enough to save lives. If anything, I have caused more destruction in my life than not.'

'There's a lot about yourself that you have yet to discover.'

The dots from the previous months start to connect. 'Did you use me, then? Bite me deliberately so I could join you?'

Nova places her glass on the table. 'No, no. I promise. I had been told about you and wanted to meet you that night. And when I got near you, something strange happened. I couldn't control myself, and I attacked you. That's the truth.'

'This isn't adding up! I only became a Wolf Walker after the bite – before then, I was a human.'

'Not according to Florence. Your destiny has been marked from the start.'

This is bullshit. 'No!' I get to my feet, livid. 'Look at me, you said so yourself: I am not fit to join you.'

'Honestly, I wasn't sure you were either. I've had my doubts, believe me. And I wanted to be sure that it was you before I let you come fully into the fold.' She stares ahead, trying to find the words.

'So, let me get this straight. All this time you have known, or at least suspected, that I am somebody special – and now you have convinced yourself that I am. What now? Give me a gun and send me out to war?'

'War is not here yet.'

'Yet?' I shriek. 'I need some air.'

'Get back here,' she commands.

Ignoring her, I reach for the front door handle, but in a flash Nova has apprehended me, blocking my way.

'Stay. If they find you, I don't know what they'll do to you.'

I push her off me and reluctantly return to my chair. I take a final swig of my whisky, and then I pounce on her, using all my force. She flies on to the dusty rug, but pulls me with her, so I'm straddling her again. I am so angry I want to put my hands around her neck and squeeze the life out of her. But the fury shapeshifts into another simmering feeling before I can do anything about it. Like they have minds of their own, our mouths find each other. This time, I push myself closer to her body, which feels toned and strong as she takes me in her arms. Pushing my curls out of the way, she kisses and licks my neck until I'm so dripping wet, I can feel my soaking underwear sliding in between my legs. When Nova's mouth finds mine again, I wonder if it's possible to orgasm from kissing alone, because I feel dangerously close. Every kiss and touch from her sends waves of pleasure crashing all over my body. I feel like I'm mercury, dripping everywhere. A volcano of lust, with burning hot lava spilling out of me.

Nova shoves me off her, then grabs me, pushing me on to the couch on all fours. She yanks off my cargo pants, and my hands sink into the old cushions, leaving finger marks in their wake.

And when I feel her teeth close to the side of my underwear, a surge of excitement cascades through me. She drags off my panties with her mouth and rolls them into a tiny wet ball before shoving them into my mouth. I think I might explode. I am shaking so much; I am not in control, and I don't care. I hear a zip being pulled down and I turn to see she has undressed now, her body taut and pale, and covered in tattoos and scars.

'Turn back around,' she barks, and I do as she says. I focus on my fingers, now digging so hard into the couch I might tear the fabric. I can taste myself from my underwear, and feel a dribble of saliva travel down my chin and neck. Tilting my head down, I see a pool of my own juices forming on the cushion between my knees, and wonder if anyone has ever been this turned on. It can't be possible. And then I feel her beautifully round breasts push against my back as she leans over me, her lean body wrapping around me and her fingers exploring my vulva. Even though it's the first time they have been down there, they seem to know their way around. I can't even picture how she is moving them; all I know is it feels incredible. Euphoric. Nova wraps her free arm around me, and our skin slides together, my peachy bum rubbing against her juicy clit. I'm shaking so much now it's like I've been electrocuted. The sensation of her fingering me pushes me quickly over the edge, and then I feel her coming with me, hard and strong behind me. After the waves turn into ripples, I spit out my underwear, and it sits, curled up in a sodden black ball. I am glistening with sweat and cum as I turn on to my back. I want Nova to hold me now, to take me in her arms and kiss me. Not like before – tenderly and sweetly. But just as I pull her towards me, there's a noise from outside. The snap of a twig. As if someone or something has stepped on it.

'Get dressed,' Nova orders, yanking on her clothes, and I hurriedly follow suit.

Behind the netted curtains, all the windows are blacked out, so we can't see who or what is out there.

Nova flings open a tall wooden cabinet in the corner of the room. It's lined with an array of dangerous weapons: nun-chucks, a bow and arrow and various guns, including a large hunting rifle, which she grabs and loads.

'Grab the axe,' she says. I pick it up with two hands, like a golf club, gripping the curved, smooth wooden handle and letting the metal head swing.

'Stand behind the door, and if someone runs in, swing it down on their head.'

'I can't do that.' I start to shake again, but this time in fear.

Nova puts a hand behind my neck and pulls me close, giving me a short, hot kiss.

We hear another twig snap; this time, it sounds nearer to the cabin. Someone is definitely outside. Fear curls around me.

'Is it them?' I whisper. Nova puts a finger to my mouth to silence me as she twists the radio dial to off. The absence of the fuzzy music heightens the tension. Nova cocks the rifle expertly, and I flinch as the metal shell falls to the wooden floor and rolls across the room. She creeps towards the door with the skill of someone who has done this many times before. I stand behind the door and lift the heavy axe over my head, feeling my triceps ache under the weight. I grimace at the thought of having to crash this down on someone, but it's time I stood up for myself. If these bastards are going to be merciless to me, then I'll be merciless to them. I try to summon bravery, but I am terrified. Suddenly, I think about my parents, and the unbearable idea of them losing a second daughter. I grip the handle of the axe tighter. I cannot let that happen, no way in hell.

There's another rustle and a snap, and then somebody raps on the door. Nova and I share a confused look. Are soldiers of the opposition really this polite?

Nova quickly swings open the door, her finger suspended over the trigger of the gun, which points out into the dusky evening.

'It's me!' a woman's voice says.

I slowly peer through the crack of the door's hinges to see Phoenix with her arms outstretched. She's covered in mud and cuts.

'I can see that.' Nova spits the words out, keeping the gun where it is.

'Will you lower that thing, please?' Phoenix sounds exasperated.

'Who says it's safe to?' Nova says through gritted teeth, the gun still poised facing out, right towards Phoenix's stomach.

'Come on, put the gun down. I don't fight dirty.'

'We both know that's not true,' Nova says, not moving an inch. 'Is she in there?'

'Who?'

'Marilyn fucking Monroe. Who do you think – Brodie Bell!'

'No. Now if you don't mind, I'm trying to have some alone time, so you can piss back off to the horse stable.'

The dust in the cabin has brought on my allergies. I feel a sneeze forming, tickling the inside of my nose, and I try hard to hold it in, pulling my face into a grimace.

'Did you learn all your manners at charm school, or do they come naturally?'

Shit, I can't help it, try as I might – I'm going to sneeze. 'Aaaaachoooo!'

Nova jumps in fright at the noise and the gun fires. The sound is beyond deafening. It rings in my ears, all the way into my skull, reverberating around. I push my palms against my head and crouch down, squeezing my eyes shut until it subsides. A puff of dust and smoke fills the doorway. Nova drops the gun angrily.

'Fuck!' she shouts.

'Did you kill her?' I eventually ask, too terrified to look out, imagining Phoenix's body, blown to bits across the forest.

'No, she didn't; terrible aim.' Phoenix invites herself in and slams the door behind her.

'Maybe I was trying *not* to shoot you.' Nova's anger seethes to the surface as Phoenix steps over the gun and regards me, still crouched on the floor, my hands covering my ears.

'Bless you.'

I stand up and wipe my nose, dropping the axe to the floor.

'What is it with you and inflicting blunt trauma to my head?' Phoenix chides. She and Nova begin to size one another up.

I've already witnessed what a fight looks like between them, and I'm in no hurry to see it again. Especially not in such a confined space.

'What are you doing here? And, more to the point, how did you find us?' Nova demands.

'I am here to make sure nothing happens to her.' Phoenix points a finger at me. 'Aren't you going to offer me a cup of tea?' She strolls towards the couch, observing with a wry smile our post-coital scene, with the cushions all messed up. 'Looks like I interrupted a little party.' She sticks out her bottom lip, feigning a huff. 'Why wasn't I invited?'

'We don't have tea, but I can offer you something stronger.' Nova gestures to the whisky bottle.

I grab my soggy underwear and shove it into my pocket.

'Why the hell not?' Phoenix chirps.

'Make yourself at home.' Nova's jaw is clenched in annoyance as she prepares a drink for Phoenix, who sits on the couch like she owns the place. She wriggles around, reaching behind her back and pulling out my grey and tired bra. I go beetroot and look at my feet.

'Woah, maybe it was a big party.'

Nova ignores her and passes her a whisky, sitting in the chair opposite. I hover around, not sure where I am meant to be.

'Brodie, join us!' Phoenix pats the empty space beside her. I shuffle over and sit down, barely able to look Nova in the eye.

'The Illvirkjar have launched a surveillance mission,' Nova says in a clipped tone.

'Duh, why do you think I'm here?'

'Until you arrived, this was one of our best hiding spots.'

'Sorry, but you'll need to try harder next time. Are you sure this was the best place to hide, or did you just want somewhere cute and cosy so you two could cuddle up?'

'Don't be absurd,' Nova shoots back.

Phoenix spreads her legs, enjoying making Nova uncomfortable. 'What are we to do?'

'We've cleared the underground tunnels and the Den back at HQ. We can't go back there. Or to the Faol People. They'll be on to you next, if they aren't already.'

Phoenix sighs, as if bored by Nova. I feel almost embarrassed for her, that she has someone treating her like this. Phoenix takes a little smoking tin from her waistcoat and goes to light a cigarette on a nearby candle.

'No – outside, please.' Nova stops her.

'You know what, Nova, you really should learn to live a little. It's not healthy being this uptight.'

'You want to speak to me about health when you're huffing on one of those things?'

'Have you got one for me?' I ask, surprising both Nova and myself.

'Sure do, pretty gal.'

'Let's go out the front.'

'I'll shoot you if you take her,' Nova reminds Phoenix brightly as we stand up.

I look between them, finally understanding what it might be like to be a child of divorce. 'Listen, I'm not a kid. Or a toy. I can speak for myself.'

Phoenix claps me on the back, impressed.

When we step around the side of the cabin, the night is drawing in. Phoenix lights a cigarette, passes it to me, then lights a second one, shaking the match then casting it behind her. The filter is slightly wet from her lips, but I don't mind. In the pale evening light, I get a better look at her features. The day she kidnapped me, I was in too much shock to really take in what she looked like, but standing here, I can see she's really quite beautiful.

'Don't let her push you around,' Phoenix warns.

'I don't,' I say defensively.

'If you say so.'

A few moments of silence go by. This cigarette tastes absolutely horrible, so I just hold it by my hip, hoping she won't realise that I'm not smoking it.

'Are you really here to protect me?' I ask her.

She blows some hoops in the air expertly. Like a cool girl in the year above who I could never quite reach. 'I am.' She faces me, her shiny green-brown eyes catching the glow from the end of her cigarette. 'Trust me,' she adds. And for some reason, I do.

When we re-enter the cabin, Nova is busying herself counting the cans of food. The radio is back on, playing an upbeat tune. But the atmosphere is far from that. Nova addresses us sternly. 'With three of us here now, our provisions won't go as far. But we can always hunt rabbits and such at night. We have enough to get us by for two weeks. Two of us will sleep in the bedroom while the other one keeps watch. We'll take it in turns.' Her brisk, matter-of-fact tone is jarring to hear so soon after we fucked.

Phoenix kicks off her cowboy boots. 'Fine by me. Have you lit a barbecue out back?'

'Why would I—' Nova stops herself and takes a big, deep sniff, her nostrils flaring. And then I can smell it too. Something's burning. It's then I see the cabin is filled with a thin but undeniable smoky haze. Nova peels back the covers on the windows to look out to the back decking, her face glowing orange with the reflection from outside. 'Oh, shit!'

For the first time tonight, even Phoenix looks shaken.

The fire spreads fast and furiously around the exterior of the cabin, thanks to the abundance of wood. Judging by how smoky it's getting in here, it won't be long before it gets to us. I grab some dust sheets, and we wrap ourselves up in them and duck down.

'We're trapped!' I yell, helplessly.

'We'll run out the front together – even if you see fire, you run through it. Keep your head down. Do you hear me?' Nova shouts. I nod, whimpering as the growing heat surrounds us. 'Go on three,' she adds. But just as we approach the front door, we hear an almighty crash as the porch collapses in on itself and completely blocks the doorway.

'Shit. Follow me.' Nova opens the back door to expose the decking, which is in flames, juxtaposed against the moody sky. Nova dives out first, expecting us to follow.

I want to follow her, but I can't. I freeze. I picture myself as a little girl, falling through the air, tumbling, with Grace beside me, screaming silently. I can't do it. I can't go out there.

'Let's try the front again?' I say to Phoenix.

'It's completely blocked.'

I swallow my fear. We wrap our dust sheets around us and run through the flames, out the backdoor and on to the decking.

I look around frantically, trying to find Nova, my heart pounding and sinking at the same time. Where is she? And just as I start to believe the unimaginable, that she has fallen off one of the incinerating sides in to the valley below, I see her. She's trapped at the far edge of the platform. A blazing beam from the cabin separating us and her.

'Brodie!' she yells in a tone of voice I've never heard from her. Vulnerable. Scared.

Phoenix yells out, 'Watch out!' Another huge wooden beam swings out from the smouldering cabin roof. I dive out of the way and it crashes into the decking and whacks Nova, pushing her to the ground, unconscious. When I glance down, all I see is the blackness of craggy rocks. If I fell, they would swallow me up. Or worse, skin me alive on the way down. The handrail designed to safely separate us and the drop has caught fire, threatening to burn away any minute now. I look behind me and panic as I see the door back into the cabin is now completely blocked. But I need to save Nova.

Phoenix grabs me by the elbow. 'No!'

I struggle, trying to wrestle free from her grip, but it's no use.

The heat and the flames are drawing nearer. Yet the real heat comes from Phoenix's stare.

'I can't let you go again!'

'Why not?' I scream over the roaring flames.

'Because I'm your sister!'

All of a sudden, the air escapes from my lungs. Phoenix's words have sucker-punched me, right in the solar plexus. How could anyone be so cruel as to make up a stupid lie like that?

'No!' I scream back in her face, anger boiling as hot as the fire that closes in around us.

She pulls my arm, bringing me close, and for a split second I wonder if she is leaning in for a kiss. But she pushes her nose against mine. *Nosey, nosey*.

'It's me – Grace.'

CHAPTER TWENTY-SEVEN

Explore how Jim Hawkins takes a leap of faith in
Treasure Island by Robert Louis Stevenson (1883).

gape at her like a goldfish.

'But I remember the blood; I remember you dying.'

'That was your blood, Brodie. It got all over me, but it was yours.'

The words ignite a firework inside me – I don't know what or how to feel, but I know deep in my soul that she's telling the truth.

'We can talk later!' I shout, and she releases my arm.

You can do this. You can do this. Just don't look down.

'It's too late!' Phoenix shouts.

'If she dies, I die!'

Phoenix tries to reply, but I have already started to make my way carefully towards Nova. I hear the creaking and straining of burning wood below my feet.

I try to climb to her, but I can't. The flames are licking higher and higher. Impossible to see her now, although the image of her lying there, unconscious and minutes from death, was unbearable. I start to yell and cry like a wounded animal. I get on my hands and knees, screaming and crying, and then I howl. A low, guttural, animalistic howl. I start to feel my body pulse and yield. My muscles expand and contract as my spine arches, and I buckle down until I'm on all fours. I burst back up, standing on strong back legs. My hands have grown to five times their size, human-adjacent but with hair, and sharp, chrome-coloured nails poking from each fingertip. A layer of brown fur covers my entire body, and between my hind legs, there's a small tail. I breathe and see that I have a long, thick snout. I wrinkle my leathery nose. I bare my teeth and feel knife-sharp fangs and a weighty tongue.

I need to save Nova. Now. Trying to pretend that I am not about to fall to my death, I swallow my fear and edge nearer to her. Then my left paw goes straight through a weak slat of wood, which splinters and cuts into my skin at the ankle. I yelp in pain, trying to wriggle it free, but it feels stuck, with some of the wood lodged in my flesh.

You can do this, Brodie! Come on!

I won't let it end like this. I twist and yank my leg up and out of the hole, deep-red blood dripping out of it. *Don't look down. Don't look down.* But then I do. I glance down through the hole into the deep abyss of the valley. It's hypnotising and deadly in all its mystery and darkness. Fuck it. I leap across the wall of fire, not knowing if there is a ground to catch me on the other side. As I fly into the flames, my fur singes.

Dozens of images flash before my eyes like a slideshow. Me and Grace eating candy floss at Thistle Bay. Dad in his Speedos and the pink blow-up whale. Mum twirling in the kitchen, singing Dolly Parton out of time. Mum sobbing in bed. My swimming competition at school, where Kirsty Bigwood cheated by kicking me out of the way. The sting of my bumblebee tattoo, administered by a guy with a tongue piercing. Unpacking my books at Bucky Place, wondering briefly if I should put them in alphabetical order, then deciding I'm not that type of person. Meeting Nova and looking into her one green eye and one blue, and realising how much more of the juice of life's fruits I had yet to taste.

I land on all fours, beside where Nova lies. She is crumpled up like an old pile of laundry, and is bleeding from her temple. When I reach her, I nudge her with my snout; her body falls limply back in to place. I carefully take her jacket in between my jaws and hoist her up so she's hanging from my mouth, like she's my cub. To our right, the balcony itself is beginning to crumble, with pieces of wood dropping down into the valley, like little orange glow sticks.

Just then the mezzanine creaks and groans, and a lightning-shaped split forms, all the way down the middle, with one side threatening to snap off and succumb to the valley. The railing has completely caught ablaze now, surrounding us with a deadly ring of fire. The deck snaps in two, with the other end falling to its demise. It makes the hole my leg fell through look like a walk in the park in comparison. I scramble backwards, taking Nova with me, but the wooden panels have tipped, causing me to slide. The sheer drop below us is almost begging to swallow us both up. I gain purchase with my hind legs and, gripping Nova as tightly as possible with my jaws, I jump through the air. Surrounded by fire and ash and smoke, we fly together and, after a few seconds, land on the moist bark of the forest floor. Behind us, I hear a series of deafening cracks as the cottage collapses in on itself.

I find Phoenix there, smeared in charcoal from the smoke. 'Let's go,' she says, and she transforms into a werewolf, her clothes ripping and her brown fur glowing.

And so we pad quickly through the forest, balancing Nova between us, twigs snapping under my paws, until we reach a series of small waterfalls leading to a glistening pond. I place Nova on the bank and slide into the pool of water, hearing my fur hiss and singe, steam billowing from me like I'm a hot pot.

Phoenix paces the water's edge, panting and snarling. I jump back out of the water and turn back into myself, feeling my muscles contract and adjust back to my small naked human body. I feel like a lobster without its shell. Drained and squishy. I put my bony, wet arms around Nova's lifeless body and sob.

'She's not breathing,' I cry. I stand up and point an accusatory finger at Phoenix, who is now back in her human form, her unclothed body standing under a tree. 'You!' I snarl.

Phoenix doesn't move.

'This is all your fault. Coming here, uninvited. We would have been fine, just us. It was meant to be just us. And then you came here with your stupid plan and your stupid cigarette that probably started this whole fire. You stupid bitch!' The vitriol flies out, venomous and untethered. Emotion and worry finally exploding.

'Hey,' Phoenix offers weakly.

I cup the back of Nova's head and sob and sob and sob.

And then I hear a deep rattling, a large intake of breath and a hacking cough. Nova rolls on to her side and coughs and splutters, her eyes red and wide in shock as she rejoins the conscious.

After letting Nova rest briefly, we find a cave behind a waterfall to shelter in. Exhausted is an understatement. The cave is tall enough to stand up in, with dimpled walls full of holes. It's not exactly the Ritz, but it gives us relative shelter from the weather. A few times in the night, I wake up with a start, my mind reeling about Phoenix, or should I say Grace? She's been alive this whole time?

In the morning, Phoenix is nowhere to be seen. Maybe she's disappeared out of my life again. Nova is still fast asleep, so I leave her to rest. My cut ankle – now wrapped in a big leaf, secured by some bendy twigs – has seen better days, but I can still walk on it, more or less. I climb out of the cave, through a gap in the waterfall, squinting in the bright morning sun.

I limp down the knoll to find Phoenix sitting in the long grass, surrounded by a smattering of rainbow wildflowers. She looks like a painting.

'Morning, sunshine!' she calls.

I survey her body with a polite curiosity. I had pictured how Grace would look if she'd had the chance to grow up a thousand times. It's such a strange feeling to be confronted by the real thing in the flesh. Her petite yet sculpted shoulders, built up from years of vigorous exercise. Her white bottom is a similar flat shape to my own. Her pubic hair has a tinge of ginger in it. She puts her hands into a diamond shape and dives in with ease. I dive in after her, ducking my head under the clear cold water, and emerging with a small gasp.

We swim to a shallow area and face one another, our heads bobbing in the water. Now Phoenix's hair is wet, its true texture shows – unruly curls that she pulls away from her heart-shaped face.

She swirls her hands through the water, then comes towards me and cups my face.

'So, you're not dead,' I say, pulling away from her.

'Doesn't look like it.'

'But I remember the accident.'

'You probably remember what Sheryl and Doug told you.'

Hearing her distance herself by calling my parents – our parents – by their names hurts. 'No, I remember. I went to climb out of the window and you tried to stop me. To save me. We both fell. I've replayed the fall many times. I think . . .' I stare off into the distance and watch a tiny glittering fish leap out of the water and dive back in, causing circular ripples to dance in our direction.

'You didn't try to jump out of the window for no reason. You were trying to escape from me.'

My gaze drifts slowly back to her. I notice the skin on her chest and neck is dimpled with the cold.

'Why was I trying to escape?' I ask, although the answer is already dawning on me, as clear as the water we are swimming in.

'Because I bit you.'

My hand flies up to my scar, my fingertips tracing the ridges like they have done countless times before. They are teeth marks.

'You were a werewolf then.' I mean it as a question but it comes out as a statement.

'That's right. Most people aren't bitten until they're way older. Why pick a small starter when you could have a big juicy main, you know? But I reckon I was bitten by accident, or maybe in desperation.'

'Where? When?'

'On our holiday in Butlin's. Remember the second-last day of the holiday?'

Her words rouse a faraway memory, still slightly out of reach in my mind.

'I remember you not being yourself.'

'You can say that again.' Phoenix laughs, shaking her head. 'The next full moon, I went nuts. Tried to maul my own sister. You jumped and I fell chasing you, but I don't blame you. You were trying to survive. Even at four years old, you knew that was the only way out. You've always been so clever.' Her comment warms me from the inside.

'But at the hospital, they told me you died.'

'Sheryl and Doug panicked. They thought I was bad. So they sent me away to a young offenders institute. It marketed itself as a place to nurture and reform "bad kids". God knows if they believed that, but they were just trying to do their best by me and you.'

'And was it? A place to nurture and reform?'

'It was a breeding ground for problematic behaviour, if you ask me.'

As she speaks, my hand has remained on my scar, feeling the familiar ridges of it with my wet fingertips.

'That is a scar from a werewolf bite. I would have finished the job if you hadn't jumped. Sorry.' She speaks so casually as her arms sway in the water. As if she were apologising for putting unwanted sugar in my coffee. No need to feel bad.

Considering my whole life I've been riddled with deep, core-eating shame, her words do a good job of making me feel better. I feel so light now, I could bob away like a birthday balloon. Yet it's almost too difficult to believe. A couple of painfully average people like my mum and dad, coming up with an extravagant lie. 'So they've been lying to me my whole life. Let me believe that I lost a sister.'

'Well, that's not a lie. You did.'

It's quiet, apart from the rushing sound of the waterfall behind us and a bird singing in one of the trees.

'Don't hate them, please.'

So many things start to make sense now. The fact that I don't remember Grace's funeral. And my parents changed the subject whenever I brought up the night of our accident.

'They've been through enough,' she adds.

'You sound so . . . resigned.'

'Time heals. And I've had a lot of it to mull this over. I left when I was six. I eventually found a new family. The Faol People.'

'Don't you miss Seafall?'

'I did when I was little, but not anymore.'

'Don't you miss us? Me? And Mum and Dad?' The hurt rises in my throat.

Phoenix knows I'm getting upset, steps towards me and pulls me close. 'Hey, don't be sad. Of course I missed you. Look.' She extends her wrist to show me she's wearing her little bumblebee bracelet. 'I've not taken this off.'

'Since you stole it. After kidnapping me,' I joke, laughing my tears away. Phoenix wipes my face, then gives me a tender kiss on the forehead.

'I wanted you back in my life. I wasn't sure how to do it. But you could join the Faol People, you know? There will always be a place for you there.'

'I don't know. I've got to say, it was pretty cool becoming a werewolf last night.' I smile wickedly.

'It's fun, right?'

As I break into a giggle, I get the sense I'm being watched. I turn and see Nova standing at the water's edge. Her mouth is drawn in a tight, straight line, her fists balled at her side.

'Does she always act like she has sand up her twat?' Phoenix laughs.

I quickly swim to the edge and rest my arms on the grass, treading water.

'I didn't mean to interrupt your moment.' Nova looks down her nose at me, icily.

'Oh, it wasn't what you think,' I protest, kicking my legs behind me.

'You're your own person.'

Phoenix swims up beside me.

'I didn't think she'd be your type,' Nova says, her lip curling in disdain.

'Nova, we need to tell you something,' Phoenix offers.

Nova folds her arms. 'It's pretty obvious to me.'

'I doubt that,' Phoenix mumbles.

'You can tell me in the truck. Get dried off, it's time to head back.'

'To where? Edinburgh?' I can't hide the excitement in my voice.

'The Illvirkjar have retreated. They caught wind of the Glasgow and Edinburgh cohorts joining forces, and realised they'd be outnumbered. For now. So yes, we can return to Edinburgh.'

'What about Zainab and everyone at Clyde Cove?'

'Everyone's safe.'

I heave myself out of the water, sore but elated. Nothing can stop me now. 'Come on, Phoenix!' I yell excitedly over my shoulder.

CHAPTER TWENTY-EIGHT

After the disciplinary committee decide to give me a second chance and not kick my ass out of uni, I get my head down and really study for my resit, which comes around a month after the Illvirkjar's retreat.

When I turn over the paper and see the question, I light up inside.

In **The Strange Case of Dr Jekyll and Mr Hyde** *(1886) by Robert Louis Stevenson, there is a running theme of two conflicting sides. Please explore at least three of these using examples from the text.*

And then I get writing, the nib barely leaving the paper in the ninety-minute time frame. I don't hear anything else – no writing, no clock ticking. I'm completely lost in my own world. I barely notice Ted hovering around me, ensuring I don't cheat this time. Time flies. I finish writing with just enough time to read over my answers. Then it is over. 'Pens and pencils down.'

I stretch my hand, which is aching from the writing, then give Ted a brief nod goodbye and step out into the sunshine. I squeeze my eyes shut, welcoming the warm rays on my face.

'Brodie!' I open my eyes and spin around to see Killian. He's wearing a crinkled summer shirt and a wide smile. I can't help but give him a big hug.

He stumbles back, not expecting the sudden assault of affection, and pats my back awkwardly. I release him quickly.

'It went well, then?' he asks, beaming.

I radiate pride. 'I nailed it!'

Killian punches the air in triumph. 'Knew you would.'

'Thanks for everything.'

'It's my job.' He tries to bat away my gratitude, but I can see he's tickled by my success. 'You turned it around.'

'No – thanks for everything beyond your job. For believing in me when nobody else did.'

'The problem wasn't that nobody believed in you. It was that you didn't believe in yourself.'

I stand tall. 'Well, now I do.'

Killian puts his hands in his pockets, grinning from ear to ear. 'I can see that. How about I take you for a coffee to celebrate?'

I am about to reply when I see her, past Killian's shoulder, sitting on the concrete steps at Bristo Square.

'Oh, I'd love to, but I have plans with a friend.'

'No worries. Well, well done again! See you next semester, alright?'

I nod and give him a little wave goodbye as I walk towards her.

'Hey, you,' I say, standing behind Nova. She gets to her feet. 'Are you following me again?'

My question makes her go almost shy.

'Don't flatter yourself. I was out for a walk, and I remembered it was your final today, so . . .'

I spot a bouquet of sunflowers lying by her feet. 'So . . . are you going to give me them or not?'

'Right. Of course.' When she picks them up, a small section of blonde hair falls into her eyes. I step nearer to her and brush it out of the way, tenderly stroking her ear and neck. Electricity bubbles between us.

'Shall we go somewhere more private? There's something I need to tell you,' Nova says.

'What now?' I ask. 'I've had enough earth-shattering reveals for one year, don't you think?'

Nova bristles. 'Come to the Den?'

'I'm meeting Autumn and Zainab for drinks later.'

'Don't worry, Cinderella, I'll have you back in time.'

So we walk, my arm looped around hers, to Rock Bar.

In Nova's quarters, she takes me through a door that leads to a magnificent bedroom, with a huge sunken bed, tall ceilings and minimalist and futuristic finishes. Our palace of countless orgasms.

'And the rest.' Nova takes off her boots and pulls me on to the edge of the bed.

I launch myself on her, ready to fuck her brains out. But she stops me, pushing me down, pinning my wrists to the black silky bedsheets. Then she kisses me, and it is just as amazing as the other times. More. When I'm with her, I get lost in my own body; I don't think, I just am. After removing my underwear, she dives in between my legs, and my back arches and writhes as her tongue brings me to the edge, as fast and as overwhelming as an unstoppable tidal wave, crashing inside me. I yell out in ecstasy as I come, my legs trembling, my face covered in a sheen of sweat.

Nova stays down there, licking her lips. Staring at me.

I feel suddenly self-conscious. 'What is it?'

'There's something I need to ask you.'

I sit up, hug my knees and search her face for clues. 'You're freaking me out. What is it?'

Nova moves stealthily up beside me on the bed, props herself up on her arm to face me sideways. 'Juniper looked over your tests again. You have two small strains of Were blood in you. Phoenix's and then mine.' She pauses to ensure I'm following, so I gesture for her to continue. 'Instead of working in harmony in your body, they're at war with one another.'

'A bit like you and Phoenix.'

'We have a truce now. But our microcells don't know that.'

'What are you saying here?'

Nova stands up and faces me. 'In order to move forward, as a werewolf, the best idea would be for me to bite you again, and that would tip the balance, as it were. Then you would be able to use your power. Really become one of us.'

I let this sink in for a few moments. 'And if I don't?'

'You can probably live a perfectly ordinary life. If that's what you want?'

I gaze around the bedroom. This exotic and alluring world that I could be a part of. A place where I belong. Where I am wanted. Special. But then . . . 'What about university?'

'Look at Zainab. It hasn't stopped her from getting an education.'

'I don't know. I'm not sure . . .' I trail off.

'There is no going back, I should add. You would be giving up your human life, effectively. I understand if it's not right for you. Or if you're scared.'

The old Brodie would be terrified. Shitting herself every second about the most horrendous possible outcome. But something deep inside me is telling me to go for it. I've never felt quite right in my own skin as a human – maybe this is meant to be. It feels right.

'Let's do it.' I stand up, exhilarated, and take her hands.

'There is one small risk, however.'

'What?'

'It might kill us.'

'That feels pretty big, no?' I knew this was too good to be true.

'If a soul spirit bites their fellow soul spirit, it could cause an irreversible reaction that leads to death. Both of our deaths. It probably won't, but I have to be honest.'

I look into her eyes. And I see hope, not fear.

'I don't know.'

Then I remember all the times I've been too scared to take risks, or worried about what others think. That was the old me. The new Brodie grabs life by the throat!

'I don't care; let's do it. I don't want to live a life without you. I can't.'

'Are you sure?'

'Yes,' I say courageously.

She gives me one last, achingly hot kiss, so gorgeous I lose myself again momentarily.

Nova transforms almost immediately. There's no going back. You can reason with a human, but you can't reason with a beast. She is more majestic and way bigger than I remember. In the confines of a bedroom, she looks huge. At least twice the size of a Bengal tiger. My body starts to shake as adrenaline pumps through my veins, but I remain as still as I can, still sitting at the foot of the bed.

Nova sniffs, her snout twitching. She licks her lips, her tongue large and pink. She eyes me like a prize piece of meat. *Please don't kill me. I have so much to live for.*

She can't take her eyes off me, and I don't dare look away. One blue. One green. I have to remind myself it's still her, it's still Nova. I sit still, awaiting my fate.

'I'm ready.' I shut my eyes. Before I can even count down from three, the mattress puckers and bows as she climbs onto the bed. I feel her breath, warm and wet. And then everything goes black.

EPILOGUE

Grace and I are playing with big pieces of chalk on the sidewalk outside our flat. Grace has drawn lots of different pictures. A big yellow sun. A blue flower. A pink house. I can't draw very well; I am just doing squiggles and circles.

'Well done, Brodie! That's amazing!' Grace says encouragingly. She gives me a big hug and a kiss, and my heart fills with love.

*

'Brodie!' *Beep. Beep. Beep.*

'She's waking up!'

'Brodie? Can you hear me? Brodie!'

A blurred bright light shines on me.

'Am I in heaven?' I slur.

I hear Juniper's deep laugh. 'Close enough.'

Everything's blurry. I see Juniper leaning over me.

'Where's Nova?' I ask, my tongue sticking to the roof of my mouth.

'I'm right here.' I feel her hand, decorated with her cold metal rings, and then I see her. 'You made it. We both did.'

I grasp for Nova's arms and feel the cold of a silver pendant on my chest. I inspect it closely; a little engraved wolf stares back at me. I pull Nova in, and I know I am home.

ACKNOWLEDGMENTS

My amazing, patient editor Jack who was with me every step of the way, thank you for supporting and believing in me from day one of this project.

My sunbeam nephew, baby Leo, who was brewing at the same time as the first draft of this book; nice of you to join us.

My Dad, the first writer I ever knew, and my guiding light. To spare our blushes, I hope this is the only part of my book you read.

Dr Reid, I appreciate you very much for taking the time to answer all my medical-related questions, no matter how bonkers they were.

Zara and Katherine for letting me sleep in the princess layer at the mad hoose, during my own long dark night of the soul.

Zoë, thank you for all the chats, encouragement, and girl dinners: exactly what I needed to get me over the finish line.

Kina, my unofficial manager – everyone needs a number one cheerleader, and I am glad you are mine.

Kerr, I will be forever grateful for you letting me turn our closet into a novel-writing story cave. Thanks for everything.